A LILITH NOVEL

BLOOD INK

BLOOD INK

A LILITH NOVEL

DANA FREDSTI

TITAN BOOKS

BLOOD INK
Mass-market edition ISBN: 9781785656156
Ebook edition ISBN: 9781785652639

Published by Titan Books
A division of Titan Publishing Group Ltd
144 Southwark Street, London SE1 0UP

First mass-market edition: February 2020
2 4 6 8 10 9 7 5 3 1

A CIP catalogue record for this title is available from the British Library.

Printed in the USA.

To my mother, Dorothy Carol Galante.
You had the best laugh in the world, and I'd travel
through hell dimensions to hear it again.

The ads all call me fearless, but that's just publicity.
Anyone who thinks I'm not scared out of my mind
whenever I do one of my stunts is crazier than I am.

—Jackie Chan

The art of stunt-making is not about falling down; it's
about getting the shot. Creating stunts is creating heroes.

—Chad Stahelski

I do all my own stunts. I'm kidding.

—Dwayne "The Rock" Johnson

PROLOGUE

It was born of love, but transformed by hate. Now it dwelt in chaos.
And it dwelt alone.

The thing's unimaginable form alone was enough to provoke insanity. The hint of serpentine tentacles, the insane clusters of its eyes, its skeletal, grasping limbs, and its proportions too horrible, too terrifying, too mind-wrecking for the crude animal brain of a human to comprehend.

Its predecessors had emerged from the primal chaos long eons ago—from the same unfathomable dimension in which it now swam—a place of exotic nebulae and roiling cosmic pandemonium, where physics ran amok, where space and time, existence and nothingness, sense and madness all had strange new meanings.

Here, in the vast infinite space of this utterly inexplicable dimension, it moved and intermingled with myriad bewildering entities. Cold and unsympathetic ancient intelligences. Frightening beings born of nightmares, and all manner of unearthly creatures high and low. Some paid it no heed whatsoever, others gave it a wary kind of respect, and still others it hunted and feasted upon when it encountered them.

It had no equal. Nothing that could provide conversation or companionship. It had been this way ever since it had consumed its mate.

Virtually no single aspect of the thing could be safely encompassed by the human mind. But even while it undulated in the black depths of its howling abyss, the thing would at times contemplate its existence, and the barely remembered shape it once possessed, so very long ago.

It recalled, with difficulty, many strange sensations. The constant tug of gravity. The garish brightness of solar radiation warming a gaseous atmosphere. Swimming in an ocean of salt water. Sand beneath its feet. When it was… different.

It seemed to remember, with difficulty, experiencing several alien emotions, though it no longer possessed the words for them. Existing in a much simpler, weaker, short-lived terrestrial larval form… being human. *A peculiar warm and engaging state… being* loved. *Having something, another being separate from itself, that provoked that state…*

It could—and still did—experience one vestigial emotional state left over from that nascent embryonic stage. It felt loneliness.

It missed its mother.

CHAPTER ONE

RISE OF THE VAMPSHEES: THE NETHERWORLD CHRONICLES, PART II

EXT. THE DOCKS – NIGHT

A full moon SHINES down on a wooden dock being buffeted by a stormy sea. Waves surge over the sides. A SEAL washes onto the dock... and stands up, seal skin puddling around now human feet. The skin shimmers as masculine hands pick it up.

We SEE the back of a well-built man, GALEN, striding up the dock, wearing form-fitting pants the same color and texture as the sealskin. His footing is sure and swift despite the waves threatening to sweep him back into the ocean. Behind him, other seals converge on the dock, shedding skins as they morph into men and women, and follow the first selkie to...

...A DILAPIDATED WAREHOUSE at the end of the dock, windows boarded up, strips of paint peeling off the exterior.

CUT TO:

INT. WAREHOUSE – NIGHT

The interior of the warehouse is as ramshackle as its exterior. Wooden catwalks line the upper perimeter, and dozens of extraordinarily attractive vampires clad in black leather line the edges. They all stare with glowing red eyes at the floor below, where an equal number of selkies in human form—all dressed in transformed seal-skin garments—glare up at the vampires above them.
Galen steps forward. He stares up at a tall, imposing figure in a black duster. VIGGA, vampire queen with the beauty—and treachery—of a fallen angel.

>GALEN
>My people are here, Vigga! Many traveled from selkie courts hundreds of miles away. Let us hope the terms of this treaty are worth their journey.

>VIGGA
>I promise you, Galen, that this... treaty will once and for all end the hostility between our two races.

>CONNOR (o.s)
>Vigga lies!

All eyes, selkie and vampire alike, turn to the door. CONNOR, handsome half-werewolf, half-selkie, stands in the doorway.

CONNOR

She means to slaughter the selkie folk, not make
peace with our people!

Cries of outrage come from both sides at Connor's words.
Vigga smiles.

VIGGA

Surely this intruder is not one of your people, Galen.
Since when do werewolves claim kinship with the
selkies?

CONNOR

Galen and I are brothers.

GALEN (bitterly)

We are half-brothers. Born of the same selkie
mother, but this half-breed whelp's father was a
bastard werewolf.

LELA (o.s)

This "half-breed whelp," as you call him, is the
savior of your people!

CU CONNOR'S FACE...

...as he looks up at the catwalk opposite the one where Vigga
stands. He stares in disbelief at a hooded figure.

CONNOR (in a whisper)

Lela? You're... You're alive?

CU HOODED FIGURE...

...as she pushes the hood away from her head to reveal LELA, beautiful half-vampire, half-banshee. She stares down at her former lover with sadness and longing.

> LELA
>
> Yes, Connor.

Vigga hisses in fury and hatred.

> VIGGA
>
> It cannot be. You killed yourself. You are dead, you half-vampire, half-banshee abomination!

> LELA
>
> I am difficult to kill, even by my own hand...
> (dramatic pause)
>
> ...Aunt Vigga.

> VIGGA
>
> Kill her!

> GALEN
>
> Destroy the half-breed whelp!

Selkies close in on Connor even as vampires converge on Lela. Lela leaps up and over the catwalk railing, duster billowing out as she drops to the floor, landing in a crouching position, feet wide apart and supporting her weight with one hand on the floor, the other hand outstretched diagonally upward.

> **LELA** (looking at her lover)
> Hello, Connor.

Connor stares at her, disbelief and love blazing from his eyes.

> **VIGGA** (in fury)
> Nooooooooo!

†

Now, that's where I *should* have come in. But I didn't, because on the first movie's film set, a stunt had gone wrong and I'd ended up in the hospital. When they'd been hiring for the sequel, the stunt coordinator hadn't thought I was ready to do falls or jumps from any height taller than a bunk bed at the time of production, so the job of doubling Kayley Avondale—perky British ingénue turned action heroine—went to somebody else. The fact that I disliked this "somebody" made it all the harder to be okay with the situation.

What I was doing instead?

†

DRAGON DRUID MAGES: FIRES OF CHANGE

EXT. DRUID CLAN CIRCLE – AFTERNOON
A clearing. Dozens of white-robe-clad Druids, holding torches, ring a dais of obsidian rising five feet above the grass. BALTHAR, 30s, darkly handsome in black leather and dragonscale armor, stands in the shadows, watching the ceremony with a sneer.

> **HIGH MAGE**
> Druids from every clan gather here to decide who,

by rite of passage and right of lineage, will lead the people of this land, the northern tribes.

                    BALTHAR (stepping forward)
Nay. The only rights belong to the strong. To those not afraid to fight!

He addresses the rest of the Druids.

                    BALTHAR
Step away from this antiquated test and join me. Together we will lead the tribes to bloody victory against the Roman conquerors!

                    MARISA
No!

MARISA steps out of the shadows, face concealed by the pure-white hood of her Druid's robe. A RED DRAGON is embroidered on the front. She ascends the dais.

                    MARISA
Balthar speaks half-truths and cleverly concealed lies!

Marisa pushes the hood away from her face, revealing strong yet beautiful features. The face of a virgin warrior queen. Pure yet powerful.

C.U. BALTHAR...
...glaring at her with a mixture of hatred and desire.

MARISA

Balthar will lead us to only death and dishonor. As
he attempted to dishonor me with his touch.

BALTHAR

The only lies come from you and your antiquated
gods, Dragon Druidess.

He strides up until he is standing face to face with her.
Armed warriors on both sides draw their swords. Bows are
raised, arrows notched and ready to fly.

BALTHAR

You will not win this fight, Marisa.
                    (to someone behind him)
Show her the child.

A look of horror crosses Marisa's face.

MARISA

You cannot mean...

Balthar laughs as two of his warriors drag ILLIAD—five
years old—out from behind them.

ILLIAD

Mother!

Marisa turns on Balthar, perfectly shaped lips now
contorted in a snarl, the feral look of a lioness whose cub
is threatened.

MARISA

Illiad!

Throwing off her white robes to reveal chainmail and leather battle armor, Marisa launches herself off the platform, her staff a lethal whirling weapon of fury and vengeance as she attacks the men holding her son.

BALTHAR

Take the boy to Black Keep!

He joins the fight, driving Marisa back so Balthar's men can drag Illiad away. All around them, Druids are savagely cut down until only Marisa is left standing.

BALTHAR

You cannot win, Marisa. Surrender now and I will spare your son's life.

MARISA

Allow me to don my robes of station and I will surrender.

Balthar hesitates, then nods. Marisa returns to the platform, dons her robes, then suddenly lifts her arms to the sky.

MARISA

I invoke Breath of the Dragon!

Flames envelop her, keeping Balthar and his men at bay as she transforms into a dragon, then vanishes into the fire.

BALTHAR (face contorting with fury)

Noooooooooo!

†

This is where I came in—to film Marisa's leap to the ground and her "lethal whirling weapon of fury and vengeance" as she whomps the crap out of a few tackily clad soldiers before battling Balthar. The wardrobe department had raided a Cosplay'R'Us for the cheap fantasy armor. Perhaps they'd hit a cultists' discount warehouse for the generic white poly-cotton mage robes.

Gina, the actress playing the titular Dragon Druid Mage, happily handed over her staff and stepped to the side as I took her place on the platform. She was not one of the many actors who want to do their own fights. "I bruise way too easily," she'd told me. More screen time and more money for me.

I tried to resist the need to tug the chainmail and faux leather bikini either up or down. It wouldn't cover any more flesh either way.

"Armor, my ass," I muttered.

"You *wish* it covered your ass, huh, Lee?" Tommy, the actor playing Balthar, quipped.

He was not wrong. He was also one of the main reasons Gina didn't want to do any fight choreography. When learning theatrical combat, some people do just fine and dandy with the choreography, but are about as convincing as robots when it comes to selling the fight. Other people put plenty of verve into it, but have less control than five-year-olds chasing each other around with sticks.

Tommy was just a little too enthusiastic with the fight choreography without paying quite enough attention to details like remembering where his targets were. Annoying, but any bruises would fade in a few days, and at least Tommy didn't have anything to prove—unlike Axel, a Priaptic demon I'd worked with a few months earlier. Tommy just needed to dial it down a few notches whereas Axel had wanted to hurt me.

Three hours later, it was time for the last shot of the day—Marisa's Dragon Breath hot flash.

Some stunt performers really love fire gags. They say there's a rush to it that they don't get from any other stunt. I am not one of these people. My rush comes from the moment right after the flames are extinguished and I realize I am alive and—hopefully—unsinged.

With the crew and a Los Angeles County fire marshal standing by, I slid into the flesh-colored Nomex "long underwear." Long-sleeve top, long pants with drawstring, gloves and booties. A hood that covered my hair and neck. The Nomex had been soaked in flame-retardant gel and kept in a cooler full of ice, so putting it on was not fun. We were experiencing a warm SoCal September, but it was still a gooey, cold shock to my system. Still, I was glad to have it slathered on as this was going to be a "hot burn," meaning I wouldn't be moving around during the stunt. The flames burn hotter when you're standing still, which increases the risk of losing eyebrows or worse. I could take feeling like I'd been hit by Slimer in *Ghostbusters* if it meant keeping my eyelashes.

When I stepped out from behind the makeshift dressing room, the stunt coordinator and his assistants slathered me with more of the gel, making sure my face and all other bits not already protected by Nomex were well covered. Over that went Marissa's Druid robes. They had been treated with flame-retardant spray. Another lighter version of the Druid robe went on over all of that. The outer layer would burn, but theoretically the under-layers would not. This way we would achieve the effect of the flames without Marissa's clothes—or me—going up in smoke.

The dragon FX would be added in postproduction. At least the director was committed to getting some of this as a practical effect instead of trying to do the entire thing with CGI. The overall look of it would be less cheesy. Unfortunately, the dialogue, plot and cardboard characters could fill up multiple cheese boards.

Before my accident, things had been very different. I'd been part of the Katz Stunt Crew, one of the top stunt teams in the Industry. It's run by my Uncle Sean, who's actually my godfather, but "uncle" rolls off the tongue easier and doesn't bring to mind the Mob. Most of the team are supes—that's "supernaturals" for those of us too lazy to use five syllables—I'm one of the few exceptions. Since my fall I'd lived at Sean's ranch and trained newbies, but I was currently a free agent when it came to stunt work, though not by choice. Sean didn't think I was ready to get back on the horse, so I'd had to find my own work. Hence *Dragon Druid Mages*.

If this had been Sean's kind of production—one aware of their supernatural hires and/or one where my uncle was running the stunt show and could handle second unit shooting with a small, select crew—we probably would've used Dion, our fire gag expert. He was human-phoenix and there is nothing like that particular combo to achieve some kickass practical effects. It's also cheaper and quicker in the long run because you don't need the gel, Nomex, or fire extinguishers. Dion would just go all "flame on" in a spectacular ball of fire or a slow burn, depending on what was desired, and then calmly emerge from the ashes when the take was over. *Dragon Druid Mages*, however, was a NSA (non supe aware) production, so we'd do the stunt the old-fashioned way and I'd get the small pay bump that came with the dangers of being covered in goo and getting set on fire.

This was my last day on the film and as soon as the fire gag was completed, I was officially done. After two weeks of fourteen-hour days, I was ready for a break, but I'd had a blast. The cast and crew knew they weren't making art and it was a fun shoot. Even better, I did not have to work with an asshole Priaptic demon and there were no shadows with teeth and claws slaughtering people.

Be grateful for the little things, right?

"You ready, Lee?" Norris, the stunt coordinator, stood by with a plastic pitcher full of gasoline. His assistants, Mark and Mikey, both held blowtorches.

I nodded. "Light me up and put me out."

Norris grinned. "Let's go."

He doused the robes, covering my arms, legs, and back with the gasoline. I wrinkled my nose as the acrid fumes rose into my nostrils and then hopped back up on the platform, where a gel-soaked furniture pad had been placed to prevent an actual conflagration and to give me a semi-protected place to land when it was time to be extinguished.

"And... action!"

Raising my arms above my head, I intoned, "I invoke Breath of the Dragon!"

Whoosh!

Flames rose on either side of me, running up my arms and down my body, the fire dancing over my body without any real sense of heat. The fire crackled and snapped as it followed the path laid by the gasoline. The heat suddenly penetrated the protective layers, slamming into me like a super-heated punch from behind. I fell to my knees and then forward onto the pad, hearing the welcome hiss of fire extinguishers as Mark and Mikey put out the flames.

"Great job, Lee. How ya feeling?" Norris grinned down at me. I gave him a gooey thumbs-up.

"I wouldn't say no to a beer."

†

If anyone had ever told Celia that a tattoo would kill her, she would've laughed it off. It sounded like the kind of urban legend parents liked to feed their kids. Get them to behave by freaking them out. Shitty parenting.

Sure, she'd heard of some people getting staph infections. Having to have pieces of their flesh cut out to save the rest of a limb. But they'd gone to questionable parlors, had their tattoos done by people who didn't clean the needles. Stuff like that.

LeRoy's Ink Shop had been totally recommended by more than one of her friends. Well, at least one of them. Or maybe it was her boyfriend. She couldn't quite remember. Whatever, the place had been clean and there'd been nothing hinky about it at all.

Celia had the idea that she'd get a tattoo like the cloisonné butterfly on her favorite necklace so that when she wore her low-cut jeans, the wings would emerge partway. Something pretty and feminine. Maybe in pale pinks and tangerine. The head tattoo artist—LeRoy himself, and, wow, he was hunky for a man who had to be at least thirty—had liked the idea, but talked her into a butterfly with iridescent purple and blue wings. He'd pulled a portfolio out from behind the counter, something he didn't leave out for just anyone to see.

"Special people deserve special ink," he'd said with a smile.

Celia felt very special at that moment. Not like she usually did, with her friends. They weren't exactly mean girls—well, Tiffany was—but they were cheerleaders and prom queens, the kind of girls who never paid for their own drinks. Whose boyfriends bought them expensive jewelry. Friends who lived in expensive mansions in the center of New Orleans' Garden District, not at the edge of it in a small raised cottage, like Celia's family. Friends who sometimes forgot to include her in their plans.

No, she was getting something special. Because she was special. She just knew once she showed it to the gang, they'd all want one too.

LeRoy had shunted off other customers to the other tattooists in the shop. There were three of them, all women. Two could have been twins—maybe they were—with large liquid green eyes the color of swamp water, almost snub noses, wide mouths and receding chins. Celia couldn't decide if they were pretty or freakish. They sure were different. The third looked to be about her age, petite and kind of goth-y, but really nice. She smiled at Celia and complimented her necklace.

When it was all over, LeRoy had given her a jar of ointment that he said would help promote the healing process, prevent flaking, and minimize scabbing. That way she wouldn't have to come back for touch-ups. He also told her that it would itch. That it would feel like a mild sunburn on and around the site of the tattoo.

This felt like the mother of all sunburns. She'd been burned badly in her teens, when she and her friends had gone to a tanning salon. The girl working that day had been new and let her stay in for too long. Celia had gone from deep pink to angry red to almost purple, unable to stand even the lightest cloth on her body. Within two days, the skin started peeling off her butt and breasts, which had gotten the worst of it. Instead of strutting around in her bikini with a golden tan, she had spent a few weeks of enforced indoor time, slathering lotion on raw, peeling skin.

That had hurt, had, in fact, been some of the worst pain she'd ever experienced—until now. This was worse. He hadn't said it would itch and burn straight down to the bone, like acid eating its way into her bloodstream. Like something was burrowing in there, biting her, plucking on the nerve endings. He hadn't said that it would feel like the skin was peeling off and acid was dripping onto each point of the tattoo.

No, LeRoy hadn't warned her about that.

Finally, she went into her mom's bathroom, grabbed the Valium out of the cornucopia of prescription meds, took two, and went back to bed. After a while, she drifted off and dreamed of insects drilling into her spine.

CHAPTER TWO

Randy and I sat on his couch, drinking beer and watching a bad movie on his big-ass flat-screen television. The TV took up most of one wall of the living room in his Encino apartment. The other walls sported a few John Carpenter movie posters—*The Thing*, *They Live*, *Big Trouble in Little China*—and a very tasty poster-sized photo of Randy with his shirt off. While he wasn't quite as buff as, say, Thor or some of the other Avengers, he was in good enough shape that he could probably get there pretty quickly if the right job came along.

The movie—*Marauders: Grid Wars*—was what you'd get if you took *Avengers* and *The Matrix*, mashed them together with none of the humor of the former and no red pill option to escape the latter. The busty heroine, Anya—dressed in a low-cut corset, matching thong, sexy garter belt, black stockings and four-inch heels—was currently in the grip of two cyber-thugs in black suits, several others lurking in the background. The villain, Evon, stood in front of her, exuding low-budget sexual menace. Anya's face was totally serene, the result of too much Botox on the part of the actress playing her.

> **EVON**
>
> It doesn't have to be this way, Anya. Tell me where
> Osprey is hiding, and I'll let you go.

Randy snorted. "Osprey?"

"At least they didn't call him Pigeon or Hummer. Now listen or you'll miss really important dialogue."

That got another snort.

> **ANYA**
>
> You know that will never happen, Evon. The
> Marauders are going to take down the Grid. It's
> only a matter of time.

"Does she ever move her upper lip?" Randy said.

I shook my head. "I don't think she can. Now hush."

> **EVON**
>
> You and I have something, Anya. Something real.
> You can see it in the air between us!

He reaches out, and CGI electricity visibly crackles in the air between them.

Randy and I both giggled.

> **EVON**
>
> Can you really throw this away?

On "this" he touches Anya's face and she closes her eyes, visibly stirred.

At least as visibly stirred as the actress could convey without working facial muscles.

ANYA (softly with regret)
There's nothing real in the Grid, Evon. Not even us.

Anya suddenly explodes in a flurry of movement, knocking Evon back with a brutal kick to his solar plexus. He falls backwards, winded. Anya's hands, arms, legs and feet, her entire body, become deadly weapons as she takes out the cyber-thugs holding her. Others whip out weapons and fire. Time SLOWS DOWN and Anya leans into an impossibly deep back bend, twisting to one side to let the cyber-bullets flow past her and—

"How the hell do you gals do that shit in those heels?" Randy asked, staring in bemusement at the scene playing out.

I shrugged, the gesture barely moving Randy's muscular arm, which was draped around my shoulders. "It's a definite skill set," I said. "One that most of us would rather not have to utilize quite so often."

"So… what's the deal? They think the higher the heels, the more kickass the heroine?"

Awww, bless his little lycanthropic heart…

"Below a certain budget level, yeah. Ooh, check it out." I leaned forward. "This is the bit where Jan sprained her ankle because the goddamn director wouldn't back down on the stupid heels."

"He made her do the *whole* fight scene in four-inch heels?"

"It's a Crazy Casa film."

"Ah," Randy said. "Say no more."

Crazy Casa Productions is known for cheap knock-offs of high-budget films and even cheaper original movies with mutant monster combos. Think *Pandaconda*. They pay for shit. As in they hardly pay anything, and they get exactly what they pay for. They also go through actors *way* too fast—what I not-so-nicely refer to as Barbies and Kens. They have an in-house stunt coordinator who cycles through young and eager stunt players almost as quickly. If you survived more than one Crazy Casa production as a stunt player, you were either really good at your job or had the luck of the Irish with a shit-ton of four-leaf clovers on the side. And, until you proved yourself under a reputable stunt coordinator, you were also considered potentially dangerous.

I hadn't worked on *Grid Wars*, but I knew Jan, the stuntwoman doubling Anya, and she'd fought the good fight against heels, and lost. I felt for her. The director I'd worked for before *Dragon Druid Mages* had pushed for the female police officer in his micro-budget movie *Woman in a Blue Dress Uniform* to wear high-heeled boots when she was on duty, including during an extensive chase sequence culminating in a fight against six muscular thugs. Said director was shouted down by the lead actress with my full support as her stunt double. I'd shaken my head and said, "Ain't gonna happen."

And it hadn't, but Jan was getting a lot more work than I was these days.

Dragon Druid Mages was only my fourth job since healing

from my fall on the high-budget piece o' poo, *Vampshee: The Netherworld Chronicles*. It had taken me half a year to recover from the injuries to the point where I could get back to work, and I was still dealing with a newly formed—and highly inconvenient—fear of heights.

The first job, *Steel Legions*, barely paid for my gas driving back-and-forth to set. It had been, however, the first stunt work I'd gotten since my accident, and despite dealing with Axel—the aforementioned Priaptic demon who'd played the villain—it hadn't been all bad. It had been Randy's first job as stunt coordinator and I'd gotten to know him as more than an irritating newbie at the Katz Ranch and discovered that underneath an annoyingly cocky veneer, he was actually a nice guy.

He'd stunt-doubled a variety of generically good-looking actors—the ones that were probably cloned in a vat somewhere and then dispersed to the various television networks to populate their shows. I'd never found the type particularly compelling and hadn't thought too much of Randy when he first showed up to train at the Ranch with Sean's crew. There was a lot more to him than first met the eye, however, including an unexpected dash of shifter. He'd never talked to me about his heritage, and I didn't want to be nosy. Information offered was one thing, but digging for it was another—in the supe community, it wasn't considered polite.

A lot of supernaturals flock to places like Los Angeles because the entertainment industry makes it easier for them to make a living without having to hide in the shadows all the time. Unfortunately, there are purebloods among the various races with major attitude problems, like Death Eaters in the Potterverse. That bullshit didn't play with Sean Katz. As long as you could do the job—whatever that job might be from one day to the next—he didn't care if you were, say, a vampire-banshee hybrid, a were-bunny, or a zombie.

Okay, maybe not zombies. Way too much cleanup involved if they took any sort of impact, not to mention the risk of infection. There'd been a scandal a few years back when zombie movies were all the rage and some idiot producer on a low-budget film had gotten into major trouble for using them as expendable extras. Careless cleanup had led to an outbreak on the set, luckily contained by the isolated filming location and a weapons handler with a cache of firearms, live ammo, and great aim.

Randy and I continued to watch *Grid Wars*, washing the badness down with excellent craft beer. "Did you know," I said conversationally, "that the director originally wanted to call it *Dark Noir Night*?"

"Uh, doesn't that translate to *Dark Black Night*?"

"Uh huh. Kind of like *Manos, Hands of Fate* translates to *Hands, Hands of Fate*."

"Wow."

Grid Wars took itself as seriously as *Man of Steel*. Anya and Evon continued their battle, transitioning from the slow-mo backbends to some uninspired aerial moves. Flying kicks, flips, the usual. Nothing that hadn't already been done to death. *Yawn*.

"Jeez, this is stale," Randy said dismissively. "I remember when the wirework in *Big Trouble in Little China* was a big deal."

"How do you remember that?" I peered up at him skeptically from my comfy position under his arm. "Were you even born when that was released? I don't think so."

"How old do you think I am?" he retorted. "My sister and I saw that in the theater at least a half dozen times when it came out."

"I stand corrected, Methuselah."

We finished watching *Grid Wars* and I got up to stretch, shutting my eyes as I rolled my head in slow circles to loosen the muscles in my neck. I opened my eyes and caught Randy looking at me, his brow furrowed. When he saw that I'd noticed, his forehead straightened out as if a magic wrinkle remover had been applied.

I raised an eyebrow. "Okay, Squid, what's up? You're looking at me funny."

"Everything's good," he replied. "I was just wondering if everything was okay." He scratched his head and looked uncomfortable.

O-kay…

"Why wouldn't it be? I mean, bad movies, good pizza, great beer. What's not to like?"

"You're sure you're feeling all right? No headaches or anything?"

My eyes narrowed. "Did Sean tell you to keep an eye on me and make sure that I'm not gonna go into convulsions or something? Even though I'm seeing a neurologist and haven't had any kind of seizure since the accident?"

Randy took a big chug of beer to hide his embarrassed expression. "Yeah, he kind of did, but I would've done that anyway. Just because you haven't had any kind of seizure or whatever doesn't mean it couldn't happen. Nothing bad's gonna happen to you on *my* watch."

I did my best to hide the fact that I was more than a little touched by his words even though they also made me nervous. I wasn't ready to settle down with anyone and I liked the casualness of our friendship. It made me comfortable in a way that intense emotions and commitment did not.

"You're not getting all mushy on me, are you?"

Randy's face flushed just a little bit. He shook his head vigorously. "Hell, no." He drank more beer. "I know better than that."

I guess he did. He'd told me before that he really liked me, but he didn't expect anything more than friendship with benefits. I knew he wouldn't mind seeing where things went if I were onboard, but he didn't want me to run screaming in the other direction. I didn't know if he was dating anyone else and I didn't ask. Maybe I didn't want to know. Maybe I was just a big fat weenie who couldn't handle emotions but still wanted everything my own way.

Thanks for that, brain.

"So…" Randy trailed off, giving his beer bottle an inordinate amount of attention. I mean, he wasn't drinking from it, he was just staring at the label.

"What?"

"Sean say anything about you and me?"

I shook my head. "Nope."

"Oh." His tone was flat. He was still studying the beer bottle.

"Trust me, that's a good thing," I said, poking Randy in his well-muscled stomach. Not a lot of give there in either his abdomen or his expression. "Seriously," I reassured him. "Sean doesn't say much about my personal life unless he's got an issue with it."

Point of fact, Sean had been conspicuously quiet about my dating Randy, other than a response to a pithy comment I'd overheard Seth make about some of my late nights. Sean's brief reply had been, "Be thankful, why don't you? Randy's at least a few steps up from her last choice in men."

Somehow I didn't think Randy would understand why that was a compliment. According to Seth and Sean, my previous boyfriends had been less than stellar. I had to take their word for it—large chunks of my life before the accident were still a blank.

He downed the rest of his beer in one quick swallow. "You had enough of dumbass films yet, or do you wanna move on to the next piece of crap?"

Was it my imagination or did he seem a little hurt?

"Let's move on," I said, making a quick decision. "But let's improve the quality of the entertainment a little bit, shall we?"

I leaned down, wound one hand in his thick brown hair and pulled him closer so I could kiss him. He gave a low growl deep in his throat, the vibration sending a pleasurable shiver through me. Randy was good at more than stunt work.

†

Celia struggled to pull herself out of the cobwebs of a drugged slumber. It felt like she was wading through a room of cotton candy—sticky, cloying, and endless. She'd get through one section, pull herself free of the strands around her, only to stumble into a fresh batch.

Even worse was the sensation that her mouth was filled to bursting with gum. She'd stopped chewing bubblegum years ago after a nightmare where no matter how much gum she pulled out of her mouth, she couldn't get rid of it. Pulling great sticky, stretchy swaths of the gum as more formed in her throat and oozed forward. This was like that. But so much worse.

Because when she woke up, her throat and mouth were still clogged with some gummy substance.

"Mommy?"

At least that was what she tried to say. The sound was muffled, her jaws only able to open about an inch before something snapped them shut again.

Celia tried to sit up, throw the covers off her body, but she couldn't move. Pinpricks of white-hot agony flared up and down her body, as if something was stitching her legs together at the inner thighs and calves, and her arms to her torso. Her bedroom, large and well ventilated, now seemed unbearably confined, the air humid and stale at the same time. Kicking up with both legs with the greatest of effort, she hit a solid surface a few inches above her.

She struggled, trying to scream, to get help, but even as she tried to cry out again, pinkish strands like spun sugar drifted across her face, and inside her mouth, nose, eyes, cocooning her from the inside out until she could no longer move at all, not even to blink her eyes.

She could still feel everything.

CHAPTER THREE

I stood on top of a towering cliff, a storm brewing overhead, oily clouds roiling around with slashes of deep red and a poisonous orange. As if the clouds were embers still burning on the inside, looking for the chance to burst into flame.

"Lee…"

His voice, like rough velvet, called to me, rippling through my nerve endings, promising such pleasure if only I'd step away from the edge of the cliff. If only I'd turn around and go to him. If only I'd let him touch me.

If only I'd let him kill me.

"Lee…" Louder this time, more insistent.

I stepped off the edge of the world into the void.

†

I woke with a start, bathed in so much sweat I was surprised I didn't just wash right out of my bed. And yet I was freezing, my body wracked with chills. It didn't help that I'd thrown the covers off at some point during the night. I slept with my window open, no matter the weather, and it had been unseasonably cold last night.

It was still dark outside. I reached for my iPhone, charging on the bedside table. 5 A.M. Time to get up. Then I remembered I didn't have to get out of bed and drive to

37

Angeles Forest. My body and brain were still inconveniently on early-morning film-shoot schedule. I *could* get up and be productive. Or I could play bed slug a while longer.

I retrieved my covers, snuggling under the down quilt and luxuriating in the warm bedding while I thought about the nightmare that had woken me up. When I'd first gotten out of the hospital, I'd had plenty of dreams about the fall that nearly killed me, but a few months ago my subconscious decided that reliving a near-death experience—including the pain of smashing against unyielding concrete—wasn't enough. It decided to switch things up with new and exciting locations straight out of a Hieronymus Bosch painting. It also saw fit to add a sexy shadow-figure that I knew wanted to kill me, but with a promise of mega hot sex first. Possibly during. Maybe even after. These dreams really were that fucked up.

The details of the dream changed, but with variations of the same theme in each iteration. I was always on the edge of some place uncomfortably high. A cliff above an angry ocean. A snow-capped mountain peak. Once I even stood at the open door of an in-flight airplane. It was always dark and stormy, with fiery, black clouds filling the sky.

There was also always a man—or something that looked like a man—behind me. Face in the shadows, eyes glowing with the same banked flame as the clouds. Palpable waves of hate rolled off him, combined with undeniable lust. I could never tell which emotion was the stronger. Maybe my dream stalker didn't know either.

He would call my name, try to get me to turn around. Sometimes he'd caress me, his touch an icy-cold fire spreading through my body. Part of me always wanted to pull away from the death drop and go to him. Rather than let him touch me, though, I took the step into the abyss every time. Falling into an endless night. Waking up before I hit bottom.

Each time I had the dream, however, the urge to turn to him grew stronger, and the subsequent fall seemed that much longer. Was there even a bottom in these new dreams? If I found out... would I wake up?

And an even scarier thought... What would happen if I stepped away from the endless drop and let him claim me?

The smell of freshly brewed coffee and bacon with an overlay of maple wafted under the crack at the bottom of my bedroom door. The enticing and down-to-earth aromas drove the last lingering shreds of death drops and scary, sexy men out of my head, replacing them with visions of breakfast.

I sniffed again, then took a deep inhale. Yup, time to get out of bed. There was work to do in the kitchen. I wandered down the hallway in Black Watch-plaid pajama bottoms and a baseball-style jersey with Grumpy Cat on it, fuzzy socks protecting my feet against the cold hardwood floor.

My godfather, Sean, sat at the kitchen table playing on his iPad, a mug of coffee giving off steam in front of him, while his son Seth was in the command position in front of the stove, three separate burners going. A rugged blond with blue eyes, Sean could have been anywhere from late forties to early fifties, but his nephilim heritage meant he might be many years older. It also meant he and Seth were naturals for high falls—when your ancestor's an angel, the laws of gravity aren't a problem. I had no idea what Sean's actual age was, and he wasn't telling.

He got up at the sound of my footsteps, and gave me a hug and a kiss on the cheek.

"Hey, hon. How did you sleep?"

I gave a jaw-cracking yawn in reply. Sean looked at me knowingly. "Out late last night?"

"Not *too* late." I'd gotten back from Randy's a little before two. A normal bedtime when I didn't have to get up the next morning was generally midnight, especially when any of the regular crew stayed after training.

I helped myself to coffee, pouring a generous dollop of cream into my mug.

Seth cast me a glance. "You do realize that this coffee is over twenty bucks a pound, right? The flavor stands on its own. Why are you adding cream?"

Even in sweatpants and a faded red T-shirt, my quasi-cousin looked like a movie star. Cheekbones most supermodels would kill for. Eyes the rich brown of bittersweet chocolate, framed with long, thick lashes. An artfully tousled mane of dark brown hair that you'd think a team of stylists had spent hours working on. His eyelashes alone made it hard not to hate him, especially since he was a jerk ninety percent of the time.

Ignoring Seth's kibitzing, I sat at the table across from Sean, enjoying that first precious life-giving sip of coffee. A blissful smile spread over my face. Like everything Seth made in the kitchen, the coffee tasted better than it should have. He'd used a French press this morning, but he could have used a Mister Coffee and gotten the same results. Rich and smooth, with notes of caramel lurking underneath. It almost didn't need cream. Almost.

"So. Out with Randy last night?" Seth spoke with a studied nonchalance that would have failed totally had he not been busily tending the stove.

My smile faded. Last thing I wanted to do was discuss any details of last night's date with Sean and Seth.

"Uh huh," I said noncommittally.

"That's nice," Sean chimed in.

"How late did you work?" Seth again.

I shrugged even though I knew he couldn't see me. Or maybe he could. I caught a glance of his eyes reflected in the shiny steel of the stove backing.

"Got done around five." I drank more coffee. A big gulp this time.

I could almost feel father and son calculating how many hours I'd spent with Randy. Suddenly the thought of cooking my own breakfast wasn't so bad.

"Did you two go out to dinner?" Sean asked.

Translation: *Were you out in public, away from a bedroom?*

"No, we watched movies and had pizza at his place."

"Oh." A slight pause. "What did you watch?"

Translation: *Do you remember what you watched or were you too busy indulging in original sin?*

"*Grid Wars* and some other piece of crap film. It had zombies in it." Okay, a little white lie there, but we'd *planned* on watching the zombie movie. Besides, twenty-seven was just a little too old to deal with the *Dating Game* interrogation.

Seth plunked down a plate in front of his father and then one for me. I stared at the beautifully plated scrambled eggs with tomatoes and feta cheese, perfectly crisp bacon, and a short stack of fluffy homemade pancakes with maple syrup and butter pooling on top and drizzling down the sides.

One of the few things that endeared Seth to me—and possibly why I haven't killed him—was his improbable love of cooking shows. He watched them all, even the ones with lots of yelling and artificially created drama. *Yeah, I'm looking at you, Gordon Ramsay*. Seth's favorite was *The Great British Bake Off*. He liked to try out recipes. I liked to eat them. So very dangerous. I had a fantasy about reaching a point in my life where I no longer worried about the size of my jeans. Until then… well, only the fact that I spent more hours exercising than eating saved me from obesity.

My stomach growled, making its opinion known.

"Thanks," I muttered even as I filled my fork and took my first bite.

Ambrosia.

"So. Good."

Seth gave a little satisfied *huff*. He and I may not get along most of the time, but I never failed to show proper appreciation for his cooking skills. He served himself and sat down at the table, digging into his food with enthusiasm. My shoulders relaxed. The gentle inquisition was over. At least for now.

"When's your next gig?" I asked casually.

"Two weeks off and then we start pre-production on the sequel to *Twitch*."

Twitch was the first book in one of the silliest YA dystopian series out there. It made the plot twists of the *Labyrinthine Walker* series seem logical. Still, I felt a little drop in the pit of my stomach. I should've been working on this film. "What's it called?" I asked, just to be polite.

Seth gave a snort. Sean grinned. "*Spasm*," they replied at the same time.

I almost did a spit take, but that would have been a waste of good food, not to mention gross. "You have got to be kidding. Please tell me you're kidding." They weren't. "Is the third film gonna be called *Seizure*?"

That actually drew a smile from Seth. "Well, of course. Because, you know, metaphor and symbology and all that shit."

Seth and I started snickering even as Sean frowned at his son for his use of the "s" word. He gave us both a half-hearted glare, shaking his head as he tried not to smile. He's always happier when Seth and I aren't at each other's throats. Luckily there're plenty of other things that make him happy.

It's not that I enjoy fighting with Seth. In fact, it's one of the things that makes my life much more stressful than it should be. We've always squabbled, but over the last few years our minor disagreements had transmogrified into bitter wars. I hated it, but I didn't know how to fix it. My friend Eden opines that Seth has feelings for me that go beyond those of a protective pseudo-cousin. I opine that too much chardonnay has killed off some of her brain cells. We agree to disagree.

"What about you, hon?" Sean speared a forkful of pancakes. "Got anything else lined up now that *Dragon Druid Mages* has wrapped?"

"A couple of possibilities in the works, but nothing definite." I kept my answer deliberately vague but I knew that they'd be able to translate it to "no prospects" without any problem.

I hate feeling pathetic.

"Well," Sean said after a beat, "I'm sure that something will come through."

I gave a small inward sigh. I guess—no, I *knew*—I wanted him to say, "Look no further, because there's some stunt doubling that you'd be perfect for on this stupid piece-of-shit, high-budget film."

Although he would never say "shit." Sean frowns upon bad language. Not sure how he's managed to make it as Papa Bear for the Katz Stunt Crew for so many years without his ears falling off. Most stuntmen and stuntwomen are not known for their lack of vulgarity.

At any rate, part of me totally got why Sean didn't want to have me on a production until I'd gotten over my problem with heights. The KSC—and no, I'm not the only person who thinks it's funny to call Sean "the Colonel"—was known for radical wirework, high falls, and near-insane aerial stunts that few others would try. If I couldn't keep up with them, I could be a liability if a director suddenly wanted a female character to dangle from a helicopter. Another part of me, however, was pissed off and hurt that he wouldn't even bring me in as a fight double.

Oh well, I've been working on my high falls again and could now take a dive from more than twenty feet without freezing in place or holding onto the practice tower like a scared kid on a high dive board.

The back of my legs still crawled and my stomach flipped over, mind you, and it was still an effort of sheer willpower to go any higher, but I was doing the work. I just wasn't doing it fast enough or good enough to earn my place back on the crew.

"What's next for you after *Spasm*?" I asked with forced lightness.

"We're talking to Spielberg about some space opera project. Pirates in space, that kind of thing."

"Any chance you think I'll be ready to work with you if this one goes through?" Wow. I hadn't known I was gonna ask that until the words had already tumbled from my mouth. Whatever, the question clunked like a brick dropped in the middle of the kitchen table, leaving an awkward silence that I hustled to fill. "I mean, come on, pirates in space? They'll have to have swords or light sabers, right? You know you don't have anyone better than me on the edged-weapon side of things."

"Well, hon…" Sean paused, evidently trying to word his reply with care. Which told me the answer was going to be either, "I don't know," or just, "No." I barged ahead before he could prove me right.

"What, then?" I took a deep breath and finally brought up the subject I'd been avoiding for the last two months. "I'm just expected to sit around and wait for monsters to find me so I can kill them? Because, seriously, I need to find paying work and I doubt there's a lot of money in demon killing. Although I guess I could put up an ad on Craigslist and see if I get any takers."

Seth choked on a mouthful of eggs and bacon, covering his mouth and coughing until he'd managed to swallow without asphyxiating himself.

Sean set his fork down.

My first impulse was to apologize. Instead, I pushed away from the table with a mumbled, "Excuse me," and left the room before the hot tears welling in my eyes could escape. I fled to the bathroom and let them spill out for a few minutes, long enough to release some of my frustration and regain a little bit of equilibrium. Oh, it was hard, though. My heartbeat thrummed in my ears, at least twice as fast as it should have been, and I didn't know if I was going to throw up or punch the mirror above the sink. Possibly both.

This whole fucked-up situation was *not* my fault and I was tired of acting as if life was normal. Because it wasn't. It never would be again. I'd trusted Sean and he'd pretty much lied to me most of my life. He'd raised me since I was five, taking me in when my parents had died in what I'd been told was an auto accident, but what had actually been a hit job by a pissed-off demon. And it was only a couple of months ago, after a film set I'd been working on had fallen under demonic attack, that Sean had finally told me the truth—there were plenty more demons in my future. Not only that, but I was a veritable demon magnet.

Turns out that El—also known as Yahweh—a god with

serious anger-management issues, had put a curse on my ancestress Lilith when she decided to ditch Adam and choose her own mate. As punishment, El turned most of Lilith's kids into demonspawn, and then cast her into a hell dimension. Only a few of her descendants remained human, and El ordered them to clean up the mess *he'd* created—hunt down the monsters and kill them. Talk about harsh parenting.

My personal opinion? El was a total asshole with a big helping of crazy on the side.

Along with the training, each lucky human descendant also got an amulet engraved with ancient sigils that imbued pretty much anything with the power to fight demons, giving the bearer the ability to take out creatures that would otherwise be near impossible to kill. Each demon taken out of the game supposedly brought Lilith one step closer to release from her prison.

As if things weren't complicated enough, there was so much interbreeding amongst demons, monsters, lesser gods and what not over the years that any number of supernaturals could be considered Lilith's children. Many of them, however, are not evil. Hell, I work with a lot of them. And most humans have at least a little supe blood in them. A lot of hardcore surfers, for example, have at least a trace of selkie, kelpie, or *taniwha*. Scratch a fearless horseback rider and you'll find some centaur or *púca* way back in the family tree. And so on. In most cases, the bloodline is so diluted it would show up in 23&Me as "unknown genome of Middle Eastern origin" or something along those lines. So not only did I have to worry about potentially killing a harmless creature by mistake, but there was also no retirement plan.

Some mornings, there just wasn't enough coffee in the world to make it easy to rise and shine. I heaved a deep, shuddering sigh and splashed some cold water on my flushed face, taking a quick peek in the mirror to see how bad I looked. A little red in and around the eyes, and my long mane of dark-brown hair needed a brush in the worst possible way. Taking a few more minutes, I tamed my hair into a Dutch braid that fell past my butt, smoothed the fragile skin under my eyes with some cream, and ran a Burt's Bees tinted balm over my lips. It'd do.

My mother's amulet—yeah, that one—rested a few inches below the hollow of my neck, the gold metal gleaming dully against my skin. For all I knew the ancient sigils stood for "Eat my shorts, demonspawn!" Whatever, it had been Mom's, it was now mine, and it worked.

Taking a deep breath, I headed back down the hall toward the kitchen. I stopped short of the door when I heard Sean say, "How is Lee doing on the falls?"

"Better," Seth replied. "Much better. Up to forty feet without hesitation. Maybe we should consider bringing her in on *Spasm*, give her a chance to ease back in."

Holy shit, did I just hear Seth advocating to use me on a film? Hope my ancestress had some winter clothing to keep her warm in her prison in hell, because it just froze over.

"Now, Seth, you know that's not practical right now."

"Yeah, but—"

The floor creaked as I shifted my weight. Seth stopped mid-sentence. *Rats.* I went into the kitchen, poured myself more coffee and sat at the table. I didn't bother to pretend I hadn't been eavesdropping.

"Do you not want me on your films because you're afraid I'm a monster magnet and people could get hurt? Because if that's the case I guess I understand, but it would be really nice if you'd just tell me."

"That's just—"

Sean held up a hand, cutting off his son's predictable insult. "It's a fair question, Seth, and a thoughtful one." He ran the same hand through his hair, then dropped it to the table to retrieve his coffee cup. "There will always be the risk of one of Lilith's children seeking you out if they're close enough to sense you, but the chance of another one showing up on a film you're working on?" He shook his head. "Not likely."

"Then what's the deal?" I tried to keep the frustration out of my voice. I really did. The fact that it was an epic fail was not for lack of effort on my part. "If even *Seth* thinks I'm ready to work again, why the hell won't you put me back on a film?"

"Look, hon," Sean said patiently, "considering the double whammy of trauma you had, first with the accident and then what happened on *Pale Dreamer*, it seemed prudent to keep you away from the work until you could get your head back in the game." He reached out to put a hand over mine, something I used to find comforting. Calming, even. Now it felt more like a cursory "there, there" gesture. "You've been taking work that's in your comfort zone, and you've been doing a good job. That's a great start."

"So how long will it take before you decide I've weathered all the trauma?" *And how come you get to decide this and not me?* I added silently.

Sean and Seth exchanged a quick glance. They did that a lot these days.

"Guess I'd like to see how you keep your head next time you take on a demon."

"And what, exactly, should I be doing to find one?" *I will not blow up.* My frustration felt increasingly like lava bubbling deep inside a seemingly dormant volcano—just because I had a lid on it didn't mean it still couldn't go off at any time. "I mean, we haven't talked about this at all since you guys dropped the 'worst family tree ever' bomb on me."

"Well, Lee, you haven't brought it up either," Sean said gently.

He had a point. I'd tried to ignore it and get on with my life. Except the whole getting on with my life thing was happening with the speed of a lazy glacier.

"Okay, fair enough. So let's talk about it now. If this is something I'm supposed to do, maybe I should be more proactive about it. You said yourself they're not likely to show up on a film set. Should I put out ads in the paper? Print business cards that read 'I'm here to kill your monster'?"

"There's no telling how many are out there or how often you'll run across them. With your mom…" Sean rubbed a hand across his brow, as if to smooth away his nearly non-existent wrinkles. "When Lila first found out her destiny, she searched for demons, kept an eye on the papers. Watched the news. Listened to radio shows. Keeping an eye and an ear out for anything that might be out of the ordinary. People gone missing. Cattle mysteriously slaughtered. Small towns and villages where urban legends originated. She and your dad loved to travel, so they'd choose their destinations accordingly. When two years went by without any sign of one of Lilith's spawn, they decided it was safe to have a child. You."

"She stopped looking," I guessed.

"She did. And then another homicidal demon turned up again and your mother realized it wasn't over, and never would be. She and your father decided to run."

"And they were bushwhacked."

"Yes."

Which led me to the big question. "How do I find the demon that killed them so I can go all Inigo Montoya on its ass?"

"That's something we need to—"

Whatever else Sean might have said was lost in the sound of a *very* loud engine as a car roared up the drive leading to the carport out front. Brakes screeched in harmony with the sound of tires skidding on pavement. There was a brief silence, broken by the slam of car doors and then the sound of the front door bursting open. Heavy footsteps thudded on the tiled floor.

"Holy shit, that was fucking *perfect*," a familiar voice crowed in complete self- satisfaction.

"Yeah, not too bad," came the laconic reply. "Hey, I smell bacon!"

The footsteps headed our way and two men built like WWF wrestlers on steroids clomped into the kitchen. Joe "Drift" McKenzie and Jim "Tater" Tott. Both sported close-cropped beards and mustaches and wore workout gear, including athletic shoes that could double as small kayaks. The two weren't related, but looked like they should be. Drift had some cave troll in his family tree and while Tater didn't talk about his supe heritage, I was pretty sure it included something big and scary. Both of them could take hits and falls that would break the average stuntman without more than a bruise or two to show for it.

I smiled despite the frustration of *conversation interruptus*. Two of the longest-standing members of the KSC, Drift and Tater are on my shortlist of favorites. Drift is one of the best stunt drivers in the business and Tater, a former Army Ranger, thrives on anything as long as it's dangerous. Somewhere between uncles and big brothers, they'd taught me a lot of the ropes when I'd started training. More recently, they'd helped me keep my sanity and sense of humor through the long months of rehab, and watching stunt players less talented get jobs that should have been mine.

"You guys are early," I commented as Drift ruffled my hair with a hand of the size of a dinner plate on his way to the stovetop to see if there was any food up for grabs. He had a brown paper grocery bag tucked under one muscular arm.

"Figured one of these two would be cooking up grub before the morning session starts."

Planting a kiss on the top of my head, Tater hugged me with one arm while his hand did a sneaky-snake maneuver towards my last piece of bacon. I successfully snagged it from under his questing fingers and popped it in my mouth. We had played this game before.

"What makes you think you two are going to get any?" Sean eyeballed the two meal crashers with a mock-stern look.

Drift promptly pulled a case of Stella Artois out of the grocery bag and deposited it on the counter.

Sean gave a satisfied nod. "Okay, then. I think there's still some eggs on the stove."

"Is there more bacon?" Tater asked, poking his head in the fridge while Drift grabbed clean plates and coffee mugs from the cupboard and popped a couple pieces of bread in the toaster. A triumphant hoot signaled the successful discovery of more bacon.

"I'll just fry this up," he said, with a sideways glance in Seth's direction.

"No, you don't." Pushing back his chair, Seth grabbed the bacon and growled, "No one touches my cast-iron but me."

Drift and Tater exchanged satisfied smiles behind Seth's back as he fried up more bacon and made fresh coffee. They had played this game before too, and always won. Seth was a much easier mark than me.

†

Tater and I started the morning training session by introducing the newbies to basic broadsword, while a couple of the more advanced students got to practice sword and shield. My way of training newbies in swordplay is to teach them the parries and target areas along with basic footwork and safe distancing first. Nothing fancy. After they show that they can handle a broadsword without whacking their partners on the extremities or, even worse, the head, I move them onto more complicated weaponry where there's pointwork involved. The goal is to get them to do the moves safely and realistically, making a fight appear scary with a minimum of risk. It is not always successful.

Take Jada, for instance. She's perfectly safe as a fight partner, but there's absolutely no fire, no realism. She thinks if she yells or grunts every time she cuts, thrusts, or throws a punch, it'll make it look real. It doesn't. The smattering of air elemental in her DNA that makes her excel at aerial stunts doesn't do a damn thing for her fighting skills. Not that she'd agree with my assessment. We don't play well together.

Jada and I are similar physical types. Long dark hair. Strong, regular features. Skin that tans easily. My eyes are a blueish violet whereas hers are hazel. I also have more of a melting-pot appearance and can pretty much pass for any ethnicity. Still, Jada is at least two sizes smaller than me, and we've been up for the same job more than once. Until my accident, I usually got the work, even the wirework and falls. Not because of nepotism, but because I'm better than she is. And I don't just say this because I think Jada is a bitch.

Although she totally is.

I mean, first thing she said when she showed up for the afternoon session? "Lee, are you gonna be able to come back and work on *Spasm* with the rest of us?" Her oh-so-faux concerned tone told me she already knew the answer was "no."

Giving her a friendly smile, I replied, "Nah, but it'll be okay. Sean can make do with you until I'm ready to come back to work."

"Well, that'll be a while, won't it?" Jada returned my smile with a saccharine-sweet one of her own. "Because I guess you still can't get past the twenty-foot falls, right?"

I looked at her. "You really haven't been paying attention, have you?"

Then I used the pissed-off adrenaline to climb to the sixty-foot mark of the practice tower and throw myself off without hesitation, stepping into the void and doing a slow forward flip until—

Whomp.

I landed dead center of the airbag on my back, eyes shut, a huge grin on my face as I heard Drift give a loud celebratory whoop.

"Good job, Lee."

No way.

My eyes flew open to see Seth standing next to the airbag. I scanned the sky for four horsemen because Seth praising me is one of the signs of the coming apocalypse. Nothing up there but a few clouds and a red-tail hawk. He extended his hand to help me up off the airbag. I took it gingerly, half-expecting a buzzer to go off and shock me. But nothing happened other than him pulling me to my feet. Oh, and Jada stomping off in the other direction, which was almost as satisfying as Seth's reaction.

"So… that was okay?" *Jeez, could I sound any needier?*

"I'm proud of you," he said simply. "You owned that."

Before I had a chance to find out if I was going to thank

him or burst into tears, Drift picked me up and twirled me around like I was made of straw, hooting and hollering in glee the entire time.

"Holy shit, Lee, that was awesome!"

"It sure was," Tater chimed in, giving me a hug as Drift set me back on my feet.

I smiled, and not just because Jada looked like she'd bitten into the world's bitterest lemon.

Maybe it was time to be proactive and go see my agent.

Hell, if I could impress Seth, I could do anything.

CHAPTER FOUR

Monday late morning I sat across from Faustina Corbin on the other side of a big dark wood desk, at Mana Talent Agency in Beverly Grove. It may not have had the more popular Beverly Hills zip code attached to its address, but MTA was still *the* agency for supes in the entertainment business. Sure, there were other agencies that handled supernatural clients, but none of them had the same clout or reputation as MTA—probably because none of them were owned and run by a former Dacian goddess of the harvest.

The name of the agency—Mana, originally spelled "manna"—was pretty much an in-joke. Faustina once told me the backstory. Manna by itself is neither good nor bad, kind of like the Force. It's also, quite literally, the food of the gods. When the cosmos was created out of chaos, those gods and Titans who came into being the first million or so years lived on it. When they discovered every mortal who believed in them, who offered worship and sacrifice, increased their manna and thus their power, they fought over it, using their worshipers as pawns. They sent them on quests to feed the glory of their chosen deity. Some of the gods still crave the raw power they used to have. Some reinvented themselves. Changed their names to fit whatever mythos people believed in. Some are real bastards. Yahweh comes to mind.

Today Faustina wore a simple cream-colored suit that hugged bounteous curves and a slender waist. Her glossy dark hair was drawn back in a ballerina bun. A few wrinkles on her forehead and the barest hint of crow's feet gave her just enough character without making her look old. I wondered if it was something only ex-goddesses could get away with.

Given my non-supe status, I'd wondered at first why Faustina wanted me as a client. I'd assumed it was because I was good at my job and that I accepted the supernatural element in the world—and in the Industry—without problems or prejudice. After Sean filled me in on my family history, however, I couldn't help but speculate that the whole "descendent of Lilith" played into her decision as well. Whatever the reason, I considered myself lucky. Except all the luck and clout in the world evidently wasn't enough to get me work any time soon.

"Basically, what you're saying is you've got nothing for me right now," I said. "Can you tell me why?" *Or, more to the point, will you?*

"It's slow right now, Lee." Faustina smiled sympathetically, inviting me to agree with her.

"It's not that slow," I argued. "I'm not asking for the impossible, but can't you even get me another piece of schlock like *Dragon Druid Mages*?" Even to my own ears, I sounded like an ungrateful teenager. Faustina graciously chose to ignore my sullen tone, partly because the door to her office opened and her assistant Tracy appeared bearing two venti-sized Starbucks cups.

"Sorry to interrupt, Miss Corbin, but I have your lattes."

She walked as if she were balancing on a tightrope and spilling a drop would mean death. Faustina inspired this kind of over-the-top devotion in her staff.

"Ah, Tracy! Excellent!" Faustina smiled brightly, the kind of smile that chases clouds and their shadows away. Tracy practically blossomed in front of us, the tired lines in her face smoothing out, brown eyes sparkling with pleasure. She carefully set one of the cups in front of Faustina as if presenting Baby Jesus with myrrh and frankincense, putting mine down with less reverence, but equal care.

I thanked her, and she shot me a quick, "You're welcome," before her attention swung back to Faustina—a sunflower shifting to face the sun.

"I'm so sorry about the Nespresso machine." Tracy wrung her hands apologetically. "They still haven't sent the replacement hose for the—"

Faustina cut her off with a wave of one hand. "Please don't worry about it, Tracy. We'll make do with Starbucks for the time being."

Tracy wilted just a little bit, but another smile from Faustina gave her enough energy to leave the room, shutting the door ever so quietly behind her. My agent waited a few beats before saying, "I wish she'd take more vacation days. A lovely girl, but she really needs to get a life outside of the office. Bless her patience with the lines at Starbucks, though."

I sipped my own drink, waiting for Faustina's attention to return to the subject at hand. Before that happened, however, her phone rang. "Well, hell," she said, throwing me an apologetic glance. "Tracy wouldn't bother me unless it was important. Do you mind? I promise I'll just be a few minutes."

How could I say no to an apologetic goddess? "No worries."

She punched the blinking line. "Yes, hon? Oh yes, good

call. Put her through." A pause. "*Hel*-lo, Irina. What can I do for you?" Tucking the phone against one ear and tapping her French manicured nails on the desktop, Faustina listened to a stream of monologue from her caller, giving encouraging "mm hmms" and "I see" at what I was sure were perfectly timed intervals. After a few minutes of this, she finally cut in with, "So you need someone who can ski and has a resistance to frostbite. In their twenties. Not a problem. Jasmine Basnet, quarter Yeti, gorgeous, very athletic, and will have absolutely no trouble shooting a scene while skiing in her skivvies." Another pause. "I'll email her résumé and headshot before lunch. Mm hmmm. Ciao." The receiver went back into its cradle.

Faustina heaved a little sigh, took a sip of her latte and turned back to me. "Now, where were we?"

"Talking about why you can't get me work right now, even jobs that have crap for pay."

"Ah yes, that." She tapped her nails on the desktop again. "As to compensation, I know the pay rate on the jobs you've had aren't what we'd hoped for—"

"But you know I appreciate the work, right? And if it means taking a lower pay rate versus not working at all, I'm okay with that. At least until things pick up."

"I'm sure there will be other projects coming down the pipeline."

"Just not right now," I said bitterly.

"I'm afraid not."

"Dammit." I scowled, deciding anger was a better coping mechanism than despair.

"Be patient, Lee." Faustina stared at me over the rim of her cup. Except it was now a mug, a very pretty piece of hand-thrown pottery with a gold, red and orange glaze that reminded me of a vibrant sunrise. My paper cup-turned-mug was in blues and greens, like the ocean. Nice trick, that.

"We need to let the furor over *Pale Dreamer* die down a bit," she continued. "The lawyers and publicity team managed to hide the worst of things, but the project still has a little bit of—how shall we say?—the stench of death on it."

And there it was—the decomposing elephant in the room.

"Yeah, but it wasn't my fault."

"I know that, hon." Faustina's manner was more sympathetic than impatient—a distinction for which I was grateful. "Problem is, word gets out. And you *did* kill a producer."

I stared at her. "Again, *so* not my fault."

"The people in the know realize that, but his lawyers threw a lot of money at this to preserve reputations. Mainly his."

"What about everyone else who worked on the film? Ben Farrell just got a role on a big-budget horror flick. And what about the crew? I know for a fact that Connor Hayden isn't having trouble getting hired. I saw his name listed under a few things in preproduction." Nothing like following someone on IMDB to make a girl feel like a stalker.

Connor had been the director of photography on *Pale Dreamer*. He was a little full of himself, but good at his job. We'd locked horns at first—figurative horns, since Connor's human—but by the last day of shooting I'd thought we could at least be friends, maybe even a little bit more. Hell, I'd saved his life—I'd expected at least a little gratitude. Other than a get well card after I'd ended up in the hospital, however, I hadn't heard a peep from him. Then again, this *was* Hollywood, the land of "what did you do for me five minutes ago?"

"They didn't kill the producer," Faustina pointed out reasonably.

Well, hell.

"Now you know I'll continue to submit your name for anything that comes up."

"Hell," I said with a sigh, "I'd even go for a Crazy Casa film about now."

Faustina opened her mouth to reply, then hesitated.

Oh, you've got to be kidding me...

"They already said no, didn't they?"

She nodded reluctantly. Now I knew what it felt like to truly hit rock bottom, when the bottom feeders turned their noses up at me. My expression must have shown my feelings because Faustina hastened to say, "You *know* you don't want to work for them. Truth be told, I regretted submitting your résumé the minute I hit the 'send' button." She reached across the desk and patted my hand. "Give it a little while, Lee. When enough time passes, I know we can get you back on some projects with a little bit of clout."

And that was that. I thanked her for seeing me, and gave her a hug. Even ex-goddesses like to feel appreciated.

✝

I decided to stop at Ocean's End for a quick drink to cheer myself up. Once that thought crossed my mind, I gave Eden a quick call to see if she could meet me there. She could, and she would. At least the day wouldn't be a total loss.

Ocean's End is a quirky bar off Ocean Front Walk in Venice Beach, just a few blocks north of the boardwalk. It's not for everyone. I mean that literally. It's in between a bike rental place and craft brew pub, only accessible through a charming little alley that you won't even see unless the owner, Manny, likes you or your timing is exceptionally good.

This was the first time I had been there on my own. I

hoped I wouldn't have any problem finding the entrance. You didn't necessarily have to be a supe to get in—although it helped—but you did have to be aware of their existence… *and* be cool with it. Otherwise the concept of an entrance that worked kind of like a gateway into Fae-ville meets Monster Mash could cause some serious mental damage.

I was pretty sure that Manny liked me, but I couldn't help the little rush of anxiety that rose in my chest as I walked down Rose Avenue and turned right on the boardwalk. The anxiety disappeared when I walked past the brewpub and spotted the alleyway. I smiled in relief when I didn't hit an invisible force field or encounter a bearded man in robes intoning, "You shall not pass!"

A wooden sign with "Ocean's End" carved into it hung above a wood-planked door. It creaked gently as if blown by a nonexistent wind. I pushed the heavy door open and went inside.

Mellow Celtic music played softly, less soporific than Enya, but nothing that'd make a person want to kick up their heels in a jig or a highland fling. The décor alone—a grim selection of seascapes, all storms and ships foundering in white-capped water—was enough to make Michael Flatley hang up his dance shoes and drink himself to death.

The bar was practically empty, most of the wooden tables and booths scattered around the dark wood interior currently unoccupied. Only one of the booths near the front was occupied, by a pair of pale *bardha* having what appeared to be a very earnest discussion. Both had majorly frou-frou cocktails in front of them. You know, the type with umbrellas and pieces of fruit on sword-shaped skewers. Not surprising considering how much *bardhas* love sugar. There were also a couple of Nereids at the bar, water dripping from their long green gauze skirts. Hard-core regulars, they'd been there every time I'd come into Ocean's End.

I headed to the bar, a twenty-foot length of smooth redwood at least six inches thick, with another piece about five feet long creating an L shape at the far end. The top had been polished by years of hands and elbows resting on its surface, but I had no idea how old Ocean's End—or Manny—really was. I also wasn't sure *what* he was, but my gut told me there was something big league in his origin story.

The man himself was, as usual, behind the bar, reading a magazine. Flaming red hair, mustache and beard, all at least a foot long—he kept the front of his 'stache neatly trimmed, but the sides flowed into the beard like tributaries flowing into a river. The front of his hair was pulled back in braids on both sides, with shells, silver beads and pieces of frosted, multicolored glass woven in. He put hipsters and their ironic facial hair to shame.

When we'd first met, Manny had been about as welcoming as the Cthulhuian nightmare pulling a wooden ship down into a storm-tossed ocean in the painting hanging up behind him. Luckily, he'd warmed up to me quickly, possibly because of my ability to spell "Cthulhu" without googling it. Considering his stellar beer list and the generosity of his pours, this made me happy. Although I still question his taste in artwork.

He looked up from his magazine as I approached, eyes currently a shade of green I'd call seafoam. I say "currently" because his irises changed color to reflect his state of mind, like an ocular mood ring.

"Hey, Manny," I greeted him with a little wave, grinning as I got a peek of his reading material—the Fashion Police section of *US Magazine*.

"Mistress Striga," he said with a nod, his thick Irish accent almost sexy enough to offset the facial fur. "And what may I be pourin' for you this afternoon?"

I studied the What's on Tap list, written in chalk on a blackboard next to an old-fashioned register. "How's the Triple Threat?"

"Strong, with enough hops up front to put hair on your chest, but malty and almost sweet on the finish. Nectar of the gods, lass." He poured me a taste. It was everything he'd promised and more.

"Yes, please."

He promptly filled a good-sized snifter and set it in front of me. I handed over a twenty-dollar bill, blinking when he gave me fifteen bucks in change. "Happy hour," he said off my surprised look.

I gave him a sharp glance. "I thought happy hour didn't start until four."

"It's my bar. Happy hour is when I say it is." He glared at me, eyes darkening from seafoam to seaweed.

I held up my hands in surrender. "If you're happy, I'm happy."

He gave a *harrumph* of satisfaction.

"Eden's meeting me here. She never lets me treat so can I just pay for her chardonnay now so she can't argue with me? Pretty please?"

Manny nodded. "Happy hour prices apply, though."

I gave him another five, put down a couple of ones for a tip, and went to the other side of the room, claiming one of the empty booths. Once there, I went over the conversation with Faustina in my head, trying to find anything positive to give me even a small injection of badly needed optimism.

My career, while not entirely in the toilet, had at best moved into a low-rent neighborhood. Sure, I was getting jobs here and there. With production companies that realized they were getting high-quality stunts dirt cheap. Like a four-star dinner at McDonald's Happy Meal prices. Not the kind of paychecks that could afford me a place of my own in any neighborhood I'd want to live in without 24-hour security. And now it seemed that the people whose lives I had saved were afraid to hire me or even recommend me for fear that the stench of death might stick to their clothes as well.

Hypocrites. Like none of them had ever fantasized about snuffing a producer or two.

There was no help for it. If Faustina couldn't—or wouldn't—get me work, I was going to have to do some schmoozing and see what I could do to fix my reputation. While I waited for Eden, I made a list on my phone of stunt coordinators who might want to hire someone with experience. I'd do some research, make some calls, and find out what they were currently working on. And if need be, I'd pay a few on-set visits. Not something I enjoyed, but without the safety net of the KSC, I would have to work on my hustling chops.

Ugh, with a side order of "screw this."

As I scraped the bottom of my brainpan for likely suspects, I realized how insular my professional life with the Katz Stunt Crew had been. I knew more than a few stunt people by reputation, sure. I'd met a lot of them at the annual Taurus Stunt Awards. Some had even offered me lucrative work in the past. But would they be so gung-ho to hire me without my former willingness to throw myself off very tall buildings or dangle from moving helicopters? This was assuming they'd overlook the whole "killing a producer" entry on my résumé.

I had another twenty minutes before Eden was supposed

to arrive. I took a deep breath followed by a big swig of beer, and started making calls. Fifteen minutes later, I'd scratched off at least three-fourths of the names on my list and was too discouraged to try the next one down. I heaved a dejected sigh and put my phone away, even more depressed than I'd been during the months of rehab and physical therapy after my accident.

A large hand plucked the empty glass out from under my nose, setting a fresh one filled to the brim in its place.

"You look like you could use another Triple Threat." Manny smiled down at me. At least I thought the flash of teeth between beard and mustache was a smile. I was touched—Manny didn't usually come out from behind the bar.

"And this—" he set a glass of white wine on the other side of the table "—is for Eden, when she deigns to honor us with her presence."

I started to pull out my purse, but he shook his head. "You already paid for the wine, and the beer is on the house." I nodded my thanks, not trusting myself to speak without getting all choked up. "I'll just add a little extra to Marty's tab," he added. "He's always stingy with the tips."

That made me grin. Marty was a real demon of an agent. A Scaenicus demon, to be precise. They can change their appearance, which is a good thing considering their true form is butt-ugly. In Marty's case, the ugly went all the way through. He was always after Eden to jump ship to his talent agency, couching the offer in the most skin-crawling terms imaginable.

"Can you do that? I mean, is it legal?"

Manny gave a great bark of laughter, the shells and bones woven into his hair and beard rattling like castanets. "Do you think Marty would have the balls to argue with me?"

I laughed. "I think it's debatable that Marty *has* balls."

"Well then." Manny gave a satisfied grin and turned back toward the bar. Then he stopped and swiveled back around to face me again, his irises now swirling in stripes of blues, grays and greens. The colors expanded and retracted, each shade blending into the next like two pinwheels while pupils as black as onyx spun the other direction. *Uh oh.* Last time this happened, Manny had gone into a mini trance, prophesizing doom and gloom like a scary-ass, hirsute Cassandra, and I'd been on the receiving end.

"It's starting again, lass," he intoned. "Repeating the past, doomed to forget each mistake made unless you learn to break the chains that bind."

Here we go again. Unless I was mistaken, this was a similar song and dance to the last time Manny had done his spooky prophet routine, before I'd started work on *Pale Dreamer.*

"You thought him dead," he continued, "but he was only resting. Healing until the wheel of time once again turned in his favor. He is stronger, seeking to bring back that which has been lost—that which must not return. Shapes will form where none lay before. Harbingers to usher in a new age of darkness. Beware those who would betray you for their own glory. Be careful of spilling your beer."

Huh?

Looking down, I saw that I was in danger of pulling the full glass off the table and onto my lap. "Oh."

"Are you all right, lass?" Manny raised one bushy eyebrow in question, concern lacing his tone. His irises had settled back to seafoam green. He hadn't remembered making with the second sight last time either.

One of the Nereids swiveled on her barstool, holding up an empty glass and giving a sad look in Manny's direction.

He nodded and went back behind the bar, leaving me to cradle my beer and wonder how much I should worry about what had just happened.

Last time he'd gone Oracle of Delphi, Manny had warned me about shadows that tore flesh. Nothing metaphorical about it—not long after his warning, there had been much rending of flesh and bone by some nasty shadow demons known as Davea. This latest round of prophesizing didn't sound nearly as gory, more like a demonic amber alert. Although I didn't much like the sound of a "new age of darkness." Didn't I have enough on my plate already?

I took a long pull of the Triple Threat. *God damn, this is some seriously good stuff.*

As the second high-octane beer and Manny's generosity hit my system, my muscles relaxed. My shoulders dropped at least an inch and I heaved another sigh, a contented one this time around. I'd worry about harbingers and what not later.

"Well, you look much happier than you sounded on the phone!"

I looked up to see Eden standing next to the booth. As usual, she was wearing something in a shade of pink, this time a halter-top dress in a deep rose color that offset her natural beauty perfectly. Eden Carmel—pronounced Car*mel*, as in Carmel-by-the-Sea—could be glamorous or she could be the girl next-door. Golden blonde with cornflower-blue eyes. Tall and curvy, like a young Marilyn Monroe. Broad where a broad should be broad. She could probably stop traffic on the 405 freeway—when it was actually going the speed limit.

"I don't know how you do it," I said, shaking my head.

"Do what?" She slid into the seat across from me, plunking a large rose-pink leather bag next to her. One of her knock-off Coach purses. Eden was a great believer in bargain luxuries.

"Look at you, all fresh and cool and spring-like." I gestured in mock disgust. "You should be walking on the beach holding hands with a hunky guy, both of you wearing white, or in a bikini getting ready to go for a swim while talking about confidence in your choice of feminine protection, and how you feel fresh as a daisy."

Eden gave a distinctly unladylike snort of laughter. "That's a compliment, right?"

"Duh."

"Well, thank you." Glancing around, she heaved a contented sigh of her own. "I love it when it's quiet like this. Manny's always so mellow when he doesn't have to deal with throngs of sweaty demons." She glanced over at the Nereids and lowered her voice. "Or soggy sea nymphs."

"Have you ever asked him why he got into the barkeeping business when crowds make him anxious?"

Eden raised an eyebrow. "Even if I summoned up the courage to ask him, the odds of him giving me a straight answer are definitely *not* in my favor." Her gaze fell on the glass of wine. "You got me a drink? You didn't have to do that."

"You're always picking up the tab these days," I said. "I figured I'd get a round in before you could argue with me."

"Lee, you're not working much right now. Not to rub it in, but I just wrapped up a national commercial. I can afford to treat you and I don't mind doing it."

"Yeah, but I don't want you to think I take it for granted, y'know? Besides, sometimes you have to show the universe a little bit of faith to get it to move its ass and help you out." I didn't add that the more I held on to what little money I had, the poorer I felt.

Eden smiled. "I don't think I've ever met anyone who surprises me all the time the way you do."

"Is that a good thing?" I hoped I didn't sound as insecure as I felt. This whole friendship thing was new to me. I had work buddies, sure, but I didn't remember ever really bonding with another female… well, ever. I couldn't remember going to a slumber party as a kid, or even shopping at the mall with girlfriends in high school.

"It's a good thing, you dope. In a town where rich assholes don't even bother to leave tips, it's really nice." She lifted her wine. "Here's to you."

We clinked glasses and drank.

"I got an email from Kyra a few days ago," Eden said casually. Kyra had been the makeup supervisor on *Pale Dreamer*. We'd bonded over our dislike of Portia, the lead actress, but I hadn't heard from her since I'd gotten out of the hospital.

"How's she doing?" I asked somewhat grudgingly.

"She's working on a low-budget indie in Mexico." She paused, then added, "Connor's the DP."

"Oh. That's nice." I tried for nonchalant, but ended up sounding stilted.

"He never contacted you, did he?"

"Nope. But why should he be any different than the rest of the gang. After all the 'Lee, you saved our lives, you're so awesome,' I'm now totally *persona non grata*."

"I'm sure that's not—"

"Oh, it is," I insisted, not even trying to hide the bitterness. "Do you realize you're the only person from that production who still talks to me? It's like having professional leprosy. No one wants to catch it."

There wasn't much Eden could say. She knew I was right. She gave a disgusted huff and shook her head. "Well, that's their loss. And they're stupid. I haven't had any problems getting work."

My turn to shake my head, even as I laughed. "Eden, you'd get hired even if you were besties with Hitler."

"Well, I wouldn't go that far, but—" Eden's attention suddenly shifted as the front door creaked open. "*Hel*-lo…"

I turned and saw a tall, well-built man with his back to us, a long-sleeved cotton thermal doing little to disguise the musculature underneath. Designer jeans hugging an exceedingly nice butt. Dark auburn hair, a more sedate shade than Manny's fiery mane. I could see why Eden's jaw hung ajar, although not enough to be unattractive. I don't think her face is programmed for unflattering expressions.

Eden stared appreciatively. "He's tasty, am I right?"

"Did you get a look at his face yet?" I asked.

"Actually, he *backed* into the room."

"So maybe that's his best side."

Mr. Hunky Butt called to someone still outside the bar, voice deep and pleasantly raspy. The hackles rose on the back of my neck as it stirred some weird and unpleasant sense memory. I recognized the voice, but hell if I could remember the specifics.

A couple of giggling starlets—probably actresses-slash-waitresses-slash-models—sauntered in, draping themselves on the redhead's shoulders and arms like expensive custom-made accessories. You know the type. Six feet of impossibly slender limbs and torso—although if you took their high heels away, they'd lose four inches. Heavy makeup—too heavy for this early in the day—carefully applied. The kind of hair that didn't need a fan or a slow-motion headshake to look like it'd just escaped from a shampoo commercial.

"What's wrong?" Eden raised an eyebrow.

"His voice sounds familiar, but I don't recognize him."

"Maybe you only saw him from the front before," she said with a smirk.

She had a point.

Hunky Butt and his entourage finally came all the way inside, neglecting to shut the door behind them.

Then he turned around, light from one of the wall sconces next to the door falling across his face. Strong, almost coarse features. Pale-blue eyes, tan skin. I knew exactly why I'd recognized his voice. I'd run into him at Arlo's a few months back. He'd been a condescending jerk, oozing both confidence and arrogance while dissing my taste in beer—although to be fair, I'd tossed in some PBR for the boys along with the good stuff. He'd just moved into a place up the road, the DuShane mansion, a genuine 1920s movie-star palace that was rumored—most likely correctly—to be gruesomely haunted.

Figures, I thought. Typical Hollywood show-boater, making sure to be seen with not one, but two hot babes on his arm before lunch. How many women did he take with him on a typical *night* on the town?

Never mind. I didn't really want to know.

"I've definitely met him," I said, still looking at the man. "He may have a magnificent backside, but the man's an ass."

I wondered what kind of supe this guy was. I had a pretty good radar when it came to picking supes out of a crowd of humans, but I couldn't always identify specifics. It's kind of like wine-tasting, except instead of trying to identify grape varietals, you're trying to figure out if someone is a naiad or a dryad.

His companions most likely had a dollop of succubae in their genetic makeup, but they seemed more insipid than sexy. Proof that even supes weren't perfect. There was no denying he was attractive, however. A real bad boy—for those who went for the type.

Not me, though. Nope.

"Well, hell," Eden said.

I pulled my attention away from the newcomer. Eden was smiling, but it was as if someone had made a facial cast of the expression, not the real thing. This was the first time I'd ever seen my friend appear less than authentic. She *looked* like she was acting, like Nicolas Cage on most of his movie posters.

"Do you know him?"

"I'm familiar with him," Eden replied. "Cayden Doran. He does stunts. And also maybe directs. Or writes. Or something." She waved a hand in a gesture as vague as the information she'd just imparted.

The stunt part did not surprise me. There was something edgy about him, the same kind of vibe I'd gotten off a lot of other stuntmen in the past. Willing to try or do anything no matter how dangerous. Extreme. I'd bet he'd climbed and jumped off of more than one figurative mountain just because it was there. The only real question was why I hadn't run into him on a job before now.

I glanced over my shoulder, feeling the weight of someone staring at me. Sure enough, Doran was looking in our direction. He said something to his companions, pointed to a table, and headed our way.

"He's coming over here," I said in an undertone.

"I'm going to run to the ladies' room," Eden said suddenly.

"But—"

"Be right back." Standing, Eden walked quickly past the far end of the bar, vanishing into a hallway that led to the restrooms, leaving me feeling abandoned as Cayden Doran approached the booth.

I stiffened in my comfy padded seat. Last thing I wanted to do was to talk to this guy, especially without Eden to run interference. He'd been an arrogant jackass during the few minutes I'd spent in his company the first time we'd met. When he stopped in front of my booth, I didn't smile or give any indication that his presence was welcome. He sat down across from me in the seat Eden had vacated.

"Too dark to be PBR," he said with a nod toward my glass. "Guess you managed to upgrade since the first time I saw you."

I glared at him with open dislike, not flattered he'd remembered me. "I didn't invite you to sit down."

"Waiting for an invitation means running the risk of not getting invited anywhere interesting."

"So, what? You're a professional party crasher?"

"Not anymore." He leaned toward me, managing to invade my personal space even with a table between us. "These days I'm invited everywhere. There are even people who would pay to have me at their parties."

"Wow. You super-sized your ego when you ordered it, didn't you?"

He shrugged. "Is it ego if it's true?"

"Is it true if it's delusional?" I shot back.

He grinned at me, something not entirely sane dancing in those blue eyes.

I didn't bother to hide my distaste. "How about you go back to your own little party?" I jerked my thumb toward the table where his two companions sat pouting, probably because he was paying attention to me instead of them. "I don't think they like being ignored, whereas it would delight me no end."

He ignored my hint. "I'd rather talk to you."

"Honestly, does the fact that I don't want anything to do with you matter at all?"

That grin again. "Did you know that most of the time when someone starts a sentence with 'honestly,' it means they're lying? In your case, you're lying to both of us."

I could have thrown my drink in his face. But that would've been a waste of damn fine beer. For the first time in my life, I wished I had Pabst Blue Ribbon in my glass. Heresy, I know. Mortals have been struck down for less blasphemous thoughts.

"Is there a point to any of this?" I asked, forcing myself to stay calm. "Because my friend will be back any minute and you're in her seat."

"You're Lee Striga." It wasn't a question as much as a confirmation.

"And you're Cayden Doran. What of it?"

"I might have a job for you."

Oh, there were so many other things I expected him to say, things that would've enabled me to slam the metaphorical door in his face. After the demoralizing conversation I'd had with Faustina, however, I was interested despite myself. This pissed me off no end.

"This looks good," he said, picking up my glass and staring into the dark caramel-colored depths. "What is it?"

"Triple Threat."

"Triple Threat, eh?" He raised the glass and he—

Oh, he did not just take a sip of my beer. But he did.

"Not bad," he allowed. "Are *you* a triple threat, Lee Striga?"

I stared at him, a death stare that should've disintegrated him where he sat.

"You just drank half my beer," I said. "I wouldn't let my boyfriend get away with that, let alone some jackass I barely know."

He smirked. Either he liked to be insulted or didn't care what anyone thought. My money was on the latter. "You've been hanging around the wrong kind of men. The type of guys who drink PBR. The type without the balls to do much of anything without asking first."

"Which is why they're all still alive."

"Really? You seem like the kind of woman who doesn't mind a little danger. A little uncertainty."

"Really?" I mimicked his tone. "And you've figured that out in the space of two random encounters, both of which have taken up less than ten minutes combined?" I shook my head. "You'll have to forgive me if I tell you you're full of shit. Scratch that. I don't give a flying fart if you forgive me or not."

He laughed, unoffended despite my best efforts. "Did I give you my card the first time we met?"

I shrugged. "Sorry, don't remember. You didn't make that much of an impression on me."

As if by magic, a black business card appeared in one of his hands. He slapped it on the table in front of me. "Don't lose it. I don't hand these out to just anyone."

I stared at him. "You really think you're something, don't you?"

"Oh, I know I am."

"If you know as much about me as you seem to think you do, then you'll know some people are actually afraid I might kill them. In your case, it would be a temptation."

He gave a roar of laughter. "Oh, sweetheart, it's been tried more than once."

"No real surprise there." I looked over at the table where his companions alternately pouted and glared in my direction. "Are we done? You're in my friend's seat and I'm tired of getting the death glare from the Barbie twins."

"Call me." With that, he stood up and rejoined his companions without a backward glance.

I didn't bother answering, but I tucked his card in my purse.

†

"Is this the place?" Liz gestured toward the alley with a wide swoop of one hand—the one holding her plastic cup. Pink slush went flying, spattering her three friends. Star shrieked as frozen daiquiri dripped down her ample cleavage, staining her formerly pristine white blouse.

"God, Liz, you are such an asshole!" Tiffany said, emerald eyes flashing annoyance. The slush had splashed her shoes, which she swore were Manolo Blahniks. Her friends already suspected they were knock-offs, and this confirmed it. If they'd been the real thing, Tiff would have ripped Liz's drunken ass a new one.

Cherry took her fair share of daiquiri splatter too, but didn't care. She was just happy she'd worn black this evening and didn't have to waste time being pissed at Liz. She'd rather just enjoy the evening.

Bourbon Street was a notorious tourist destination in the French Quarter of New Orleans—certainly not the place where locals went when they wanted to get drunk without spending too much. They also carded, and all three girls were a few months shy of their twenty-first birthdays. Still, it was a fun place to hang out and meet cute guys there to party. Some of them—usually older ones—didn't mind sharing their to-go drinks in return for some flirtation.

"Girls Gone Wild missed out," Cherry's stepmother Jazz sniped as the girls had been heading out the door.

"They're just high-spirited," Cherry's dad had replied, not for the first time. Dad had more tolerance than her stepmother. Then again, he'd known the girls since they were kids, pre-cleavage and attitudes.

"Sluts, more like." Jazz's comment had been just loud enough to be audible. Cherry had heard it, and so had her friends.

"Your mom is such a bitch," Tiffany said now, as if reading Cherry's mind.

"She's not my mom," Cherry said for the umpteenth time. "I swear, I don't know why Daddy married her. She's, what, like four years older than me?"

"Careful, Cherry," Star said. "You sound like Chutney in *Legally Blonde.*"

"I don't need to perm my hair," Cherry said with the smugness of truth.

"C'mon, you guys!" Liz gave another drunken wave, and the four entered the alley, teetering on uneven cobblestones not meant to accommodate three-inch stiletto heels. Tiffany and Cherry clung to one another, following Liz and Star to a door set into a weathered brick wall that looked too old to house an establishment named LeRoy's Ink Shop.

Going inside, the girls expected to find some sort of pirate tavern, men with beards wearing puffy shirts and boots, with busty wenches on their laps, swigging from huge tankards of ale. Instead there were walls covered with artwork, tattoo samples, and a sign that read: IT'S ALL ABOUT THE PAIN. THE TATTOO IS JUST THE SOUVENIR. Chairs that could almost belong at a dentist's office and a long counter with portfolios on top. Three women, two of which were working on clients. Those two could be twins—long brown hair, huge muddy green eyes and receding chins. Like frog princesses. Pretty in spite of themselves. Both smiled at the newcomers, then went back to their work.

The third woman, a petite brunette who looked like she spent too much time in libraries, was currently unoccupied. She smiled and said, "Can I help you?"

Tiffany, as usual, stepped forward and took charge. "Yes," she said in her best "you are the help and don't forget it" voice. "My friends and I want to get tattoos."

The girl's eyebrow shot up at Tiffany's tone, but she kept her own voice civil. "Well, you can see some examples on the walls."

Tiffany gave the girl and the artwork in question a quick disparaging glance. "If that's the best you have, we're wasting our time." Cherry actually thought the art was way cool, but Tiffany never liked anything unless she knew she had the best of the best.

The girl opened her mouth to reply, but before she'd begun, a deep, rich voice from the back of the store caught everyone's attention. Her mouth snapped shut on whatever pithy insult she'd been intending to unleash.

As for Cherry and her friends, even Tiffany's attitude melted in the face of the warmth and charm oozing from the man stepping out from the back of the shop. Tall. Strong, aquiline features. Complexion an olive-toned tan. Eyes the color of smoky topaz. He smelled like spiced coffee and forbidden fruit.

"We…" Tiffany gulped, staring into those dark eyes. "We'd like tattoos. All of us."

The man smiled and nodded. "I'm LeRoy. I will be happy to help you lovely ladies choose the perfect ink for each of you."

Tiffany gave a self-satisfied smile that made Cherry want to slap her. "Our friend was here," Tiffany continued. "She said she got a special tattoo."

Star nodded. "From a special book."

"That's right," Tiffany agreed. "She said the book wasn't something that just anybody could look at."

"Ah," LeRoy breathed. "Your friend chose the blue morpho design."

"Is that a butterfly?" Cherry asked. "If that's a butterfly, that's what Celia got."

"It's really nice for a tramp stamp," Tiffany added.

LeRoy smiled. "I know just the book you speak of." He pulled a thick book bound in brownish-red leather on the counter. "Here. My own special portfolio. Take a look and see if anything strikes your fancy."

All four girls felt like he was talking just to them alone. Had he placed one portfolio on the counter or four? None of them could remember, but when all was said and done, Tiffany chose an exotic flower in vivid shades of reds and purples that might be found in the heart of the Amazon. Liz was drawn to a stylized heart surrounded by black lace, like a Gothic valentine. Star, appropriately enough, chose a star in a simple design that seemed to glow with a life of its own, and Cherry picked a delicate pair of wings, like an angel's, but black.

All four girls wanted LeRoy to ink their tattoos—after all, they were his designs. He smiled apologetically and said that he could only do one, but his three apprentices—the three women in the shop—were more than up to the task. Tiffany insisted that she be the one to be inked by LeRoy himself. The other three girls grumbled, but knew better than to argue. Tiff was a total bitch when she didn't get her own way.

When all four tattoos were finished, and the girls were back on Bourbon Street, it didn't seem as if any time had passed at all.

The eternity of pain came later.

CHAPTER FIVE

I knew I was going to call Cayden Doran. I had a feeling in my gut—the kind of churning that feels like indigestion, but is actually certainty that a course of action, however distasteful, is the right and necessary thing to do. Just in case I was wrong, though, I took some Pepto-Bismol. Then I forced myself to do something I'd never had to do before.

I hustled.

In stunt parlance, hustling is networking on steroids. If you're not lucky enough to belong to a crew like KSC, which gives priority to its own members before bringing in outside stunt players, you need to get your face and résumé in front of working stunt coordinators. Which means first you find out when and where they're working. Then you have the fun of sneaking onto the set—avoiding sometimes very over-zealous security—finding the stunt coordinator, and then trying to find a good time to introduce yourself and hand off your résumé without pissing anybody off.

I hoped that the in-person touch might have a more positive outcome than calling. A voice on the other end of the phone was easier to dismiss than someone standing right in front of you, right?

Doing my research with a little help from Randy—who I

know would have hired me if there'd been any female parts in *Deadly Emancipation*, the low-budget high-testosterone *Deliverance* rip-off he'd just scored as stunt coordinator—I started with Bogle McNabb, a long-time crony and friendly rival of Sean's. The only thing supernatural about Bogle was his name, which came from a mischievous spirit that haunted the McNabb family manse in Scotland. Bogle's parents had given him the nickname because he liked to do scary things, like jump off buildings and crash cars. He was tall, thin and pale, but not particularly scary or mischievous. He took his job seriously and was someone that Sean spoke of with respect.

I successfully hunted Bogle down on the closed set of a television spy thriller at Warner Bros, lurking by craft services and doing my best to look like a harmless production assistant until cast and crew broke for lunch.

"Lee, good to see ya!" The warmth in Bogle's hug was genuine, but his smile was a little too forced to give me optimism. "What can I do you for?"

"I just thought I'd see if you might need an awesome stunt woman." No point in wasting time with false modesty, right?

Bogle's smile slipped a notch. "Gee, Lee," he said, scratching his head with long white fingers. "You know I'd love to work with you, but we're full up right now, and it's a mainly male cast and all that."

I nodded even as I gave an inward sigh. I had a feeling that even if the show had called for a cast of more Amazons than *Wonder Woman*, he would not hire me to work on it.

"That's too bad, Bogle," I replied, keeping my tone upbeat even as another chunk of hope broke off and sank into the pit of my stomach. "I'd love to work with you. Know anyone looking to hire?"

Bogle scratched his head again, pretending to think really hard. "Not offhand, Lee." No surprise there. "If anything comes up, I'll be sure to pass on your name."

I didn't let on that I knew the key word here was "pass."

"Thanks, Bogle." I handed him an envelope with my résumé and he took it with promises both of us knew he couldn't or wouldn't keep any time soon. Then I left, walking off the soundstage with the purposeful stride of someone who had someplace to be. Another trick for staying under the radar of security guards. Mentally crossing Bogle off my rapidly shrinking list, I psyched myself up for a drive to Sun Valley and another stunt coordinator I fully expected to turn me down.

Sometimes I really hate being right.

†

A few hours later, I'd officially gone through all the remaining stunt coordinators on my list. I'd done a good job keeping my spirits up until my third miss, on the set of a little pissant studio off of the 118 freeway in Sun Valley. I'd dropped in on a stunt coordinator I only knew by reputation, but whose right-hand man happened to be a woman. I'd thought this might make him more open to taking a chance on me and maybe it would have, but his assistant was not happy to see me and didn't bother trying to pretend that she was. So much for female solidarity in the Industry.

It looked like I'd be holding down things at the Ranch while the rest of the team worked on *Spasm*. Randy was going to help out when his schedule allowed, along with any of the core team not needed on any given day on set, but it would mostly be me running the training sessions.

It made me feel slightly less guilty when I knew I was contributing to the household even though Sean had told me more than once he didn't expect me to pay rent. Still, I needed to earn real money and get my own place instead of feeling like one of those little birds that lives on the scraps it cleans out of crocodile teeth. Besides, as far as Seth was concerned, job-hunting didn't count—the end result was all that mattered to him. He'd never lacked for work a day in his adult life and certainly didn't know what it was like to be repeatedly rejected—how that wore a person down. If he'd ever been rejected by anyone for anything in his lifetime, I'd eat an airbag.

I almost called Randy to see if he wanted to get together, but then I remembered he was working today. Just as well—I didn't want to become reliant on him, or for him to think I was relying on him to cheer me up whenever I was down. In my current state, that would be a full-time job. Something a boyfriend would do. But if I wasn't willing to commit to that type of relationship, it wasn't fair of me to expect him to do the work without getting the perks.

Okay, he got some of the perks, but still… I didn't want to dial our relationship up any higher at this point.

I'd already hit Eden up once this week for cheer-up duty, and I was nowhere near her neck of the woods anyway. Instead, I drove home to an empty house, tired, depressed and hangry, hoping that there were still a couple of bottles of decent beer in the fridge. There was. Dogfish Head 90 Minute tucked away in the back behind one of Drift's six-packs of Stella Artois. And, wonder of wonders, there were also a few slices of leftover pizza. Nothing special, just from a local delivery joint, but it would do me fine.

I threw a couple pieces in one of Seth's beloved cast-iron skillets, covered it with a lid, and turned the heat on low. Then I popped the top off a bottle of Dogfish Head, finishing half of it in two greedy gulps.

I pulled the pizza out of the cast-iron, adding a drizzle of truffle oil on top. Seth could be a dick, but he'd taught me things about cooking that turned cheap delivery pizza into something just short of gourmet. I made sure to wipe the pan out, mainly because I wasn't up to getting reamed out. Besides it would've been a dick move to leave a mess.

Who says I can't be mature?

Retrieving Cayden's card from my bag, I stared at it while I ate a slice of pizza, finished my first beer, and opened another. Stared some more. And finally decided I had reached bottom and had nothing left to lose.

Taking a deep breath, I dialed the number on the card.

One ring and it went straight into voicemail.

"Leave your name and number. Tell me why you're not potentially wasting my time." *Beep.*

I recognized that voice. All husky and deep and full of arrogance. My first instinct was to hang up. My second? To say "fuck you," and *then* hang up.

What I actually did?

"Lee here. You know why I'm calling. And if your phone isn't smart enough to have stalker vision in this industry, talking to you would be a waste of *my* time." I hesitated, then added cheerfully, "Have a great day!"

Click.

Well, that's the end of that, I thought.

My phone rang. The theme from *Jaws*, meaning someone calling for the first time. I checked my own caller ID. Cayden.

Okay then.

I hit the button. "This is Lee."

A low, smoky chuckle. "I know."

"That's good," I said. "Saves us both time."

"I like that."

"Uh… good?"

Another chuckle. "You want the job."

It was a statement, not a question.

"Depends."

A pause, but not a silence. Amazing how a lack of words could fill the space so eloquently.

"Good enough. We'll talk it over. Meet me at my place in an hour."

I thought about it. I mean, really gave it some consideration. I'd always wanted to see the inside of the DuShane mansion, because who can resist a good, old-fashioned horrific tale of ghosts and murder? But this was not the time or the occasion for indulging in ghost house porn.

"How about we just meet at a coffee shop?"

"I'm surprised. You don't strike me as being timid."

"Yeah, well, you don't strike me as necessarily trustworthy. And for the record, I prefer 'prudently cautious' to 'timid.'"

There was silence at the other end of the line, but I could swear he was laughing.

"Fine," Cayden finally said. Yup, I definitely heard a slight quiver of amusement in his voice. "Meet me at the Starbucks at Trancas Country Market at 10 A.M. tomorrow."

"Okay." I paused, then added, "What's the job?"

"Just be there."

Click.

He'd hung up.

Asshole.

†

"Dude, hurry up and pick a fuckin' tattoo already. Bourbon Street, booze and bitches are waiting!" Simon let out a raucous belch to punctuate his words. Looking up from the portfolio he was flipping

through, Charlie saw Tia, the tattooist working on his friend, wrinkle her nose in distaste. Simon didn't notice. She wasn't his type, Charlie could see that—no makeup, oversized glasses, brown hair pulled back in a single braid. Real bookworm type. If she'd had decent tits, Simon would have been flirting with her, but those were A cups at best under her plain black tank top. Not worth the time.

Charlie—an on-campus DJ whose shock jock persona was only slighter cruder than Charlie himself—was Simon's best friend. Their frat house had just been reinstated after a year's suspension, and both of them were in a mood to celebrate. They'd come to New Orleans to get drunk and—if possible—get laid. They had a free place to crash close to the French Quarter with Simon's cousin, and three days to do the town—which pretty much meant Bourbon Street, as far as they were concerned.

Charlie had been the one to spot the little tattoo parlor tucked away in a side alley off the ass end of Bourbon Street, and they'd had just enough potent hurricanes earlier at Pat O'Brien's to make spending time and money on tats seem like a good idea. Luckily this tattoo shop, unlike many, didn't have a hard and fast rule about their customers being sober.

Simon had quickly picked out a Greek symbol meaning "strength" to go on his left deltoid and the work was already underway. Charlie was still skimming the portfolios, trying to find something that caught his fancy. The buzzing of Tia's tattoo gun sang in the background, like a chorus of quiet hornets.

"What about that one?" Simon pointed to a photo on the wall of a hammerhead shark tattoo. "You're always hammered, am I right? Or you could shave your mustache and get 'pussy eater' tattooed there instead." He guffawed at his own joke, shoulders shaking with drunken laughter.

The tattooist paused in her work to avoid a potential blowout, even though the urge to ink the kanji for "anus" on the frat boy's skin was nearly irresistible. If LeRoy hadn't been lurking in the back room, keeping an eye on her work, she might have done it. But she knew better. She was lucky to be LeRoy's apprentice. And one of his favorite sayings was, "Do not fuck with the integrity of the ink, no matter how unworthy the canvas"—even if the canvas was shitfaced.

Charlie shook his head. "Lame, bro."

"Dude, not supposed to use that word, remember?"

"Do me a favor," Charlie said. "Go into your safe space and fuck yourself."

Simon belched again in reply. Charlie flipped him the bird and continued his search for the perfect tattoo. The shark had been kind of cool—he liked the idea of a predator inked on his skin. But it wasn't quite right.

"Nothing catching your eye?"

Charlie looked up from his dissatisfied perusal of a stylized tiger to find a smiling man with dark hair standing behind the counter. Later—after his skin burned and peeled, crusted over and then hardened into scales—all Charlie could remember was the man's smile, with lots of crooked teeth.

"See if you find anything more to your taste in here."

The man slapped another binder down on the counter, although this one had a much nicer cover than the others—dark brownish-red leather. Charlie found his fingers caressing it even though there was something unpleasant about the soft, almost oily texture of the leather. Unpleasant and yet…

Charlie opened the binder, revealing a world of vivid colors and unforgettable images. The noise from the streets faded into the background as he flipped through the pages, marveling at the depth of imagination that went into each piece of art. Even the simplest of drawings crackled with a life and animation that none of the other samples came even close to having. An ouroboros done as a stylized Celtic knot… A Chinese dragon with red and gold lacquered scales... *A blue butterfly so realistic it seemed to be suspended in flight... A phoenix in a nest of flames, beak outstretched in a cry of agony and rebirth... The face of a woman in mourning, a black tear tracing down her cheek, the skin splitting where the tear had already passed... A man eating his own arm...*

He finally paused when he came to a drawing of a crocodilian head rising from dark water rendered in dark-green ink. Its reptilian jaws stretched wide to reveal jagged rows of teeth and its eyes seemed to glow with endless hunger. And was that a human hand caught in those jaws? He peered more closely. It was. Ribbons of flesh seemed to float between its teeth.

"Oh yeah," he whispered.

The man behind the counter nodded in satisfaction.

"These are my own designs," he said, the slightest hint of a French accent evident in his voice. "I'll do the work myself."

"Awesome," Charlie said absently.

"Tia, you good to mind the shop till Hyla and Polli get here so I can ink this boy?"

"Sure, LeRoy," Tia replied.

"Give me a few minutes to set up in back and we'll get to work." He grinned at Charlie with more teeth than the reptile.

Charlie nodded, unable to take his eyes off the drawing. The rest of the world was irrelevant.

†

LeRoy pulled out the ink he only used for the special tattoos. Whenever these were necessary, he tried to find the joy and glory of knowing that out of the bearer's agony would come a harbinger— and that his skill was an integral part of the process. But still, the gods did not always choose vessels deserving of the suffering that went with their fate. The young girl who had picked the butterfly, for instance—her personality had been as fragile and beautiful as the symbol she had chosen. Her soul as pristine as her milk-white skin.

When she had gravitated to the special book and pointed at the blue morpho, what was left of LeRoy's soul had curdled a little around the edges. But there was nothing for it. All harbingers decided upon their own vessel.

Her fate had been sealed once he'd laid down the last of the ink.

When the time had come for her transformation to begin, he'd removed her from her home in the silence of the night and placed her in an oven vault in La Fayette Cemetery No. 1 for the gestation period. The girl would be aware of the changes being wrought to her body for every agonizing second, right up until the point when the harbinger finally ate its way out of her skin. It was on this sort of insufferable pain that the harbingers drew enough strength to bring back He Who Eats Worlds from beyond the stars into this dimension.

He might have spared the girl if it had been up to him.

Others, like her four friends… Well, he had no pity to waste on them. As for this youth, he wore his corruption and bad intentions like a badge of honor. Was it any wonder that he'd been drawn to this particular image? Of all the harbingers, the one that would come forth from this oaf's screaming flesh was the key to the most important door of all. Without the Thaumaturge as the central beacon, He Who Eats Worlds could not find His way through the frozen stars and hell dimensions to finally reach the Earth.

If the other vessels suffered agonies of the damned during the gestation process, this youth's suffering would eclipse it all. What was the quote? Oh yes. His suffering would be legendary, even in Hell.

LeRoy couldn't wait to begin the process.

CHAPTER SIX

Some film execs liked to meet prospective employees in plush offices, secure behind their big-ass desks, like in *The Big Picture*. I preferred the informality of restaurants or coffee houses. I might not get the job in question, but at least I'd usually get a decent cappuccino. Starbucks wasn't the world's best coffee, but it was reliable. As Miles from *Sideways* put it, "quaffable but not transcendent."

I arrived at Trancas Country Market at nine-thirty the next morning, a half-hour before I was due to meet Cayden. A surge of nervous energy had woken me at five, so I'd surfed that wave and given myself plenty of time to shower and dress. I wore jeans and a form-fitting gray AleSmith T-shirt from my ever-growing brewery collection, this one advertising Evil Dead Red Ale. I'd got on the road with time to spare—enough to show I was serious but not so early as to appear desperate.

Checking my minimal makeup in the rearview mirror of my Saturn, I ran a brush through my hair, which I'd worn long and loose today. Then I wandered around the uber-quaint and rustic shopping center, killing time by admiring jewelry, casual beach wear and household items I couldn't afford. At nine fifty-five I headed over to the Starbucks and went inside, planning on getting my drink and snagging a seat before Cayden arrived.

I felt an irrational surge of irritation when I saw that he was already there, ensconced at a corner table that allowed him a view of the parking lot, as well as both entrances to the Starbucks. Which meant he probably saw me arrive early, and fix my hair and makeup. And of course he'd assume I cared what he thought of my appearance.

A-a-a-nd I need to stop overthinking.

Cayden looked up from the script he was reading and nodded at me, a half-smile playing on his lips as if he knew what I'd been thinking.

I gave a half-hearted wave in return and got in line behind a teenage boy with clothing so artfully distressed you could almost hear it whisper, "Please kill me," and a thirty-something Suit in the middle of a Very Important Call.

"I don't care if he's not available," the Suit said loudly, "you *make* him available and you do it now, or the only job you'll get in this town will be slinging lattes at Starbucks!"

Wow, lacking basic survival skills. The barista doing the slinging in this particular Starbucks shot him a quick but heated glare. The odds were good the Suit would get a little something extra in his latte.

When it was my turn, I pulled out my credit card to pay for my cappuccino and toasted Everything bagel with cream cheese, but the cute twenty-something cashier shook his head. "The gentleman there already paid," he informed me, with a nod toward Cayden.

I didn't bother correcting his judgment of Cayden's character, instead asking, "Out of curiosity, how did he pay when he didn't know what I was going to order?"

"He left more than enough money to cover whatever you got," the barista replied.

"O-kay… Do you want me to take him his change?"

"Oh no. He said that whatever was left we should put in the tip jar."

Damn.

There's nothing I hate more than a rich asshole who doesn't tip well, and Cayden Doran had to go and *not* fall into the stereotype. Didn't he realize I didn't *want* to like anything about him?

"Well, that was nice," I said stiffly.

"I know, right?" He cast an adoring glance in Cayden's direction. Couldn't really blame him. Good-looking and generous was a heady combo—and the cashier obviously hadn't met the self-centered jerk I'd encountered twice before.

After a quick internal debate, I decided it would be less awkward to go say hello than to stand and wait for my order, knowing that Cayden was watching me. I walked over and set my portfolio on the table across from him.

"Hey there," I said. My tone had gone from stiff to paralyzed.

"Miss Striga." He stood up and held out a hand, very formal. I was pleasantly surprised that he didn't try using an overly macho Kung-Fu grip to impress me with his strength.

"How was traffic?"

Really? Small talk?

I shrugged. "Not bad. But then you probably had the same drive that I did, since you live up the road."

"I had a meeting in Santa Monica earlier this morning," he said. "The kind of traffic made for audio books. The drive back on PCH, on the other hand, was made for fast cars with good traction."

"And speeding tickets."

"Haven't gotten one yet," he said, somehow managing to sound matter-of-fact instead of smug.

The barista called my name. When I came back with my latte and bagel, I took a seat across from him. "Thanks for picking up the tab," I said, not wanting to be ungrateful. Still, I couldn't help adding, "Appreciated, but totally unnecessary."

"Hey, it's the thing to do." Cayden shrugged and flashed me that grin again, the one that combined dark humor with the promise of trouble. Dangerously attractive.

Nope, no more bad boys.

I decided to get down to business. "So, tell me about the job."

He raised an eyebrow. "What? No more small talk?"

"We already covered traffic," I said, smiling sweetly at him over my latte. "Besides, I thought we agreed neither of us likes to waste time."

"Fair enough. I see you brought your portfolio. Unnecessary, but appreciated." He threw my own words back at me, hoisting me on my own snippy petard without breaking a sweat.

Touché.

"Let's see it." He held out a hand.

"I thought it was unnecessary."

"Wouldn't want you to feel like you wasted the effort." His hand remained outstretched.

I studied him for a moment. "You know," I finally said, "I get the impression you think you know me a lot better than you do."

He shrugged. "Maybe. I've seen some of your work. And you know how close-knit the stunt community is. People talk."

That they do.

I handed him my portfolio case without another word. He unzipped it, putting it down in front of him after carefully moving his coffee and pastry out of the way—a fact I appreciated.

Double dammit. I didn't want to like anything about this man.

As he flipped through the various photographs of me in action, I tore off a piece of overly toasted bagel, smeared some cream cheese on it with a wobbly plastic knife, and took a bite, following it up with more latte. I found myself strangely comfortable, a stark contrast to the level of irritation and dislike I'd felt during our encounter at Ocean's End.

When he finally finished perusing my portfolio, he zipped it shut and handed it back to me with a satisfied nod. "It appears you're everything I heard you were. You've done some acting as well, right?"

"Yeah," I said. "Unfortunately, the film didn't get finished." I figured he knew what film I was referring to if he knew so damned much about me.

"I saw some footage." An irritating little half-smile played on his mouth.

I wanted to ask him how he'd seen the footage, where it was, how I could get some of it for my demo reel. Even Faustina hadn't been able to manage that. Instead I took a deep breath and waited for him to follow up on that statement.

Contrary bastard that he was, Cayden cocked his head to one side and said, "You were trained by Sean Katz."

Fine. I nodded. "Since I was seven."

"I can assume you're comfortable working with supernaturals."

"Absolutely," I assured him. "Some of my best friends are supes." I wasn't even being facetious.

"Good. Our cast and crew is a mixed bag, but most of them are supes, and those that aren't don't have a problem with it."

"What about you?" The words popped unbidden out of my mouth before I could stop them. My face flushed red with embarrassment at the *faux-pas*.

"I'm surprised you didn't work on *Wonder Woman*," Cayden said blandly, changing the subject as if my last question never happened. "I would've thought you'd be a natural for all the sword-fighting and wirework in that."

"I took a bad fall," I answered, both grateful and annoyed at the easy out Cayden had offered me. "It put me out of commission for a good six months. I like to think I would've made the cut for that movie, but I was in physical therapy learning how to walk again." The back of my neck itched. I absent-mindedly scratched it, a fingernail snagging on my necklace chain.

"That's right. I remember reading about that when it happened." His eyes were on me, appraising me. "Give me an honest answer here. Do you think you're back up to speed?"

I chose my words carefully. "Yes. The only reservations I have right now are with high falls or wirework, depending on what kind of heights we're talking. Still working on getting back into the swing of things."

He nodded, and seemed to be deep in thought. I didn't regret being honest. I'd either get the job or I wouldn't. What surprised me is how much I suddenly hoped I would.

"There are a couple of falls," he finally said, "two to three stories, tops. Do you think you can handle that?"

"We're talking thirty to forty feet?"

"If that."

My turn to mull things over. I could now easily take falls off the tower at the Ranch from forty feet with no problem, not even counting the sixty-footer I'd taken over the weekend. I'd since repeated it, albeit without the pissed-off adrenaline that Jada had supplied. The backs of my legs had crawled and things had churned in my stomach, but I'd been able to let go and do the fall without clutching onto the tower like a kid afraid to step off a high dive for the first time.

I took a deep breath. "Yeah, I can handle that." Wonder of wonders, I wasn't bullshitting either.

He nodded as if I'd answered a very important question. "So. The job. We're filming in New Orleans. It's a fast-paced action period piece about voodoo."

Seriously?

"A fast-paced action period piece about voodoo?" I repeated. I couldn't help it.

"If Snyder can turn *Batman versus Superman* into a film with the pace of an unambitious glacier, and moodier than an emo teenager…" He shrugged. "Well, then we can make Marie Laveau an action hero."

"Is her mother's name Martha?"

Cayden laughed, showing his teeth. He had a lot, all of them very white. Then he reached down by his chair, pulled out a script, and slapped it down on the table in front of me. The title did indeed read *Voodoo Wars*. I did not snort or roll my eyes, both of which could be construed as rude and inappropriate—although totally justified—responses, especially since the "written by" was followed by two names, one of them Cayden's, the other someone named Devon Manus—a line of text below informing me it was the property of Berserker Productions. Instead I put on my best "I am very serious about this job" face and asked, "Not to be rude, but since when does a screenwriter get a say in hiring the crew?" I smeared more cream cheese on my Everything-but-fresh bagel.

"Partly because I'm also the stunt coordinator and second unit director," he replied. "I'm also one of the executive producers."

"Ah."

"Ah, indeed," he agreed. "Director's a buddy of mine. We co-wrote the script. We've been looking to work together on a project for a few years and…"

Cayden's voice faded into the background. The sky seemed to darken as if a sudden storm full of ominous clouds had moved in from the ocean. The sky was cloudless, though. Just… gloomy, like someone slipped a filter over the sun. A reddish tint glazed the horizon and things suddenly grew very quiet. The air felt uncomfortably still, like riding in a car with the vents closed on a hot day. The back of my neck itched even more, like someone had slapped a patch of poison ivy there.

Shit.

This had happened to me twice before—once at the Ranch and once on the street in Venice Beach. Both times I'd had the sense of time almost standing still—and of being in mortal danger. This was no different. White-knuckled, I clutched the flimsy plastic knife.

"Am I boring you?" I looked up to find Cayden staring at me, one eyebrow raised.

I shook my head, my skin buzzing with electricity, the amulet around my neck suddenly tingling against my skin. "Something—"

Someone screamed.

I twisted around in my chair just as a teenage boy in board shorts stumbled through the front doors, gasping for breath. Skin the deep tan of a dedicated surfer. Bare arms, legs and torso oozing blood from multiple lacerations, as if he'd lost an argument with a rose bush, the terrified expression on his face completely at odds with the beautiful sunny day. A look like this one belonged in the shadows.

He swayed back and forth before collapsing to his knees. I

leaped to my feet, knocking the chair over backwards in my hurry to reach him. It spoke unflattering volumes about the clientele in Starbucks that most of the people backed away, as if they were afraid of getting blood on their clothes. Only one other person joined me as I ran over to the injured boy.

Cayden.

Mentally adding a tick to the "pros" column of taking a job on *Voodoo Wars*—stunt coordinator not afraid of blood—I knelt by the kid's side, gingerly putting an arm around his shoulders to prevent him from falling face forward onto the floor. Slowly I eased him back against the wall into a half-sitting/half-lying position.

"Someone call 9-1-1," I said harshly.

A rail-thin blonde in expensive designer yoga-wear took out her phone. "What's the number?" she asked in a no-nonsense tone.

You've got to be fucking kidding me. She wasn't.

"9-1-1," I snapped, then turned back to the kid. "Can you talk?"

He coughed in reply and a thin spray of blood misted out. Not good.

Cayden grabbed a bottle of water from the open cooler against the wall, twisted off the lid, and handed it to me. I held it up to the boy's mouth. "Here," I said gently.

He took a sip, and then another, stark terror in his pale-blue eyes.

"It's coming," he said, coughing again. Drops of blood clung to his lower lip.

"What's coming?"

Even as I asked the question, the back of my neck started itching again, practically buzzing.

"We were surfing," the kid replied weakly, "me and Robin.

There was a ton of seaweed today, all over the fucking place." He drank more water, then continued. "Robin wiped out, went straight into a kelp bed. At first I thought she was tangled. She started yelling for help. And then I saw the kelp move, wrap around her arms and her head, and pull her down. I saw blood… I thought maybe it was a shark, y'know? I tried to ride in, get help. But… it followed me. Seaweed on the skeg…"

What the hell did that *mean?*

"Oh God…" He struggled to sit up, rolling his eyes like a panicked horse. "I saw it coming out of the water!"

Cayden crouched down next to me, putting a hand on the kid's shoulder to keep him in place. The contact seemed to calm him.

"What was it?" Cayden asked.

The kid shook his head. "I don't know."

Fresh screams from outside the Starbucks told me that we'd know soon enough.

CHAPTER SEVEN

I ran to the front door. People stood in the parking lot, shouting and pointing toward the Pacific Coast Highway in front of the marketplace. Two cars heading north slammed on their brakes to avoid hitting a nasty pile-up on the highway directly in front of the main entrance. At least a half-dozen vehicles were involved, locked together as steam hissed out from under crumpled hoods.

Closest to the marketplace, the front bumper of a red Prius was buried into the driver's side of a silver RAV4. The prognosis looked bad for both drivers. They must have both braked to avoid an obstacle in the road and the RAV4 had spun sideways, the Prius barreling into it. Something greenish-brown clung to the undercarriage of the RAV4, maybe a tumbleweed or something.

Then I noticed the stuff moving, writhing up and around the dented metal of the cars.

The passenger door of a Mercedes opened and a woman tumbled out onto the asphalt, falling heavily to her knees. Almost immediately, tendrils of the greenish-brown mass shot out and wrapped around her thighs and torso. It looked like a giant pile of seaweed, all strands and ribbons and pods. She screamed, trying to tear it off, but even as she peeled the thick slimy ribbons away from her waist, another one slapped down next to it. Blood seeped out from her skin between large flat, furry fronds, only to vanish. Gobbets of flesh dropped on the road as the woman seemed to shrink before my eyes.

My amulet burned with cold fire against my skin.

Well, hell.

It seemed my wait to meet another demonic relative might be over.

More screams emanated from the other cars involved in the smashup as the thing sent exploratory strands into the interiors. I could see the people trapped inside, trying to open crumpled doors, hammering on automatic windows that would not open. In the blink of an eye, the people were obscured by a seething mass of greenish brown, their screams muted but still audible.

Even as I took a step forward, strong fingers wrapped around my elbow and jerked me back. Cayden again. Before I could snap at him, he tapped my right hand and said, "If you're going to fight it, you need a weapon. A better one than that."

I still clutched the knife from Starbucks, cream cheese smeared on the black plastic. Amulet or not, I just couldn't see myself tackling vicious, carnivorous ambulatory seaweed with a plastic utensil.

"Car," I said.

Cayden and I had the same idea pretty much simultaneously. He took off at a lope to a silver Porsche 911 Turbo even as I dashed to my Saturn, flung open the driver's side door, and popped the trunk release. Rooting around, I found a heavy-duty L-type lug wrench and pulled it, not bothering to shut the trunk before taking off at a run for the highway.

I skidded to a halt, however, as I realized the screams in

the cars had stopped. My heart sank because it was too late to help any of those people. Even as I watched, the mass of tendrils and ribbons pulled away from the cars, coalescing into something that looked like the lovechild of a pile of seaweed and a Chinese dragon—slender and sinuous, covered with glistening scales. The undulating tendrils grew out of long stalks, semi-translucent pods hanging off them like pieces of fruit. Some of the pods were small, and others the size of golf balls. Red liquid sloshed around inside, made darker by the translucent exterior. It had brought pieces of its meal with it—some recognizable as body parts, and others unidentifiable lumps of bloody meat. Several frond-like appendages were wrapped around a shapely female calf, which ended in ragged flesh and bone at the knee.

The pods near the chunks of flesh expanded like balloons on a helium machine. Elsewhere pods deflated, the blood inside disappearing as if sucked by a straw into the main body of the creature. The stalks near that pod seemed to rejuvenate, growing thicker and darker as they fed on the blood.

Was this one of my ancestral relatives coming to call, or was it something entirely different? *Oh, this is just fucked up.*

The seaweed dragon started toward us, slithering and undulating its way across the Pacific Coast Highway, leaving bits of its victims strewn in its wake. People at the edge of the lot stared as it drew closer, transfixed by the sight as it neared the curb. I couldn't entirely blame them—this was one crazy-ass monster—but they needed to get the hell away from ground zero.

Why the hell aren't they running?

"Move closer," a pushy male voice insisted.

Oh, no fucking way, I thought.

"No fucking way, Ron," another man said. "It's—"

"Just do it," Ron snapped. "Don't be such a pussy, Kyle."

I looked over in disbelief at Ron—a total bro-dude sporting a backwards baseball cap over a shaved pate and goatee, wearing a black tank top with the words "Do you lift?" spread out across an impressive beer paunch—urging Kyle, his sensibly reluctant companion, to stand at the edge of the parking lot so he could take a picture with his smartphone. As far as I was concerned, Ron was one Snapchat away from a broken jaw.

The seaweed dragon surged up and over the curb, across the sidewalk, and straight into the parking lot. Before I could react, it unfurled more ribbon-like tendrils and snatched Kyle off his feet, dragging him screaming into its center mass. Pods quickly filled up with blood even as Kyle's screams faded into a gurgling moan. Unbelievably, Douche-Bro continued to take pictures even as the rest of the onlookers finally scattered, screaming just like a coached crowd of extras on a film set.

Douche-Bro wasn't fast enough. One of the tendrils lashed out and wrapped around his ankle with a sharp tug, jerking the man off his feet and pulling him toward the same mass of fronds and pods currently feasting on his now silent and limp friend. Douche-Bro screamed again, and I saw that the thing had wrapped another frond around his leg and was now feeding.

Shit!

I vaulted over the hood of a car directly in my path, raising the lug wrench as I hit the ground running. The thing reared up as if to greet me, a noise emanating from it—like the roar of a lion, if it could breathe underwater. Several of its frond-like appendages reached for me, giving me a closer look at the undersides—sucker-like mouths ringed with sharp, jagged teeth, some still stained with blood and scraps of flesh.

I ducked under the appendages whipping towards me and stabbed the sharp end of the lug wrench into the stalk connected to the frond suckling on its victim's leg. The seaweed dragon roared again, sounding even more pissed off, but it didn't let go of its current meal. I reach down and tried to pull the man away from its grasp, but his scream took on notes of agony as the tendril tightened. I need something to slice through the stalk above the tendril, and the lug wrench wasn't gonna cut it.

Even as this thought ran through my mind, another ribbon unfurled and snatched the wrench from my grasp, tossing it to one side as a tendril slapped itself on my left arm, wrapping around my biceps. I felt an exploratory nuzzling of the suckers and then teeth on my flesh. The nuzzling turned into needles of agony as it started to feed. I didn't have long, but the guy next to me had even less time—I needed to do something fast.

I reached into the pocket where I'd shoved the plastic knife, thanking whatever weird reflex made me pocket it instead of tossing it on the ground. Pulling it out, I slashed the edge right across the stalk above the frond currently snacking on my arm. A gash appeared in its flesh, a clear viscous fluid almost jelly-like in texture oozing out of the wound as the thing gave a roar of what I hoped was pain and not just "I'm gonna kill you, bitch" rage.

Gotcha.

I dug the edge of the knife into the gash, sawing back and forth until I'd cut all the way through. The teeth digging into my flesh went lax as I separated the toothy tendril from the rest of the creature. Pulling it off my arm, I cast it to the ground, wincing as it took some of my flesh with it just as Cayden joined the fight.

"Can you keep it off me?" I yelled. He nodded with what I can only call a crazy-ass grin on his face. Wielding his crowbar with almost barbaric abandon, he dodged in between the stalks and tendrils with the brutal grace of a toreador, his face glowing with the sheer joy of battle, like a berserker of old.

I started sawing away at the tendrils feeding on Douche-Bro. The monster was less willing to give him up without a fight, more fronds slapping on and around the man even as I sliced through one and then another. Hacking and slashing as if clearing a path through a jungle, I still couldn't quite believe that Starbucks plastic cutlery could hold up to this abuse, amulet or no amulet. Finally, I detached all the ravenous suckers, grabbed Douche-Bro under his arms and yanked. We stumbled backwards, just out of reach of the thing as it tried to reclaim its lunch.

Several people ran over to help as I got to my feet. The man groaned, his face ghastly pale. I had no idea how much blood he'd lost, but it didn't look good.

"He needs an ambulance," I said, turning him over to the good Samaritans, "but in the meantime, try and stop the bleeding."

"Gigi, no!"

I turned at the sound of the sharp, panicked scream, my blood turning to ice as a toddler, hair a mass of soft brown curls like an adorable little hobbit, ran towards the monster.

"Doggie!" she cried, chuckling happily. "Big doggie!"

I swear the thing snapped whatever passed for its head around, focusing on the child like a lion scenting its prey. I gave an incoherent yell, knowing I wouldn't reach her in time.

Cayden vaulted over the back half of the creature, scooping the little hobbit up his arms just as its tendrils descended. They missed the little girl, wrapping around Cayden's torso instead. He gave a roar of pain and rage that matched the level of bone-rattling fury of the thing attacking him.

The creature seemed to be focusing all its malevolent attention on Cayden. Frond after carnivorous frond wrapped itself around him as he shielded the little girl with his body and arms, creating a protective cage around her and letting the tendrils attach themselves to him instead. It would only be a matter of time, however, before they found their way through. I could hear the little girl screaming, although whether from fear or pain I couldn't tell.

Screw that.

Giving a battle cry of my own, I jumped in and began the task the slashing through the seaweed dragon's pulpy flesh, severing stalks and ripping the tendrils off Cayden even as the pods expanded with his blood. As I chopped, I noticed an especially fat blood pod shrinking, and the stalks near it revitalizing, as if they were getting some high-quality plant food.

Right.

Rolling to the side, I seized the lug wrench and stabbed the business end straight into the pod. It burst, spraying blood all over the place like the cheesiest of special effects. The stalk immediately withered.

"Cayden!" I shouted. "We have to take out the blood blisters so the fucker can't heal itself!" I popped another juicy one with the plastic knife, taking a vicious satisfaction as another stalk lost all its vitality, its tendril dropping from Cayden's arm. He grinned at me, eyes shining with the light of battle as one hand tightened around the crowbar and he began puncturing any pod within the reach of that arm while the other one still sheltered the toddler. I went to town on the rest of the blisters, the amulet cold fire against my skin, the back of my neck burning and itching like supernatural psoriasis as I punctured pods and chopped through withering stalks. Tendrils that tried to attach themselves to my flesh shriveled and dropped.

As the freshly ingested blood ran out of the last deflated blister, the seaweed dragon staggered. A ululating keening emanated from its core. It slowly crumpled to the asphalt, its cries fading into a pitiful mewling. The tendrils in front lifted again, one of them reaching for me, the tip of it brushing my face before falling limply into what now looked like a mass of bloody seaweed.

"It's dead." I managed to choke out those two words between pants of exhaustion.

Pushing myself up onto hands and knees, I rolled over so I was sitting, hands propping me up into an upright position. The pavement was hot against my palms, but I wasn't ready to move quite yet. Cayden was still shielding the child with his body, his designer shirt ripped in more places than I could count, blood oozing out of numerous abrasions and puncture wounds.

He slowly straightened, the crowbar falling to the asphalt with a metallic clatter as his arms dropped to his sides, revealing the crying toddler. Totally unharmed. My heart slowly unfroze and unshed tears burned my eyes.

Hell, I don't even like kids, I thought even as several fat teardrops escaped and plopped onto the ground.

Sobbing hysterically, the mother ran over and scooped the child up in her arms. She said something to Cayden that might have been "thank you," but it was hard to tell what with all the crying. Cayden nodded and then collapsed onto the pavement next to me, breathing heavily. A short distance away from us, Douche-Bro's iPhone lay in a puddle of blood.

"Good job there," I commented, surreptitiously dashing my tears away.

He nodded. "You didn't do too badly yourself."

We sat for a few minutes in an oddly companionable silence while everyone around us talked in loud voices, trying to digest what they'd just witnessed. It wasn't often that something from the dark side crawled so blatantly out into the light of day.

I grimaced in disgust as I caught a glimpse of my clothing. "This is gonna be a fun one to explain to Sean," I said, as much to myself as my companion. My jeans and tank top were totaled. What wasn't ripped and/or shredded was coated in a viscous mix of brownish goo and blood. I smelled like two-day old seafood leftovers left out in the sun. My only consolation was that Cayden's clothes were in the same shape.

"Want to use a shower at my place?" A pause, and then, "There are at least five."

We looked at each other. My breath caught in my throat as the sense of stillness closed in until it seemed to encase just the two of us. Oh, I was tempted. So very, very tempted. But there was smart and there was stupid, and jumping into bed with a guy who'd just hired me fell solidly into the latter category. Hoping that the temptation I felt wasn't blazing out from my face, I shook my head and smiled.

"Nah," I said. "Although this would have been the most action-packed first date I've ever had, let alone a job interview."

He laughed, showing white teeth. Lots of them.

"Fair enough."

All around us, people were standing or sitting in dazed

shock. I wondered how the Kolchak Division—the LAPD's "this shit ain't right" weird case unit—was going to handle this. The odds of all these survivors knowing about the supe community was small to zilch.

"Some of them won't even remember it," Cayden said.

Had I spoken out loud? "Huh?"

"These people," he replied, his gaze seeing something so far in the distance I couldn't begin to fathom what it might be.

"How do you know that?"

"The canopy of darkness. You can see it, probably feel it as well. Most people can't unless they're part of the supernatural world or open to the possibility. If they're not, they'll most likely only remember what just happened as a horrific traffic accident. That's how it will be reported."

"What about people like you and me?" I wiped a smear of foul-smelling glop off my face. "We'll remember what really happened. What if we decided to report it?"

"Would you?"

"No, but that's beside the point. What about that poor stupid jerk with the iPhone? If he lives, his video will be all over social media."

He shrugged. "You know how easy it is to cry Special Effects Wolf."

He had a point.

"So." Cayden looked at me speculatively. "Was it just me, or was that thing gunning for you?"

I seriously considered lying. I mean, the truth was a lot to unwrap, even after battling a carnivorous kelp creature. But I owed it to the guy to let him know what he might be letting himself in for if he hired me. No, lying definitely wasn't an option.

"It wasn't just you," I said reluctantly. Then I stopped,

uncertain what to say next. Cayden waited patiently, as if he had all the time in the world and we were seated on a comfy couch instead of on hard, hot asphalt.

Here was my quandary. How much should I tell him? Sean hadn't given me any guidance as far as who to tell and who not to tell about my fucked-up family legacy, and I hadn't asked. It wasn't something I wanted to share with anyone. Now, however, the demonspawn was out of the bag.

I took a deep breath, but before I could say anything, sirens wailed in the distance as if in a dream, increasing in volume and substance until the sound finally penetrated the strange cone of silence. Cayden and I watched as police vehicles, including the distinctive khaki-colored Ford Crown Victoria of the Kolchak Division—the logo of a straw pork-pie hat with a red-and-black band nestled unobtrusively in the lower left corner of the rear window—pulled into the driveway at the south end of the market.

I groaned when I recognized Detective Maggie Fitzgerald in the driver's seat. Not that there was anything wrong with her—unless you pissed her off and then she'd go all banshee on your ass—but she was bound to recognize me too. She'd been the detective in charge when people had started dying on *Pale Dreamer* and considering the fallout from *that* little slice of cinematic hell, the last thing I needed was more notoriety or a reputation for being the Jessica Fletcher of Hollywood. With my luck, the dead seaweed dragon would turn out to be a famous director's distant relative, thus getting me banned from the Industry in perpetuity.

Cayden grinned. "Don't worry," he said as if reading my mind. "I have connections."

"Can you keep me off social media?"

"I'll make sure your name stays out of the papers, the

columns, Facebook, Instagram, Snapchat, all of it. There'll be nary a tweet connecting you to this unfortunate event."

"And in return?

"Promise me we'll continue this conversation later."

He held out a hand. I took it, looked into those blue eyes, their expression just this side of crazy, and said, "Deal. Do I have the job?"

Cayden's mouth curled up in a smile.

"Yeah. Yeah, you do. Are you sure you want it?"

"Yeah," I said. "Yeah, I am."

"Good. We'll need you to fly out to New Orleans for rehearsals in the next few days. The sets and locations are already in place. You'll meet the rest of the stunt crew, start choreographing and rehearsing with the cast. I'd like you to take on training the actresses playing Laveau and Perrine, and you'll be doubling Laveau. You up for it?"

I nodded, trying not to seem too excited, because Cayden seemed like the type who'd make fun of me for being anything other than blasé.

"I'll be in touch with your agent."

"That's Faustina—"

"Faustina Corbin, I know."

Of course you do.

"Is this yours?" Cayden held out a hand, a leather cord draped over his fingers, gold disk dangling from it. I snatched it from him, heart pounding as I realized how close I'd come to losing my mother's amulet...

And my ability to fight Lilith's demonic rug rats.

"Thanks," I finally managed. The leather cord had snapped, so I tucked it away in a pocket of my jeans. I'd have to get a replacement. Until then, I'd put it in one of my neoprene pouches that I used on set. Maybe that was safer all the way around these days. Today was an object lesson that I could never be sure when unexpected relatives were going to show up.

†

"Will it be safe?" Polli's voice was hoarse and oddly liquid at the same time. No surprise there. She and Hyla—most of their family, really—always sounded two steps away from a frog chorus.

"Of course." LeRoy was irritated by the question. "The lagoon is behind the Veil. The Thaumaturge will stay here until the metamorphosis is complete and it's time for the summoning."

"What about the others?" Hyla asked.

"It has been taken care of," he replied shortly. Taking a deep breath, he exhaled very slowly. He really needed to work on his anger management.

Walking to the small shimmer that marked the border of the Veil and crossing to the other side, LeRoy cast a derisive glance, as he always did, at the shacks that passed as houses for the Castro clan, all of them beyond ramshackle. Weathered boards, gray and tinted with green moss, sagging porches and spider webs festooning the railings and rafters. Yet even the most dilapidated shack had a satellite dish on it.

LeRoy sneered with barely veiled disgust. Even deep in the Bayou modern technology insisted on creeping in and taking a hold of things. He hoped the faith of the Castro family was strong enough to aid the harbingers in the summoning.

At first glance, the kids running around playing kickball seemed perfectly normal, the sound of their laughter and screams the same thing heard at any happy gathering of children… but if you stopped and really listened, the laughter sounded like croaking, the screams and squeals guttural, as if something got stuck in their throats before the sound was forced out. The children's skin was so pale that they seemed tinted green. Thick, rubbery lips. Large watery eyes.

Underslung chins, practically nonexistent. These were the effects of inbreeding—not surprising in a backwoods clan like the Castros.

LeRoy despised them.

Years ago, before his first failure, he had approached the Marcadet family, sworn enemies of the Castros, in hopes of gaining an alliance with them instead. They were more intelligent and certainly more pleasing aesthetically, especially the women. His offer had been slapped down hard, and he'd sworn someday he'd have satisfaction for the insult. Then again, the Castros had been worshipping ancient, diseased gods for as many decades as they'd been inbreeding. He would take what he would get. Soon it wouldn't matter.

CHAPTER EIGHT

The reception of the news of my upcoming job was what some would call a mixed bag.

Randy: "You have got to be fucking kidding me. Cayden Doran is bad news!"

Sean: "That's great, sweetheart."

Eden: "New Orleans? Holy shit, that's awesome! What's the production? Are they still casting? I wanna go!" Then I told her the co-producer's name and it was, "Well, maybe I can swing a visit while you're filming. I haven't been to New Orleans in years."

Seth: Silence.

These, of course, are the short versions.

When I told Sean and Seth I'd been offered a job shooting in New Orleans with good pay and a real budget, Sean's feature-length response had been, "Hon, that's great news!" while Seth just stared at me, stone-faced.

"See?" Sean continued. "I told you time would make the difference."

So far so good. "But it means I'll be out of town same time you're working on *Spasm*, so someone else is gonna have to deal with training here."

"We'll figure it out," he answered with a wave of one

hand. "What's the job?"

"It's a historical film about Marie Laveau called *Voodoo Wars*."

A snort from Seth. Sadly, I couldn't blame him.

"Who's the stunt coordinator?" Sean asked.

"Cayden Doran."

Silence. I glanced up at both their faces and gave an inward groan. They'd definitely heard of him and whatever they'd heard was not favorable.

If telling Seth and Sean had been unpleasant, giving Randy the scoop on my new gig was a little slice of unexpected hell. We had our first actual fight since we'd started hanging out—I didn't even like to think of it as dating—and it left me angry and upset in equal doses.

"Seriously?" Randy stared at me with the kind of expression I normally only received from Seth. "You're not stupid, Lee. I know you're not. Why the hell would you agree to work with him? Do you even know the kind of reputation Cayden Doran has?"

"His rep can't be worse than Crazy Casa's."

"If it were Crazy Casa, it would be different. At least I'd know what kind of shit you were going to get into. With Doran, though…" He shook his head, his expression a combination of concern and anger that didn't sit well with me. What right did he have to be worried and angry on my behalf? I was more than a little tired of well-meaning concern from the men in my life. Didn't anyone trust me to make decisions for myself?

"Doran is bad news."

"How do you know?" I wondered how much of Randy's reaction could be attributed to sour grapes. "I hadn't even heard his name before."

"That's because he's been in Australia the last ten years or so. He hasn't done a film here in years. People die on his films." The last uttered with the "cross my heart and hope to die" solemnity of a kid telling a spooky story around a campfire.

"Oh yeah? Like who?"

I wouldn't quite say that Randy glared at me, but I'd only ever seen those gold flecks in his eyes when he was either aroused or upset. Suffice to say I did not get laid after this conversation.

"I can't remember," he finally replied, "but rumor has it people get hurt on his films."

I rolled my eyes. "Okay, 'rumor has it' is up there with 'they say.' Let's not forget the kind of crap that's been circulating about me, which we *both* know isn't true. Until I know who 'they' are, and whether or not 'they' started these rumors—which may or may not be baseless—don't you think we should give him the benefit of the doubt?"

"Okay, fine, you could be right," he conceded. "But I still would feel better if you didn't take the job."

How to describe the panic that flared up inside me? As if someone was trying to shove me in a tiny box and seal it up with chains and padlocks I couldn't break? Yeah, that was about it.

Randy must have seen something in my expression. "Look," he said, putting a hand on mine, "you know I'm not gonna tell you not to do anything. That's not what we're about. That's not what *I'm* about. I'm just asking you to think about it a little longer, okay?"

I gave a bitter little laugh. "No one else is offering me work, including Crazy Casa. In fact, they turned me down. How's that for pathetic? Doran is the only person willing to take a chance on me, and I need to be working."

Randy's muscles visibly tensed under his forest-green Henley. Normally I'd have admired the view, but not this time.

"Dammit, Lee, you know I'd hire you in a heartbeat if there were any women in the cast."

"Well, there aren't, so I'm gonna have to take a chance working with Doran. You can either trust me to take care of myself or not. Your choice."

Silence. And then, "What did Sean have to say about it?"

"We agreed to disagree." It was only half a lie. We'd disagreed. No agreement had been made. Bottom line, I was old enough to make my own decisions and this just intensified my need to get my own place. I was going to New Orleans.

The thought of beignets and chicory coffee at Café Du Monde had, of course, no bearing on my decision.

†

I was standing out on the front porch watching the sun go down behind the mountains, enjoying a cold beer when I became aware of someone standing next to me.

"Randy, what are you doing here?" I asked, trying to keep the irritation out of my voice. We'd already fought and I didn't want any more bad blood between us.

He didn't say a word, though. Just shook his head sadly, as if I'd disappointed him.

"If you think you're going to get me to change my mind about going, it ain't happening."

Still no answer. He shook his head again, taking a step and closing the gap between us.

I tried one more time.

"Seriously, Squid, this is not cool. I—"

He stepped forward again, and I took a corresponding step backward, suddenly finding myself pressed up against the porch railing. For the first time since I'd met him,

Randy was making me uncomfortable. Almost afraid.

Finally, he spoke. "That's not why I'm here."

The wind whipped up out of nowhere, the last glow of sunlight setting the tips of the mountains on fire.

"I know you won't change your mind." Randy shook his head in disgust. "You never do what you're told, do you?"

"What are you—"

"I'm not here to change your mind." His voice dropped to a low growl and his eyes burned as if lit by flames from the inside. He grabbed my shoulders with fingers that burned with the painful chill of dry ice. "It's too late for that."

The railing at my back suddenly fell away into nothingness, tumbling into an endless black chasm that stretched down for miles. I started to go over the edge after it but was saved by Randy's hands on my shoulders. Except… his features were gone, blanked out by shadows. His fingers dug in painfully, holding me there, suspended over the drop, my feet dangling into empty space.

"What'll it be, Lee?" Not Randy whispered.

I didn't answer. Couldn't speak. He opened his hands and let me fall.

My screams echoed in my ears as I tumbled head over heels down, down, down…

†

"Lee?"

My eyes flew open and I jerked awake in the front seat of Seth's car, mouth open as if in mid-scream.

"Lee? You okay?"

"I…" My voice trailed off as I tried to shake off the shreds of the nightmare that still clouded my brain. Without another word, Seth handed me a bottle of water, which I drained dry in two gulps. Then I let my head fall back against the headrest and heaved a long, shuddering sigh before saying, "Oh, that sucked."

"Bad dream?"

"Oh yeah."

"Wanna talk about it?"

"Oh no." The last thing I wanted to do was discuss the possible Freudian implications of my subconscious mind. "You'd just tell me sometimes a cigar is just a cigar."

That got maybe an eighth of a smile—just the slight lifting of one corner of his mouth. "Fair enough."

Seth had actually volunteered to drive me to LAX, despite the fact my flight left close to midnight. Randy would have probably played chauffeur, but I didn't want to ask him considering how unhappy he was about my taking this job. I also could have taken a Lyft, I suppose, but until I cashed my first paycheck from the production company, I didn't want to spend money I didn't have.

Eden, my other option for a ride, was working on a film called *Officer Dutch and Mr. French*, a gritty police comedy— not my description—about a cop from the Netherlands working with a French PI, and all the hilarious and gritty misunderstandings between them. According to Eden, hilarity did not ensue. She had the role of the PI's secretary. Written and directed by an American who thought being Dutch meant an unhealthy love of tulips, while all French people lived on brie and wine.

I shut my eyes again in the hopes of drifting back off to a hopefully dreamless sleep, but the adrenaline rush from the latest nightmare had me well and truly awake. I glanced over at Seth, who had his eyes on the road with the focus of someone taking a driver's test. For a stuntman, he took safety in mundane activities very seriously. I surreptitiously studied his profile for few minutes, wondering why we couldn't seem to get along anymore. I also wondered, not for the first time, if he had any idea how good-looking he was. Vanity was not one of Seth's personal sins.

We passed the Trancas Country Market, all traces of the seaweed dragon and its victims either wiped clean or invisible in the dark. That made me think of Cayden, which made me turn to my cousin and ask, "Have you actually met Cayden Doran or do you only know him by reputation?"

"Both," he replied, his gaze never straying from the traffic on the road.

"Is there any truth to the rumor that people have died on his stunt crews?"

"Would it make a difference to you if the answer to that is yes?"

And we'd been doing so well. I tried to ignore Seth's judgmental tone—after all, I could be looking for condemnation where none existed—and answer him truthfully. "It would depend on whether or not the deaths were caused by recklessness or carelessness on his part, or on the part of someone he hired specifically to prevent shit like that from happening."

Seth gave a little nod. "Then you're in luck because as much as I'd like to blame his arrogant ass for the shit that went down, I've heard that the two deaths were freak accidents."

"So, aside from Cayden being an arrogant ass—and please note I am not disagreeing with that description—there's no reason my taking this job should flip people out, right?"

"If you're worried about Sean, he's not flipped out. Just concerned. If you're worried about Randy, on the other hand—" His eyes flickered briefly in my direction before shifting back to the dark highway. "I'm a stuntman, not a relationship counselor."

"It's not a relationship," I shot back. "We're friends and we're hanging out, but we're not exclusive."

"Friends with benefits." Seth gave a derisive snort. "Can't quite make up your mind one way or the other, so you have your cake and eat it too, right?"

I took a deep breath and counted to three. "You think it's better to dive straight into a relationship instead of taking the time to get to know each other? Or is it because only men are allowed to have sex outside of the sacred bonds of marriage?" Except I pronounced it "mawage" à la Peter Cook in *Princess Bride*.

"No, it's just—" He shook his head. "Never mind." I could feel the tension thrumming through him.

A year ago I would have insisted he finish his thought, no doubt resulting in an ugly argument that would have lasted the rest of the drive. Now, however, after all the crap that I'd experienced since the accident, I didn't have the energy or desire to argue. I took him at his word and moved past the topic of Randy and sex.

"So," I said casually, "you're fine with me working on *Voodoo Wars*?"

His shoulders relaxed. "Aside from the dumbass title, sure."

"Well, it's no *Spasm*, I'll grant you that."

That got a bark of laughter. The rest of the hour-long drive was passed in mutually agreeable silence other than classical music played at a soft, soothing volume.

When we pulled into the terminal at LAX, Seth shut the radio off and placed a hand on my arm as I opened the door.

"You be careful, Lee."

"I'm a stunt woman," I replied lightly. "We get paid to do dangerous things carefully, y'know?"

Seth shook his head. "That's not what I meant. All of the

stuff that's been happening—" he waved his hand "—well, nothing might happen, but anything *could*."

I was touched in spite of myself. Gently voiced concern from Seth was as rare as snow in Los Angeles—not unheard of, but extremely rare. "Okay," I said, "I'll be careful."

I got out of the car, and Seth popped the trunk. To my surprise, he also got out of the car and pulled out my monster suitcase for me. I wondered if I should tell Sean to look for a Seth-shaped pod in the backyard.

Seth set my suitcase down in front of me. "Remember, Lee, if you get into trouble out there, you call me."

Yup, Sean definitely needed to be on the lookout for pods.

"Seth, I'll be fine," I assured him. "Besides, you're going to be working on *Spasm*. Even if I *did* get into a metric butt-load of trouble, you wouldn't have time to fly out."

Seth shook his head. "Anything happens, you call, do you hear me? And I'll be there."

Then he gave me a rough hug, like he didn't really want to do it but couldn't help himself. Before I had a chance to be touched by this unexpected Hallmark moment, he added, "Do your best not to sleep with Doran, okay?"

I pulled back and punched him in the arm, hard.

"Thanks for the ride," I said, and went into the terminal without a backward glance.

Okay, that was weird.

How sad was it, though, that Seth behaving nicely— other than that last potshot about Cayden—was a cause for suspicion? Pretty damn sad.

Oh well, it didn't do any good to speculate on what exactly was going through his head. That could take years to untangle and I needed to focus on this job. If it went well, then maybe I could wipe the stink of producer-cide off my résumé.

CHAPTER NINE

"Can I offer you a drink? Some champagne, perhaps?"

I smiled up at the flight attendant and nodded. Champagne? Hell, yes. A sense of well-being washed over me, all of my muscles relaxing into the cushy comfort of first-class seating. Red-eye flights usually suck, but a red-eye flight in first class is an entirely different matter and the seat next to me was empty. Free drinks, a comfy seat, plenty of leg room, soft blankets and pillows. I could actually get some sleep.

Well, I could have done if I weren't so wired after Seth's parting words. Why did he have to be such an asshat? Oh well, I'd take advantage of the unwanted adrenaline rush and give the script a good read—I hadn't had the chance until now for more than a cursory look. Pulling out my copy of *Voodoo Wars*, I sipped some very nice bubbly and flipped through the pages.

It was actually pretty horrific in places. The titular voodoo war was between Marie Laveau, a well-known real-life voodoo queen who'd lived in New Orleans during the 1800s, and her younger rival, Perrine. There was a subplot about the LaLauries, a wealthy Creole couple who want to summon a demon to help them gain more wealth and status. Louis LaLaurie has the hots for Marie. Perrine has the hots for some guy named Étienne. There are some horrific torture scenes that reminded me of *The Island of Doctor Moreau*. A potboiler of love, lust, vengeance, torture and—oh yes—demon summoning.

"More champagne?" The flight attendant smiled down at me and my empty glass.

"Sure, why not."

I felt a little light-headed, but what the hell. I went back to the script, highlighting any parts where it looked likely I'd be doubling Marie. The high fall Cayden had talked about was part of a dream sequence, where Marie uses astral projection and possesses the body of a young house slave, who falls from a balcony when running from Louis. The scene shows Marie falling and hitting the ground before cutting to the lifeless body of the slave.

I can do the stunt, no problem, I thought. Hell, give me another glass of champagne and I could fly off the balcony.

My eyelids drooped and I caught myself jerking awake, my head snapping upright after my chin touched the top of my chest. This happened a couple more times before I gave in to the inevitable, set the script on the seat next to me, and adjusted my own seat for maximum comfort— they reclined almost all the way and wasn't that sweet?— letting myself get sucked into slumber.

†

Darkness pierced by flickering torchlight. Voices chanting. A rhythmic thumping, flesh on flesh, hands clapping, feet stomping on the ground. The musky scent of sweat and sandalwood, cinnamon and sage hanging in the air. A less pleasing odor underneath. Coppery. Rank. Rotten.

Blood, so much blood. The torch flames died down, then flared up, one at a time, each one revealing a mutilated figure.

Some missing eyes. Some with their mouths stitched shut. Arms sprouting from torsos. Feet attached to knee stumps. Blood everywhere. Pus oozing slowly out of infected wounds. A rich, terrible smell. I gagged on it, choked on it. Stumbled around in the dark until another torch flared up, revealing a horribly mutilated figure, made all the more horrifying because he was still alive.

And I knew him.

†

I jerked awake, heartbeat racing double time, sweat pouring down my face and between my breasts. My hand smacked into the champagne flute and sent it flying into the aisle. Luckily it bounced instead of breaking. Didn't even wake up my snoring neighbor across the aisle.

"Damn," I muttered, glaring at the script. If the finished movie had even half the nightmare-inducing qualities of the script, Cayden and his partner would have a hit on their hands.

CHAPTER TEN

As I deplaned and made my way through the gates of Louis Armstrong Airport, my carry-on tote slung over one shoulder, the smell of brown sugar, melted butter and cinnamon from praline stands wafted through the air, managing to overpower the usual airport funk of body odor and cheap food.

Grabbing my suitcase from baggage claim, I stepped out of the terminal into the palpable humidity of autumn in Louisiana. "Holy shit," I said as sweat broke out on my forehead, chest, and back. I fanned myself with one hand.

A man glanced at me with a look that combined pity and condescension in equal parts. "It's only eighty degrees," he drawled. "You should be here in the summer."

"Oh no," I said, shaking my head. "I definitely should not."

A half-hour and a Lyft ride later, I stepped into the lobby of the Hotel Monteleone.

Oh wow.

I stopped and gazed around me. Polished parquet floors. Dark wood furniture, including an ornate grandfather clock, which was supposed to be haunted. Display cases filled with treasures—antique oyster plates, books and letters from literary figures. Old-world decadence and elegance combined. To the right was the Carousel Bar. I planned on checking it out later that evening after I had done a stroll around the French Quarter and hit Café Du Monde.

I'd flown in a day early—with Cayden's financial blessing, of course—because I wanted the chance to see some of New Orleans before it all became viewed through the lens of a camera. I'd watched *The Big Easy*, *Angel Heart*, and a few other shows set in New Orleans just to get an idea of what to expect, even though I knew that Hollywood's idea of realism was generally either idealized or just plain incorrect. I wanted to see the *real* New Orleans—although I confess I really hoped someone, somewhere, called me *cher*.

Cajun food, Creole cuisine, zydeco music, beignets at Café Du Monde, strolling through the Garden District, visiting at least one or two of the famous above-ground cemeteries… I had a bucket list and I was determined to cross everything off before the shoot was finished and I headed home to Los Angeles.

My low-heeled boots clicked on the parquet flooring as I walked under a huge crystal chandelier sparkling from the ceiling. I quickened my pace, my SoCal earthquake radar kicking in even though Louisiana was more likely to be hit by a hurricane than an earthquake. After all, the last big quake that had hit the south had been in the 1800s… but that one had been big enough to temporarily change the course of the Mississippi River.

Why do I even think of these things? I wondered, as I joined the line for the registration desk, my monster suitcase rolling behind me like a faithful dog. Two heavily made-up women in their fifties clickity-clacked their way behind me in four-inch heels. Both had the bouffant and lacquered hairstyles of former beauty queens and wore skirts and jackets in pastel shades that looked like they'd been barfed up by the Easter bunny.

"I swear," Bouffant A said in a Texas twang, her voice set at a pitch that could cut through iron and break glass, and made eavesdropping unavoidable, "this place is spooky enough to turn an atheist back to God. Just thick with spirits and evil haunts! You remember Lonnie Jenson, right, hon?"

Bouffant B nodded, fanning herself with a pink-nail-tipped hand. "I sure do. Her sister was always a bit of a troublemaker, wasn't she?"

"*Oh* yes, she certainly was! You just listen to this now. Well, Lonnie told me she and her sister came to New Orleans, spent all sorts of money on the plane fare and deposits, and Lonnie didn't even unpack her bags at the hotel. Lonnie said the air was so thick with satanic energy she told her sister, 'You do what you want, I'm leaving right now and flying back home. Some places are closer to hell than others and this evil city is one of them.'"

Both women shivered with delight at the thought.

"Did they get their deposit back?" Bouffant B asked.

"As far as I know," Bouffant A replied, "the sister stayed behind while Lonnie went home. She's always been that way, though, her sister. More interested in saving money than saving her soul."

Her friend tsk-tsk'd. As far as I was concerned, the much-maligned sister had done the sensible thing and probably enjoyed herself a lot more once killjoy Lonnie was out of the picture.

"Now," Bouffant A continued, "I've got us booked for a vampire tour, a ghost tour, and a voodoo tour, one each night, so we'll need to…"

I reluctantly stopped eavesdropping as a clerk waved me

forward to the ornate front desk. Five minutes later I was checked in and headed up in the elevator to my room, keycard in hand. A hot shower was calling my name, loudly.

†

My room was around the corner and way down the hall away from the elevator, which made me happy. Nothing like being in a room by the elevator or the ice machine to make a person aware of how sound carries through most hotel doors, even in luxury hotels.

Inside the room, more old-world, luxurious charm met my gaze. King-sized bed, covered with pillows and bedding in rich blue and golds. Walls alternating a pale yellow and cream stripe. Chairs that could have come from a high-end antique store—no shabby chic here. Curtains and swags draped over windows that looked out onto a view of the Mississippi River—which was running the right direction, thanks very much, brain. Even the paintings were a cut above generic hotel room art.

A pricey-looking bottle of red wine stood at attention in the middle of a small round table with a marble top, an envelope with my name on it next to it. Pulling out the card—cream-colored vellum that screamed "expensive but tasteful"—I read the message: "Compliments of Berserker Productions."

Further exploration uncovered a garden tub, thick cream-colored towels folded neatly on a marble counter.

Wowza.

Cayden and his partner obviously had money to burn if they were putting out-of-town cast and crew up here, not to mention booking the flights in first class. I wondered how big of a crew we'd have on location—Cayden had said "small," but that was relative when some films had end credits that lasted almost as long as the movie itself.

I opened the fridge, giving a low whistle of appreciation when I saw two four-packs of Boulevard Quad, another high-calorie bourbon barrel-aged beer. There was another note tucked into one of the packs, this one scribbled on a piece of hotel stationary. *This one's on me*, a large C scrawled underneath.

Was he attempting seduction by craft beer or just being thoughtful?

Immediately I heard Seth's voice saying, "Try not to sleep with Doran."

"I wasn't planning on it," I muttered. And I wasn't. No matter how good the man's taste in beer might be.

"Sure, Lee," Imaginary Seth replied in a tone that said he wasn't buying it.

I slammed the fridge door with more force than necessary, determined to kick Seth out of my head. This extremely snazzy hotel was my home for the time being and I was gonna enjoy it to the fullest, starting with a nap and then a shower. Later tonight after I explored the French Quarter, maybe I'd take advantage of the tub—crack open the wine, light some candles. I couldn't remember the last time I'd done anything that decadent. Hell, I couldn't remember if I'd *ever* done anything that decadent.

Living in Katz Stunt Central didn't lend itself to things like long soaks in bathtubs. While I had my own bathroom off my room, it only had a shower stall—the bathroom off the hallway had the tub. Nothing like trying to relax in a hot bath while Drift hammered on the bathroom door, wondering if I'd be out before he "exploded."

Thinking of Drift made me think of home, which reminded me it was time to let people know I'd made it safely. I texted Sean first, adding Seth to the recipients right before hitting "send." I immediately regretted the impulse, but it was too late to take it back. I hit Eden's dial button next. She picked up after one ring.

"Are you there yet?"

Grinning, I lay back on the bed and took a swig of sparkling water. "I sure am. Right in the French Quarter."

"Where are you staying?"

I told her and then grinned at her indrawn breath followed by, "Oh, I am so jealous! I love that hotel!"

"Have you stayed here?"

"More than once."

"Then don't be jealous," I said reasonably. "This is my first time."

"Yeah, okay, fair enough. Have you been to the Carousel Bar yet?"

"I just got here, but it's on my list."

She heaved a tragic sigh. "*So* very jealous!"

"Well, what's your schedule like?"

"Finishing up shooting over the next few days and then as free as the wily trout."

"You wanna come hang out in my big ass hotel room and help me explore the town?"

"Hell, yeah." A pause. "As long as I don't have to see Doran."

I had to ask. "You gonna tell me what that's all about?"

An even longer pause. Finally, "It's complicated."

"Like, holding meetings wearing a bathrobe and trying to get a blowjob type complicated?"

"He's not that kind of a creep," she answered. "Like I said, it's complicated. I'd rather not talk about it on the phone."

I could tell she'd rather not talk about it at all. I decided not to press the matter for the time being. I shrugged, then realized she couldn't see it.

"Just come hang out and help me fill in some of my off hours, okay? You don't have to see him, talk to him, or even breathe the same air as him."

"Deal."

"Cool," I said, right before a huge yawn nearly cracked my face in half.

"I'll check flights," she said, "and let you know what's what. Now get some rest."

I planned on doing just that, but first I called Randy. I dialed his home number instead of his cell, knowing that he'd be working, thus avoiding a possibly contentious call. All I wanted to do was hear his voice and remind myself of one of the very good reasons I needed to keep my distance from Cayden, emotionally and physically—at least as much as possible while working with him.

Randy's answering machine picked up. "This is Randy. I'm out crashing cars, falling off tall buildings, or getting set on fire. Leave your name, number, and any other important info and I'll call you back as soon as the flames go out."

I gave an inward groan, same as I did every time I heard that voicemail—which, by the way, was the same message he had on his cell phone. Very cheesy, and yet adorably Randy.

"Hey, Squid," I said after the beep, "just me. Safe and sound in New Orleans. Feeling like hammered shit after that red-eye and…" I paused, then quickly finished with "… and kinda missing you. Talk to you later."

I hung up before I had a chance to say anything else that might give him ideas of things like "commitment." I was already regretting the "missing you" comment. Although I hoped if and when the time came that I was ready to commit, that I'd choose someone as… well, at least someone as nice as Randy. I couldn't help but notice that even with a theoretical scenario in the unknown future, I still didn't actually *choose* Randy.

Sometimes I really didn't like myself.

Screw it, I thought, breaking off the mental self-flagellation session before it really got underway. I was in New Orleans. I had a job that had nothing to do with Sean, Seth, KSC, or anyone connected to it. The pay was more than good and I had a fridge full of excellent beer. I officially gave myself permission to not give a fuck about anything or anyone else until tomorrow.

"Winter is coming," my phone intoned in Jon Snow's voice. "Winter is com—" I switched the notification off mid-sentence and glanced at the screen.

> Dinner at 7:00. Onc Cochon. See you there.
> Cayden

I didn't speak a lot of French, but I knew enough to translate "Uncle Pig."

Uncle Pig. Really?

Guess I needed to give at least enough of a fuck to show up for dinner tonight.

My phone told me it was 10 A.M. I'd lie down for a quick catnap, take a shower or even a hot bath, and then head out for a few hours of exploration before meeting Cayden for dinner. Maybe by then I wouldn't even be pissed at his high-handed summons to dine with him. Maybe.

I texted back a quick thumbs-up emoji and set my phone to "do not disturb" before stripping off my now aromatic travel clothes and crawling in between the covers of a bed obviously made of marshmallows and the softest down plucked from angel wings.

Maybe I'll just read for a few minutes. My eyelids, however, had other ideas. They shut with a nearly audible *clunk*, and I was asleep almost as soon as my head hit the pillow.

†

"Lily…"

Strong hands rubbed the aching muscles in my back and shoulders as I lay on my stomach, slowly bringing me from a deep sleep to the edge of wakefulness. I smiled, eyes still shut, and enjoyed the feel of my lover's hands on my bare skin. He knew just where to touch in order to soothe me. To help dissolve the knots in muscles tight from sitting at a pianoforte for hours. To ease the tension earned by keeping my tone level and respectful while I taught the spoiled children of the white Creole families. As a violinist and music teacher, Étienne knew all too well the frustrations that came with our lowly position in the social circles of New Orleans society.

He also had very talented hands and fingers, his touch changing subtly from the deep soothing massage to something more sensual. His fingers drifted from my shoulder blades over the sides of my body, caressing the outer curves of my breasts. I gave a small smile but was not inclined to give up my massage quite yet. I continued to pretend to sleep.

"Lily…" His voice, deep and masculine, repeated my name. Softly at first, then more insistent. He crouched over me, careful to keep his weight evenly distributed for my comfort.

Oh, how I loved this man.

His fingers continued their teasing drift, this time sketching circles down my spine as he leaned forward, mouth against my ear and whispered, "Lily… *pssst!*"

I giggled. I couldn't help it.

"Ah, you are awake! Minx."

I felt and heard the smile curving his lips, his touch becoming more teasing and less tantalizing as he began tickling me. I shrieked and wriggled until I managed to flip over onto my back, grabbing his wrists to stop the relentless torture.

"Brute," I said in between gasps of resentful laughter, trying my best to glare at him. "You're an hour later than you said you'd be."

Étienne grinned, stretching full length on top of me. He still had on the dress clothes he wore when performing with the quartet. They'd played at one of Delphine LaLaurie's soirées that evening. As always, I felt nothing but relief when he'd left that woman's mansion none the worse for the wear. Madame LaLaurie was shallow and vindictive, with a reputation for mistreating her slaves. Even though Étienne was one of the many *gens de couleur libres* of New Orleans, like myself, I didn't trust her to respect the boundaries of decency or of the law. And her husband Louis plain made my skin crawl.

He kissed me, stilling both my laughter and my complaints. "I'm sorry to be so late," he murmured against my neck. "Madame LaLaurie insisted we played until the last of the guests had left for the night, and there's always one or two gentlemen—" he rolled his eyes at the word "—who have to have just one more glass of port or claret to go with a final cigar."

I wrinkled my nose, smelling the lingering cigar smoke on his clothing. "These must go," I insisted, tugging at his shirt.

Étienne obliged me by stripping off his clothing, only climbing back into bed when he was as naked as I was. I wrapped my arms and legs around him, savoring his scent, a mix of sandalwood, leather, and cinnamon.

"She wants us to play again Thursday," he said against my lips as we kissed.

"But you can't!" I exclaimed. "It's Erzulie's ritual and—"

"I told Madame 'no,' never fear. I would never risk offending Marie or the loas." He kissed me again. "But most of all, I would not want to upset you. I know how important this ceremony is to you."

"Was she angry? Madame Bitch, I mean."

Shrugging, Étienne rolled onto his back, wrapping one arm around me. I rested my head against his chest. "You know how she is," he replied, a small frown line between his eyes the only sign that he was even slightly concerned. "She might find another violin teacher for her daughters."

I didn't say anything at first, knowing that if I had managed to hold my temper I would still be teaching those girls piano. Louis LaLaurie, however, had pushed a boundary with me and I had not been able to let it go. I was no longer in the employ of the LaLaurie family.

"Would that be such a bad thing?" I finally asked.

"We would miss the money."

"There are more important things than money." Familiar words in a familiar argument.

"Hush, Lily," Étienne rolled over on top of me, choosing to end a possible quarrel before it began. I chose to let him. This time.

†

I slowly became aware that my alarm—currently the theme from *Jaws*—was going off next to my head. Grabbing my phone, I hit "stop" and then lay there for a few minutes, body heavy and relaxed as though I really had just had some totally killer sex with as handsome a man as I'd ever seen—and one that smelled like some sort of pheromone-infused candle. Fragrance of Cinnamon and Sex. It was a welcome change from the increasingly frequent nightmares I'd been having with scary death-drop dude, and I wanted to wallow in it a little while longer, impress the details into my mind before the dream fragmented and vanished from my memory.

Glancing at the time, I reluctantly dragged myself out of the oh-so-comfy bed and into the shower. I emerged from the bathroom, redolent with the combined scents of bergamot, sandalwood and geranium, courtesy of the hotel's high-end complimentary bath products. Then I threw on a violet tank top over a black gauze skirt and black gladiator sandals, slathered on some lip balm, and declared myself ready to take on the French Quarter.

†

When the pain first started, Charlie had gone out to the nearest bar, hoping that alcohol would dull the itching, burning sensation under his skin. Patches of red had flared up on his arms, legs, and torso, as if he'd rolled in poison oak. Three double-shots of mezcal hadn't touched it, so he'd tried two more.

Head spinning, he'd staggered out of the bar, intending to go back to Simon's cousin's. Instead, he'd passed out on the sidewalk and woken up in the trunk of a moving car. It felt like acid-dipped mites were burrowing through his body, the pain so off the charts, Charlie barely registered the fact he'd been kidnapped.

They'd dragged Charlie out of the trunk and down a dirt path, the sound of frogs and crickets so loud it hurt his ears. When his captors finally dumped Charlie in a swamp, the cool water and soothing mud felt so good on his cracking, peeling, scaling skin he'd almost welcomed it. He thrashed about, churning up mud and water as his mouth opened impossibly wide to voice inhuman howls of pain, the sounds of his agony almost primordial. Startled flocks of birds took flight from the cypress trees, while frogs and lizards quickly hopped and slithered away to comparative safety. Even the copperheads and alligators shunned the pond, instinct telling them that these waters were no longer safe—even before the otherworldly shimmering haze settled over it, creating a barrier between the pond and the rest of the bayou.

Now he—it—rested just below the surface of the brackish water, blending into the greens and browns of the swamp.

The scales crusted over, then cracked open as the creature's new form expanded, then crusted over again. The pain took a back seat to hunger, which in turn set up a gnawing agony. At first it could do nothing to assuage the ache, the only relief coming when tadpoles, water striders and bottom feeders inadvertently crossed its path, mired in the viscous jelly oozing between its scales. Once stuck, the unfortunate creatures dissolved in the acidic slime, digested even as they struggled to escape.

As the sustenance gave it strength and it continued to morph, the Thaumaturge sent out exploratory tendrils past its center mass, ensnaring insects and small fish, then moving onto frogs and the occasional baby gator. With each feeding, its bulk grew larger until it occupied nearly two thirds of the swamp. Soon even the full-sized gators stayed away, recognizing a predator more dangerous than themselves.

CHAPTER ELEVEN

The concierge had kindly furnished me with a map of the French Quarter, quickly and efficiently marking the way to Café Du Monde. "Now you definitely want to go to the Café Du Monde because it's a piece of this city's history," he'd said. "But tomorrow try Café Beignet instead. They're just as good, not nearly as crowded, and right down the street."

My stomach growled, informing me that it was running out of patience. It did not like the fact that I kept passing by restaurants and cafés with all sorts of enticing smells wafting out of their doors. As I walked, my head swiveled side to side, moving up and down like a bobble head in a moving car. I didn't want to miss anything. I loved the architecture, the wrought-iron scrollwork on fences and balconies that looked almost delicate enough to be lacework.

I paused as I came to the Café Beignet, breathing in as wonderful smells wafted out the door right into my nostrils. I was sorely tempted to stop there and do Café Du Monde another time, but no, I was going to follow the concierge's advice. My stomach could last another few blocks. Still, it was with a reluctant backward glance, like a woman parting from her lover, that I continued down Royal Street.

It felt familiar. It smelled familiar. The air, the odors—

good, bad, and kill me now—all tapped on the shoulder of my memory, even though there was no reason for them to do so. I also found myself smiling for no reason, even though sweat pooled between my breasts and dripped down my back. The expression "it's a dry heat," did not apply in New Orleans. Still, I felt totally at home. How weird was that?

Hungry as I was, I took my time—the warm, humid weather provided no incentive to pick up my pace. The streets were crowded, and no one else seemed to be in much of a hurry, so I let myself go with the flow of the pedestrian traffic and checked out the boutiques along the route. My budget didn't really run to antiques or art right now, but it was fun to pretend that someday it might. And who knew—maybe I'd be able to do more than pretend if I got more jobs like this one down the road.

I continued onward, following the concierge's precise directions, skirting the edges of Jackson Square and the street musicians, fortune-tellers, artists, and living statues, until I found myself standing in front of the Promised Land.

The terminus of the French Market, the café sported jaunty green awning with brown trim running the length of the building, "Café Du Monde, Original French Market Coffee Stand" lettered across. A short black iron fence and railing separated café from sidewalk, stuffed with as many tables and chairs as I'd ever seen in one space. The seating was packed with what I guessed was the early afternoon lunch crowd, a line of customers waiting for a table to open up. I hadn't expected anything less. From all accounts, it was worth the wait.

I stood there for a moment and inhaled deeply, letting the aromas of sweet fried dough and chicory coffee torment me for just a moment longer. As I was about to join the end of the line, however, a couple of young men nudged by me as a couple vacated a nearby table, snagging it without shame. My jaw dropped. *Really?*

"That's how the locals do it," a low, feminine voice said with a distinct mid-western accent. "Only tourists wait in line at Café Du Monde."

I turned to find a sylph of a girl standing next to me, light-brown hair pulled back in a no-nonsense braid. She wore mid-calf black boots over leggings, topped by a long, plain black sleeveless T-shirt, conspicuous only in its lack of ironic quotes or band logos. A black backpack completed the ensemble. I put her in her mid-twenties, if that.

"Did I say 'really' out loud?" I asked.

"No, but your face kinda screamed it." Her expression sharpened, her gaze fixed across the patio seating with the same focus as a hunting dog that's scented its prey. "Okay, there's a table about to clear out. Follow me if you want to eat." She immediately dove in, weaving her way between tables, chairs, and people with practiced ease. *What the hell.* I gave a mental shrug, and followed her as best I could.

Sure enough, a table for two opened up as if by magic and my new friend slid into one of the chairs, shrugging out of her backpack and putting it at her feet. I sat down across the table, looking around guiltily. "Are we gonna get in trouble for cutting?"

"Nope," she said, "at least not from the servers. I've gotten stink-eye from tourists before, though." She studied me for a moment. "Is this your first time here?"

"Is it obvious?"

"Well, you do kind of have that whole dewy-eyed 'everything is new and exciting' expression going on."

Oh dear.

She shrugged. "On the other hand, you seem pretty comfy in your skin here."

"Thank goodness for small favors," I responded drily.

Further talk was prevented by the arrival of a server, for which I was totally unprepared.

"What can I getcha?"

"Um... beignets?"

"Two plates of beignets and two café au laits, please," my companion said with the matter-of-fact air of someone who'd done this many times. "Or, if you don't like coffee, you can get hot chocolate or orange juice," she added quickly. The server paused, eyebrow raised.

"Oh no, coffee is good," I assured both of them. The server nodded and continued on her rounds. The two of us sat there for a moment in an only mildly awkward silence.

"I'm Lee," I said, holding out a hand.

"Tia," she replied, giving my hand a quick shake with long, strong fingers. "You on vacation?"

I shook my head. "Work."

"Oh? What do you do?" The question was polite, with no real interest behind it.

"I'm working on a movie that's going to start shooting in a week."

"Are you an actress?" Slightly more interest this time, but still unimpressed.

"No," I replied, grateful that she didn't immediately ask if the production was hiring. There's something about the entertainment industry that turns some people into clueless morons with no boundaries. "I'm a stuntwoman."

"That's so cool!" she exclaimed, sudden enthusiasm cutting through her world-weary "I've seen it all and done it all" expression and making me revise my first impression of her age—if she was over eighteen, I'd be surprised. "Have you ever been set on fire?"

I was in the middle of telling her about my fire gig on *Dragon Druid Mages* when the server returned with our order. The aroma of fried dough and powdered sugar was almost intoxicating, and I could smell chicory rising from the café au lait.

I took a bite of beignet, hissing as the still-steaming dough threatened to burn my mouth until the powdered sugar cooled things off. "Omigod, that's amazing," I mumbled.

Tia gave a delicate snort of laughter, the kind that sounds cute instead of like a pig at a trough. "I know, right?"

I finished the first beignet in record time and then started in on the second at a more leisurely pace. "So," I said after a few minutes of contented eating, "are you local?"

Shaking her head, Tia swallowed her own bite and replied, "Nah. Originally from Michigan. But I figured that traveling around was the best way to do what I wanted to do."

"What is it you want to do?"

"I ink," she said. Off my blank look she continued, "Tattooing. I've always been fascinated by skin art, and one of the best ways to learn is apprenticing and studying under different masters."

She only had two tattoos, at least that I could see—a beautifully rendered hummingbird on the left side of her neck, the colors iridescent blues and greens, and a delicate faux bracelet that wrapped around her right wrist. She gave a rueful smile at my surprised expression and said, "I guess I'm not anyone's first idea of a tattoo artist."

"Well, most of the ones I've met or seen or imagined all have—" I gave a little wave with one hand "—more tattoos, I guess. Like ones that cover an entire arm. What are they called... sleeves?"

"That's right," she said with a nod, "and one of these days I'll probably go there, but I'm taking my time. I want to make sure every line, every brushstroke of ink I have put on my body is exactly what I want it to be and *where* I want it to be. I don't want to have any regrets down the line. If I'm gonna be an eighty-year-old covered in ink, I wanna own every single inch of it. It may sag someday, but it'll still have meaning for me, you know?"

I thought I *did* know, and I really liked her for it.

"So how did your family take this, if you don't mind my asking?"

Her mouth twisted into something between a wry grin and a pained grimace. "They didn't. I haven't been back home since I left three years ago."

"I'm sorry."

"Don't be." She ripped a piece of beignet off with what seemed like unnecessary force. "It was never great with my family. And before I left, it got really bad." I didn't ask what she meant by "really bad" and she didn't offer the information. I changed the subject back to her tattoos.

"What do these two mean? And you can totally tell me if I'm being too nosy." Even as I said that, I hoped she wouldn't. I was fascinated by the artistry of both tattoos, and also by what I suspected was the old soul of my new friend. There was a lot of past pain there, but she'd somehow managed to keep a core of herself protected and... well, "pure" seemed a little dramatic, but it somehow fit.

"I don't mind. This one—" she lightly touched the hummingbird "—symbolizes freedom, at least to me. It reminds me to always look for the bright spots in life, no matter how shitty things get. To keep trying for my dreams even when I want to stop. Did you know their wings move in an infinity pattern?"

I shook my head. "I did not."

"They do," she asserted. "I love all birds, even the ugly ones, but hummingbirds… If there's such a thing as a totem animal, that would be mine."

"What about this one?" I pointed to the unbelievably delicate jewel-toned art around her wrist.

Tia gave a small smile. It was not a happy one. "My sister used to steal from me. If it was mine, she wanted it. I had a bracelet I'd inherited from our mom, and Dee wanted it. She'd gotten a necklace, but it wasn't enough." She paused briefly, shaking her head before adding, "Sometimes family can really suck, y'know?"

"I do," I said, adding silently, *even when they think they're doing something for all the right reasons.*

She touched her wrist as if playing with the bracelet that was no longer there. "Anyway, Mom's bracelet disappeared and there wasn't anything I could do about it. Dad either didn't believe me or didn't care. I got this so I could have a piece of jewelry no one could take away from me."

"It's beautiful," I said simply.

"There's a tattoo artist called Dr. Woo," she said, "who does these incredibly detailed, delicate pieces—jewelry, constellations, and stuff like that. I'd kill to apprentice with him," she added wistfully, "but that's about as long a shot as a shot can be."

"He did the bracelet?"

"I could never afford him," Tia said bluntly. "Meghan, the gal I went to for this one, was totally inspired by Dr. Woo's work. I got lucky because she's really talented but still working her way up to becoming a name. She gave me a fantastic deal because this was a relatively new style for her. The design is supposed to offer the wearer protection. Meghan figured I could use it." She looked down with a small smile. "She also let me apprentice under her for a while and that was amazing."

I got a feeling there was more to that story, but an insistent beeping forestalled any further confidences.

"Oops. That's my alarm." Pulling an iPhone out of her purse, Tia glanced at the time. "I'm due at the shop in ten," she said, getting to her feet almost reluctantly and gathering her things. "I'd better get going." She gave me a shy smile. "Thanks for keeping me company."

I smiled back. "Well, thanks for sharing your table with me."

She reached back into her purse and extracted a ten-dollar bill, tucking it under the edge of her plate. "Here. This'll cover my part of the check and tip."

"Thanks. How far away is the tattoo parlor?"

"Hah!" She actually said "hah" wrapped up in an explosive little laugh. "Tattoo parlor. That sounds so sleazy."

"Isn't that what they call them?"

"Most of the places I've worked just call it a shop or a studio, but I guess it's still a thing. It just makes me think of some not very clean hole-in-the-wall in Shanghai or somewhere sailors go to get anchors on their arms and the inker is some dude drinking whiskey and using dirty needles."

My turn to laugh. "You may have seen too many movies, but 'studio' does sound more modern. Next thing you know tattoo spas will be a thing."

"Don't laugh," Tia said darkly. "I can see it happening."

"At any rate, how far do you have to walk?"

She grinned and replied, "Just to the other side of Jackson

Square near the old prison and the Cabildo. It's off an alley that's off another alley. A real hole in the wall that's hard to find unless you know it's there."

"How do you get any walk-in business?"

"Word of mouth." Tia shrugged. "LeRoy—he's the owner—is crazy talented. He's also crazy serious when it comes to the art, which means being on time, which means I'd better take off."

She stopped to pull a card out of her purse. "Here," she said, handing it to me. "If you decide you want to get inked while you're in town, let me know. I'll give you an extra special discount for people who share their tables." She smiled again, the expression lightening those solemn features.

"I might just do that." I waved as she hurried off, weaving her way through the crowded foot traffic like a ninja.

The server came back. "You want anything else, hon?"

I didn't even have to think about my answer. "Another order of beignets and another café au lait, please."

CHAPTER TWELVE

Being a tourist is exhausting work, although it's no doubt easier in a more temperate climate. Sure, it was only eighty degrees, which isn't so bad unless paired with semi-tropical humidity.

I had a few hours to kill before meeting Cayden at Onc Cochon, so I decided to wander around the French Market to start. The air was sultry, redolent with a heady, rich floral smell mixed with all the culinary scents, and a hint of ozone. People moved at a leisurely pace, and were more inclined to smile at random passersby than the LA crowd. I found myself smiling back more often than not.

There were also a lot more plus-size people without any of the almost furtive shame I'd seen in Southern California. Health concerns aside, it was a welcome change from skinny-obsessed Hollywood. I could eat beignets and po-boys to my stomach's content and no one would think twice about it. I felt lazy and happy, although if the temperature had been much higher, "lazy" would have to be upgraded to "comatose."

I strolled around the open-air flea market and bought a blood-red rayon sundress for a fraction of the price I'd have paid back home. I sampled pralines from Aunt Sally's, buying a box to eat at my leisure. Finally, I followed a pedestrian walkway along the Mississippi for a little while before sitting on a bench and staring at the mighty river. It didn't look particularly turbulent on first glance, but below the surface strong currents were detectable. I continued my stroll, soaking in the sights and sounds, stopping in shops as the whim took me.

When my iPhone's alarm went off at five, I reluctantly decided to head back to the hotel for a quick freshen-up before making my way to meet Cayden for dinner. I followed Esplanade Avenue back up to Royal, figuring that would be the quickest route back to Hotel Monteleone.

About two blocks down, I stopped in my tracks to stare at a large mansion hunkered down on a corner lot, the structure stretching down the block on each side. Three stories of gray stone mellowed by age, with ornate scrollwork galleries running the length of the building on either side between the first and second stories. It was beautiful.

Why, then, was it giving me chills up my spine?

Something tugged at the corners of my memory, but I couldn't quite pull it into the light of day. Right now, the only thing I knew was that the place, as gorgeous an example of antebellum architecture as it was, gave me an uncomfortable sense of déjà vu.

"Some places are closer to hell than others and this evil city is one of them." I could hear the woman's Texas twang loud and clear as her words echoed through my head.

Someone brushed by me, heading down Royal the way I'd just come, and I realized I'd been standing in the middle of the street and was about to miss the light and possibly get hit by oncoming traffic. I hurried across the rest of the way, pausing in front of the mansion to stare up at it yet again.

Why was it so damn familiar?

"Interested in the gruesome tale of Horror House, young lady?" I jumped at the voice right at my shoulder. "Sorry, didn't mean to startle you."

I stared at the man in front of me, my heartbeat racing double time. Cute, mid-twenties, dressed like an extra in *Interview with the Vampire*, all waistcoat and breeches and frockcoat. Younger than me, making his "young lady" greeting seem like pandering. He really did look apologetic, though, so I made a valiant effort to stifle the impulse to punch him. I hate being taken unawares.

"Can I help you?" My tone was a little frostier than normal to hide the fact my heart was still doing a quickstep.

"You seemed interested in the LaLaurie mansion—"

I started at the name.

"—so I thought I'd give you one of our coupons. Best ghost tour in New Orleans at a discount!" He grinned apologetically even as he held out a brochure, adding, "We're doing one of our tours right now, matter of fact. That's us over there." He nodded across the street. A group of about fifteen people leaned against an iron fence outside a townhouse, listening to the female counterpart to my Brad Pitt wannabe while they took photos of the mansion.

I took the brochure. "Ghastly Ghost Tours of NOLA" at the top, a lurid drawing of a man being strangled by a pissed-off-looking ghost below, and a coupon for ten bucks off at the very bottom.

"We also do vampire tours, if that's more your thing," he said.

"You're dressed more for vampires than ghosts, if you don't mind my saying so," I commented.

He grinned. "Vampires, ghosts, zombies. It's all pretty much the same to our boss's wardrobe budget."

"How long is the coupon good for?" I asked, more out of idle curiosity than any real desire to go on one of their tours. I mean, it could be fun, although I didn't want to take the tour on my own. Like bad movies, I suspect it was an experience more enjoyable when shared.

"No expiration for you." He gave a gallant little bow to punctuate his words. Very nice touch, even though I suspected he'd say much the same to anyone. "Just ask for Christian."

"Thanks." I tucked the brochure in my bag. With one last glance at the building looming above me, I continued down Royal Street. I wanted to do some research before dinner.

†

Once back in my room, I checked to see how far of a walk Onc Cochon was from the hotel. It was outside the French Quarter, in the Faubourg Marigny. Basically, back the way I'd just come, on the other side of Esplanade. I *could* walk it, but I'd have to do it at a brisker pace than I cared to, and I'd be all sticky and sweaty when I got there. I decided to Lyft it instead, which gave me some time to do a little research.

A quick glance verified that the Ghastly Tours brochure gave the name of the so-called "Horror House" as the LaLaurie mansion. Yup, same name that Cayden and Devon used in *Voodoo Wars*. I quickly pulled out my laptop and googled LaLaurie and immediately got hits with sensationalized titles like "Horror House in New Orleans," and "Madame LaLaurie, Sadistic Slave Owner of the French Quarter." Delphine LaLaurie was a French Creole woman who, along with her surgeon husband, Louis, was infamous for allegedly torturing and disfiguring her slaves. There were pictures of the mansion on the corner of Royal and Governor Nicholls Street, and a lot of photos of Kathy Bates as Madame LaLaurie and Angela Bassett as

Marie Laveau in *American Horror Story*. The actual LaLaurie mansion, however, wasn't used in the series—the current owners weren't interested in cashing in on their residence's infamous history. I remembered the flock of tourists across the street, phones and cameras out as they took pictures of the house. That had to get old fast.

I took the script out and flipped through it again, looking for the scene introducing the LaLauries—a French Creole woman and her surgeon husband. *Ah ha*. In the script, they're torturing slaves in order to summon demons, which incurs the wrath of Marie Laveau and Papa John—not to be confused with the pizza chain by the same name—but it was obvious Cayden and his co-writer Devon had based parts of their story heavily on the history of the LaLauries and the horrors that supposedly happened within the walls of the mansion on Royal Street.

Putting the script down, I carried on surfing the net. There were several accounts of the supposed history of Delphine LaLaurie. At worst, she was one of history's greatest monsters—there were stories about the dreadful condition of the LaLaurie slaves found locked in the attic, victims of Delphine's sadistic whims and her husband's experiments.

One internet historian speculated that she was a typical example of the white Creole women of the time—they lacked control in other areas of their lives, and took it out on their slaves. Other accounts were relatively moderate, saying the stories were greatly exaggerated because people love a good horror story.

None of which explained why I'd gotten an honest case of the heebie-jeebies when I'd seen the LaLaurie mansion.

CHAPTER THIRTEEN

Onc Cochon was on a quiet street, nestled between a used record store and a boutique wine shop. The restaurant front was painted a subtle beige-pink, with a small sign in the shape of a winking pig in one window. My stomach growled. Beignets, however tasty, are not a substitute for lunch.

Inside, I looked around the restaurant in surprise. Everything I'd expected from a four-star establishment was missing. No snooty maître d's, for a start. Instead of white tablecloths and tasteful candles, there were cramped tables and booths with plastic red-and-white checked covers, and autographed photos of musicians and actors on the walls. The low-watt bulbs flickered and buzzed like anemic bug zappers. Hmmm, maybe they *were* bug zappers. The place was crowded, stuffed to capacity with all sorts—families with kids, couples holding hands across the tables—and the sound of animated conversation competed with zydeco music piped through cheap speakers.

In other words, *so* not what I expected when Cayden invited me to join him for dinner. My shoulders relaxed, tension draining from my body without even the benefit of a beer.

A twenty-something hostess in jeans and a violet T-shirt greeted me with a warm smile, sparkling white teeth set against rich brown skin. Her irises matched the violet of her shirt, a slightly lighter shade than my own eyes. She wore her hair, black and curly, in a French braid, tendrils escaping to soften the strong lines of her face. A cheap plastic nametag read "Angelique."

"What can I do ya for, *cher*?"

Cher. I silently and happily checked that off my bucket list. I wondered if she was Cajun.

"Um, I'm meeting someone here," I said. "A Mr. Doran?"

She nodded, her smile growing wider. "Oooh, yeah, he's a tasty one!" She looked me up and down. "Not sure which of you is getting the better deal here."

My face burned, no doubt bright red. Hopefully the dim lighting hid it.

"Right this way," she added, oblivious to my embarrassment. *Take the compliment*, I told myself, and followed her through the crowded room, admiring the skillful way she evaded the bustling waitstaff who passed us bearing heavy trays of food and drink. She moved with almost animalistic grace, which made me think she might be either a shifter or a dancer, maybe both.

She led me into a narrow hallway, past the kitchen, where the enticing smells became almost overwhelming, and out onto a patio surrounded by a wooden trellised wall on three sides, flowering bougainvillea growing thickly on the trellis and trailing the wall. Other flowering plants and prehistoric-looking ferns vied for space, permeating the air with a heady perfume that somehow complimented the rich aromas of food.

The patio held about a dozen tables of various sizes, most of them for two to four people except for one long plank of a table that could fit at least a half dozen people. Cayden sat at the far end of this one, a bottle of beer in front of him. He got to his feet when we approached, giving Angelique a small yet intimate smile.

Hmmm.

Deciding I didn't care whether the two already knew each other in the biblical sense or otherwise, I accepted Cayden's very Hollywood greeting—hands on my shoulders as he kissed my cheek a scant inch away from my lips.

"Enjoy, *cher*," Angelique said with a bright smile as she set a menu down in front of me. Whether she was talking to me or Cayden was a toss-up, but I got the feeling that she meant it both ways.

"Now, Angelique," Cayden said with a shake of his head, "how come you're working tonight? You're going to be busy enough on the film in a few days."

Really? I looked at her with renewed interest.

Angelique rolled her eyes. "I told you they couldn't get anyone for tonight. I wouldn't be a very good person if I turned my back on the people who gave me a good job." She gave me a wink. "Don't let this man talk you into anything you don't wanna be talked into, *cher*." With that, she vanished back inside the restaurant.

"Not a succubus," I said, more to myself than my dinner companion.

"No, she's not," Cayden agreed. "Shifter clan. She's playing Perrine," he continued before I could ask the question. "She's going to be doing her own stunts and you'll be the one training her."

"I can do that."

He gave me a bland smile at odds with those eyes. "You planning on sitting down any time soon?"

"Isn't this table a little big for two people?" I said as I sat down across from him.

"Thought I'd introduce you to some of the team."

"Do they work here too?"

He laughed. "No."

I looked down at my skirt and camisole with a frown. "I would have dressed up if you'd given me fair warning."

"Trust me when I say you'll fit in just fine."

All hail Cayden, the king of ambiguity.

"We have about a half-hour before they get here," he continued. "How about we order some beer and appetizers and talk about our close encounter with the carnivorous seaweed?" It wasn't a question so much as a decision. I had no quarrel with a plan that involved food and beer sooner rather than later, even if I did have some hefty reservations about the subject matter.

Reasons for not telling him about my unusual legacy? I'd been warned by Randy, Sean, and Seth not to trust the man. Eden had bailed on me and hidden in the restroom when he'd showed up at Ocean's End, and her interest in visiting New Orleans had noticeably cooled when she'd found out Cayden was part of the deal. My own early reactions to him had been negative—he'd been an ass both times—but then he'd favorably surprised me more than once and... well, my instincts were now telling me to trust him. Besides, I'd made a promise and I planned on keeping it. After I had something to drink.

"So, what's good as far as the beers go?" I asked.

"What are you in the mood for?" Cayden leaned back in his chair, fingers curled around his beer bottle, hand nearly engulfing it. "Their beer selection is extensive."

"Let's start with that," I said, nodding to it. "What are you drinking?"

"A rye pale ale aged in bourbon barrels." He uncurled

his fingers so I could see the label. Abita, Louisiana's best-known craft brewery. "It's a limited release. Go ahead and try a sip. See if you like it."

Okay, I could either take his gesture as a little too intimate, or I could try a sip, one craft beer aficionado to another. I opted for the second choice, figuring it would be less weird in the long run. Besides, it was a beer I hadn't tried before. Priorities, right?

I took the bottle, trying *not* to go out of my way to *not* to touch his fingers because I wanted to prove this was casual.

Try not to sleep with Doran, my cousin's voice intoned in my head.

Oh, fuck you, Seth, I silently retorted.

I took a quick sip of the Abita, enjoying the smooth sweetness of malts and the yeasty taste of bread integrated with all the oaky, bourbon goodness of bourbon barrels. I then took another, larger swallow, totally guilt free considering how much of my Triple Threat he'd downed at Ocean's End. "That's tasty," I concluded, handing it back to him. "I can totally drink that."

"Looks like you already did," he said wryly. I smiled sweetly and said nothing.

A waitress, attractive and comfortable with her forties, appeared as if telepathically summoned. "What can I do for you?" Her accent wrapped the words in honey.

Cayden gave her a slow grin. "Bring us two more of these and a large order of crawdads." Glancing over at me, he added, "You okay with that?"

I gave him a thumbs-up and smiled at the waitress.

A beer and a hefty share of fried crawdads later, my appetite had gone down to a low roar and I'd relaxed. "I like this place," I said, downing the dregs of my Abita.

"Figured you would."

"Did you?" I stared at him over my glass.

"Yeah. I also figure you were expecting something different."

I raised an eyebrow, stonewalling him. "I didn't have any expectations one way or the other, but I admit this place pleasantly surprised me."

Cayden didn't ask why. Instead he glanced at his watch. "We have about twenty minutes for you to explain why the sea dragon was gunning for you."

Fortified by beer and crawdads, I told him. When I was finished, he raised a hand and, as if by magic, the obviously smitten waitress who had brought our crawdads reappeared with another round of beers and a pitcher of ice water. After she'd left, Cayden said, "So, this thing, this sea dragon, was related to you."

"If Sean is to be believed—and I can't imagine him lying about something like that—then, yes."

"So if this asshole god really did turn most of Lilith's kids into demons and they all had little demonic rugrats... wouldn't all supernaturals be related to you on some level or another?"

I nodded glumly. "The thought has occurred to me more than once."

"Then why did the sea dragon attack you whereas Angelique brought you back here instead of trying to rip your throat out? She's got shifter blood in her, a lot of it."

I shrugged. "I guess the older the monster, the more likely it has a reason to try and eat me. Maybe they know Lilith's human descendants are gunning for them."

"You have no plans for slaughtering our cast and crew, right?"

"Not unless they try to kill me first. Then all bets are off."

Picking up his beer, he rolled the bottle between his

palms. "Then there shouldn't be any problem."

My laugh held no amusement. "What if another one of Lilith's unhappy offspring shows up while we're filming? You saw what happened at Trancas. If it *was* after me, a lot of innocent people died just because it was hungry and they happened to be in the way."

"Do you expect one to show up on set?"

I shrugged again, angry in a directionless way. The whole situation pissed me off all over again. "Sean doesn't think so. I mean, he said they'll always be drawn to me, that there's a risk if they're close enough to sense me. I don't know if they have some sort of familial GPS or if it's just luck of the draw, but I don't want people to die because of me."

He leaned back in his chair and regarded me. "How many people have you told about this?"

I shook my head. "So far, you're it." Although I was pretty sure Faustina knew. She *was* a goddess, after all.

"Not your friends? Your boyfriend?"

"No one," I reiterated, choking back an almost kneejerk urge to deny having a boyfriend. *Sorry, Randy.* "It was easy to pretend the Janus demon was a one-off. That maybe Sean was wrong. The whole family curse thing didn't seem real until the other day, and I guess I hoped it wasn't. But it was and it is. I'm telling you because you were there when that thing attacked, and because you deserve to know the risks of hiring me."

He nodded, still looking at me with those disturbing— and compelling—eyes.

I played with my glass, cradling it between my palms as it sweated cold moisture on my warm skin. "So that's it. Are you sure you want me on this film?"

"Oh yes," Cayden said with another of those near-manic grins. "After all, it won't be boring."

"You're joking, right?"

He leaned in across the table, expression suddenly deadly serious. "I never joke."

The sudden electricity between us was not a joke. I wasn't ready for it, so I used words as a shield. "That's kind of like saying 'everything I say is a lie' and watching some poor android's head explode."

He laughed and relaxed back into his chair as if nothing had happened. Maybe it hadn't. Maybe I needed to get over myself.

"What's call time tomorrow?" I asked, figuring I'd better budget my alcohol intake. I'm lucky in that I generally wake up headache-free regardless of how much I whooped it up the night before. If I'm not exactly sparkly and ready to sing, "Oh, what a beautiful morning," I'm at least reasonably alert. Coffee helps. But I still didn't want to overdo things the night before my first day on a job, especially not when Cayden was signing my paycheck. I might not dislike him the way I did during our first two encounters, but that didn't mean I felt comfortable getting drunk around him.

Cayden didn't appear to have any such inhibitions. When the waitress appeared yet again—she was one of the most attentive waitstaff I'd ever encountered, though I doubted I had anything to do with that—I shook my head. Cayden, on the other hand, drained his bottle and nodded. He was a big man, and a stuntman. That earned him two hollow legs.

"You're not having any more?" He raised an eyebrow. "You were tossing back some pretty high-octane bourbon barrel stout at Ocean's End."

"Oh, I will," I assured him, "but unless this is some sort of bizarre initiation rite where I'm expected to match you drink for drink, I'll take my time. You still haven't told me when and where I'm expected to show up bright-eyed and bouncy tomorrow morning."

"Tomorrow's all about sitting down with the rest of the stunt team, the FX coordinator, and the director while our line producer does any last-minute finagling needed for locations, rentals, all that." He gave a vague wave of one hand. "We'll be starting early enough when shooting begins. We're giving people a break tomorrow. 10 A.M."

I could live with that. "Okay, I'll have another when I'm finished with this one."

"Drinking contest?"

"Oh, please," I scoffed. "We're not in college anymore."

"Were you ever in college? It doesn't seem like your thing."

"I went to community college for a year before dropping out. I already knew exactly what I wanted to do, which was stunts. I really only went to satisfy Sean, who wanted me to 'explore all my options' before committing to KSC."

Cayden let out a guffaw.

"What's so funny about that?" I asked defensively.

"It's such a cliché," he said with a scornful shake of his head. "'Explore all your options.' Authority figures, parents, uncles, gods, whatever, they never give people the benefit of the doubt, never believe we might actually know exactly what we want to do without exploring any of their perceived 'options.'"

"A lot of kids don't really know what they want, though, do they?"

Another shrug. "Some of us did."

"Does this mean I'm gonna get some backstory on you?" I leaned forward almost unconsciously.

"No."

The bluntness of his reply and uncompromising tone pushed me back into my seat like a physical shove. I waited for him to follow it up with some sort of apology, something along the lines of "Not to be rude, but…" but all I got was that damn grin.

I shook my head, my mouth twisting into an exasperated grimace. Why had I expected him to act like a normal person? Or even a semi-normal one? Was he ever not an asshole?

The waitress returned with not one, but two more Abitas. Cayden poured mine into my glass with a practiced skill that was oddly graceful for someone his size. His hand engulfed the glass. Long fingers, strong.

A killer's hands…

Now where the hell had that thought come from? Had I made a huge mistake taking this job? Were Randy, Sean, and Seth right?

Hell, no, I immediately answered myself. Maybe if I'd had any other offers in the works, the answer would be different. Besides, there were directors and producers out there much worse than Cayden.

CHAPTER FOURTEEN

A few minutes later, the others began to arrive. First to appear was Langdon Pinkton-Smythe—a name only slightly more pretentious than the actor who claimed it. Wearing trousers and a white silk shirt with a cravat, he looked like he'd wandered off the set of a Noël Coward play. Popping an Altoid into his mouth, he tucked the tin into his jacket pocket and offered a pale hand, long fingers outstretched like spider legs. I shook it, managing not to react to the feel of Langdon's cold, clammy skin, partly because I knew he was a ghoul and also because I didn't want to offend him since we shared Faustina Corbin as our agent.

There'd been some trouble a year or so ago when Langdon had allegedly tried to take a bite out of an extra who'd passed out from low blood sugar—one of these twenty-somethings trying to work her way to a size two by not eating. Langdon swore, however, that he didn't do it. "Why would I eat someone when they're still alive?" he'd said in an interview for one of the few Industry websites that was exclusively for supes. "It would be like eating kimchi before it's buried in the ground to marinate." I remember thinking it was a valid, if somewhat gross analogy. This was his first decent job since that incident.

Tall and lean, Landon had a thin, almost gaunt face that just skirted the edges of handsome. If he played his cards right, he could follow in the footsteps of Lance Henriksen and Steve Buscemi.

Part of me wanted to ask Langdon if the rumors about him trying to sample the extras buffet a little too literally were true. The more mature side of me knew that it would be rude. And as long as he stuck to his prepackaged ghoul Happy Meals, it didn't really matter.

But, man, all the Altoids in the world could not quite cover the sweet-and-sour scent of decay that wafted out of his mouth.

"Langdon's playing Louis, Delphine LaLaurie's husband," Cayden said casually.

"Her third husband," Langdon amended. "The surgeon. And the villain of the piece."

"Ah," I said. "Do you think he had any part in the torture of their slaves?"

"*So* hard to know truth from fiction," the actor replied in an affected drawl, "but for the sake of a good story, I'll err on the side of him being at least as evil as his wife, if not the true evil genius behind the atrocities."

Regardless of whether or not he'd tried to eat an extra, there was no doubt Langdon was a total drama queen.

"Langdon has done some stunt work," Cayden informed me.

The actor nodded. "Got my start in the *Alive or Zed* series a few years back," he told me with a toothy grin. "Whenever they needed someone to be buried alive or to break out of airless tombs or coffins, I was their go-to."

"Uh… nice," I said politely. It made sense, though. When you wanted to get a zom crawling out of its grave and had a limited budget, the shots were easier when the actor or stunt player didn't have to breathe. "Do you consider yourself a stuntman who can act or an actor who does some stunts?"

"Same thing, yes?"

I shook my head. "Not necessarily. If you go the *Hooper* route," I said, referring to director Hal Needham's iconic film tribute to stuntmen and stuntwomen, "you're a stuntman who can act. Burt Reynolds, for instance, started out as a stuntman. On the other hand, there are actors out there who are physically capable of doing some of their own stunts."

"Like Tim Journey?"

"No," I said emphatically. "I mean, yes, he kicks ass doing his own stunts, but aside from being more than a little crazypants, he's also unseelie Fae, which gives him some mad skills."

"Am I late?"

I looked up to see a statuesque woman standing at the patio entrance, a long-sleeved, forest-green sweater dress clinging to curves Jayne Mansfield might have envied. A fall of wavy dark hair and startlingly green eyes made her irregular features beautiful.

Slowly and deliberately, she walked toward our table. The way she moved, her eyes, her attitude… all screamed, "I am feline, hear me meow!" Don't get me wrong. It wasn't like she was trying too hard to be Cat Woman or the kind of girl who thinks *Black Magic Woman* is her personal anthem. Unless I was mistaken—and I wasn't—she was the product of actual feline therianthropy. In other words, what we had here, folks, was some sort of werecat. And she was totally working it.

As a general rule, I like cats, but I got the feeling this little kitty was one of the ones that gave felines a reputation for being assholes—you know, the ones on YouTube videos that are always deliberately knocking shit off counters or ambushing people or dogs. I'd definitely keep my eyes open. Our werecat, however, currently had eyes only for Cayden. The rest of us might as well have been part of a matte painting backdrop.

"Ah, Leandra," Cayden greeted her. "Trust you to make an entrance."

"Always, darling," she purred.

"Leandra Marcadet," he continued, "this is Lee Striga. Leandra is playing Marie Laveau. Leandra, Lee here will be stunt doubling you." Glancing back at me he added, "Leandra and Angelique are cousins, by the way."

Leandra finally tore her gaze away from Cayden and looked at me, the smoldering fire in those green eyes dying down until they seemed to be rimmed with frost. My stomach gave an unpleasant flip, as if the crawdads were turning against me.

Oh, she does not like me.

Then she smiled, surprising me by swooping over to give me a hug, pressing her cheek against mine and enveloping me in a dark, opulent fragrance. Sandalwood, cinnamon, something with a spicy floral note. Geranium, maybe. Or possibly the inside of a Venus flytrap.

"We will be friends," she murmured, like a five-year-old at summer camp.

Or not. Her tone was warm, but my gut didn't believe it. Although maybe I just needed some Tums. Out loud I said, "Looking forward to working with you," trying to infuse my own voice with some warmth. Even to my own ears, however, I sounded stilted and overly formal, like someone at a really boring high tea.

Leandra Marcadet sauntered around the table and sat next to Cayden, scooching her chair as close to his as possible.

"I hope you'll forgive the assumption," I said, "but if you don't mind my asking—" *or even if you do*"—why do you need a stunt double? You obviously have the physical capabilities to do pretty much anything, much like your cousin."

"I'm an actress, *cher*," Leandra replied. Now why did *cher* sound so nice coming from Angelique and so condescending when spoken by Leandra? She looked me up and down with a sneer disguised as a smile—yeah, I could tell the difference. "You, on the other hand, are a stuntwoman. You get paid to risk yourself. To fall from buildings or set yourself on fire. I get paid to act, and to be beautiful. I cannot afford injury or harm to my face or physique. You and Angelique, on the other hand…" She gave a small, tinkling laugh as her words trailed off.

Oh yeah, we were gonna be bestest buddies.

"Well," I replied, "someone has to make you actors look good."

Her eyes narrowed and damned if her ears didn't flatten a little. *Score.*

I fully expected her to start wriggling her haunches and attack me, but instead she pulled her chair as close to Cayden's as possible without actually sitting in his lap. He looked bored and smug at the same time.

Cayden, thy name is ambiguity.

Catching Langdon's eye roll, I hid a grin of my own. Compared to the lead actress on *Pale Dreamer*, who'd lived up to her reputation as the diva from hell, Leandra would be a piece of cake. Not particularly good cake, but cake nonetheless. It was kind of like going from Voldemort to Dobby. One was evil, the other just irritating.

Besides, I only had to double Leandra—I didn't have to like her.

†

"Sorry, Tiff, but I'm just not up to going out." Star paused to cough, then added, "I feel horrible. Momma thinks I have the flu or something."

Tiffany rolled her eyes even though there was no one to see her. Star's momma worried all the damn time, coddling her daughter so much it was a wonder she ever let Star leave the house. Not like Tiffany's mother, who couldn't be bothered to keep track of her daughter's comings and goings.

"You know I'd love to go out, but I'm just so tired—"

"Fine," Tiffany interrupted with a petulant edge to her voice. "I'll just call Liz." She'd already tried Cherry, but she hadn't answered the phone.

"Liz isn't feeling so good either," Star replied. Her voice sounded feeble, as if it took real effort for her to talk.

That would be a first, Tiffany thought.

"Anyway," Star continued, "I have to go. Momma says I need to sleep because—"

"Yeah, whatever."

Tiffany hit the "end call" button and tossed her phone onto her bed, heaving a put-upon sigh that turned quickly into a nasty bout of coughing. The deep rattling in her chest took her unpleasantly by surprise. She'd felt fine a moment ago.

What the fuck? She was seized by another racking coughing fit. This time, when she lowered her hand, it was covered in red phlegm. She almost yelled for her mother but changed her mind. Her mom wouldn't know what to do if Tiffany was really ill, even if she cared enough to try. Besides, now that she thought about it, Momma had gone out for drinks with friends, which meant she wouldn't be home for hours.

If Tiffany was honest with herself—something she rarely indulged in—she would have admitted her disdain toward Star and her momma's overly protective attitude was pure jealousy. But that would involve self-introspection, and that would not end well. Narcissism ran in the family.

Throwing herself on the bed next to her phone, Tiffany wavered between the impulse to call Liz despite Star's words or—a more sensible choice—giving up and getting some sleep. She really didn't feel well. Before she could make up her mind, however, her phone's text tone went off. She rolled over and looked at her text messages.

What R U doing?

Blaise. Not exactly a boyfriend—his family didn't make enough money to put him in that category. He was definitely more of a Juan's Flying Burrito date than someone who'd take her to Commander's Palace. But, oh, he was mighty pretty. She thought briefly of telling him she was too sick for company, but dismissed the idea before it was fully born. Even if she was coming down with whatever grunge Star and Liz had, she certainly wasn't going to pass up a chance to have sex with Blaise. She'd make it up to him if he caught something from her.

Nothing. Bored. Wanna come over?

U actually gonna be there?

She'd promised to meet him the other night and had been an hour late. He'd been pissed but hadn't done anything like hit her.

Just told her in no uncertain terms that being late was disrespectful of his time, and if it happened again, they were over. She still hadn't made up her mind if she wanted to test his resolve. Tiffany had a lot of confidence in her sex appeal, but Blaise was stubborn. He didn't put up with her temper tantrums and she liked that—at least where Blaise was concerned.

> I'll be here. I promise.

> Cool. C U soon.

Getting slowly to her feet, Tiffany went over to her antique dressing table and peered at herself in the mirror. It was one of those old mercury ones that gave back a soft, flattering reflection. Not that Tiffany usually needed any help from a stupid old mirror. Now, however, she looked like crap, all dark hollows under her eyes, almost bruised. She tried a smile on for size, frowning when she saw what looked like brownish stains on her teeth. She leaned in to examine them closer, wincing as she caught a whiff of her breath. It smelled sickly-sweet and sour at the same time. Like daiquiri vomit.

Ugh.

First things first, and that was to brush her teeth. Then she'd do some magic with makeup and light some candles. Her momma always told her that candlelight hid a multitude of sins.

CHAPTER FIFTEEN

We were joined in short order by Devon Manus, the director and co-writer of *Voodoo Wars*. A well-built man in that ageless sweet spot somewhere between thirty and fifty. Sun-burnished blond hair, dark tan. Brown eyes with sunbursts of copper around the pupil. If Leandra smelled like the inside of an incense factory, Devon smelled like he'd rolled in a bale of hay and rubbed his pulse points with leather. Definitely a more pleasant aroma than the faint but distinct whiff of decomposing meat that wafted out of Langdon's mouth.

I stopped my brain from going down a ghoul-related "you are what you eat" wormhole and brought my attention back to Devon "Manly Man" Manus. He had all the attributes I associated with someone in stunts, although his crisp khaki pants and white cotton shirt were too clean and too expensive to fit the profile. Still, I fully expected him and Cayden to reenact Ah-nold and Carl Weathers' bromantic arm-wrestling match from *Predator*. They both had the biceps and forearms for it. Instead, Cayden just nodded and said, "You've met Leandra and Langdon." He nodded in my direction and added, "This is Lee Striga."

"No, please don't get to your feet," Devon Manus said, even though I hadn't actually made a move to do so. His accent was pure *Crocodile Dundee*, and if that wasn't a crocodile tooth dangling from the leather cord around his neck, I'd eat vegemite.

Well, no, I really wouldn't.

"After all," he continued, "you'll be doing plenty of that when we start filming."

How he managed to make something so innocuous sound suggestive was a mystery I didn't care to solve.

"I see why you and Cayden are friends," I said neutrally.

Cayden laughed. "In case you were wondering, Dev, that wasn't a compliment."

"Didn't think so." Devon looked at me appreciatively. "You didn't exaggerate. She's a right feisty one."

Oh, spare me.

"So," I inquired sweetly, "are you really Australian? Or do you just play one on TV?"

Both men roared with laughter, Langdon chuckling politely to avoid being left out of the male camaraderie. Leandra raised an eyebrow as if shocked at my bad manners.

Hypocrite.

"Half Aussie, half Irish," Devon admitted cheerfully, taking the accent down a few notches. He slid into a chair next to me without an invitation. Fair enough since this was his film. "My Irish half is *gancanagh*, if you're curious." He pronounced it "gan-KHAN-och." Whatever, it's basically a sexed-up leprechaun.

"What's the Australian half?" I asked, even though I knew better.

"All man," he said with a grin.

"Seriously," I said, "are you and Cayden related?"

"We're all related if you go back far enough, *acushla*," he replied with a grin and a practiced twinkle in his eye.

Laying the Irish on thick didn't help his cause as far as I was concerned.

"Er, Dev…" Cayden gave a very small shake of his head.

"Ah, my apologies, Miss Striga." He paused, then added, "Or do you prefer Ms.?"

"You can call me whatever you want as long as you accept the risk that I might haul off and punch you if I don't like it."

If this had been a sitcom, the audience reaction would have been all indrawn breaths and "ooOOOoooh!" Maybe a "oh no she di'n't" tossed in for good measure. Instead we got a well-timed interruption from the waitress bearing an overflowing tray of drinks. Beers for everyone except Leandra, who preferred white wine spritzers.

I bet she used the pink weights at the gym.

I turned back to Devon. "You come from a stunts background, right?"

"See, Cayden, you bastard, I *haven't* lost it." He flexed a biceps and kissed it. I rolled my eyes, but still grinned.

"It's the attitude," Cayden drawled. "Everything about you screams 'cocky son-of-a-bitch.' Although it's gotten worse since you started directing. I think your head has gone up two hat sizes at least."

"Three," Devon corrected him, "but who's counting?"

"So how big a crew are we looking at?" I asked, hoping it would break up the male bonding.

"It's a small crew," Devon answered. "You look at movies from the seventies, even some from the eighties, and there was none of this half-hour's worth of credits with everyone who even thought of working on the film listed. We don't need a cast or crew of thousands to make quality films. Just the right cast and crew, eh, Cayden?"

Cayden nodded, somehow implying neither agreement nor disagreement. More like he didn't give a shit one way or the other. His eyes were on me as if gauging my reaction.

I shrugged. I'd worked on both types of productions and plenty in between, and it all depended on the competence of those in charge, and who they hired.

"Who else do I get to meet tonight?"

"The Ginga brothers," Cayden said. "They'll be doing any rigging needed, plus they're on the stunt team. Worked with them on three films to date. And speak of the devil…"

"Oy!" Devon jumped to his feet and waved enthusiastically at the two men entering the patio, nearly smacking Langdon in the face and totally clueless at his own near-miss. The actor chuckled again with the same painfully fake bonhomie that again went unacknowledged.

The Ginga brothers were short and well-built, one in cargo shorts and a souvenir New Orleans T-shirt, the other in a teal button-down shirt worn untucked over black jeans. Both men had dark, weathered skin and curly dark-brown hair shot through with bronze and blond highlights that would cost a fortune to get in a salon. They looked as if they spent equal amounts of time in the sun and working out.

"Lee Striga," Cayden said, "meet Illuka and Miro Ginga. I've worked with them on three different Australian films, and they're solid."

"Dependable *and* versatile," Devon added.

Their last name joggled something in my memory, but I couldn't quite place it.

"Nice to meet you both." I stood up, holding out a hand to the brothers in quick succession. Their eyes were an unusual shade of yellowish gold and I caught a brief glimpse of a reptilian slit to the pupils that reminded me of the Eye of Sauron. Then I blinked, looked again to find that the pupils rounded out to a more human appearance. The skin of their palms was rough, almost scaly, and their smiles showed way more very white teeth than necessary.

They both beamed at me with those wide, toothy grins.

"We go by Mike and Ike on set," said the one in the cargo shorts with a strong Aussie accent.

"Like the candy?"

"Exactly right," he agreed. "I'm Mike. Pleased to meet you."

"*Dingo Lake*," I said as my brain suddenly made the connection. "You two worked on *Dingo Lake*, right?" *Dingo Lake* was one of several torture porn films that came out of Australia on the heels of the success of *Wolf Creek*. Not my type of film, but the action sequences had been crazy good. The lake location they'd used was next to abandoned oil derricks, and there'd been some really cool wirework and high falls that almost compensated for the "Abandon all hope, ye who watch this film" body count.

"You two did the stunt coordinating and at least one of you played a victim," I continued. "The guy who gets his hand stuck in an animal trap and then dragged into the lake by a crocodile, right?"

"That was me," Ike piped up with the same accent as his twin. "Mike was locked in a shed with an improbable number of redback spiders."

"Oh yeah, I remember that bit." Despite the title, there weren't actually any dingoes in the movie, but there'd been plenty of crocodiles, poisonous snakes, and venomous spiders, all unrealistically utilized by the homicidal villain.

"Lee Striga," Mike—or was it Ike?—exclaimed, grinning from ear to ear with what looked like genuine pleasure. "I know your work in *Vampshee*. You're the best thing in that movie."

His brother—definitely Ike—nodded. "He speaks the truth."

I smiled at the compliment, accepting it without argument both because it was the polite thing to do and because I totally agreed with them.

"It would be a pleasure to meet Sean Katz as well," Ike added.

"If you make it out to Los Angeles, you'll have to come out to the Ranch," I immediately offered. They beamed happily at that, taking seats across from me next to Devon.

"You didn't invite *me* to the Ranch." Cayden leaned across the table, grinning at me. Leandra glanced suspiciously between the two of us. I'd seen cats with that look right before they smacked a rival feline in danger of getting too close.

"You didn't mention wanting to meet Sean," I replied sweetly.

"Oh, we've met."

I glanced at him sharply. "Sean didn't mention that."

"I'll wager Seth didn't either." Cayden wore a small smile that made my fingers itch to slap it off his face.

I wasn't sure who I was more pissed off at—Cayden or Sean. Since I couldn't make up my mind, I decided to crumple my anger into a tiny little bitter ball for later. I turned my attention back to the Ginga brothers.

"Is 'Ginga' an Aboriginal name?" I asked, hoping they wouldn't be offended. They weren't.

Mike nodded. "It's a name for the first crocodile, Old Man Ginga." He leaned in. "One day, when Ginga was still human, he was sleeping by a fire near a billabong. He slept too close to the flames, poor bloke, and caught fire. So he dived into the water, and the mix of water and fire raised up big blisters on his back."

"In order to escape the pain," Ike continued, "Ginga turned himself into a giant crocodile. Now you can see the ridges and lumps on Ginga's back in the water and along the shores of billabongs, rivers, and the oceans."

"You see, our family is descended from Ginga," Mike added. "We can cross rivers and estuaries that are infested with crocodiles and our cousins will grant us safe passage."

Ike nodded. "Especially useful when we're filming in the Northern Territory."

"Does that work with alligators as well?" Langdon asked.

"Oh yeah," Ike replied. "Caimans too, although they're not really much of a threat. Not like salties or alligators."

"Was… Was the Crocodile Hunter related to Ginga too?" I couldn't resist the question. Both brothers nodded, big grins on their faces as if pleased I'd figured this out.

If I ever got a chance to visit Australia, I wanted to make sure these two were my tour guides. I might be able to take on demons, but crocodiles were another matter. There was something primordially horrifying at the thought of being ripped to pieces by a reptile, especially one that did a death roll first.

"Lee Striga," Mike said thoughtfully. "Yes. You're the one who got hurt taking a high fall, yeah?"

"Yeah, that's me." I heaved an inward sigh. How I longed for the days when I was known for taking high falls and doing kick-ass wirework rather than being recognized as the stuntwoman who bounced off the sidewalk.

"Hard luck," Ike commented.

"It was," I agreed. "Let's make sure it doesn't happen on this film."

"No one's been hurt when we've done the rigging or thrown down the airbags," Mike assured me.

"I'll drink to that." I held up my glass. Almost magically the waitress appeared yet again, carrying extra glasses, a large pitcher of beer and a fresh wine spritzer for Leandra. In a blink of an eye we were all raising a toast to *Voodoo Wars*.

†

"You like this, baby?"

Tiffany stared up into Blaise's face, trying to match his rhythm as he moved on top of her. He had startling good looks, a mix of Louisiana Creole and Cajun heritage, with striking bone structure and full lips a model would envy. Jade-green eyes against smooth umber skin. Wavy dark hair. He knew he was handsome and regularly exploited this to his advantage. Tiffany didn't care. She did the same thing every day. She loved his features, the fact they could be twins—if her skin was just a few shades darker.

Normally all she needed to get off was to see Blaise's face when they fucked. Tonight, though, even though she felt a growing heat in her belly and groin, it was unstable. As if she was going to both come and vomit at the same time. She swallowed as her gorge rose, forcing it back as she tried to focus on Blaise.

"Tiff, what's wrong with your stomach?" Blaise paused in his thrusts.

"Huh?"

"It's all… squishy. Soft. Maybe you should lay off the booze, spend some time at the gym."

"Fuck you," Tiffany shot back, but there was no real heat in her voice. She didn't have the energy.

Blaise shrugged. "Sure thing." He continued his rhythmic thrusting with a distinct lack of imagination common—if not unique—to young startlingly good-looking men. A few minutes later he paused again.

"Something stinks."

He sniffed the air, upper lip pulling back like a dog that smelled something bad.

Tiff shrugged, lackluster. "I don't smell it." But she did. *Sweet and rank and septic. The kind of smell that drew in its prey, then sucked the life juices out of it.* The thought spilled out of her, unbidden. If she hadn't felt so sick, she would have wondered where it came from.

"Damn, babe," Blaise said, drawing back a little further without actually withdrawing from her. "You ate something that died in there or what?"

Tiffany would have lashed out at him if she'd had the energy—and if she wasn't suddenly distracted by the sensation of Blaise's hand sinking into the flesh of her stomach, as if her organs and muscles were dissolving, melting like taffy in the New Orleans heat.

"What the f—" Blaise's words were swallowed up as his firm, muscled forearms, chiseled abs, and penis rapidly dissolved and he collapsed on top of Tiffany, his tongue and teeth rotting in his mouth. Flesh putrefying, blackening, liquefying. The juices were eagerly sucked into Tiffany's fluid-starved body. When two strange men entered her room a short time later and carried her out, she would have screamed too, but her throat clogged with thorns. The tattoo—having quietly fed on its host since the ink had been laid down—had started to grow.

CHAPTER SIXTEEN

I slept in as late as possible, since getting to the production meeting involved nothing more complicated than taking the elevator and walking down a hallway. When I knew I couldn't put the inevitable off any longer, I rolled out of the all-too-comfy bed, hit the "brew" button on the Keurig machine to start the much-needed caffeination of my bloodstream, and ducked into the shower for a quick rinse.

Berserker Productions had closed out Onc Cochon, our faithful waitress keeping the food and drinks flowing until Cayden finally slapped down a silver-embossed black credit card. One of those cards that means the bearer can afford pretty much anything. If the look on the waitress's face was anything to go by, he'd left one hell of a generous tip.

The meeting was being held in one of the hotel suites, which was serving as the production's office for the time being. Again, I wondered what kind of budget they had that could afford this type of luxury. The kind of budget that came with spiffy black credit cards, I guessed.

Devon opened the door when I knocked, hair still wet from the shower and brimming with near manic energy. "Lee!" he exclaimed, giving me an unsolicited hug. He didn't try to turn it into anything creepy, but I really wish he would've asked first.

I was impressed with how clean the suite was. Given the normal habits of film crews, I'd half-expected to find empty beer bottles littering the surfaces and used condoms in the wastebaskets. But the only thing spread out across the available surfaces were script pages and storyboards, with several high-end laptops jostling for position. There was also a tray of sandwiches on a side table, along with a pitcher of ice water and a decent-sized coffee maker.

A woman with cropped blonde hair and a dark tan sat behind a desk near one of the windows, speaking rapidly into a Bluetooth headset. Although she spoke quietly, I overheard more than one swear word delivered in a broad Australian accent. Probably the unit production manager. She had a certain predatory smile and "I will take no shit" attitude that went with the territory.

"That's Jen." Devon pointed at the blonde. "She's the UPM."

Hah! Jen raised a hand in an absent-minded wave, never looking away from her notes or taking her attention away from her phone call.

"She's also the line producer," he added, "so don't piss her off. She pretty much runs Berserker Productions."

"And I'm Daphne, the FX coordinator," a cheerful Southern-accented voice piped up behind me. I turned as a Junoesque brunette walked through the door. Smooth, milky skin, all voluptuous curves in a loose orange sun dress. Huge brown eyes with Bambiesque lashes, a tiny nose, and full lips that rivaled Angelina Jolie's. She seemed supremely comfortable in her own skin and smelled like gardenias. Not perfume, but fresh flowers. Some sort of tree nymph.

I shook her outstretched hand and introduced myself. She nodded knowingly and said, "I'm so glad y'all are on board. Cayden was determined to hire you for this film, but he wasn't sure if he could get you or not."

"Really? How long ago was this?"

"Oh, you know…" Daphne said vaguely, waving one hand as though that explained it all.

It didn't, but I managed to refrain from pushing the issue for the time being. Had I been on his radar before the encounter at Ocean's End? Or had the idea popped into his head because of that? Did it actually matter? Probably not, but I still wanted to know.

Cayden sat on the couch, staring intently at a series of storyboards and making notes on a MacBook Pro, a fifteen-inch that still looked too small for his hands. Angelique was curled up on a chair, feet tucked underneath her, one arm resting on her knees. She held a cup of coffee in one hand and a croissant in the other. Smiling, she gave me a friendly wave with the croissant.

I raised a hand in greeting, then quickly scanned the room for the source of her pastry. I had priorities. Mike and Ike were over by one of the windows, standing over a tray of various pastries perched on an end table. My eyes brightened, and I quickly snagged a plump chocolate croissant, still warm, the chocolate melting into the buttery pastry.

"Are you guys trying to hide this?"

The brothers grinned, neither denying nor confirming my accusation.

I didn't care. I had my croissant. I poured myself a cup of coffee, grateful that there was actual half-and-half instead of nondairy creamer. It's the little things in life.

Langdon arrived, along with the first assistant director, a tall skinny guy named Liam with a laconic style of speech that seemed to be the trademark of most of the ADs I'd worked with to date. A few minutes later Jen finished her call and we all settled down around the coffee table. There was room on the couch next to Cayden, but I pulled up a chair next to Angelique instead. Leandra was missing, but then this particular meeting was primarily to discuss the stunts. Angelique and Langdon would be doing their own stunts, so they both needed to be here. Leandra, thankfully, did not.

"Micah!" Angelique waved and jumped to her feet as a twenty-something guy walked in. Thick, unkempt brown hair, freckled skin, and wide-set green eyes. His lips were full. He looked like he smiled a lot.

"Micah, right on time," Jen said in pleased tone. "For those of you who haven't already met him, this is Micah, our main production assistant, runner, and driver. He will be ferrying people to and from location, he knows where and how to get just about anything in this city and the surrounding areas, and we ask that you treat him like the treasure that he is."

Micah's grin got even wider.

"Right then," Devon said, rubbing his hands together. "We have three primary locations that feature the main action sequences. All of them may or may not include a little bit of green screen, depending on how good the initial location shoots are. If we do need green screen, we have access to a local studio thanks to our FX genius." He tipped a nod toward Daphne. She didn't argue with his description.

Cayden nodded. "We're going to do as much practical effects as possible, but as you can see by the storyboards, some gags won't photograph well even if we had the combined supernatural skills to pull them off. So we'll be using a combination of practical and CGI when necessary. This scene, for instance." He tapped several sheets of storyboard, spreading them out on the coffee table so we all could see them. "This is the main action sequence when Marie and Perrine are trying to kill each other, and then realize that they have a common enemy in Louis."

I leaned in to take a look. The scene in question took place in a clearing in the Bayou. Lots of power bolts shot from open palms. Invisible spirits causing winds and striking invisible blows. Snakes boiling out of the earth. Stuff like that.

The culmination of the fight between the two women involved torches that morphed into flaming swords being wielded almost like quarterstaffs, moving in and out of the throng of worshippers.

"Lots of fire on set," I observed.

Daphne nodded. "We'll have a fire marshal on set, even though it'd take some work setting the bayou where we're filming on fire. I don't even know if that's physically possible."

I went back to the storyboards. It would take great precision and a lot of practice, and it wasn't something just anyone could do. I'd kick ass at it, and make sure Angelique was up to speed too.

After that, both women rise in the air, and then unite to attack the real big bad—Louis—who brings down torrential rains, the drops of water turning into spiders and other creepy-crawlies as they hit the ground.

"Are you using a rain tower for this bit?" I asked Daphne.

"That is still up in the air," she said. "I have an in with a local weather witch, but I need to do a test run with him to make sure he can stop the rain when we need it to stop, make sure it stays within certain perimeters, so the equipment doesn't get wet. Things like that. I have a rain tower standing by if we need it."

"Nice," I said, and went back to studying the storyboards.

"Well?" Devon stared at me eagerly.

"It looks like *The Serpent and the Rainbow* and *Big Trouble in Little China* had a love child." I spoke without thinking. Then I noticed everyone's expression, and hastily added, "I mean that in the best possible way, of course."

Cayden gave a shout of laughter. "We freely admit to having been influenced by both," he admitted.

I found a sequence where Perrine springs from the ground to a nearby tree and perches on a branch like a big cat. Marie's movements as depicted in the same scene were less feline and more suited to... well, more suited to things I excelled at.

I had to shake my head. Shifters were strong, often preternaturally graceful, and capable of physical feats beyond that of mere mortals like me. I guess some of them were also egocentric. Honestly, if Leandra wasn't such a prima donna when it came to the possibility of chipping a fingernail or something equally horrifying, she was more than capable of doing her own stunts. Not that I was complaining. I needed the work.

"Principal photography starts in five days and we're going to tackle the stunt-heavy scenes first," Devon said. "That means you'll have four days to train and choreograph the big voodoo battle extraordinaire."

Cayden nodded. "Lee, I'd like you to handle training Angelique and Langdon, teach them basics in hand-to-hand and swordplay. They won't have complicated choreography, but what they have needs to be solid."

"Not a problem," I said, flashing a smile at Angelique. She looked as excited as a kid on her first trip to Disneyland.

"Cayden says you're one of the best," she offered. "I can't wait to learn what you have to teach!"

Devon stepped back in. "Now we'll be going over the shot list for all the stunts, who's doing each one, how many people are involved, which location they're going to be shot at, all of it. We've already been to the locations and our esteemed stunt coordinator—" he nodded at Cayden "—is happy with them. If he's happy, I'm happy. If I'm happy, everyone else should be fucking delirious with joy."

Devon gave a little laugh to let everyone know he was kidding, but I somehow didn't think he was. There was a certain edge underneath his "all for one and one for all" camaraderie that flashed a hazard light—warning, dictator ahead. I'd met the type before. Jovial and fun as long as things were going his way, tantrum-throwing bully when things weren't. Everyone's best friend at the expensive and lavish after-party to help people forget what a jerk he could be on set. Still, I liked the way the shoot seemed to be coming together and the fact that Devon was open to giving his stunt team some lead time. That wasn't something all productions were willing to do.

Also, considering the amount of Marlborough Man Macho generated by Devon—I wasn't even counting the walking, breathing perfect storm of testosterone that was Cayden—it was great to see women in at least two of the key production roles. Yet another mark in Cayden's—and possibly Devon's—favor. It was one thing for a man to surround himself with arm candy to make an impression and feed his ego. It was something else entirely to surround himself with competent women on the job. I didn't get any sense that either Daphne or Jen were in any way intimidated by either of the men in charge. I doubt Jen was intimidated by much of anything.

So far this year I had met two men who were much more than first met the eye. Cayden and Randy. They were about as unlike each other as was possible, but I was starting to learn that first impressions weren't always the best indicator. I never really had the patience to dig very deeply under an obnoxious facade. That, of course, made me start to wonder what people thought the first time they met me. *A-a-and that's enough introspection.* I turned my full attention back to the meeting.

CHAPTER SEVENTEEN

Hands clapping. Feet stomping. Voices chanting. Torches burning along the perimeter of a clearing. The dark vegetal smell of the swamp mixed with burning herbs, flowers, things pleasing to the loas. Sweat poured freely from all of the participants—the summer heat and humidity lay like a damp wool blanket over the city and the surrounding swamps. Bronze John was a much-feared visitor, but had not made his presence known for two years.

I looked across the clearing at Marie, our priestess. High, strong cheekbones, smooth skin the color of café au lait. She had the bearing of a queen. Was it any wonder that we all worshiped her only slightly less than the loas? All of us except, perhaps, Perrine. Younger than Marie, beautiful and strong, but without the calm center of Marie Laveau.

But I didn't want to think about Perrine right now. I knew she was up to something bad. Something dangerous. I intended to find out what it was and stop her. But not tonight.

This was not one of the public spectacles ostensibly held for slaves in Congo Square or on the shores of Bayou St. John, where it was becoming the rage for white people to show up and watch the supposed dark rituals of "degenerate savages," as one sanctimonious newspaper referred to anyone with even a drop of black blood in them. Luckily, people like him were not privy to these more private rituals, held further away from the city limits on the outskirts of a bayou where few people dared to venture. Bayou Ef'tageux was not for the faint of heart. Supposedly, the gators that inhabited the Bayou beyond the Veil were twice the size of normal gators. Strange lights were seen dancing around through the moss-laden cypress trees, and shrieks tore through the night that could raise hair on a bald man.

It was here that the true *serviteurs* came, hoping the voodoo queen would help raise the loas and solve their problems. Me? I wanted to speak to my mother, dead along with my father these past twenty years. I barely remembered either of them, but only they would have answers to the questions that had been popping up in my life this past year. And if I couldn't speak to my mother, then maybe one of the loas would take pity on me and grant me the wisdom to answer these questions myself.

I caught Étienne's gaze across the clearing, where he stomped his feet and clapped his hands along with the rest of the devotees. I could feel that rhythm in my blood, wanting to take over.

So I let it.

Closing my eyes, I swayed back and forth to the rhythm of hands clapping, feet stomping. Felt myself start to drift out of my body as something else tried to take over. I felt wind on the back of my neck as the loa sought entrance. Mounting me. Riding me. My body swayed harder, head, arms, and legs moving with abandon. Opening my eyes, I saw Étienne standing in front of me, a wide grin on his face, eyes alight with a fire not his own. I smiled back. We had been chosen by Erzulie and Baron Samedi, and now we would—

†

The theme from *Jaws* pulled me out of my dream before I could find out what happened next. Although I suspected hot sex was involved.

Damn.

Still half-asleep, I let the images of the dream play through my head, wondering why my subconscious was so enamored of the plot of *Voodoo Wars*. Interesting that it chose not to cast either Leandra or Angelique in the roles of Marie and Perrine. And who was this hunky Étienne? I wished I had another hour to rest and mull it all over, but today was an early call time—7 A.M. early. I had to get my butt in gear. Today was the first day we'd be rehearsing at one of the primary locations and it was a bit of a drive.

A quick shower and an even quicker cup of coffee later, I met Langdon and the Ginga twins in the lobby, where we were greeted by Micah.

"Y'all set for a day in the swamp?" he said with an easy grin. He was seemingly impervious to stress, a quality highly valued on a film set.

"When you live in the Northern Territory," Ike said, "a little swamp like you have here is nothing."

"How far is the drive?" Langdon asked.

"'Bout an hour and a half," Micah replied.

Langdon shot a look at the Ginga brothers. "Now you two aren't going to start again, right?"

"Start what?" Mike asked, the picture of innocence.

I'd made the mistake of starting a chant of "Are we there yet?" the day before on our way to the rehearsal studio. Mike and Ike had embraced it wholeheartedly and managed to irritate Langdon to the point of distraction during what was only a ten-minute drive.

"Are we there yet? Are we there yet?" started the second we hit the road.

Micah simply turned the volume up on his iPod and nodded happily in time to whatever music he had playing over his headphones. Langdon, however, looked like he was sucking on lemons—instead of his ever-present Altoids. I'd have felt sorry for him if he hadn't proven over the last few days to have an insufferable superiority complex. As it was, I smiled and shut my eyes.

Today we were blocking out the action at the location that the script referred to as a "dilapidated manor and bayou." This was where much of the voodoo ceremony and titular "wars" would take place, so the stunt team needed to get an idea of what kind of terrain we'd be working with and make sure the choreography we'd come up with would work. The location, Bayou Ef'tageux, was a few acres of privately owned land an hour and change outside of New Orleans, tucked away near one of the nature preserves that promised alligators and boars. Did we really want to be filming with the possibility of either alligators or boars making unexpected cameos? I had my doubts.

I'd almost drifted off, but a jarring thump woke me up and I opened my eyes. We were no longer on the nicely paved road, but instead were on a not-so-nice dirt road, loosely scattered with gravel to prevent vehicles from miring in mud during rainy weather. Micah's ancient Cadillac hit every bump with commitment. The twins loved it, Langdon not so much. He whined every time the car hit another pothole.

The Caddy hit an especially deep rut in the road, causing all of us to rise up from our seats—Langdon hitting his head against the car's ceiling—and come back down with tail-bone-jarring force. The twins laughed as if this was the funniest thing ever.

"Are we there yet?"

"Oh, good god," Langdon snapped, "this is ridiculous!"

He pulled out the directions we'd all received—just in case someone missed their provided ride and needed to call a Lyft because this place was not on any GPS—and peered at it as if looking for lost treasure. He tapped Micah insistently on one shoulder, refusing to stop until Micah took out one of his earbuds and grunted by way of acknowledging the ghoul.

"We should be there by now," Langdon said. "It says the house is less than a mile or so off this godforsaken road."

"Almost there," Micah said serenely. He started to re-insert the earbud, but Langdon tapped his shoulder.

"How much further?"

"Maybe half a mile."

We started to pass a turnoff almost hidden by overgrowth of grass, bushes and cypress trees.

"Says to park at the end of the drive," Langdon told Micah.

"That ain't a drive," Micah drawled. "That's a dirt track." He slowed to a stop anyway, and we all looked at the track.

"Maybe it has delusions of grandeur," I suggested. Calling it a "drive" would be like calling a tract home a manor.

Micah shook his head. "This place ain't seen any love for a good ten years or more. The potholes have potholes. I hate to think of drivin' my car down there. Maybe I'll use the dolly to haul stuff in."

"Surely you don't expect us to walk." Langdon's tone was pure affronted outrage. I suspected it was totally for show since as a ghoul he'd walked in more disgusting places than this.

"You want Micah should haul you on the dolly?" I cheerfully inquired.

Langdon giggled, a sound so incongruous and creepy

it made even Micah grimace. I didn't blame him. Some supernatural types are user-friendly and some are not. Ghouls—even civilized ones—take some getting used to.

A lot of the action took place here. Perrine—Marie Laveau's rival for both the affections of her lover and title of Queen of Voodoo in New Orleans—has enlisted the help of Louis LaLaurie to offer a blood sacrifice to win the affections of Étienne and strip Marie of her powers. Little does Perrine know that Louis aspires to win the heart of Laveau, and has told her of Perrine's plans, as well as sacrificing Étienne to his gods. Marie shows up in the midst of all the blood, incantations, and throbbing voodoo drums. An over-the-top magical fight ensues, complete with swords, hand-to-hand and other shenanigans.

Angelique and I had started working with Cayden and Mike'n'Ike, choreographing a series of set pieces that would be put together in post-production and supplemented with special effects. Cayden and Devon wanted to film the magical duel next to the bayou on this property, and I was looking forward to seeing what kind of practical effects we could get away with in such an isolated location.

See, one of the benefits of a largely supe cast and crew on any production is the time and money saved on things like FX and specialty makeup, anything from transformation scenes in monster movies to irises changing color.

We had a slew of local extras coming out over the next couple of weeks—all supes, mostly shifters and those all related to Angelique and Leandra—for the voodoo ritual scenes. Lots of drums and dancing and snake handling, and utilizing their shifting to emphasize the dream-like qualities of the rituals.

Although in my dreams, the drums weren't there. The rhythm was kept by the stomping of feet, the clapping of hands...

I shook my head to clear it of the phantom smell of burning herbs and the thick scent of the bayou. Green vegetation, both fertile and rotting underneath…

"You okay, Lee?"

I glanced up to find Micah looking at me quizzically.

"Yeah, fine," I replied. "What is this place? Or what was it, rather?"

He shrugged. "Used to belong to a Creole gentleman, wanted a place to keep his mistress. His wife didn't much like her man having a bit on the side, especially one she considered inferior."

Langdon looked puzzled. "I thought Creoles were *gens de couleur libres*," he said. Turning to me, he put on his best "I am going to teach you" expression and continued, "That means—"

"*Free people of color*," I broke in before he could educate me yet again. Langdon meant well, but his tendency to ghoulsplain got on my nerves. "Yes, I know."

"Not always." Micah said, not bothering to hide his smirk at my interruption. Popping open the trunk, he pulled out a folding handcart, flipping it open. "See," he said as he loaded up the cart with flats of bottled water and soda, "*créole* originally meant someone born outside the country their folks originated from. You got white folk descended from the French and Spanish that came here back in the day. Then you got the folks who are a combo of African and French or Spanish. They're what most people think of when they hear the word Creole, especially in New Orleans."

"Are you sure?" Langdon's pale brow furrowed. "I did some reading on the subject before coming out here and…"

I edged away from the pair. I wanted some time to look around by myself and get a feel for the lay of the land, not to mention get away from Langdon's need to know everything better than anyone else.

I stepped carefully as I followed the dirt track around the bend. One misstep in any of the many potholes could mean a twisted ankle or worse, a sprain or a fracture, and wouldn't *that* be embarrassing before we even started filming, no matter how fast I healed. I hoped the clearing we'd be filming in had better footing.

Rounding the curve, I stopped and stared. The house must have been beautiful when it was built, but now that beauty was moldering. Weathered gray boards, warped so that the corners were offset like a model put together by an impatient kid. The roof was all catawampus, and I didn't even want to think about what creepy-crawlies might be lurking inside. The whole place looked and felt sad, and what was left was a case of good bones shining through even though the skin sagged with wrinkles, sloughing off in places. Just a quick glance at the veranda that ran the length of the front of the house made me wonder if it would hold my weight, let alone camera and sound equipment, lights, craft service tables, hand carts and costume racks.

I took a tentative step onto the veranda, wincing at the resulting groan as the board protested at my weight. The location scout must have tested it out, hopefully by jumping up and down on it a few times. No one in their right mind would leave something like that up to fate. I mean, Cayden alone weighed more than a lot of men and if he hadn't crashed through rotted flooring, the rest of us were probably safe.

Langdon came up beside me and stared at the structure. "We're filming here?"

"Guess so. And they need to set up craft service somewhere inside."

"I'm not much of a swamp type of guy," Langdon offered.
"Do ghouls have a preference?"

"Desert. Definitely desert."

I thought about that. "What about, like, temperate beaches? San Diego or Los Angeles?"

"They'll do in a pinch," he said with a shrug. "But give me hot and dry any day."

"Are there ghouls who like the tropics?"

"Certainly," Langdon replied. "Some prefer their meat falling off the bone. Kind of like putting a whole chicken in a crockpot. It gets slow cooked, has quite a lovely aroma."

Eeeeew. I tried not to let my distaste show on my face. To each his own, right? Except *Eeeeew!*

Going inside, I made my way through the house, trying not to look too hard at the occupants of some disturbingly large spider webs. The parlor, the dining room… and here the kitchen. A solid oak table occupied a place of prominence in the center, with an ancient stove, an enamel sink with an old-fashioned pump handle, and pitted countertops. *I'd had many a fine cup of coffee at that table with Étienne when we visited Marie and—*

WTF?

I shook my head and strode through the kitchen to the back door, ignoring the creak of the warped floorboards. The screen door hung off its hinges, an inner wooden door standing a half-assed sentinel in the face of any intruders. I wondered who'd bother to lock the doors here.

The sound of the front door creaking open was followed by footsteps and voices, Micah and the other production assistants bringing in supplies. I wanted a little more time on my own, trying to figure out what it was about this place that sparked half-formed memories at the edge of my consciousness. It certainly wasn't wish-fulfillment. I could honestly say this was not on my list of places I wanted to go. New Orleans, sure. A decaying house in a swamp? Not so much.

Pushing the screen door open, I ducked under a spider and stepped out into the backyard, a weed-choked expanse of grass leading up to the edge of the cypress-ringed bayou. Glad I was wearing closed-toed shoes, I walked slowly up to the edge of the water, marveling at how still it was. Dark green, almost soupy.

I didn't trust it. Water like this usually hid things that bit or stung—poisonous snakes and such. Or worse, things like rusalkas, kappas and grindylows that like to eat people.

I followed the water around the side of the house to a big clearing, where the grass was trimmed short. I stood there, listening to the faint buzzing of insects and the low hum of voices from the house behind me. The sounds were almost hypnotic, almost enough to put me in a trance as I stared at the lagoon. The water rippled as something swam by. Too big to be a water skimmer, too small to be an alligator. Maybe a cottonmouth. I would not be going swimming any time soon.

As I watched, the ripples abruptly stopped, as if whatever critter had generated them had been plucked out of the water. Or perhaps dived down under the surface. The concentric rings lapped out but stopped as if a glass plate had slammed down in the water.

Okay, that's weird.

I stared closer at the water, waiting for whatever it was that had made the ripples to make its presence known again. Nothing. Just the half circle of ripples still expanding out, no discernable reason for them to not be full circles.

Laws of nature need not apply here.

A cloud of red suddenly appeared, obscuring the ripples

as it spread through the water.

Something shimmered in front of the ripples, like sun hitting the side of a glass building. I shielded my eyes. When I lowered my hand, the ripples were gone, as was the shimmer. Some of the red, however, still remained, wispy tendrils snaking through the water.

I shook my head. I needed more sleep, obviously.

"Lee, you out here?"

I turned and waved at Micah. "You need me inside?"

"Nah," he said, stepping off the back porch and joining me at the side of the water. "Just makin' sure you're here and not drowned in the bayou, feedin' the gators."

I snorted—I couldn't help it. "That is so reassuring, I can't even begin to tell you."

"Hey," Micah said with a grin, "gotta be careful out here."

"What's over there, do you know?" I gestured toward the other side of the lagoon. "Is this a state park or a wildlife preserve?"

"Further south, yeah. It's private property for a few miles around here. This place we're filming, it belongs to the Marcadet family."

"Marcadet? Wait, is that Leandra and Angelique's family?"

"The same. Over there—" he gestured across the water "—it belongs to the Castros."

"As in Fidel?"

"No, ma'am, as in one of the most inbred families in the Louisiana bayous, and one you do not want to mess with."

"It would be easier to take you seriously if you weren't grinning from ear to ear," I informed him. "Only serial killers and beauty pageant contestants smile all the time."

That broke him up. He shook his head, chuckling, as he went back into the house.

I glanced back at the water, looking for any signs of movement. As still as a glass pane. I didn't trust it.

†

A kind of insanity of celebration took over New Orleans between Mardi Gras and Ash Wednesday each year, but even in September the city was alive with festivals—music, food and art. The events were quieter than those in spring, but just as vibrant.

Others preferred even more quiet and calm. Most of them didn't live in the French Quarter.

Some of the quietest residents of New Orleans could be found in cities of the dead. Most of the crypts and mausoleums in the necropolises were above ground, so that the corpses didn't float away when flooding occurred. At sunset, the cemeteries were locked up, and the only noises from inside were the call of night birds and the distant sounds of revelry, depending on the cemetery.

However, in cemeteries across the city, Tiffany, Cherry, Star, Liz, and Celia each lay in an oven vault, the remains of the previous— and legal—occupants scattered in holes beneath. Inside these vaults, the temperature was hot and humid enough to cook a body in its own juices—and to help the gestation process for the five harbingers that would eventually consume their hosts, who remained hellishly aware the entire time.

†

If anyone else had been inside St. Louis Cemetery No. 2, they might have noticed the faintest of glows emanating from almost undetectable cracks in seams of one of the vaults. Inside it, Star lay there as her insides cooked, the star tattoo on her shoulder sending the sorcerous equivalent of microwaves through her. She felt each separate microscopically thin laser of pain through every inch of her body. It wasn't white hot—no, it burned so much hotter than that. Why didn't it kill her? Why wasn't she dead?

She would've screamed, but the pain was too much. Even

though she could open her mouth, the only thing that came out was an inarticulate drone of "stop please stop please stop please stop please stop…"

But it didn't.

†

Cherry lay on her stomach inside her vault, the black lines of the angel's wings spreading out from the tattoo over and into the rest of her body, each line sprouting tiny filaments as the wings slowly took on three-dimensional form, growing and wrapping themselves around her, keeping her still, gently stroking her skin and her hair for a brief time before they sank into her flesh and made their way through her body, feeding on internal organs, attaching themselves to the veins, re-creating organs, bones, muscles… one agonizing second at a time.

†

Liz's world was reduced to the sound and vibration of her heart pulsing, slowly getting louder, each beat a lifetime of its own, the sound vibrating through her, liquefying her insides. It was like being inside a metal drum, each echoing beat threatening to crack her skull. And just when she thought it would stop, just as the echo faded to a bearable level, the drum was struck anew, the heart thrummed, the pulse reverberated until her veins were swollen and throbbing, blood ran from fingernails and eyes as her body reshaped itself, her eardrums exploded yet again, and it started all over. Again and again and again.

†

One expects graveyards to have a certain odor, a faint whiff of rot, even though in the sanitized cemeteries of modern times, that wasn't usually the case. If anyone had been standing close to a particular oven vault at St. Louis Cemetery No. 1, in just the right spot, they would've gotten a whiff of putrescence so foul that it made the smell of most dead bodies seem sweet in comparison, even ones rotting in *the heat with maggots squirming in the decomposing flesh.*

Inside the vault, Tiffany could feel her body rot. Her firm, young flesh sagged and caved in as each organ, bone, and muscle was infected by the sweet-sour poison of the flower. The stalk took root in her shoulder and the petals grew, slithering along her limbs, peeling up and tearing the flesh from her body to encase her in their poisonous, membranous folds. Like the others, she remained impossibly sentient. Never able to sink into blissful unconsciousness. Aware of every agonizing change—no matter how minute—taking place inside her.

†

Celia still lay in her own particular hell, no longer sure who or what she was, only sure that this pain had to have an end. One hand and arm, twitching non-stop, broke free of the cocoon that encased her and began scratching and tugging at the rest of it.

†

"And… action!"

I leaped off the edge of the balcony of a beautiful mansion at the edge of the French Quarter, clothing fluttering around my body as I fell three stories, turning once in the air and landing on my back, square in the center of the airbag.

"Cut!"

A round of applause burst out from the crew and cast members on set. When I sat up, the Ginga brothers were grinning ear to ear. I grinned back at them as I basked in the admiration of my peers, enjoying both the validation and the well-placed airbag. This was the first high fall I'd done on a job since the accident, and it felt oh so good to get it right.

"Beautiful, Lee!" Devon strode over, beaming from ear to ear. "Perfect! One take and that's all we need." Almost as an afterthought he added, "You good with it, Cayden? Or do we need another?"

Cayden's expression was annoyingly neutral. Oh well, I wasn't going to grovel for his good opinion. Then he slowly nodded.

"Well done, Lee," he said. "It's a wrap as far as I'm concerned."

I brightened, instantly annoyed with myself for caring what he thought. But then, of course I cared what Cayden thought. He was the stunt coordinator. *Oh, hormones, you suck.*

"It's a wrap, folks!" Liam shouted out the good news to all and sundry. They'd budgeted another two hours for this scene, so wrapping early was like a free day at school.

What to do with my free time?

After giving it some thought while changing back into my street clothes, I got my purse and took out Tia's business card—dark mauve with contrasting purple léttering and a small drawing of a hummingbird in the left side in jewel tones. Intricate and simple at the same time, nothing fussy about it.

I started to dial the number but decided to change it to a text message instead. Less intrusive if she was in the middle of a job.

"Hey there," I dictated. "Got the night off and wondered if you'd like to help me use two free passes to one of those ghost tours. This is Lee, by the way. We met at Café Du Monde." I paused for a minute, then added, "Anyway, hope you can make it."

I read it, corrected the inevitable Siri autocorrect fails, and hit "send." Two minutes later my text notification went off.

> Hell, yes! Cheesy but fun. What time you wanna meet and where?

I grinned. It's hard to read tone in texts, but Tia seemed as jazzed about getting together as I was. If so, this would be the second female friend I'd made outside of stunt circles. Not that there was anything wrong with most stuntwomen, but my friendships with them tended to be what I'd call "Industry friendships." None of them had ever extended to getting together in between jobs unless it was at the Ranch for beer and pizza after working out.

> Tour starts at seven in front of a bar called Black Penny. Meet there around 6:45?

> Sounds good! See ya then.

My text tone went off again. I smiled as Eden's name popped up at the top of the screen.

> Done with film. Bored. Flying out tomorrow. Sound good?

I texted back quickly.

> Sure. I'll give your name to the front desk at the hotel so you can get a key to my room. Going on a haunted New Orleans tour tonight.

> Fun! Maybe we can take a voodoo tour or something on one of your days off, or do the riverboat thing.

> I'm up for anything!

Well, almost anything. As long as we avoided any of my demonic kin, I'd be happy.

"So, Miss Striga, what are you going to do with your night off?"

I suppressed a grimace as the minty-fresh carrion breath of Langdon wafted in my direction. How he managed to smile and look lugubrious at the same time was a mystery. Maybe it was a ghoul thing.

I gave a non-committal shrug, not wanting to go into specifics in case he wanted to join me. A little Langdon went a long way.

"What are *you* going to do?" I turned the question back on him, a time-honored way of evading an answer.

"I thought I'd take one of the voodoo tours offered and see if I can soak up some atmosphere to give myself more verisimilitude in my portrayal of Louis." His tone was just on the edge of pompously self-congratulatory. "You see, I feel that it's vital for an actor to..."

Ghouls just wanna have fun, I thought apropos of nothing as he droned on. *Ghoul on a Train? Ghoul, Interrupted. Ghoul with the Vampire Tattoo.*

Okay, I needed to stop now.

I tuned back in just in time to hear "—so important to immerse oneself in one's role. I've always admired Daniel

Day-Lewis's commitment to his art. Did you know he insisted on wearing clothing, even underwear, faithful to the time period when he made *Last of the Mohicans*?"

I did not, but I nodded and said, "Yes," in the hopes of forestalling any more of Langdon's infomercial. His need to educate far outweighed my need to be educated.

"Well, have fun on the voodoo tour," I said before he could launch into another Hollywood anecdote that I didn't care about. "I'm gonna head back to the hotel and clean up."

"Oh! Are you catching a ride with Micah? I'll go with you."

I heaved one of those "on the inside only" sighs because I could think of no good reason to object that wouldn't be rude. Micah was there to drive any and all of the talent, not just me. Even those with bad breath.

"Fine," I said, "but I call shotgun."

†

The French Quarter was hopping when I hit the streets, tourists and locals headed toward bars and restaurants to unwind and gain a few thousand calories. I patted my stomach self-consciously, and once again thanked the universe for a job that allowed me to burn off more calories than I ate.

New Orleans had the reputation of being the most haunted city in the United States. Strolling through the streets and soaking in the atmosphere, I could believe it. History permeated the air, as if there should be sepia-toned overlays of the past, along with the sounds of horses and horse-drawn carriages instead of car engines.

The air was heavy, thick with humidity and perfumed with the scent of tropical blooms, fried food, and humanity. Thick, luscious swags of bougainvillea framed doorways, crawled through arches and wrought-iron scrollwork, the pink, fuchsia, and orange blossoms brilliant amidst the dark green leaves.

As I walked, I people-watched and played my usual game of "spot the supe" amongst the straights. Sitting at a little table outside of a sidewalk café was a family that might be wererats—father, mother, toddler, and baby strapped into a bassinet. All with underslung jaws, long noses, and a faint red gleam in their eyes when the sunlight hit them. The entire family had dark, glossy hair—even the baby—reminiscent of the sleek coats of well-fed rodents. As I walked past the café I caught their voices, improbably high-voiced and squeaky.

I smiled. Definitely wererats. The next supe sighting, however, wiped the smile from my face.

Across the street, an inordinately tall, skinny black man strode easily through the crowd—people got out of his way without anyone seeming to actually see him. It was as if he had some sort of force-field that parted the crowds before him like an invisible bodyguard. He was one creepy motherfucker—kind of like the Tall Man in the old *Phantasm* movies, but worse. I could see something writhing under his skin as if trying to get out. His real face. A face I didn't want to see if the roiling aura shrouding him—it—was anything to go by. I had no idea what, exactly, it was, but I sensed dark cravings. Saw flashes of body parts on a blood-soaked wooden floor. Small body parts, as if a baby doll had been torn apart. I gave an involuntary shudder.

Suddenly he—it—stopped in its tracks, head swiveling around with a suddenness as abrupt as a guillotine blade at the end of its drop. The people near it stumbled, either stopping short or taking sudden jags to either side to avoid touching it. I wondered if they could see what I saw, or only sensed there was something very wrong with it. Dark, hooded eyes stared straight at me. The back of my neck started to tingle, and my amulet heated up against my skin.

Shit.

It bared its teeth—long, sharp, and *so* not belonging in a human face—in a silent snarl. I braced myself as the tingling in the back of my neck increased. *Oh, this is bad.* There were too many innocent bystanders. If things went wrong, I could end up with more collateral damage than the last half-hour of *Blue Thunder*. No, this was not the time or the place to go after one of Lilith's stray demonspawn.

It hadn't seen me yet. I stepped very slowly backwards, trying not to draw its attention by using the cover of a large family—and I mean "large" in every sense of the word—to hide my movements. Slipping inside the open door of a nearby shop, I did my best to fade out of sight, even though that was difficult because the shop was an art gallery of sorts, with picture windows. There were no aisles to hide behind—everything was hung on the walls or displayed in short cabinets.

But there were curtains, claret-colored brocade curtains caught back in ornamental hooks on either side of the picture windows. Quickly pulling a section out so it covered some of the glass, I hugged the thin strip of wall nearest to me, hoping the fabric was thick enough to conceal me.

"Can I help you, hon?"

I nearly screamed at the sound of a warm southern voice, but managed to hold it in. I did jump, however, and one hand flew to my throat like a Victorian lady in need of a fainting couch.

"I am so sorry, I surely didn't mean to startle you." A slender black woman in her late thirties/early forties gave me a rueful smile. She was elegantly dressed in a black pencil skirt and royal-blue silk blouse, looking more like a model than a shop clerk.

"It's okay," I replied while trying to sneak a peek outside.

"Just got a little overheated." The thing across the street was still standing in the middle of the sidewalk, head turning from side to side and then, impossibly, swiveling all the way around as it searched for me.

"You hidin' from someone?" She drew back the curtain far enough to peer outside, following the direction of my gaze. She frowned, lips pursing in disapproval. "Now what is ol' Nal doing walkin' around so early?"

"You can see it?" I took a second look at her, using more than my eyes this time. Nothing about her screamed "supe" right off the bat, but I could sense she had at least one foot in between worlds.

"Oh sure, hon." She patted me on one arm. "I see a lot of things most people don't. That fellow, though…" She shook her head. "I'd rather be spared that sight."

"Is he—it—still out there?" I didn't want to risk looking again in case the creature either saw me or sensed my location. The back of my neck still burned, which meant it was still trying to find me.

"He's moving… Oh lord, he's coming this way."

Shit. I'd have to fight it and I didn't even know what it was or how to kill it and this nice woman might get hurt and—

"Here." She slipped something that felt like cloth into my hand, squeezing her fingers around mine. "Hold this. Don't let go."

I didn't question her, even when the thing started thumping against my skin, as if I held a tiny beating heart. I could feel the woman's pulse through her fingers, felt my own heart beating at the same rate until the three separate rhythms became one, the sound filling my ears. Pounding. Thrumming. Roaring. Until nothing else existed.

"Ah, that's better." The woman's voice acted like an

"off" switch. The triple heartbeat stopped. "He's spotted something more interesting down the street. Lord, I hope it's not that sweet little girl..." Shaking her head again, she let the curtain fall back into place and released my hand. I opened my fingers and looked at the small black cotton bag resting against my palm.

"What is it?" I asked as the tingling in the back of my neck faded away.

"A *gris-gris*," she replied. "Protection against those that mean you harm. And that thing... he never means anything good for anyone."

"You called it—him—Nal?"

"Short for Nalusa Falaya—" She pronounced it "nah-luss-ah fah-lah-yah." "He's a critter out of old Choctaw legends. Name translates to 'long black being.' Nal, he hunts in the shadows at twilight, keeps his wicked eyes open for children who've strayed too far from home." She frowned. "He's gotten bold, hunting in the city."

"He hunts for food...?"

She nodded. "Nal's an eater of flesh. Like the Ojibwa wendigo or the rakshasa of India."

I risked another glance out the window. The Nalusa Falaya was nowhere in sight. My amulet was once again cool against my skin. I heaved a sigh of relief.

"Now, hon, how 'bout you tell me why ol' Nal was after you?"

I had no idea how to answer that honestly without opening up a can of worms so large it would bury us—and make me late for the ghost tour—so I settled for "Maybe because I saw what it really was. I'm Lee, by the way," I added.

"Eugenie," my savior replied.

My gaze lit on a display on the wall adjacent to the

windows. Broken tiles with paintings on them that, upon closer inspection of the captions, were tiles that had been retrieved from neighborhoods decimated by Hurricane Katrina. Most of them were from the Ninth Ward. One of them showed an almost ephemeral tracing of a woman's face, with one word beneath it—Erzulie. Almost without thinking, I pointed at it and said, "I'd like to buy this, please."

"Of course, hon." Eugenie took the tile off its wall hanger, walked behind one of the counters, and rung it up.

"Ten dollars? That can't be right." I knew it wasn't—the cheapest of the tile art was fifty bucks and they were much smaller than the one I wanted to buy.

"Don't you be arguing with me," she chided gently. "There's something about you. You're special. If Erzulie is meant to go with you, she would want me to make it easy." She patted my hand. "Trust me."

"Thank you." I didn't know what else to say.

"You have spirits watching over you, child. The loas are on your side."

I handed her a twenty-dollar bill, accepted the change she handed back along with the carefully wrapped tile in a small black paper bag. A quick glance at an ornate and obviously antique clock on the wall told me I'd better get a move on if I was going to get to the tour's meet-up location on time, so I thanked Eugenie one more time and left the gallery.

As I started back down the street, I looked back at the shop front for the name. Curtains now blocked the entire front of picture windows and the door was shut, a "closed" sign hanging on the doorknob.

What the...?

I glanced at the bag. "Loa Creations" was stenciled in vibrant pink across the black paper.

CHAPTER EIGHTEEN

I arrived with ten minutes to spare before the tour, and I knew exactly how I wanted to spend them. I'd googled Black Penny and planned on checking out their beer selection. They sold canned craft beers only, nothing on tap, no bottles.

A few people were gathered around outside, an older couple in their sixties wearing sensible shoes and loose, comfy-looking clothing. A Chinese couple somewhere in their thirties or forties, speaking in Mandarin as they checked their watches. A cluster of twenty-somethings—three boys and two girls—who were acting like they were there to audition for a spring break reality show, with white smiles and clothing that bespoke comprehensive dental plans and the money to spend on mid-level designer labels. They'd already been in Black Penny and were all clutching cans of beer. The guys checked me out pretty thoroughly, making me wonder if they were either all just friends or the guys were all just jerks. A younger couple in matching khaki pants and dark-blue sweaters could have stepped straight out of an Abercrombie & Fitch ad.

"This is hella lame," one of the young men muttered. A girl in a white sundress punched him on his shoulder.

"It'll be fun. Don't be an asshole."

Their accents screamed Boston.

Inside, Black Penny was everything I'd hoped. Cozy, a mixture of exposed brick and walls painted a dark olive. Big-ass chandeliers dangling from the ceiling provided light, which spread out dimly through the rest of the interior. Vintage paintings, brass rubbings, and photographs filled the walls, hanging above a smattering of cream-colored booths. My gaze flickered over all of this, then stopped at shallow alcoves, cans upon cans of craft beer lining the shelves there and on shelves behind the dark wood bar.

Wow. This place could be dangerous.

After a brief but intense perusal of the beer selection, many of which I'd never heard of, I chose a Ten Fidy— another high-octane Imperial Stout—from a brewery called Oskar Blues. Seemed like the perfect way to start out a ghost tour and since it was in a can, I could take it to go. Gotta love New Orleans just for that alone. I could get used to this. I walked back outside, taking a deep, satisfying swig of the rich, malty brew.

Tia came hurrying up St. Peter Street, waving when she saw me, a smile lighting up her face. She wore the same plain black, logo-free leggings and T-shirt she'd worn when we'd met, black backpack slung over one shoulder.

"Sorry I'm late," she said breathlessly. "I had a walk-in an hour ago. Nothing fancy, just wanted a David Bowie quote on one shoulder, but I don't like rushing, y'know?"

It seemed natural to hug in greeting, so I went with it.

"No worries," I said. "If I were getting a tattoo, I'd be pissed as hell if the artist was in too much of a hurry to do a good job."

"You're a tattoo artist?" One of the college boys looked at Tia with sudden interest. Tia's lack of makeup and single messy braid hadn't attracted more than a quick, uninterested glance up to this point, though to me it was easy to see how pretty she was if one took the time to look past her almost aggressively casual style.

Tia nodded, pulling one of her business cards out of the front compartment of her backpack. "You can either call and book an appointment or take your chances and do a walk-in."

"Cool," he replied, pocketing the card.

"I didn't know kids still said that," I whispered to Tia.

"Kids?" she said, amused. "You can't be more than a few years older than any of them."

I shrugged. "Trust me. They're kids."

"What does that make me, oh world-weary one?"

"A mere infant," I said with a grin.

Tia snorted. "Well, this infant has an ID that says she can have a beer. Do I have time before the tour starts?"

"I don't see anyone dressed like a low-rent Vampire Lestat or his squeeze, so I don't think the tour guides have arrived yet." I glanced at my phone. "They've got five minutes before the tour's supposed to start."

"I'll be right back." Tia vanished into Black Penny, reappearing shortly with a can of Horny Goat Chocolate Peanut Butter Imperial clutched in one hand.

I seriously doubted she was old enough to be buying alcohol, but if her ID passed muster, it didn't bother me. If someone was old enough to be drafted, they should damn well be able to enjoy a beer if they wanted.

"Ladies and gentlemen, welcome to Ghastly Ghost Tours of New Orleans," intoned a deep male voice.

We turned to see our guides. The speaker was Christian, the man who'd given me the free passes, wearing his Goth wet dream outfit. His female counterpart seemed a lot more comfortable in her empire-waisted cotton frock. Christian gave a start of recognition when he saw me, taking off his top hat and sketching a respectable bow in my direction. "Ah, mademoiselle, so pleased you decided to join us!'

I wiggled the fingers of one hand in a little wave.

He was cute enough in his wannabe Lestat costume to garner speculative glances and giggles from the college girls. I could tell the frat boys didn't much like this, and I hoped they wouldn't be dicks during the tour and try to score points off our guide.

Christian cleared his throat and launched into his routine. "Ladies and gentlemen—"

Paris Hilton Lite hit her boyfriend on the arm. "He's not talking about you, that's for sure."

"—Welcome to Ghastly New Orleans. We are most pleased to have you as our guests. I hope none of you are faint of heart…"

His female co-host nodded with a serene smile. "That's right," she said. "We've only lost one person on our tours over five years, and she'd forgotten to take her heart medicine that day."

And so on.

They were game, I'd give them that. Even though they'd probably given this tour dozens upon dozens of times, both Christian and his fellow guide, Sasha, put energy and a gleeful enthusiasm into their spiel.

"Congo Square," Christian intoned. "Once the site of bizarre and unholy voodoo rituals, led by none other than Marie Laveau herself…"

A flash of green met my eyes. Drums. Voices raised in song and chanting, the heat of summer and many men and women dancing with complete abandon...

The loa—Erzulie—once rode me there.

The thought came from nowhere.

Heat and humidity suddenly beat down on me with a vengeance. Heard the music. Felt the drums in my very core, my body responding to the rhythm. I—

"Lee!"

I opened my eyes, surprised to find them closed. I gave my head a little shake to clear it of the phantom drums.

"You okay?" Tia stood in front of me with a semi-concerned expression.

I nodded. "Yeah," I said. "Just a weird déjà vu moment there."

"Ah, yeah." Tia patted me on one shoulder. "This whole city is filled with those if you're open to them."

"You feel it too?" I took a swig of my beer as we walked a few yards behind our group.

"Yeah." Tia looked thoughtful, then added, "I have no idea if it's wishful thinking or no, but I've felt like I've been here before more than once."

"Ancestral memories, maybe," I replied without thinking. Then I stopped. Ancestral memories. That explanation made as much sense as anything else that had been thrown at me recently. I made a mental note to ask Sean about that.

"This is the Gardette–LaPrete House," Christian said in his pseudo-English accent. "After the Civil War, the LaPrete family fortune was lost, and they were forced to lease their grand mansion in the French Quarter to a mysterious Turk, who some whispered was a deposed Sultan from a far-off land in the Orient. He brought with him a fortune in gold and used his wealth to transform the Creole house into a palace. From without, it became a veritable fortress, the doors and windows covered and barred with iron, guarded by fierce men with curved daggers in their belts.

"From within, a perfumed eastern pleasure palace, rivaling that of fabled Xanadu, filled with a harem of concubines, houris, and dancing girls. Every night, a wild orgy of decadence ensued. Until one terrible, dark and stormy night…

"When the storm cleared the next morning, passers-by were horrified to see a river of blood trickling down the front steps of the Sultan's Palace. The police forced open the iron gates, only to discover a grisly massacre. Blood splatters covered the fine walls. Corpses littered the elegant floor. All the occupants had been butchered by scimitar or axe— hacked to pieces so horribly, it was impossible to tell which decapitated head or chopped limb belonged to which body.

"The gruesome scene was so horrific the local newspapers forbore to print the shocking details. But the most chilling crime of all was outside the house. In the courtyard behind the mansion, the heavy rain of the previous night's storm had left the soil wet and muddy. Sticking out of the ground was a man's hand, the fingers in a rictus, clawing to escape the grave. The Sultan himself had been *buried alive*…"

Christian sounded positively gleeful as he continued, "Throughout the years since this horrific event, people have sworn they've heard hideously muffled screams coming from the courtyard… somewhere in the ground beneath."

The tour continued, including Lafitte's Blacksmith—"The oldest bar in America since 1772"—and the old Pharmacy, where Christian informed us that, "according to legend, America's first licensed pharmacist performed vile exploratory surgeries upon his victims, especially lovely ladies."

Then finally, now deep within the French Quarter, we arrived at the corner of Royal and Governor Nicholls Street, gazing up at an imposing building, a mansion from a bygone era. Standing three stories high, its grim rectangular bulk, ringed by black wrought-iron galleries, loomed over the rest of the block, its brick walls the color of a brooding thunderstorm…

The LaLaurie Mansion.

It still gave me the shivers.

"And now we come to the house at 1140 Royal Street, and our final stop of our Ghastly Ghost tour—the infamous LaLaurie Mansion. Ladies and gentlemen, as you probably already know, New Orleans is recognized worldwide as the most haunted city in the Western Hemisphere. But now, I must warn you… many expert authorities of the supernatural consider the LaLaurie Mansion to be the most haunted house in all of New Orleans."

Some of our fellow tour attendees glanced at one another nervously, while the frat boys nudged their friends with their elbows. Christian continued unabated.

"If you've heard anything about the ghosts and hauntings in New Orleans, there's no doubt that you've heard about the LaLaurie Mansion. How many of you saw it on *American Horror Story*? Well, I should tell you that the show's producers took a great deal of poetic license with the story—as Hollywood tends to do." The crowd chuckled.

Tell me about it, I thought.

"Actually, the majority of filming didn't even take place here, but was done over on St. Louis Street, at the Hermann–Grima House…"

Christian's voice faded out as I gazed up at the mansion. Smoke billowing out from the windows, the flicker of flames casting dancing red shadows against the glass panes. The sound of screams. An angry rumble of outraged voices. Body parts. Blood.

Horror.

"Lee, are you okay?"

I shook my head, trying to control the rapid pounding of my heart and the sudden lurch of my stomach.

"I—"

I was going to say, "I'm fine," but my body chose to throw up instead. Luckily, I managed to skitter away from the group and around the corner first, dry-heaving into a trashcan.

"Jeez, girl, if you're gonna do tha' shit, get your ass over to Bourbon Street."

"Sorry," I muttered, wiping my mouth with the back of one hand without bothering to look at my critic.

"Lee, you okay?" Tia had followed me around the corner.

"That's the third time you've asked me that tonight," I said with a shaky laugh.

Tia stared at me in concern. "Seriously, that makes it even worse. You know that, right?"

"I'm fine," I said. "Just… I think I should have had more than a donut and a protein bar to eat today."

Tia stared at me for a minute, then nodded as if coming to a decision.

"You up to a short Lyft ride?"

"I think so."

"Good. I'm gonna take you to one of my favorite bars. Best burgers in the city."

My stomach growled as if in agreement with Tia's plans. A hamburger and French fries sounded amazing about now.

†

Jordan leaned against the wrought-iron gate of Lafayette Cemetery, and lit a cigarette. American Spirit. He deliberately stayed underneath the illumination of one of the streetlights, doing his best to look like he wasn't there to cause any trouble—for once, there was truth in advertising—trying to let go of his anger toward Blaise for ditching him.

"Man, I can't believe you're bailing on me for that bitch." Jordan had kept his glare leveled at the ground, not wanting Blaise to see how hurt he really was. "Whatever happened to bros before hoes?"

"If you needed to be bailed out," Blaise had replied, "I'd be there. But you're not. You can drink beer by yourself, right?"

"Yeah, sure," Jordan muttered. "Have a blast."

"I will." Blaise had flashed him a cocky grin. "See you later."

Maybe. Maybe not. *Jordan wasn't sure anymore.*

Okay, so maybe it wasn't a big deal. Having a few beers and hanging out, nothing that couldn't wait for another time. Except Blaise always seemed to have something better to do with his time these days.

"I won't leave you behind." Blaise had made this promise to Jordan years ago, when they were just kids who lived on the same block in a crappy neighborhood. But wasn't he doing just that, little by little, every day? Jordan should have known Blaise had planned on ditching him for Tiffany when he'd suggested meeting at Lafayette Cemetery. Bitch only lived a few blocks away.

If Jordan could get rid of all the bitches like Tiffany, he would. Maybe not kill them, no, maybe not go that far, but something. Maybe scar their pretty faces so they wouldn't be so full of themselves, take up the time and attention of his friends. Like Blaise.

Fuck it. *He wasn't going to think about it anymore. At least not tonight.*

He heard that there was a time back in the day when the cemeteries were open after sunset. People used to perform rituals on the graves of voodoo types like Marie Laveau. Now, of course, wandering the cemeteries by yourself even in the daytime was practically sending a frickin' invite out to potential muggers.

Jordan knew, because he and Blaise ran with one of the gangs that haunted the cemeteries of New Orleans. Lafayette Cemetery

No. 1 was one of the safer ones. Too small and too close at the edge of the Garden District to offer more than an occasional opportunity to relieve a tourist of their valuables.

Blaise had taught Jordan to only use force if they fought back. If that happened, then Blaise would just rough the mark up enough to teach them a lesson, not do permanent damage. That was smart. Jordan didn't want a manslaughter charge on his still theoretical rap sheet. Worst thing Jordan himself had done so far was shove some stupid tourist hard enough that the guy had fallen and hit his head against a sarcophagus. Knocked him right out. There'd been some blood, sure, but the guy had been breathing fine when Jordan had left, and nothing had turned up in the news about a dead tourist.

An unexpected noise from the other side of the cemetery wall drew Jordan's attention. It sounded like a flag flapping in the wind. But how was that even possible? The night air was cool and still, only a slight breeze rustling the leaves.

The sound came again, definitely from inside the cemetery grounds. From one of the vaults.

What the fuck?

Lafayette No. 1 was a safe cemetery. Safe for tourists, safe for its residents. No graffiti, no mischief. A body laid to rest here stayed at rest—unless they were in one of the oven vaults shared by generations of the same family. Then, the bones of the last stiff were swept into a hole in the tomb when the time came for a new relative to be sealed into the vault.

What the hell could be making a noise inside one of those vaults?

Giving a quick look around to make sure no one was watching, Jordan grabbed a low-hanging oak tree branch and hoisted himself over the cemetery wall. Like it could keep anyone out who really wanted to get in.

He jumped to the ground, knees flexing as he landed. Then

he listened, the sounds of voices further down one of the nearby streets filtering through the sudden soft moan of the wind as clouds scudded across the autumn sky.

There.

Jordan followed the flapping noise down a row of raised sarcophaguses and single-family mausoleums to a bank of oven crypts. They were creepy as fuck. Jordan didn't so much mind the thought of each generation of bones being dumped to make room for the next, but the idea of bodies rotting in the heat skeeved him out. When he was a kid, his gran used to tell him that the oven vaults were openings to hell and if he wasn't good, he'd be shoved inside to feed the hungry demons. Keep them from breaking out to seek their meals elsewhere. Gran had been a terror, no doubt. He'd said the first and only heartfelt prayer of thanksgiving of his life when she'd finally died.

Flap flap flap.

That sound again. Closer now. Like demon wings beating against the brick and mortar sealing the crypts. A hungry demon trying to get out. The hairs rose on the back of Jordan's neck and arms, and his balls seemed to shrink as if trying to crawl up inside and hide.

Jordan was suddenly five again, stricken by the same paralyzing fear he'd felt when his gran had sat next to him on his bed, pinning the blankets tight around his arms with her weight so he was trapped, forced to listen to the horrors she'd gleefully recount. He'd lie awake for hours, frozen in place, afraid to move for fear that something would reach out from under the bed, seize him, and pull him down with it.

"Fuck this," *he muttered, angry at his own cowardice. His pack would laugh—Blaise would laugh—at him if they saw him practically pissing his jeans. It was probably just an injured pigeon, hitting its wings against the stone and brick.*

Flap, flap, flap.

Pressing an ear against the brick, Jordan listened.

Flap, flap, flap. Yeah, definitely a pigeon. Must have been trapped when they'd sealed the vault. The mortar around the bricks looked pretty fresh. Poor stupid bird. That was a fucked-up way to die.

Satisfied that he'd solved the mystery, Jordan turned to go back the way he came. He could use a beer or three now and—

"Help me…"

No fucking way.

No way he just heard a voice from inside a fucking sealed tomb. It was sealed, right? Still, he leaned up close to it and said, "Hel… Hello?"

A chunk of brick fell out of the wall as if pushed from within.

Jordan jumped, letting out a yelp and nearly falling over his own feet as he stumbled away from the wall. His phone hit the ground with an ominous crack. Retrieving it, he checked the screen, relieved to find it undamaged. He shone its flashlight at the oven vault.

"Shit," he breathed.

There was a gap in the bricks, crumbling around the edges.

Even as he watched, something that looked like a cartoon version of a hand—like a flesh-toned mitten with the vague outline of a thumb attached to a blob—thrust through the gap, pawing at the loose mortar to enlarge the opening. Another deformed appendage pushed through. Was it wrapped in bandages? Or—

Both fleshy blobs seized him by the neck, cutting off his air as more bricks tumbled to the ground. Before he could even try to break free, something plunged into one of his eyes, puncturing the eyeball and piercing his brain. Luckily for Jordan, he died before the brains were sucked out of his head.

CHAPTER NINETEEN

"My place is a few blocks from here," Tia told me as we waited for our burgers in a little sports bar near the Garden District. The place didn't have an extensive beer list—no fancy craft beers—but they did carry Abita, and I didn't want anything too heavy or sweet anyway. I ordered an IPA, hoppy and crisp, and exactly what my queasy stomach craved.

"It's really more of an in-law than a proper house," she continued. "Well, it's really a shack—you'd only stick your mother-in-law in there if you hated her, but at least it has running water. Most of the time," she amended. "And since it's around the back of a big house, it's got a locked gate and it's pretty safe."

"That's something," I said.

"Yeah," Tia agreed. "The landlord's son is kinda creepy—I caught him peeking in my window one morning."

"Gross!"

"I know, right?" Tia shrugged. "He looks like your typical good Christian boy—" she did finger quotes "—but he's pretty much a perv. Anyway, I bought some cheap fabric and hung it up for curtains. Solved that problem."

"Do you think he'll try anything else?" I couldn't help but be concerned. Tia couldn't weigh more than ninety pounds, even with all her clothes and her backpack on.

"Yeah, no. He's about thirteen and he's smaller than me anyway."

I lifted my bottle and clinked it against hers.

We sat in a booth near the back of the bar, some sportsball or another playing on the three large flat-screen TVs that dominated the walls at either end and in the middle of the bar. Might have been football, might have been baseball. I didn't care enough to pay attention.

A voluptuous waitress in tight jeans and an equally tight T-shirt, both of which looked painted on, sauntered over bearing two plates of food, which she set in front of us with a warm smile.

"Getcha anything else, ladies?"

I picked up my beer bottle and sloshed it around. About a quarter of it left. "Another round, please," I said.

I dug into my burger. "Holy shit, this is good," I moaned, eyes at half-mast.

Tia gave a complacent nod. "Best burgers in town, told you. Wait till you try the fries."

I did. They were thin and golden and crispy, the perfect French fries. They didn't even need ketchup.

I started feeling better almost immediately. As my blood sugar levels stabilized, it was also easier to dismiss the weird 3-D Technicolor flashes of déjà vu I'd had in front of the LaLaurie mansion. I knew better than to go on an empty stomach for any length of time. I'd let the weirdness of the day throw me off my game.

I finished my burger in record time despite doing my best not to shove it down my throat. Growing up around a bunch of stuntmen hadn't done a lot for my table manners, especially when I was hungry. I managed to slow down and eat my fries one at a time instead of by the handful, but I was done with my meal while Tia still worked her way through half her food. I tried not to eyeball her fries. No one likes a glutton, right?

Tia caught my glance and swiveled her plate around so the fries faced me. "Help yourself."

"Are you sure?" *Please be sure.*

She nodded. "I can never finish. I don't spend my days working out like you do."

As I made short work of the fries, I realized the sound of the game on the TV had been replaced by the voice of a solemn-sounding male newscaster.

"...not the first young woman to go missing in the last month. A week ago, a young woman called Celia Davenport vanished from her house after going to bed. Her parents heard no disturbance, there were no obvious signs of a break-in, and all of Celia's belongings, including ID and wallet, were still in her bedroom. A week later, four other young women, friends of Celia Davenport, vanished from their homes, all in a single night. While there is no sign of foul play, the disappearance of these five women has residents of the Garden District in an uproar."

Tia's mouth was agape as she stared at the images of the missing women on the TV. She sank back into her seat, skin pasty.

"Did you know them?" I asked curiously.

"No." She shook her head without conviction. "It's just that—" She swallowed, then took a sip of her beer. "It's just that if it can happen to people like them, girls that live in safe neighborhoods, with their parents... that can't be safe for people like me."

She picked up her beer, started to take another drink, and

then set it down again. "Are you okay if we take off? I could really use some fresh air about now." Without waiting for an answer, Tia stood up and practically ran out of the bar, leaving her backpack behind.

WTF?

Hastily settling our bill and leaving a generous tip on the table, I grabbed the backpack and hurried outside, looking up and down the dimly lit street for Tia. A slight figure was stumbling down the sidewalk further down the street, lurching from side to side as if drunk.

"Shit."

I ran after her, her backpack bouncing against my shoulder blade. "Tia!" I called as I drew closer to her.

At first, she put on a burst of speed, accompanied by an almost explosive noise that sounded as if she couldn't decide if she wanted to cry or throw up.

"Tia!" I passed a cement wall and a wrought-iron gate as Tia vanished around the corner. Stepping up my pace, I rounded the corner just in time to see her trip and fall to her knees. I ran over before she could pick herself up and take off again. I hate running. "Tia, what the hell is going on?" My voice was harsher than I meant it to be, but did I mention I hate running?

All of her energy seemed to have seeped into the concrete sidewalk beneath her. Tia stayed slumped where she was, her breathing shallow and rapid.

"Those girls," she finally choked out.

"What *about* them?" I tried not to sound impatient, but I could not think of any good reason why she would suddenly bolt out of the bar, leaving me and her backpack behind.

"I don't—"

A scream rang out, cutting off whatever Tia was going

to say. The scream itself was muffled and then cut short, as if someone had thrown a heavy blanket over whoever was screaming. The sound had come from around the corner up ahead.

Before I had a chance to do more than think about going to the rescue, someone—no, two someones—staggered around the corner toward us, arms flailing. The street lights were dim, barely casting enough light to make out details. What I could see, however, was that one of the figures wore high heels and jeans. The rest of her was shrouded in what looked like gray cheesecloth, which was also attached to the second figure. As I watched, the woman in heels stumbled and fell to her knees. The person holding her followed her down and—

"Holy shit," I breathed as I saw what was going on.

I didn't stop to think. If I had, I might've sensibly run in the other direction. Instead I dropped Tia's backpack in front of her, propelled myself to my feet, and ran toward the abomination down the sidewalk.

CHAPTER TWENTY

By the time I reached the crumpled woman, it was too late to save her. When I got a closer look at her assailant, I could still see the human form that had once been a young female inside the sticky grayish-black membrane. Her features were blurred, as if they were partially dissolved. Human arms and legs had merged with insectile limbs, but the stubs of fingers and toes still protruded, pink nail polish still visible. A double set of wings unfurled in the breeze, but instead of having the delicate beauty of a butterfly, they were scabrous and gray, like shroud-cloth left too long in the grave. Where a mouth should be, a proboscis protruded, the tip pulsing and wet, dripping with red fluid. It came out of the woman's body with a wet sucking sound, spraying little droplets into the air.

"Help me." The words, thick and bubbling with mucus, were still clear enough to understand. I took an involuntary step backward as the thing reached for me. She? There was something about the voice and the blurred features that seemed feminine.

"Help me," it said again. Even as it repeated those words, however, it lunged for me, wings wrapping around me like wet towels, slapping against my arms, torso, and legs, encasing me in fibrous folds that smelled like death. The wings wrapped tightly around my body and head exuded a sick, sweet perfume—like night-blooming jasmine with a hint of decay underneath. It made me nauseated and dizzy at the same time.

Even worse, though, was the sound of that thick, clotted voice saying, "Help me" over and over again, even as it did its best to kill me. And knowing there was still something human left inside, but not enough to stop it from feeding. I had to act quickly, before the sickly-sweet odor made me lose consciousness. It would be all too easy to succumb, if only to spare myself from the guilt I knew I'd feel when this was over.

The fibrous wings pinned one arm to my side, but luckily for me, I'd been raising the other as the creature attacked. It would have succeeded in killing me if it had managed to trap both my arms. Its proboscis snapped forward toward my chest, but I had enough range of motion to grab it right below the tip with the hand not trapped at my side.

As it squirmed in my grasp, the proboscis whipped around, the tip landing against my palm and found the fleshy part under my thumb, nuzzling, almost suckling like the world's grossest infant trying to feed. Before I had a chance to be totally disgusted, what felt like hundreds of needle-sharp teeth sunk into the meat of my palm, and almost immediately began suctioning up blood like greedy little vampires.

"Oh, no you don't, you fucker," I snarled, my ambivalence evaporating. Whatever this thing had been in its human incarnation, there was no way back for it. This creature had to die and screw any guilt attached to killing it.

Twisting my hand—doing my best to ignore the scalding pain as the flesh ripped away from all those teeth, I grabbed the proboscis and pulled, even as the wings tightened in smothering folds around me, cutting off oxygen. Flashes of red burst in my vision as I struggled for air, still pulling the proboscis as I managed to lift up my right leg and shove my foot against the thing's lower body.

As I felt something start to give, a high-pitched squealing pierced my eardrums—not just a sound but a visceral auditory assault that threatened to dissolve me from the inside out. It felt like my bones were liquefying, the muscles and tissue melting. My voice rose in a shriek of its own as I gave one last vicious, desperate yank on the proboscis. There was a ripping sound, like a thick piece of cloth being torn in two. Dark, foul-smelling fluid spurted out from the hole in its face, a gory fringe of pink and red gobbets of tissue hanging from the edges.

The creature shuddered as if hit with high voltage, its squeals thickening and weakening as it choked on its own fluids and the regurgitated blood of its last victim. The membranous wings loosened and fell away, the monster toppling to the ground. It twitched feebly and then was still.

Holy shit.

As I watched, the fluids still bubbling from the wound I'd inflicted began pouring out more rapidly, the flesh around it starting to smoke. The thing deflated and dissolved before my horrified gaze until the only thing left was a spreading puddle of pinkish slime. Turning away from the remains, I put my hands on my knees, leaning over to take a few deep breaths to clear my head and chase away the cloying smell.

Ugh.

"Are… Are you okay?" Tia hovered above me, her face a pasty greenish-white in the glow of the street lamp.

"I'll live. At least I think I will." The smell of the thing was still thick in my nostrils.

"I didn't know what to do," Tia said, her voice small and ashamed. "I just stood there and—"

I held up a hand, the one dripping with pink goo. "It's okay. Staying out of the way was actually the smartest thing you could have done. It's easier to fight when you're only worried about yourself."

"But you—"

"Seriously. I'm not saying it to make you feel better."

A glint of gold caught my attention, right in the middle of the goo that had once been a... well, a living creature, something stuck between human and insect. Overcoming my disgust, I reached down and plucked a necklace from the reeking puddle. A delicate cloisonné butterfly on a gold chain.

Behind me, Tia gasped.

She reached out, fingering the necklace dangling from my hand. I looked at her.

"Do you recognize this?" I asked gently.

Tia hesitated. "I'm not sure," she finally replied. "Maybe."

"Tia…"

She sucked in a breath, then let it out in a long exhalation. "Okay, yeah. I've seen it before."

"Where?"

Tia folded down onto the ground, like a prima ballerina playing Odette in *Swan Lake*. She rested her head on both hands, her breath coming in rapid, shallow gasps.

"Tia, what? Where did you see it?" I tried not to sound too impatient, but honest to god, after dealing with the butterfly monster from hell, I didn't have a lot of patience left.

"In the shop," Tia muttered in between gasping breaths.

"Say again?" Okay, there was my impatience shining through.

"In the shop," she repeated. "LeRoy's. There was a girl getting a tattoo. I talked to her before she went in the back with LeRoy. She had a really pretty necklace, a butterfly." She held out the cloisonné butterfly. "This necklace. Oh God, I'm gonna be sick."

And she was.

†

Somehow—I'm not quite sure how—I managed to get Tia through the iron gate and front door of a little in-law in back of the main house. She was right. It *was* kind of a shitty little place, especially when compared to the well-kept mansion in front. The interior smelled of mildew, and the short-napped gray carpet was worn and stained. Tia had attempted to brighten the place up by hanging up pieces of what looked like old sari fabric—but I could see where moisture had seeped into and stained the walls.

My glance flickered over the place. A black coffee mug on the counter. An ancient Mr. Coffee maker. A mini-fridge. A hot plate. A tiny little microwave, and a rusty old sink that made me positive this place had once been a garden shed. On the shelf above the sink were some books—a few on the art of tattooing, a Klimt art book, and a couple of novels. A battered copy of *The Girl with the Dragon Tattoo* lay open face-down and spine cracked on a futon covered by a faded purple comforter. The way that a kid would treat a book. Clothes, mostly black, littered the floor, the back of the single chair in the room, and the futon. All in all, it rated solid ten in the depressing décor category.

I unceremoniously cleared everything off the futon with a sweep of one arm and plunked Tia down. Her teeth were still chattering, her body wracked with uncontrollable shivers, so I pulled the comforter around her shoulders. I grabbed the bottle of tequila off the counter, unscrewed the lid, and poured a hefty shot into a coffee mug. As far as I could tell, it was the only thing that passed for a glass in the apartment.

"Here," I said, shoving the mug into her hands. She took it, but I didn't trust her not to drop it, so I helped guide it to her mouth and made sure she took a swallow. Then another, and one more until she finished what I poured. Then I poured some more and sat silently with her for a few minutes, one arm wrapped around Tia's shoulders, making sure that the quilt stayed in place.

"Tell me what you know about those missing girls." I kept my voice calm and level, afraid any emotion might make Tia shut down on me. I didn't think she'd answer me at first. Then she cradled her fingers around the mug and took another sip of tequila, and then another until her trembling subsided.

"The tattoos," Tia said simply. "That has to be it."

"What tattoos?" I was glad it was obvious to her, but I had no idea what she was talking about. Then she told me. My stomach curdled with horror as she talked.

"So," I said slowly after Tia had finished telling me about the five girls who'd come into the ink shop where she worked, "you're saying you think the tattoos have something to do with their disappearing?"

Tia nodded. "The last four were friends of Celia's, the first girl who went missing—the girl with the necklace. They said she'd told them about LeRoy's shop. She… Celia had gotten one of LeRoy's special tattoos too, one of the ones in his private portfolio. Since I've been working there, he's only shown it to six people—those four girls, their friend Celia, and this total dickhead frat boy who came in with his friend. I inked his friend. And… I also inked one of the girls. We all inked one of them."

"Who's 'we'?"

"Me and the Creepy Twins," she answered reluctantly,

avoiding my eyes. "That's what I call the other tattooists that work there." Her color was returning to normal—pale sure, but she no longer looked like she was Langdon's cousin. "All four of them picked designs from that portfolio."

I stared at her. "You think that the thing we saw... that I killed... was one of those girls?"

"The necklace," Tia said softly. "Like I said, she wore it when she came in to get her tattoo. I noticed it. Complimented her. So, yeah. I think... I know that was her." Downing the tequila, Tia finally looked up, directly at me. "And those tattoos had something to do with it. At first, I thought he was just being really picky about his designs. But then it was almost like he was part of a cult, or a slavery ring—marking people with special tats. That would be bad enough. But... But that thing..."

"If that's the case," I said, "there are five more people out there who may or may not be—"

"May or may not be human," Tia said dully. "And if that's true, I did the ink on one of them." She shook her head. "Fuck. I need to make this right."

I thought of what to say to her. Things like, "It's not your fault," and, "You had no way of knowing." But I didn't know if either of those statements were true—even if I suspected she really hadn't known—and I didn't want to offer false comfort. What I finally said was, "How?"

Shaking her head, Tia wrapped her arms around her knees. "I don't know. But I need to try. I'll start with the shop tomorrow."

"Do you want me to go with you?"

Even as I said it, I realized I had a full day of shooting ahead of me tomorrow. I seriously doubted either Devon or Cayden would accept amateur detecting as an excuse for putting the film a day behind schedule. Okay, Cayden *might* cut me some slack given what we'd been through together in Malibu. Devon, on the other hand, not so much.

I felt almost guilty at my relief when Tia said, "Thanks, but no. LeRoy is really weird about having anyone in the shop if they're not working or paying customers. He doesn't even like having friends of customers hanging out while they're getting inked. I'm gonna try to get there before he or the Creepy Twins do, but if any of them came in and you were there, I'm not sure what he'd do."

"Fire you?" I suggested.

That drew a wan smile. "Hell, I'm out of there end of day tomorrow, no matter what." She bit her lower lip and shook her head. "I honestly don't know what he'd do. And I don't want to find out."

†

When I got back to the hotel, I tried to slink as inconspicuously as I could back to my room, not an easy task when covered with smelly goo. The couple unfortunate enough to share the elevator with me going up moved as far away from me as possible.

"We're filming a movie," I said apologetically.

They nodded, smiled bright, fake smiles, and got out at the next floor.

Back in my room, I immediately pulled off all my clothes, wondering if it was worth trying to wash the gunk off them or if I should just toss them. I liked that camisole top, dammit! I grabbed one of the hotel laundry bags and stuffed everything but the boots in it. A small black object fell to the ground as I put the jeans in—the little *gris-gris* bag from Loa Creations. I picked it up and tucked it away with the tile I'd bought. Whether or not the charm had anything to do with me defeating the creature, it made me feel better.

†

I had been dreaming I was floating on a cloud. The sun had not yet risen, the air still pleasantly cool although I could feel the humid heat waiting to fall over the city like a sticky shroud.

I stretched, luxuriating in the feeling of cool sheets on my naked flesh. I let my limbs spread wide, hands arching skyward, then pointed and flexed my feet before curling into myself like a cat. The only problem with this picture was the bed next to me was empty, only a slight indentation in the mattress to show that my lover had indeed stayed the night.

"Étienne?"

No answer. I should get up and go find him. Instead I sank back down into my cloud and shut my eyes again, inhaling deeply to catch the scent of cinnamon and leather mingling with the tang of musky sweat. A pleasing, almost sweet smell, unlike the sour reek of so many other men.

As I lay there, myrrh, frankincense, sandalwood, and something less pleasant fought to overwhelm Étienne's familiar smell. It came from the clouds of incense now roiling in the air above me, permeating the room.

Throwing back the covers, I got out of bed, bare feet padding across the wooden floors as I tried to follow Étienne's signature scent, which wove its way like a ribbon amongst the other smells in the air. It faded in and out, sometimes lost in the mix of smoke and the heavy, coppery scent of ozone and blood—then suddenly strong and standing out on its own. I followed it as the floor beneath my feet suddenly became a dirt path, leading me into a clearing filled with shadowy figures, all of them joining in a shrieking chant that rose above the discordant sound of screeching pipes and other instruments that had no place in this world…

CHAPTER TWENTY-ONE

The interior of the shop was still dark when Tia arrived. Good. She'd beaten both LeRoy and the Creepy Twins to work.

Tia's stomach swarmed with butterflies—God, after what she'd seen, the thought was horrifying—at the thought of being caught. There was one place in the shop LeRoy had told her to steer clear of, and that was where she had to look—the room at the back of the shop. She'd never seen anyone other than LeRoy go in there. Her stomach churned in anticipation of finding out things she'd rather never know.

Polli and Hyla didn't usually arrive before the sun was at least thinking of setting, but LeRoy's schedule was unpredictable. Tia couldn't peg him as either a morning person or a night owl—he was as likely to arrive at the shop at midnight or noon. No matter what time he did show up at the shop, though, he was always dressed to impress and looked like he'd enjoyed a good eight hours' slumber, untroubled by either guilt or nightmares. The sleep of the innocent, he called it.

Tia somehow doubted that. More like the sleep of the "I don't give a fuck." Yeah, that seemed about right. She'd told Lee the truth when she'd said the initial ego rush of apprenticing with him had worn off the more unsettling both his behavior and that of the twins became. And all the hero worship in the world couldn't mask LeRoy's increasingly frequent borderline-abusive behavior. She needed to leave before she went all Stockholm Syndrome and started thinking it was normal. In a week's time she'd have worked under LeRoy for three months, long enough to give her some street cred. Maybe he'd even give her a recommendation if she didn't piss him off before she left.

So why was she even thinking of violating one of the main rules he'd set down when she'd started her apprenticeship?

She thought again about LeRoy's portfolio, the private one that he only brought out for special customers. Like the girl who'd worn the butterfly necklace.

The dead girl. The dead… thing.

Fuckity fuck.

Using her key—and oh, hadn't she been proud to be trusted with the key to the shop?—Tia let herself in, the faint tinkling of the bell sounding overly loud to her ears. Stepping over the threshold, she paused for a moment. Her time living on the streets, thankfully short as it had been, had taught her to feel for the slight vibration disturbing the air that spoke of another's presence. To listen for tiny inhalations of breath. To sense the heat of another living body.

No, LeRoy's Ink Shop was empty, except for Tia and a whole lot of spooky atmosphere. She'd never thought the shop looked eerie before, never really noticed anything off-putting about the artwork on the walls. Just your standard ink house stuff with maybe a little more emphasis on darker subject matter than unicorns, Celtic knot arm bands and such. Here the unicorns were rotting, and the Celtic knot motifs wove in skulls or screaming faces.

Giving her head a brisk shake to clear it of unwelcome phantasms, Tia strode resolutely to the inner door leading to LeRoy's private workshop. Like Bluebeard's tower, it was forbidden. And like one of Bluebeard's stupid wives, Tia knew she had to find out what was inside. This never ended well for the wives, she thought, her brisk pace diminishing as she drew abreast of the door in question. And still she reached out, turned the knob.

Locked.

Tia let out a breath she hadn't been aware of holding, more relieved than she wanted to admit that her brief foray into detective work had come to an end before it really began. Of course it was locked. Someone like LeRoy, someone who basically treated his employees like indentured servants, of course he'd lock this room. He obviously had secrets to hide—why would he trust anyone to keep them? His type never trusts, *she thought.*

She was only partly right.

Putting on an exaggerated expression of disappointment—more for herself than any audience—Tia headed to her station. Might as well settle in, maybe work on some of the new designs she'd been playing with. All of them surreal, like fever dreams. She'd be lying if she didn't admit that some of LeRoy's work had really influenced her since the apprenticeship began. He had a couple of Hieronymus Bosch-type dreamscapes that called to her. She especially loved Doorway to the Elders, a series of old-fashioned locks set into increasingly decrepit wooden doors that spiraled off into the distance—or seemed to, at any rate. She couldn't figure out how he'd managed the effect of endless doors, all connected to one another. Like Escher, LeRoy effortlessly defied the laws of physics in ways that disturbed the viewer and yet made perfect visual sense.

The matte for this particular painting was constructed of antique keys made of various metals like brass, bronze, and iron. The type of keys that belonged on a heavy round keyring carried on the belt of a spooky housekeeper. The kind that opened the locks in the painting—

—or the door to LeRoy's office.

Biting her lip, Tia raised her eyes to Doorway to the Elders *and the dozens of keys crisscrossed over one another, glued inside a dark wooden frame made elegant by its curves and subtle molding. Like a lot of LeRoy's paintings, the overall effect was that of an optical illusion, like looking through a View-Master where two flat images combined into a third, three-dimensional one.*

The keys were laid out in spiraling pinwheels, set onto the matte with clear glue. The size graduated from largest to smallest as they approached the painting itself. Tia studied it, focusing on the outer edges of the key spiral, reaching up to run her fingers lightly over bronze, iron, and—

"Motherfucker!" Tia snatched her hand away and shook it. Something had shocked her good, a hot needle jabbing into the fingers that had brushed…

That one. Black metal with red flecks, like pinpricks of blood. Some sort of iron, maybe? Tia didn't know.

Pulling open one of the drawers at her station, she pulled out a pair of purple latex gloves and put them on. Thin enough to allow her to do her inking with assured precision, yet hopefully thick enough to protect her from another jolt. Then she cautiously reached out and touched the black key. This time she felt maybe a slight thrumming sensation through the latex, but that was all. Snatching the key off the frame, she headed back to the locked door. Now she really felt like one of Bluebeard's wives—except for the purple gloves.

She stopped midway when she spotted LeRoy's portfolio resting on the counter, its distinctive brownish-red cover making it stand out next to the other portfolios. It looked wrong. Funny how Tia hadn't noticed that before. She also hadn't noticed how the cover felt warm and oddly textured—she could feel it even through the latex gloves. Like the skin of someone suffering from a high fever. Febrile and unpleasant.

Flipping it open, she scanned the pages, remembering the first time LeRoy had let her see it. She'd felt so honored, like she'd been initiated into an exclusive club.

She thumbed through the pages, smiling to herself almost unconsciously as her gaze fell upon now familiar sketches and watercolors, the details rendered with almost impossible clarity.

Here was a crouching gargoyle, expression both menacing and pathetic.

Here a python wrapped around a luckless hunter, only a purpling face, eyes wide and bugging out from the constricting pressure visible in the thick coils.

An unfurling red rose, the petals dripping with blood and revealing a demonic fetus in the center of the blooms...

A black-and-orange butterfly, arcane patterns visible in the swirls of the wings' patterns...

Tia stopped, pulling herself almost physically out of the near-hypnotic reverie she'd fallen into. Next to the black-and-orange butterfly was a blank page.

Tia knew there was something off. The butterfly was her favorite of LeRoy's portfolio. Before she left, she hoped to have enough money to get this particular tat inked between her shoulder blades. She'd also admired the blue morpho on the adjacent page. The one that that sweet, quiet girl had chosen for her tattoo a couple weeks ago. That page was now blank.

Running her fingers along the crease, Tia couldn't feel any sign that the page had been ripped out of the book. And when she turned to the next page, the Death Head moth was still there. So, either she'd imagined the blue morpho or the drawing had mysteriously vanished from the portfolio.

Impossible.

And yet... there was no denying it.

Tia flipped through more pages, finding more blank spaces that she could swear had been filled with LeRoy's artwork.

Here. Hadn't there been an irradiated star, its rays so bright they seemed to glow? Gone. And this blank page sandwiched in between a Gila monster and a nest of vipers so real they seemed to writhe as she stared at them... Hadn't there been some sort of alligator?

Thump.

Tia snapped her head to the side, staring into a darkened corner of the room. Nothing that she could see, but she felt something. A presence... or maybe it was just her nerves, stretched to breaking point. She looked at the key in her hand.

She'd reached a crossroads, even though she hadn't realized it yet. She could follow through on her intent to see what lay beyond in LeRoy's private workspace. Or she could put the key back in the painting and do what she'd done for the last couple of years—fit into the cracks and crevices of other people's lives and make her own mark one tattoo at a time until she'd finally filled the gaping hole of self-loathing left by a childhood of neglect, after her mom had died.

"Oh, fuck it," Tia muttered. She'd had enough of self-pity and inaction. Time to swim against the tide instead of letting it toss her around like a twig.

She stiffened her spine. Armed with the key—it probably was a long shot, but why not try it, right?—she once again approached the door leading to LeRoy's inner sanctum. She told herself she didn't expect the key to fit. This was just to satisfy some fucked up sense of honor so she could report back to Lee that all was well, that her suspicions were groundless and stupid, and then she could get back to her ink with a clear conscience.

The key slid in without a hitch. Tia's heart skipped a beat before starting to pound very loudly in her ears.

She hesitated. Going through with this could mean the end of her internship.

Or the end of much more, *an inner voice whispered.*

Before she had a chance to decide, the key moved beneath her suddenly nerveless fingers, turning in the lock by itself. The door opened. Only a crack, but that was enough. If Tia had felt chilled before, the blood in her veins had now gone arctic. Like she would shatter if she moved too quickly. She wanted nothing more than to run, and not just to her station. No, she wanted to get the hell *out of New Orleans, get back on the road to Los Angeles or Vegas, even Bakersfield, just anywhere the fuck away from right here and right now.*

Instead she set her hand against the door, the wood seeming to pulse underneath her palm as if it were breathing.

Fuck this.

Before she could move, something slimy coiled around her wrist and yanked her into madness.

†

"This is Tia. Leave a message."

Short and to the point. Easy to remember, especially after hearing it at least a dozen times since I first called her number when I'd woken up. She'd promised to call as soon as she'd found out anything, but what if she'd just decided to ditch town instead? I knew her guilt level was off the charts, but that could make doing a runner even easier if she were the kind of person who couldn't face their own mistakes.

Although if what she told me was the truth, she had nothing to be ashamed of—she'd been used. Even if she was correct and the tattoos were related to the disappearances and to the creature I'd killed last night… how the hell would she have known?

Still… why wasn't she answering?

Shit.

"Lee! They're ready for you on set!"

Time to get back to work. And somehow keep my head in the game instead of worrying about Tia.

†

Tia woke up to the sound of buzzing, like a swarm of bees, and felt those same bees stinging her over and over on her back, in between her shoulder blades. She made a sound of protest, slow and drawn-out, as if her vocal chords had rusted in place. Surely that wasn't her voice?

253

"Hush, Tia." LeRoy. "I'm truly sorry for this, but you have no one to blame but yourself." The stinging continued, needle-sharp.

Needles. He was inking her.

At first Tia couldn't remember why this should send a ripple of pure terror through her. Then her fogged brain drew up an image of the thing Lee had killed, the warped beauty of the faded wings and the horror of the thing's face, melted, barely human features, and those wide blue eyes filled with pain and hunger.

No. Nonononononononono!

The shriek of denial rang in Tia's head, but the most she could manage was a strangled cry. Then something stung her shoulder and she drifted away into unconsciousness.

†

"Will there be enough time for the new Cantrix to manifest?" Hyla cocked her head and stared down at the unconscious girl, watching in fascination as LeRoy created yet another masterpiece on Tia's back.

Without taking his eyes off his living canvas, LeRoy replied, "I do not know for certain. The time draws near to perform the invocation and open the gates. Each harbinger has its role to play, though, and we cannot do without the Cantrix."

"Can the invocation wait until her gestation is complete?" Polli drew closer to her twin so she, too, could watch the master at work.

LeRoy heaved a sigh and shook his head. "Polli," he said, his tone almost gentle, "if time were not of the essence I would be tempted to use you as the Cantrix's vessel for asking a question that proves to me you either do not pay attention when I speak, or that you are simple-minded to a dangerous degree." Knowing better than to try to defend herself, Polli gave an audible gulp that sounded like the croaking of a frog.

"But fortunately for you," LeRoy continued, "I will require your assistance for a while longer. A much more talented girl must suffer *and die instead. If we miss the conjunction of the stars and the gateways…"* He shook his head. *"This is not an option. They will not be in alignment again for another century or more. Our god has waited long enough."*

A pause while he finished up the final touches on Tia's back. "I will be done soon. She'll have to gestate somewhere close to the Veil so we can lead the Cantrix there quickly when it's time. Meanwhile, I want you both to check the other harbingers, make sure none of them have emerged prematurely."

Putting the first Cantrix in Lafayette 1 was a miscalculation, he thought as the twins hastened to follow his orders. But the cemetery had been close to the vessel's home and, like all other New Orleans cemeteries, closed before sunset. He knew from prior experience that the hosts' vessels sometimes grew increasingly active as the harbingers took over more and more of their bodies. No one should have been there to hear any disturbance. And as much as the gestation process hurt—agonies untold—the vessel should not have been able to cry out.

Ah well, he wouldn't make the same mistake with Tia. The land near the Veil had a small, private graveyard with an old mausoleum that would do nicely. Private property with only one access road, and that merely a deeply rutted dirt track. The Thaumaturge and the Veil would keep any possible intruders from reaching the house swampside. He would keep Tia close at hand and do what he could to encourage the harbinger to come forth quickly.

CHAPTER TWENTY-TWO

I didn't get back to the hotel until a little after ten, covered with dirt and sweat. I craved a shower the way a drunk craves a drink. And I wanted one of those too, but after the shower, preferably in my room. The last thing I wanted or expected when I walked wearily past the Carousel Bar was a chipper female voice saying, "How about a drink, cutie?"

I whirled around at the sound of the familiar voice. Eden, wearing a pale-pink halter-necked sundress and looking as fresh as someone who'd just stepped out of the shower I so desperately craved, stood at the entrance to the bar. She held a tall, frosty glass in one hand and seemed totally oblivious to the cadre of men watching her every move from their seats.

Tired as I was, I couldn't help the huge smile that spread over my face as I hurried over to greet her. "Fair warning," I said as I gave her a one-armed hug, "I need a shower."

"Don't be ridiculous." Eden squeezed me tightly with both arms without spilling her drink. "Come, let me buy you something yummy and filled with alcohol."

"I really want to have a drink here," I admitted wistfully. "I haven't managed it yet. But you smell like roses. I smell like swamp. My 24-hour deodorant gave up the ghost at least six hours ago. And I also really need to talk to you about some stuff that I'd rather not share at a bar."

"We can do the bar another time," she said without hesitation. "Here, help me finish this and we'll go upstairs." She handed me her drink. I took a cautious sip, totally unable to tell what I was drinking other than it tasted really good and had a shitload of alcohol in it. I handed it back. "This will kill me on an empty stomach."

"More for me then," she said cheerfully. She gave a little toast and then downed the contents of her glass.

"You already have the room key?"

Eden nodded. "How about I settle my bill while you go up, get your shower, and get another twenty-four hours from your deodorant. Then we can pajama up and talk."

I gave her a thumbs-up and she went back into the bar, ignoring or oblivious to the hungry looks being cast her way.

†

By the time I'd taken a long, hot shower and changed into a black tank top and blue flannel pajama bottoms with penguins on them, Eden had come back to the room and jammied up in a white tank top and pink flannel bottoms sporting winged pigs. I made a quick call to room service, and we curled up in the comfy chairs. I got to work opening the wine.

"So," I said, picking up the bottle of red wine Berserker Productions had left for me, along with a handy little waiter's helper bottle opener. "You remember what happened when we were filming *Pale Dreamer*?"

Eden laughed. We're not talking a small polite laugh, but rather a full-on guffaw, totally at odds with her appearance. I smiled and continued opening the wine, peeling the foil and jiggering the cork open while Eden roared with laughter. When her outburst finally subsided, she raised an eyebrow, and said, "You're kidding, right?"

"Well, it didn't come out exactly the way I meant it to."

"I mean, I realize that being attacked by weird shadow demons and having the film set suddenly surrounded by unworldly darkness is an everyday occurrence for some people, but, yes, I do remember it."

I poured us each some wine, just a little bit first. We took a minute to try it, both swirling and sniffing, even though I wasn't entirely sure what I was sniffing for. I was relatively new at this whole wine thing, and one didn't swirl and sniff beer as a general rule.

We both tasted it, looked at each other and grinned. "That is some good shit," Eden said appreciatively as I poured more into our glasses.

"Anyway," I said, "what I want to tell you has to do with that. Stuff I found out from Sean and Seth. Stuff about my family, and it's pretty much as totally out there as the Davea demons."

Taking another sip of what even I could tell was a really good wine, I proceeded to fill Eden in on my whackadoodle family history. Pretty much the same spiel I gave Cayden, adding on the whole fight with the seaweed dragon in Malibu. I'd just reached the point where Cayden saved the little girl when there was a knock at the door.

"Here, let me." Eden jumped to her feet and opened the door, admitting a young man bearing fried prawns and filet mignon medallions, which he deposited on the table between our two chairs. Eden sent him on his way with a five-dollar tip and a smile. He seemed equally happy with both.

"Okay. So you left off at the point Cayden saved a child."

I nodded. "You don't seem that surprised by the whole Lilith stuff."

"I'm not." Eden picked up a prawn in one pink-manicured hand and regarded me solemnly as she took a bite. "There are a lot of weird things in this world, Lee. It makes sense that they have an origin story." She swirled her wine, staring into its burgundy depths. "And this isn't the first I've heard of Lilith, or her children."

"What about the whole curse handed down through her descendants?" I asked. "I googled this whole shitstorm after Sean told me about it, and although there were some fun stories about her being a succubus, a lamia, a bad wife, a slut who slept with demons and had baby demons... none of it mentioned a centuries-old curse needing cleanup duty."

"I don't think the real story was ever written down."

"Then how did you hear about it?" The words just slipped out and I hoped my voice didn't sound as accusatory as it felt. Eden didn't seem offended.

"Tales handed down through the family," she answered. "Gossip from demons in bars, guys who were a few sheets to the wind. That kind of thing."

I nodded. Took another sip of wine. "You don't think I'm nuts?"

"Of course not," she exclaimed. "Who else have you told about this?"

"You're only the second person I've told," I admitted. "I mean, Sean and Seth know, obviously, and I think Faustina knows on account she's an ex-goddess, but—"

"Randy knows, then?"

"Uh, no."

"Really?"

"Really. Have not told him."

"So, who *did* you tell?"

Heaving a sigh, I muttered, "Cayden."

Eden's jaw dropped. "You have *got* to be shitting me."

"Nope."

"Why?"

"Let's see, maybe because he hired me to work on a film even though we got attacked by a freaky-assed sea critter that pretty much had me in its crosshairs, and—" I emphasized "and" with a wave of my fork, sending a shrimp slapping back onto the plate "—it was obvious that the thing was gunning for me, but he still hired me anyway. Considering that this conceivably could happen any time or any place—"

"Wait. You getting hired or a monster gunning for you?"

"Sadly, the second seems a lot more likely these days," I admitted. "Even though Sean didn't seem to think it would be too much of an issue, me working on films and getting attacked by monsters. Other than the fact it happened on *Pale Dreamer*—and did I mention the seaweed dragon? I'm surprised Cayden didn't have an entire liability waiver just for me to sign after that happened."

"Yeah, okay, I guess you sorta kinda had to tell him," Eden conceded grudgingly.

"Morally and ethically speaking, yeah."

We were both silent for a few minutes. Sipped our wine. Nibbled on shrimp and steak. I shot a sideways glance at Eden.

"So… you believe me?"

She looked at me as if I were batshit crazy. "Of course I believe you. I've seen you in action, remember? And even if I hadn't…" Eden shook her head and smiled. "One good thing about you—mixed up with a bunch of other good things, of course—is you're totally honest. You'd make a shit poker player."

A heavy sigh of relief escaped me, one that I hadn't even realized I'd been holding in. Telling Cayden, I'd somehow never doubted he'd believe me. Having Eden firmly on my side felt even better. Validation.

Eden tapped her nails on the table. "You haven't told Randy about any of this."

"Nope."

"But you told Cayden."

"Yup."

Eden shook her head. "Randy is gonna be pissed off when he finds out."

I sighed again, this time without the relief. "Yeah, I know."

Then I told her about the Nalusa Falaya I'd seen yesterday on my way to Black Penny.

"And it didn't attack you?"

"No, but only because I… well, I hid. If we'd gotten into it, too many people could have been hurt or killed," I explained.

"Like in all the *Avengers* movies," Eden supplied helpfully.

"Uh, yeah." She had a point.

"What about the butterfly critter you killed last night?"

"Here's the funny thing," I replied slowly. "I didn't feel any itching from the scar and my necklace didn't burn and nothing lit up like Frodo's sword. I think it tried to kill me because it was hungry and I interrupted its meal. Not because of my bloodline."

"Huh." Eden was quiet for a few minutes as she took this all in. I drank some more wine and tried to make sense of it all, failing just as miserably my second time around. I didn't know what to think about any of this.

"Well," Eden finally broke her silence, "if it's any consolation, I think you totally made the right choice not trying to take down the thin man—"

"Long being," I corrected her.

"Yeah, whatever. You made the right choice. If he'd been attacking someone and you'd let him get away with it, yeah, that's different. But he was just taking a stroll through the French Quarter. Attacking him would've endangered everyone around you, and it would have been unprovoked. The butterfly thingy was eating someone. Even if it wasn't technically a demon, you did the right thing."

"Thanks," I said simply. Trust Eden to cut through all my existential angst. "Now if Tia would just call me back, I'd feel better. We need to know if there are other weird tattoo-induced monsters out there to deal with. Even better, I'd love for her to tell me she was totally off base with that whole notion and the butterfly monster was just a one-off." Even as I said it, I knew the truth wouldn't be so convenient or comforting.

"What if she doesn't call you back?"

"I hunt down the ink shop where she works and look for answers myself."

"*We* hunt down the ink shop." She smiled serenely. "I'm going with you."

†

Pieces of bodies… pale-brown limbs mixed with those of a darker hue, strong and well-muscled, strewn on the swampy ground. A thick odor comprised of rotting vegetation, freshly spilt blood and decomposing flesh mixed with the pungent fragrance of burned herbs.

"Étienne?"

No. It couldn't be.

Here was a torso. There a well-muscled calf. And there, a forearm and hand, the fingers long and graceful. The hands of a musician. Still I kept hope alive, a small but bright flame that refused to accept what was before my eyes.

Amidst the tangle of bloody limbs, I saw a glint of silver. Slowly, I reached down and picked up Étienne's St. Christopher medal, smeared with blood.

The flame inside me flickered and died.

"Oh no…" Soft words that couldn't even begin to encompass the vastness of my loss. A pit opened up inside me and all that was good in the world fell into it, followed by any happiness and any hope I'd ever feel again. Gone forever.

Just as well because the sight that met me when I finally raised my eyes from the gory remains on the wooden floor would have crushed me beyond belief if I could have felt anything.

Men and women, chained to wooden posts, thick manacles around throats, wrists and ankles, the unyielding metal cutting into soft flesh. The sickly-sweet odor of rotting flesh permeated the air. None of the prisoners were white—no doubt these were slaves of the LaLaurie family.

Surely no slaves had ever been treated as vilely as this.

To my left, a young woman hung suspended by her wrists, which were locked in manacles. Her bare toes brushed the wooden floorboards. The skin around her shoulders was red and shiny, stretched taut over the dislocated bones. A scold's bridle had been inserted into her mouth, blood dribbling down her chin. My horrified gaze fell upon a bench covered with surgical instruments and more common tools, along with several more of the metal gags, with spikes that would dig into the tongue should the wearer try to speak. Barbaric.

Still, that was nothing compared to what lay beyond in the shadows of the attic.

The things that were shackled to bolts screwed into the wall had once been human. I recognized hands, eyes, other specific body parts as having once belonged to men and women. But they weren't in the right place.

Hands were stitched onto elbows. Feet sprouted from shoulders. Others had animal parts sewn on in place of human. There was no rhyme or reason to the mutilations.

But in every single instance, the most horrifying aspect was that each victim was still alive and aware of what had been done to them.

Including Étienne.

I recognized my lover only because his eyes were still untouched, although the rest of him had been tortured and rearranged beyond imagination. Hellish awareness was clear in his gaze, as well as his recognition of me. How was he— how were *any* of them—still alive? How could anything living endure such horrific mutilations and still draw breath?

I'd thought nothing could penetrate the layers of numbness swaddling me. I was wrong. Throwing back my head, I screamed my anguish to the gods as smoke continued to seep through the floorboards from the fire below…

†

I woke up, sweat running down my face and breasts in rivulets, heart pounding as if I'd run a few laps at top speed. "Holy shit," I whispered, throwing the covers off to let the cool temperature-controlled air take some of the heat off my body.

Sexy scary dude without a face was starting to look pretty good about now.

What the hell? I thought as I got myself a glass of water. This wasn't a coincidence. It wasn't the script playing with my head. These dreams had to mean something, but I had no way of telling what on my own. I needed help. I glanced at the bed next to mine where Eden still slept soundly and serenely.

Grabbing my phone, I went into the bathroom and hit Sean's name. It rang through straight to voicemail. "Sean…" I swallowed, my throat suddenly dry again. "I know it's early… I'm sorry. Can you call when you have a minute? It's… things have gotten weird. I could really use your advice."

I hit "end" and stared at the phone. Then I sent Sean a

quick text along those same lines, adding, "If you could call me back as soon as possible… I think it would be a good thing. Family issues."

Hopefully he'd get what I meant by that. Sometimes Sean can be infuriatingly literal.

The phone rang ten minutes later. It wasn't Sean who showed up on my stalker vision, but Seth. I hesitated for one ring, then answered.

"Hey," I said warily. I glanced over at Eden, sawing the cutest little snoring logs ever. "Hang on a sec." I got out of bed and padded into the bathroom, shutting the door behind me.

"Okay, I'm here. Um… I don't want to be rude here, but I called Sean."

"He's on a conference call with Abe O'Bannon." The producer of *Spasm*. "He got your text right before he went into the call. Passed it onto me because he thought you sounded overwrought."

"His word or yours?"

"Fine. He said 'upset.'"

I came that close to ending the call, but something—maybe common sense or maybe desperation—kept me on the line.

"Whatever, Seth. I need help, okay? Things are getting weird here and I don't know if it's related to the whole ancestral curse or if I'm just susceptible to suggestion and bad scripts."

There was a muffled laugh at the other end of the line. "Talk to me," he said.

So I did. I told him about the dreams I'd been having. "They're different from the other dreams—"

"What other dreams?" he cut in.

"Just some weird dreams about cliffs and a guy with red eyes and no face. Shit like that."

Silence. I continued.

"The dreams I've had since I got here are totally different."

"What are they?"

"There's... They're all different, but like in some fucked-up chronological order. I wake up in a room, I know it's my bedroom. Someone's missing, though, and when I try to find him, I end up in a clearing with drums and incense and chanting that sounds like something out of a... I don't even know what, but it doesn't sound like it belongs in this world."

"Is that all?"

I took a deep breath. Maybe he didn't mean to sound quite as dismissive as he just did. Maybe I was just uber-defensive. Or maybe Seth thought I was nuts.

"Well, no," I finally answered. "Five girls... well, young women, have disappeared in the last few weeks. I found what I think might be one of them. And this all feels like... It's like a super-duper case of déjà vu, really shitty déjà vu. Same with the dreams. In the last one... the one I just woke up from, I found a bunch of bodies, mutilated. Pieces of them. And then I found... in the dream, I found... they were still alive, but..." I stopped. "But they shouldn't have been."

Silence from the other end of the line.

"Look, I know this sounds nuts, but given everything else that's happened in the last few months, maybe it's not. I just want to know if I'm crazy, okay?"

Pause.

"You're not."

That was it?

"You wanna tell me how you know that for sure?"

"All I can tell you is that one of your ancestors was in New Orleans before. Back in the 1800s. You're experiencing inherited memories. They're not necessarily relevant to anything else going on in the present day."

"Not necessarily?"

"Look, I need to talk to Sean." Seth actually sounded flustered. "I'll call you back or have him call you."

"Seth, I—"

He'd hung up.

"Son of a bitch."

CHAPTER TWENTY-THREE

The next day's shoot was pretty mellow, mainly working with Angelique on the finer points of knife fighting in prep for a fight with another contender for the voodoo queen's figurative crown. Cayden had given me free rein on the choreography of this particular fight, so Angelique and I spent most of the day out at the bayou location having ourselves a blast playing with rubber knives while the set and FX crews prepped for the next day's shoot. Tomorrow would be the start of the voodoo ritual scenes, leading up to the big magic battle between Marie and Perrine.

When he wasn't working, Micah hung out and watched us, adding his two cents as we worked the choreography. "Y'all gonna mud wrestle next?" he said when Angelique slipped, inadvertently dragging us both into the muddy water of the bayou. We looked at each other, each grabbing a handful of mud and throwing it at him. He dodged my muddy bullet, but Angelique's hit him square in the face.

"Score!" she crowed triumphantly. Micah grinned, unperturbed.

Later, during the meal break, the three of us sat outside and ate our lunch together. It was obvious Micah had a crush on Angelique, and just as obvious that she hadn't noticed. She treated him with offhand affection, like you'd treat a younger brother. When she went to get some more water, the expression on his face as he watched her walk away was painfully clear.

"Hey, Micah," I said, to fill the awkward silence, "you mentioned earlier that the land across the water here belongs to another family."

"That's right." Micah gave a little nod and took a big bite of a sandwich.

"I get the feeling that this family and the Marcadets aren't exactly the best of friends."

Micah finished chewing, swallowed and said, "That's what y'all would call an understatement."

I waited, figuring he was either going to give me more information or he wasn't. I also got the feeling he enjoyed stringing me along instead of giving me straight answers. I don't like being strung along under any circumstances, for any reason.

He took his time with another seemingly impossibly huge bite of sandwich. He swallowed, wiped his mouth on the back of his shirt sleeve, and sat there for a moment. I kept quiet, nibbling on my own sandwich with an air of indifference. Or so I hoped.

"Castro family," Micah said, ending our little stand-off. "Real nasty, real strange. They're not exactly shifters, but some point in their past they had to get down and dirty with some kinda amphibian or reptile. And they stay out of the voodoo rituals, they don't even go near the places those are held. They got their own freaky shit going on, somewhere deep in the swamps where you do *not* want to be going."

I nodded, keeping my thoughts to myself for the moment. After making another impressive indentation on his meal, Micah continued. "Let's just say the Hatfields and McCoys got nothing on the Castros and the Marcadets. They even have their own star-crossed lovers and illegitimate babies."

I almost didn't want to ask my next question, but I did anyway. "What happened to those kids?"

Shrugging, Micah took a big gulp of Mountain Dew. After he swallowed, he said, "'Bout what you expect. Treated like shit by both sides of their families."

Bad as that sounded, I was relieved. I'd expected something more along the lines of "they were sacrificed to the swamp gators" or worse. I didn't ask for any more details, instead taking the conversation down a new path.

"What was it started the feud in the first place?" I tried to think back on my history lessons. Surely we'd covered something as iconic as the Hatfield–McCoy feud.

"Some say it was over land. Some say a couple of Marcadet cats got friskier than they should've with one of the Castro girls. Them cats, they sure like to play."

Well, that conjured up plenty of nasty images in my head. "One more thing. You say this feud is still going on?"

"Yes, ma'am. Just as strong as it ever was or has ever been."

Great. "Any reason to think those Castros might take it into their heads to fuck around with the filming? Seeing as we are filming on Marcadet land and Leandra is one of the lead actresses?"

"I doubt it. Now, if we were to step on their land…" He gave an unpleasant chuckle and shook his head. "*That* might result in some real trouble."

I didn't ask what kind of trouble. I had enough on my plate worrying about Tia, who was still MIA.

†

"Is this the place?" Eden pointed down an alleyway. I followed the direction of her finger to a projecting sign hanging perpendicular to the brick wall. The sign read "LeRoy's Ink Shop."

"I think so," I replied. The name LeRoy rang a sharp bell in my memory.

As we entered the alley, the temperature dropped, and I immediately experienced a strange disconnect. The sounds from the street were oddly muffled, almost as if cotton batting had been swaddled over my ears. "Is it just me or—?"

Eden shook her head. "No, it's not just you."

"It's kind of like the entrance to Ocean's End," I said slowly. "But creepy instead of cool."

We walked slowly toward the door, the soles of my boots crunching on whatever littered the cracking cobblestones. A particularly loud crunch made me glance down, and I gave an indrawn hiss when I saw what looked like finger bones sticking out from under my right foot.

No fucking way.

Taking a deep breath, I shut my eyes, counted to three, then slowly opened them again. The only thing under my feet were leaves, twigs, and the partially crushed remains of a to-go daiquiri cup.

Eden eyed me with curious concern. "You okay?"

"I officially do not like this place," I said with complete sincerity.

We reached the door. Small frosted-glass windows set into the wood. The interior of the shop was dark, and the "Closed" sign on the inside of one of the windows was weathered with age.

"Okay," I said slowly. "This is weird."

"Are you sure that this is the right place?"

"Pretty damn sure." I slammed my hand against the door in frustration. "I definitely remember the name

LeRoy. And Tia said it was off of Pirate Alley."

"Huh. This place looks like it hasn't been open for months."

I slapped my hand against the door again, this time on the glass. I didn't expect the glass to fracture underneath my palm. Yet fracture it did, jagged shards falling inside the shop.

Oops.

Still, if that didn't seem like a cosmic invitation…

"Well," Eden finally commented, "this seems like breaking and entering in the most accidental sense, don't you think?"

I thought about that for a second. Would the production and Cayden consider me worth putting up bail money for? I could lose my job over this. And then I thought about the thing I'd had to kill last night, about its victim, and about the glazed pain in its all too human eyes. If the person responsible for that was in this shop, I'd take my chances. Especially since Tia hadn't shown up. She could be in danger, and the only person who could help might be me.

Eden shrugged at my expression. "If you're looking for someone to talk to you out of this," she said, "you've got the wrong girl."

I pushed the door open and stepped inside.

"Can I help you ladies?" A man's voice with just a hint of an accent. Maybe French.

I'd like to say neither Eden or I were startled, but it would be a lie of the devil. We both let out surprised yelps, kind of like coyotes.

"Are… Are you LeRoy?" Eden recovered her composure first, stepping forward with a bright smile that had opened many doors for her in Hollywood. I just stared at him— medium height. Dark eyes. Tan, almost weathered skin. Wavy brown hair pulled back into a ponytail at the base of his skull. Totally familiar even though I knew I'd never met him before.

Maybe it was because he was a "type"—the handsome but creepy owner of a Dark Arts store in a supernatural TV show.

"The sign says 'closed,'" he said, not answering Eden's question.

"And yet here you are," she responded brightly. "We're so sorry to burst in like this, but—"

"But what?"

"But we're looking for our friend Tia," I broke in. "She said to meet her here, so we didn't think there'd be a problem if we came inside."

His expression remained borderline threatening. "This isn't a bar, ladies." His emphasis of the word "ladies" made it clear he meant just the opposite. "And Tia isn't here."

"She's not?" I couldn't hide my dismay.

"No." He leaned against one of the counters and regarded us coolly. "Tia has not been into work for the last two days, you see."

"But that's—" I stopped before the word "impossible" slipped out because then he'd ask me how I knew that, and I wasn't a particularly good liar. "That doesn't sound like Tia," I finished lamely. "Why would she tell us to meet us here?"

He shrugged. "Maybe her plans changed between the time you last spoke and this evening. She was young, a drifter. Very talented, but unstable. A substance abuse problem, perhaps." He heaved what I thought was an overly dramatic sigh. "I had high hopes for her, but… it was not to be."

I glanced up on the wall behind one of the stations where a picture of Tia and a young man that might be her brother was taped. The edges curled up, a sign that this was an older photo, one that had traveled more than a few miles. No way Tia would have left it behind if she had suddenly decided to leave New Orleans.

Nor would she have left her backpack, which lay on the floor next to the chair.

I kept my expression neutral even as my heart started pounding a mile a minute in my chest. "You said Tia hasn't been here for *how* long?"

"Two days," he lied smoothly. Then he stared at me some more. "I feel like we've met. Perhaps you were in here to visit Tia another time?"

"We haven't met," I assured him, even though it almost felt like lying.

"Then unless you ladies want a tattoo, you'll have to excuse me. The shop is, after all, closed."

"We won't bother you anymore." I smiled even though it hurt my face to do so. "If you do see Tia again, can you tell her we were looking for her?"

"And who shall I say stopped by?" His smile was smooth, oily, and as dark as the abyss I fell into in my dreams.

"Linda and Carrie," I replied. "Tia has my number."

†

Eden waited until we were well away from LeRoy's Ink Shop, safe in the crowds of Bourbon Street, before turning to me and asking, "Did you buy *any* of that?"

"Hell, no." I practically spat out the words. I did not like or trust LeRoy. "That guy gives me one of the biggest cases of the creeps I've ever had. If Tia had really decided to leave all of a sudden, I think she would have mentioned it. She definitely would *not* have said she was going to check on a few things."

"What if she just said that so you wouldn't ask her any more questions?"

"No." I shook my head. "Not even a possibility."

"Are you sure?" Eden pressed. "You said yourself she's

been on the move, and not stayed in one place for more than a few months at a time."

"Just... no," I insisted. "Tia took her work seriously. And she may even be a drifter, but she isn't a flake. Tia was working toward a future, and just vanishing without a word to anyone, especially her current boss..." I shook my head again. "Just no. I don't believe it. But I *am* sure that's what LeRoy wanted us to think."

Eden mulled this over for a minute and then nodded. "Okay, that makes sense. But what do we do now?"

"I don't know." Admitting that pissed me off. I wanted answers immediately and easily, like breaking open a fortune cookie. The hard fact was that I needed to find out more about LeRoy, but I had no idea where to even start with that. "I guess maybe talk to some of the other tattoo shop owners and employees, see if anyone knows where LeRoy came from. See if anyone will vouch for his honesty." I heaved a defeated sigh. "I have an early-morning call tomorrow so there's not much I can do about it tonight." It killed me to admit that.

Eden reached over and gave me a one-armed hug that somehow managed to be reassuring and calming at the same time. "How about we head back, have a drink at the Carousel Bar—my treat—and go from there?"

I considered this. "Fine, but it'll be my treat, okay? I've got a per diem to spend and, so far, I've been doing a piss-poor job of it. People keep buying me drinks."

"Ooh, that's a first world problem if ever I've heard one." Eden gave me another one-armed squeeze. "I'm happy to give you a hand with this."

†

Three hours later I trudged down the hall to my room, so tired I could barely see straight. Eden walked beside me, one hand on my shoulder to make sure I didn't careen into the walls like a sleepy and tipsy pinball. I'd already done that once.

"C'mon," she urged gently. "Only a little bit further."

I stumbled and kept walking. I didn't think I'd had that much to drink at the bar, but maybe the whole going around and around thing gave the alcohol a head start screwing with my equilibrium.

Or maybe I'd just had one too many drinks.

Bonk. I rebounded off the wall for the second time, taking two steps back before stopping.

"Do you think you're gonna throw up?"

"Doubtful," I replied, although it came out more like "dowful." I rarely got sick to my stomach.

"That's good. Here we are." Eden got the door open and helped me inside. I made an immediate if sloppy beeline for the bed, sprawling on top of the covers.

"You want some water?"

"Sure," I replied sleepily. "I should take my shoes off."

She gave a soft chuckle. "Yeah, probably. I'll give you a hand."

"Thanks." Gentle hands removed my shoes and then helped me get under the covers. I reached out and curled my fingers around her wrist. "You're awesome," I said with the unfiltered sincerity that only comes with lots of alcohol consumption. "I'm glad we're friends."

A pause and then, "Me too."

CHAPTER TWENTY-FOUR

"How are you feeling?" Eden peered down at me as I did my best to burrow back under the covers and ignore my alarm that told me it was time to get up and go to work.

"Did I do or say anything stupid last night?"

"Only if you count telling the bartender that he looked like Chris Hemsworth and asking if you could see his mighty war hammer."

Groaning, I pulled the covers over my head. "I didn't. Tell me I didn't."

She flashed me a wicked grin, ducking when I threw one of my pillows at her. She made up for it by handing me a cup of coffee from the Keurig to tide me over until I could get a better cup elsewhere.

Whatever other crappy heritage I'd inherited from my parents, one of the pluses was an apparently iron stomach and a constitution that laughed off the other ill-effects of alcohol. It would be nice if my resistance to hangovers also included an inoculation against saying things I might regret later, but, oh well.

Jumping into the shower, I washed away the last of the mojito cobwebs from my brain, letting hot water sluice over me before ending with a cool rinse that finished the wake-up job that the coffee had started. I then threw on yoga pants and a pale lavender T-shirt with the words "I'm a delicate fucking flower" on the front, pulled on athletic shoes, and grabbed my tote bag. Eden, meanwhile, brewed a cup of coffee for herself and lounged on the sofa, legs curled up underneath her. She looked like a 1940s movie star in her pink satin pajamas, impossibly fresh-faced. Especially that early in the morning.

"What are you gonna do while I work?" I asked, tossing my phone into my tote bag and heading to the door.

"Well," Eden said, taking a sip of her coffee, "I thought I'd check out a few tattoo parlors and see what I can dig up on our friend LeRoy." She smiled slyly. "Sound like a plan?"

"A plan only slightly less awesome than you," I replied sincerely. "I'll call you from set when I can, okay?"

†

> No real info on LeRoy. Store is relatively new, he hasn't pissed anyone off enough to badmouth him. Except Barney at Dark Art says he's a dick. Does that count?

I texted back, standing in the shade of a cypress, out of the bright morning sun.

> Hell if I know. Thanks for doing the legwork. See you later.

"Important?"

I turned to see Leandra smirking at me, all voodoo hot-to-trot in her white dress, which matched my current wardrobe.

"Maybe," I replied neutrally.

"But not as important as making me look good, yes?"

I laughed. I couldn't help it. "Seriously, Leandra? There are so many things in life that are more important than making you look good, but luckily for you, my job right now is doing just that. If I answer a text or a call in my spare time, it is none of your business. Are we clear?"

She growled. A real liquid growl, like a big cat would make in the wild, a lion in the veldt. I could see the hair—fur—on her arms stand on end as she stood straighter, taller, and took a step toward me.

"And stop trying to make yourself look big." I shook my head. I was *so* not gonna play submissive kitty. "It's just silly and I am not getting in a cat fight with you." I stood my ground as she took one more step in my direction. Her irises shimmered, flashing gold, and her pupils grew long and slitted like a cat's.

All I could hear in my head was Cartman from South Park's voice saying, "Bad kitteh!" and that was enough to make me laugh. Which didn't go over well. Cats do love to stand on their dignity.

Tough shit.

"He's mine," Leandra growled. "Just remember that." I didn't need to ask who she was talking about.

Did we just experience a wrinkle in time and jump back to high school?

"You could just pee on him, y'know." I spoke in a cheerful undertone.

"Only males mark their territory that way," she replied in all seriousness.

"Everything okay, ladies?" Cayden appeared as if out of nowhere. He looked as if he'd stepped out of the cover of an old men's adventure magazine—olive-drab cotton shirt, khaki pants tucked into well-worn leather boots. He even wore a sizeable knife tucked into a scabbard on his belt.

I suspected he knew he'd interrupted a disagreement. Bad feelings and malice leave traces in the air, no matter how good the acting talents involved.

I'm not sure if Leandra would have pushed the issue any further if Cayden hadn't appeared. Sure, I could take her, but probably not without hurting her. I was on this film to prevent her from putting herself in any danger of being injured or bruised. Oh, the rich, rich irony.

"Lee, the extras for the voodoo ritual scenes are wrapping up in wardrobe and makeup," Cayden said. "We need to make sure their placement doesn't interfere with the initial physical confrontation between Marie and Perrine, so I'll need you and Angelique to run the choreography while the second AD wrangles them into place." He turned to Leandra. "Why don't you come inside the house and have some coffee? No need for you to be out here until it's time to do close-ups."

Leandra pouted. I couldn't stand that expression on anyone older than five and even then, it was questionable. Cayden, however, seemed to find it acceptable. Maybe that was because she'd sidled up to him and was now running a finger up and down one well-muscled arm. Not that I cared about his build.

"Don't you want me to stay on set to help keep your spirits… up?"

Angelique, fresh and gorgeous in a white cotton shift, came out of the house just in time to catch Leandra's question, and promptly stuck a finger in her mouth and mimed throwing up. I immediately felt better.

"How did you two get along when you were kids?" I asked her as soon as Leandra had moved out of earshot.

"When we were younger I used to drive Leandra crazy, always following her around, wanting to dress like her, be like her." Angelique gave a rueful smile and shook her head. "I wanted to *be* her."

"What happened?"

She shrugged. "I grew up and developed better taste."

"Or recognized a lost cause," came Leandra's voice behind us. "Smart little kitten knew she was outclassed." She gave a little laugh and sauntered off toward the house. I could practically see a tail swish back and forth.

Note to self. Earshot for shifters was slightly further away than I'd thought.

"Bitch," Angelique muttered. "One of these days I swear I'm gonna jerk a knot in her tail."

The extras started trickling out of the house, where makeup and wardrobe were staged, until there was a small crowd out back. There were people of all ages, from little kids to a woman who had to be over eighty. They all wore a variation on white shifts, skirts or pants and tops, as voodoo *serviteurs* would have worn in the 1800s.

Two things were true of everyone there. They were all excited to be a part of the film, and they all looked like they were related. Same strong cheekbones, a certain slant to the eye that screamed feline, and the same grace that both Angelique and Leandra had in abundance. Even the little ones had it, although they had the same kind of ungainly bumbling style of play as kittens. They would tackle one another, and pop up again like gravity did not exist for them.

I watched in amusement as the cubs tumbled around

on the ground, then dashed up into a tree, the pursuer becoming the pursued, and then switching back again in seconds. I briefly wondered what would happen if I married a shifter. Would I end up with a kid that was part kitten or cub? That might be fun. But would they need diapers *and* litter boxes? Never mind, too much work.

I watched the cubs tumbling and rolling around for a few minutes, trying to catch the moment when their human form morphed into feline. The sounds of little kids giggling and cubs making those adorable nurgling growling noises were too cute for words, especially when combined with their antics on the grass. A YouTube sensation waiting to happen, if the supernatural and normal could handle the collision.

I heaved a sigh of contentment, feeling a rare moment of happiness that I was lucky enough to be part of both worlds. If Tia would just get in contact, things would be about perfect right now.

One of the cubs evaded a pounce by one of its kin, rolling into my legs. I laughed, reaching down to scoop it up into my arms. Its tawny fur was spotted, four stubby little legs waving in the air as I cradled it upside down, dropping a quick kiss on its triangular nose. It stopped squirming, a deep rumbling purr vibrating through its entire body. As I watched, the fur shortened, the nose lengthened while the whiskers retracted, and soon I found myself holding a chubby little girl with large green-gold eyes and a grin so mischievous and adorable that it melted even my hard heart.

Okay, yeah, my heart isn't particularly hard, but I've never been much for kids. Kids that are crossed with kittens, however...

Oh my god, ridiculously cute.

She reached up and threw her arms around my neck,

rubbing her cold and wet nose against mine, the rumbling of her purr still vibrating through her.

"You are disgustingly cute," I said. "It shouldn't be legal."

The little werecub giggled, morphed back into a feline, and clambered up onto my shoulder. Her claws dug in as she pushed off, leaping back to the ground.

"Ouch," I said with no real heat, watching as my little pal was pounced on by her playmates.

"Lee, you ready?"

I turned my attention back to the job at hand.

†

As the Thaumaturge grew larger, it explored the boundaries of its new home. While it had plenty of space in the water, it grew hungry and bored. Wildlife had started to avoid its territory. It reached further, trying to find an opening in the invisible yet solid barrier that surrounded it.

It discovered two things.

If it stretched its tendrils deep enough in one direction, there was a tiny little opening below the muck in the bottom of the lagoon. It could only send out very small pieces of itself, but that was enough to catch the occasional unsuspecting frog or fish swimming on the other side.

Then it also discovered if it reached up in the same area, there was another, larger hole where it could crawl along one of the cypress trees and its roots. It couldn't hear, but it could sense. Something was moving on the other side. The Thaumaturge stretched further…

†

Angelique leaped up in the cypress tree, landing in a little crouch on the overhanging branch with the effortless ease of… well, of a cat. It was a great stunt, one that would require wirework for most non-supes, myself included. I had seen similar things done where the filmmakers rolled the film backwards, but I always thought that looked cheesy. This, on the other hand, was pure poetry in motion. I'd forgotten how much fun it was to work on a film like this, even if some scenes could only be filmed in secret, remote second unit locations to avoid the public eye.

Devon gave Cayden a satisfied nod. They conferred while Angelique collapsed onto the branch with her arms and legs hanging off, looking for all the world like a leopard lounging on a tree limb.

"That was pretty much perfect," Cayden said. "But let's get one more like that for safety."

Angelique gave a thumbs-up from her prone position on the branch.

In the water underneath, ripples spread out in concentric rings as something leaped out of the water and fell back in again, a small fish or maybe a frog.

Pushing herself back up to her hands and knees, Angelique pushed off with her legs and cleared the water to land on solid ground. She made it look easy.

I gave her a high-five.

"Why doesn't Marie do things like this?" Leandra said with a frown. She'd stayed inside for all of ten minutes before coming back out to watch the action. "I don't want Perrine to be more graceful than Marie." She threw a dissatisfied glance in my direction as if saying, "See what I have to work with?"

"Leandra, darlin'," Devon began, barely hiding his impatience. "We talked about this before."

I wasn't too surprised to hear it. I bet she'd tried to get me fired already.

"We talked about it, but I still don't understand why you want Marie to seem less than her rival."

"Perrine is younger, not as experienced," Cayden

interjected. "Marie's strength doesn't come from flashy tricks or trying to defeat her rival by leaping all over the place." I saw him drop a quick wink in Angelique's direction. "She is strong. Stronger inside, and she's building up that strength while Perrine tires herself out." He put his hands on her shoulder. "Don't worry. Lee is going to make you look exceptional when Marie fights. There will be no doubt in the audience's mind who is the true Voodoo Queen."

"Taking the whole thing a little too seriously, our Leandra is," Angelique whispered next to me.

"No kidding," I whispered back. "Hey, when you jerk that knot in her tail, can I help?"

We both started laughing.

A sudden screech sent all of our heads whipping around toward the cypress tree. Three of the shifter kids had taken advantage of the brief lull in filming to clamber up it, trying to imitate Angelique's stunt. Two of them tumbled out of the tree to the ground, morphing from cubs to little boys as we watched, while the third, my little pal still in her cub form, huddled on a branch above, one that stuck out over the water. She stared below with wide eyes, her tail puffed out the size of a small Christmas tree.

"What now?" Angelique uttered. "I swear, those cubs are more trouble than—"

"Something is trying to eat Tikka!" shouted one of the boys.

The cub gave a high piercing wail.

As we watched, something that might've been a snake slithered up the cypress trunk, curling around tree limbs and branches, headed toward the cub.

"Oh my God," Angelique breathed in horror. "It's one of those goddamn boas!"

The three of us dashed over to the edge of the water,

staring up as the cub, apparently frozen in place, wailed again, hissing and spitting in between cries of fear.

Cayden turned to Angelique. "You get Tikka. I'll take care of the snake."

Angelique leaped up the tree, shifting form halfway as she did so. And as fast as she moved, the snake was faster. I couldn't tell if it was its mouth or what, but it snapped out, grabbing the cub around its midsection. Angelique's scream of panic and fury pierced the sky. In seconds, Cayden pulled a wicked-looking knife out of the scabbard on his belt and hurled himself into the air like an action hero, grabbing onto a tree limb with one strong hand, muscles in his arm and shoulders flexing as he brought the knife edge across in a flashing arc, slicing into the snake below. He stabbed it several times until he succeeded in cutting the thing in two. The cut piece went limp and, as it fell, still wrapped around the helpless cub, Angelique reached out, grabbing Tikka by the scruff. The piece of boa fell to the ground, and Cayden dropped back down next to it.

Except it wasn't a part of a snake. There was no mouth, no eyes, nothing but rubbery gray tentacle, like that of a squid or an octopus, but with no suckers. Even as we watched, it dissolved into liquid that rapidly evaporated in the heat.

"Tikka!" One of the women came running over, scooping up the squalling cub in her arms. It was an odd déjà vu of the encounter with the seaweed dragon, Cayden once again heroically saving a child.

Before we could all breathe a collective sigh of relief, there was another yell from the cypress tree, from Angelique this time. Even as we watched, another mud-colored tentacle whipped up the tree, wrapped around her ankle, and jerked Angelique off the branch and into the water below. Except

I didn't see her hit the water and there were no ripples circling out to show where she'd fallen in. She had vanished.

Cayden and I exchanged a quick look. Scrambling up the roots of the cypress, I pulled myself up by one of the lower branches—less graceful than a shifter, but just as efficient—until I was on the same branch that Angelique had been perched on, Cayden right behind me. The branch easily bore both of our weights.

Using my arms to balance like a tightrope walker, I made my way out to the end of the branch and looked down. What I saw was almost beyond belief.

The pond was below me, but it was as if an invisible shield cut it in half, creating two totally different bodies of water. While the water on one side was smooth and glassy, the water directly below was a sickly gray-green, roiling as Angelique thrashed in the grip of something I could not see beyond the tentacles wrapped around her waist and legs. My mind skipped back to when I had looked out over the water the first time I was here. How the ripples had radiated out in half circles instead of full—and how something had spilled blood in the water.

"Angelique!" I yelled.

She looked up, eyes wild, nostrils flaring in panic, and her arms and hands now the furred and claw-tipped legs and paws of a large predator. She used her razor-tip claws to shred at the thing trying to pull her under the water.

Dark fluid bubbled out where her claws slashed the tentacles. It wasn't blood as we knew it and I couldn't tell if she was hurting the thing or not. I did know that we had to get her out of there because I could see more undulating tentacles breach the surface of the water, reaching for her.

"Here." Cayden tossed his knife to me and I caught it by

the hilt. Dropping to his knees, he hooked his legs around the branch and hung upside down. Reaching up, he grasped my ankles and then swung me down so I dangled below him, right above the frothing, bubbling water.

Even as I reached for her, Angelique went down again. She shot back up, spitting water and gasping for air. We locked gazes. Her eyes were filled with fear—she knew she was fighting for her life.

"Grab my hand!" I yelled as my body pendulumed back and forth above the Lovecraftian horror. Angelique reached out frantically with her free hand, fingertips brushing mine but not close enough to get a good grip. The creature whipped up tentacles, but before it could grab me, I cut it with Cayden's knife, not quite separating the gray slimy thing from the rest of it. I slashed again, this time having the satisfaction of seeing the suddenly limp tentacle fall back into the water. Another one almost immediately took its place, dragging Angelique once more below the surface, which was now turning an ominous red.

"No," I growled. I was not going to lose her. Not to another one of my fucking ancestors.

"Can you lower me any further?" I shouted up to Cayden.

Almost immediately I dropped down another few inches, and that was all I needed. This time, when Angelique's grasping hand rose up out of the water, I managed to grab her around the wrist. I held on for dear life, using the knife to hack at the tentacles holding her. I saw something else come out of the water, something that looked like it might be an eye, but I couldn't be sure. I stretched my arm out as far as I could, plunging the tip of the knife into it. A high-pitched squeal rose from the water, the sound mingling with a bubbling noise. At the same time, all of the tentacles gripping Angelique became momentarily flaccid.

"Pull us up! Pull us up!"

I had never been more thankful for my regime of weightlifting and all the other exercise I'd done all of my life, because I now held the full weight of Angelique's limp body with the strength of one arm alone. My arm felt like it was going to pop out of the socket, but I thought of Cayden who was bearing both our weights, gritted my teeth and held on, the knife clutched tightly in my right hand in case the thing tried again. Angelique's white dress was splattered with ribbons of red, and there were slashes and gouges along her arms and legs. I couldn't tell if she was breathing.

My own knees and shins scraped along the bark as Cayden pulled me back up onto the branch, reaching over me to grab Angelique's arm above my own grip on her wrist. Grunting with exertion, he took some of the weight off of me until all three of us were draped over the tree limb like wet laundry.

I wanted nothing more than to lie there, my arms and legs dangling down, and just rest for a minute, but below us the water started to bubble and froth again, and gray tentacles began questing toward us. "We need to get off this tree right now," Cayden barked.

I didn't argue with him. Pulling myself up so I was kneeling on the branch, I looped an arm around Angelique's waist while Cayden gathered both of her legs. I carefully scooched backward as he moved toward me, and between the two of us we slowly inched our way to safety.

Devon and the Ginga twins were at the base of the tree to catch Angelique's limp form as we lowered her down. Jumping to the ground, I followed as they carried her over to the porch and set her gently down on the wooden flooring.

Leandra ran over to Angelique's side. All traces of the bitchy diva were gone, replaced by frantic worry. She knelt by her unmoving cousin, tears creating runnels of mascara down her face.

"Is she dead?" she sobbed, reaching out to touch Angelique's face.

Please, no, I begged to any number of unspecified deities.

"We need to clear any water out of her lungs," Devon said. He gently but firmly moved Leandra out of the way so Ike could perform CPR. After less than a minute, Angelique began to cough and choke. All the tension—and any remaining strength—ran out of my body as she spat up a quantity of murky water.

Leandra's frantic sobs changed to deep, wrenching tears of relief as she gathered her cousin into a fierce hug. She looked up at me, green eyes filled with unmistakable gratitude. "You are part of our family now," she said simply.

I put a hand on her shoulder and gave a gentle squeeze, and then walked back to the tree where Cayden was just now climbing down.

"How is she?"

"She's alive," I said. "Other than that, I'm not sure. One of her ankles is pretty swollen."

He nodded. "We'll adjust the shooting schedule if necessary."

"Are we going to be able to film here?" I asked, shooting a wary glance up into the tree.

"I think so." He followed the direction of my gaze and added, "I took some temporary measures to seal off the opening until I have the proper tools to make it permanent."

"Do you know what that thing was?" I asked. "Or where that opening led to?"

"I have some ideas," Cayden replied, "but—"

"But it has something to do with whatever's coming through the Gates." The words came out of nowhere, cutting him off. He cast me a puzzled look.

"What gates?"

"He Who Eats Worlds is coming," I whispered. "It comes from beyond the stars, through the Gates opened by harbingers created through sorcerous transformation, through blood and tears, pain and suffering."

"Lee, what—"

I held up a hand as words continued to spill out of me. "This isn't the first time someone has tried to summon He Who Eats Worlds from his home. And once the way is open for Him, it will open for others who also dwell elsewhere. Our world will be devoured. Those who are not eaten will be enslaved, kept alive to breed more food for our new masters."

I stopped abruptly, like someone had hit the "off" switch on a recorder playback. My knees suddenly went weak, wobbly. I swayed and wilted like a southern belle.

Cayden caught me before I hit the ground face-first.

CHAPTER TWENTY-FIVE

There are many horrible ways to die. Some might argue there are no good ways, but some are kinder and gentler than others.

The deaths offered by the four harbingers as they cut a deadly swath through New Orleans from their incubation tombs to the ceremonial grounds hidden in the swamps were not kind or gentle. If they had broken free during daylight hours, perhaps they would have been stopped. Or perhaps more people would have died. As it was, some parts of the city didn't close until the dark hours of the soul—a bad time to encounter creatures with origins as dark as theirs.

Born out of unbearable pain and fear, the harbingers had taken over all that used to belong to their hosts, who were now little more than pain-maddened husks carried along by the newfound appetites of the harbingers. The four—the Lucifer, the Haruspex, the Augury, and the Adjurix—carved their own paths, instinct guiding them the quickest way to their destination, but they all found sustenance. The corpses they left behind did not concern them.

The bodies the Lucifer left in its path looked as though they had been microwaved, skin blackened and flaking on the outside, the whites of the eyes gone as if they'd exploded from the inside, and they glowed an unhealthy green. Even if someone had the slightest inkling of what was happening and why, it would be too late to make a difference.

The *Adjurix*—what was once Tiffany— left behind several rotting bodies, the flesh and organs dissolving as if the victims had all gotten a super-accelerated dose of Ebola.

Outside of Lafayette Cemetery No. 2, a couple of gangbangers stumbled across the body of one of their friends who'd gone around the corner to relieve himself and met the *Haruspex*. Weird sucker marks pocked his flesh. His heart, liver, and intestines had been ripped out. What flesh was left was leached of all color.

As for the *Augury*, it took to the sky, its spiky black wings glistening with amniotic fluid. Its flight was unsteady at first, but then the mouth at its core opened wide as it passed over an old man sitting out on his back porch, enjoying a pipe in the quiet of early morning. The pipe was found by his granddaughter a few hours later, the only clues to his fate a few ugly black feathers covered in a thick fluid, and the hand still clutching the pipe. Her screams woke up the neighbors, even though this was a neighborhood used to screams in the night.

The harbingers fed, gaining strength both for their journey and for the task ahead. They grew strong on flesh and blood, and on the fear and pain of their victims as they made their way ever closer to the Veil.

†

With the help of his sorcery, LeRoy watched their progress in the surface of the *Thaumaturge's* pond. This was something LeRoy realized he'd missed before. His surgically created harbingers, while they'd suffered the torments of the damned up until their transformations, had not fed. Had not been able to spread the fear so necessary, so sweet to He Who Eats Worlds. Maybe this was why things had gone so badly back in the 1830s. Maybe he would have failed even if Lily Chouette had not discovered his secret before he'd had a chance to complete the ritual. Perhaps it was just as well he hadn't had the chance to complete it—if the Elder God had been displeased with his method of summoning, there would have been no reward—only a slow, painful death as one of the Elder God's first meals. And while it would be a great honor to feed Him, LeRoy preferred this honor to go to someone else. Anyone else, really, as long as it was not him.

His wife, Delphine, would have been easy to give up. He had, in fact, offered her to He Who Eats Worlds as soon as it was clear the harbingers had not been successful at summoning him. The offering had not been accepted, however, and LeRoy had been forced to feed Delphine to the hungry harbingers before they looked to him for sustenance.

No, he would not make that mistake again.

The timing had been bad—Delphine had insisted on throwing one of her tedious dinner parties for the local Creole society. He could not skip the dinner without an excuse, so his plan was to plead a bad humor of the stomach, slip out, and ride quickly to the bayou for the ritual. The harbingers had been kept at his secret dwelling on the edge of Bayou Ef'tageux. He'd created these in the bayou rather than at his home, so he would not have to transport them to the Veil. Too much risk in that. He also hoped that creating them within the influence of the Veil and the Gates would mean success. He simply needed to give himself enough time to travel to Bayou Ef'tageux and enact the summoning ritual before midnight.

It would have worked. It should have worked. Instead, one of their slaves—ungrateful animal—had deliberately set a fire in the kitchen, ending the dinner party in chaos. Even worse, it had led to the discovery of his trial patients in the attic when, intent on rescuing the household slaves, the inevitable good Samaritans intruded. It was bad luck that the first person up there was Lily Chouette, who had been haunting the streets near their mansion ever since her lover had vanished. He had come to the mansion to give the girls piano lessons and, one day, never left. She hadn't believed their story that Étienne had left as usual after the lesson. But ultimately the authorities chose to believe the rich and powerful LaLauries over an octoroon, even a free one.

The cursed bitch had somehow known where to find him, find the Veil. She had also somehow managed to destroy the harbingers before the ritual had been completed. Her strength and skill had been more than human, and their structural integrity had not held.

He had barely escaped the same fate, slipping away into the waters of the swamp, risking alligators, copperheads, and whatever other creatures lurked in the bayou. All preferable to facing the grief-fueled wrath of Lily Chouette. He did not think she was entirely human.

And to see that same face with those dark violet eyes… to have her knocking on the door of his shop? It was not to be tolerated. Lily's smart-mouthed descendent would not spoil this for him. He would make sure of that.

†

I was woken up at 7 A.M. by the sound of my text notification going off. "Winter is coming. Winter is coming."

I really need to change that, I thought, reaching for my phone. It was from Micah.

> Yo, Lee. Downstairs waiting for you. What's up?

Huh? I texted back:

> I thought we had the day off.

> Nope. Cayden and Devon wanna work on some new fight stuff. Thought you knew.

Well, hell. So much for resting.

> Give me ten minutes and I'll be right down.

With no joy in my heart, I got out of bed, took the quickest shower of my life, and threw on yoga pants, tank top, and running shoes. I left a quick apologetic note for Eden, still soundly sleeping, letting her know our plans for a day of playing tourist had been spoiled by my workaholic director and stunt coordinator, and then ran out the door.

Micah and his Cadillac were waiting for me outside the hotel.

"Hey," I said as I got into the front seat.

The Caddy slipped out easily into the traffic. Micah was a damn good driver, good enough that I didn't get all control-freaky and push on an imaginary brake pedal while hanging onto the "oh Jesus" handle.

I yawned, my jaw cracking with the force of it. Between my concern for Angelique, worrying about Tia, wondering what the hell Cayden and I had gone up against yesterday, and another horrific dream involving tentacles, dismembered bodies, and voodoo drums, I'd barely slept.

Micah chuckled. "You want me to stop for some coffee?"

"Slept like crap," I admitted. "Some nights there's not enough ibuprofen or Epsom salts in the world to take the aches out. And yes on the coffee, please."

He swung into a little drive-thru kiosk on the outskirts of the city. One side of it was for cars, and the other for pedestrians. There were a half-dozen cars waiting their turn in the drive-thru lane, but only one person at the walk-thru window. "Probably faster if we park," Micah observed. "How 'bout I go get it and you can wait here and maybe catch a few winks."

I gave him a grateful thumbs-up, asked for a Depth Charge with three shots, cream, and sugar, and shut my eyes. I didn't think I'd slept, but when the car door slammed, I jumped, eyes flying open. "Sorry about that," Micah said with a laugh. "Guess you really needed that nap."

"Guess I did."

He handed me my Depth Charge. "Three shots, cream, and sugar. You are gonna be flyin' high after this." I sipped my coffee while Micah turned the stereo on, pushing in one of his zydeco tapes. Between the caffeine, sugar, and lively music, you'd think I would've perked right up. Instead I found my eyelids drooping until they were too heavy to keep open any longer. I fell into a deep, dreamless sleep.

†

I woke up to a pounding headache and a mouth that felt like I'd eaten a bunch of stale rice cakes with nothing to wash them down—"dry" didn't begin to cover it. The air was stale, hot, and humid, and the sound of buzzing flies was impossibly loud. Sweat dripped off my face. I was lying on my back, something sharp digging into my lower back.

What the hell?

"What the hell?" I said out loud. My voice emerged as a hoarse croak. When I finally mustered up the energy to open my eyes the first thing I saw was Micah's concerned face hovering over me. Behind him I saw an ancient-looking shovel leaning against a wooden wall. We were in some sort of tool shed.

I tried pushing myself up on my hands, but things instantly started spinning. I lay back down and shut my eyes again until the spinning stopped.

"Lemme help you," Micah said. He put an arm around my shoulders and helped me sit up.

"I think I'm going to be sick," I mumbled.

"Here." He handed me a can of ginger ale. "It'll help."

I took a few deep breaths and managed to keep the nausea at bay long enough to take a sip of the soda. It was lukewarm, but right now it tasted as good as craft beer.

"What happened?" I asked when I was sure I wasn't going to throw up.

"Your breathing went all funny and you passed out in the car," Micah said.

"How long have I been out?"

"'Bout six hours, give or take."

"You've got to be kidding. Tell me you're kidding."

Micah shook his head. "Nope."

I groaned. My call time had been noon. We'd left the hotel at ten, stopped for coffee around 10:30. That meant it had to be at *least* four o'clock. "Where are Devon and Cayden?" I asked. "They're going to kill me for fucking up the schedule."

The door to the shed suddenly opened and watery light shone inside.

"You are indeed going to die," a familiar voice said from behind me. "But they won't be the ones to kill you."

CHAPTER TWENTY-SIX

LeRoy stood in the doorway, towering above me. Micah's expression turned to fear.

I pushed myself unsteadily up to hands and knees, then got to my feet with Micah's help. I'd be damned if I'd cower on the ground while this asshole tried to intimidate me.

"It's obvious we're not on set." I kept my voice steady.

"Smart girl," LeRoy said with a condescending smile. "We are still in Bayou Ef'tageux… but now we're in the part that lies beyond the Veil." I could tell he was waiting for me to ask what the Veil was, so I didn't. That didn't stop him from telling me.

"The Veil is like a curtain," he intoned grandly. "Something only a powerful few can conjure to separate the mundane from the mystical. The earthly from the arcane. It can be left open to allow passage between the two, or sealed, as it is now, to insure the ritual is not disturbed. And now," he added with a smirk, "allow me to introduce you to the harbingers. You've nothing to fear from them either… other than what they'll summon."

"He Who Eats Worlds," I supplied, taking a small bit of satisfaction at the frown of surprise on his face.

"How did you—" He stopped, shook his head. "Never

mind. It doesn't matter." He gestured with one hand toward the doorway. "After you."

I went outside, Micah still holding onto one arm as if afraid I'd fall without his support. And what lay outside the shed was almost enough to make my knees go weak.

We were in a clearing ringed with cypress trees. A large pond was at the center, but instead of the murky green of the bayou, this water shimmered. Rainbow colors, but a sickly rainbow, like an anemic oil slick. The plant life in the water and on the banks was equally bizarre, flourishing, with thick fronds and large leaves. Instead of healthy green and rich browns, the leaves were a flabby, leprous gray. The tree bark looked more like slime-encrusted scales and the Spanish moss like tiny writhing snakes. Unnatural things that should have died before they saw the light of day. Although, looking up at the sky and the diffused light that made it through the bloated trees, I wondered what sort of daylight, if any, had shone on this part of the bayou in recent times.

This place was not sane. If I were religious, I'd say it wasn't hallowed. But I wasn't… and it was worse. Somehow I knew it was no longer part of this world either. And neither, I thought, were the two dozen or so people ranging around the clearing.

"The Castro family," I said softly. Micah nodded, his expression sickly and scared.

"They're cultists," he whispered.

If Cletus the slack-jawed yokel had mated with a frog and spawned dozens of slack-jawed chinless offspring, they'd look like the Castros. We're talking an entire inbred family, generations maybe, of huge swamp-green eyes, almost non-existent noses, thick lips that owed nothing to collagen, and… well, no chins. Batrachian didn't even begin to cover it.

Even worse, though… the things that stood on makeshift

wooden daises at equidistant points around the pond. There were five of them.

"Ah yes, the harbingers," LeRoy said in pleased tones. "First, the Adjurix."

The harbinger on LeRoy's right was a parody of human form, with parts of its sagging limbs either strangely bloated or elongated and twisted. The distorted skin hung loosely on the skeleton within, irregular bags of flesh bulging like water balloons. Noxious vapors constantly rose from the pores in its skin. The ghastly, cloying corpse reek of its body was horrifying, as if its entire insides had broken down and collapsed internally, only to be liquefied, and finally putrefied in some unspeakable alchemical process.

He pointed to the next one. "The Haruspex."

The Haruspex was barely recognizable as human-shaped anymore—it looked more like a walking, engorged heart muscle with outstretched arms. With every loud thumping beat of its massive pulse, its entire body, bloated and grossly veined, pulsated as well—changing color from a sickly pale oyster to a flush of dark red. Its once-human face was lost now, sunken down into the swollen flesh—except for the vestiges of the mouth, which had devolved into an oversized, crude lamprey maw, just like the thing's fingertips and palms of the hands. What eyes it once had were now little more than a pair of beady crimson slits, like open wounds.

"The Lucifer."

This harbinger looked like nothing so much as a mummified corpse, although instead of wrappings, it was covered in ragged layers of dried-out papery skin, a brittle husk the same gray, lifeless color of ancient burial rags. In the black pits that had been its eyes and mouth came an eerie white ghost-light glow that pierced the overall pale azure glow that came off of its entire body like a ghastly beacon of doom.

"The Augury."

The Augury looked as though a human being had been shaped, pulled, and twisted like saltwater taffy, its body and limbs elongated. Greasy black feathers had grown through the skin, forming long, powerful wings ending in clawed hands with exquisitely elongated fingers. The unnaturally wide mouth on its gargoyle face was filled with cruel teeth, slavering continuously.

"And of course, the Cantrix." LeRoy's voice was filled with a sick, gloating tone as he gestured to the harbinger directly across the water.

I looked at the Cantrix. What seemed to be a silken cloak of pale orange and gray velvet was, in fact, its enormous moon-moth wings. Its wasp-waisted torso was supported by three pairs of limbs. There was nothing human about its two upraised beetle-like forelimbs, but the chitinous arms and legs weren't fully insect yet. One arm, in fact, was still free of the orange and gray membranous cover that had taken over the rest of the body. I recognized the fragile jeweled tattoo that laced around the wrist.

Oh god. Tia.

Slowly I raised my eyes to the thing's head, looking into its eyes and seeing the half-mad gaze of my friend. The folds of its wings had grown into her body, become a part of it, even as parts of her were still contained in a cocoon of tightly woven filaments that reminded me of crystalized spun sugar. As I watched in horror, part of the cocoon that swaddled the left arm fell off as her fingers flexed, showing how the threads had gone into the skin. God, that must have hurt.

LeRoy nodded as if reading my mind. "The harbingers

can only be created when their hosts feel fear and the kind of agonizing pain we can only imagine. The more horrific and profound their suffering, the stronger the harbingers and their aspects."

"Their aspects?" My tone was dull. I had failed to save Tia and it was most likely my insistence that she try to find out what LeRoy was doing that had brought her into his grasp. If she hadn't gone back to the tattoo shop, she would still... she would still be Tia and not this poor creature.

"Tia had to suffer a lot in a much shorter time," LeRoy went on, enjoying my horror. "Losing the original Cantrix was a blow. It shouldn't have been able to leave its womb until I summoned it. And it shouldn't have been able to be killed so easily."

"Surprise, surprise," I muttered.

He shot me a dark glance. "This is not the first time you and yours have interfered. But it will be the last. He Who Eats Worlds will be brought through the gates tonight and you will know what it is to suffer."

I looked into the pain-glazed eyes of what had been Tia and felt a small ember of rage light inside me and begin to blaze.

"Why do you want to summon something called He Who Eats Worlds?" I asked, keeping my voice level. "I mean, what is the percentage for you when this thing is going to bring eternal torment to all mankind... or just eats us? What do you get out of this?"

"The Old Ones are not without gratitude to those who help them."

I gave a derisive snort. LeRoy either didn't hear or ignored it as he continued. "He Who Eats Worlds has been trapped for millennia in a dimension he long since devoured, and those who free him shall rule what is left of humanity."

"Unless he eats it all," I shot back. "The only thing worse than evil is stupid evil. And the only thing worse than stupid evil is gullible stupid evil. Congrats. You win the triple crown here."

He frowned. "I want you to bear witness, bitch. What your ancestress stopped before, you will experience firsthand. If I had known you were here, I would have gladly chosen you to replace the Cantrix and let you feel the exquisite agony as the tattoo took over your body from the inside out. As you lay in one of the oven vaults, unable to move or scream, feeling things pierce your organs and muscles. Thirst and hunger would be ever-present, driving you mad until all you would think about was a cessation of the pain and the hunger. That would ensure that when you were summoned to the place of the ritual you'd rip a swath of death all the way here. Fear and pain, both the hosts and their victims."

I flashed on the dream where I'd stumbled on the experiments in the attic of the LaLaurie mansion. That terrible dream…

"It was you," I whispered, like some idiot heroine in a Gothic romance. "You tried this before. You're Louis LaLaurie. You turned those people into monsters—"

"Slaves, not people," he corrected me.

"You are one fucked-up little monkey." Disgust dripped from my voice. "How did you justify using them?"

He shrugged. "They are subhuman at best. Not like us."

"And these?" I gestured toward the harbingers, feeling an unearthly heat pulsing from the Lucifer as I did. "I've seen their pictures. They were human. I knew—know Tia. How do you justify that?"

"I don't have to justify it." LeRoy's smug expression nearly caused me to lose what little calm I still clung to. I so wanted to punch him in the middle of his face.

"That you waste your time lamenting the fate of those destined to take this path shows me you are no better than your ancestress. She too mourned the fates of those chosen to open the gates."

Étienne may have been my ancestress's lover, but through the dreams I had shared both her joy in his company and her grief at the discovery of his fate. I'd felt her outrage at the inhuman horrors that had been inflicted on those in the LaLaurie attic. And her fury that Louis LaLaurie and his wife had escaped punishment.

"Did you really return to France?" I asked slowly. "Or did you plant that rumor, as well as the one blaming Delphine for your work?"

LeRoy laughed. Long and hard, a rich, full sound that should have been appealing. Instead it made my skin crawl.

"Delphine was not a perjured innocent," he said when his laughter finally died down. "She handed over her slaves to me without a second thought and never asked what became of them. Never questioned the fresh graves. Delphine only cared that her needs were met. Anything else was so far removed from her world, it might as well have been a fairy tale. Today you would call her one of the one percent."

"What does that make you?"

He smiled. "Divide that one percent into ten thousand more, and I am the only one who will be left standing. The rest, if they survive the coming of the Old One, will serve me."

The harbinger that had once been Tia made an incoherent sound. I could swear she said, "Kill me." Or maybe that was just wishful thinking on my part because I didn't know how long I could stand to let Tia's harbinger live.

"I'm sorry I got you into this," Micah whispered, his voice quavering in fear. Something about it didn't ring true, however, like someone acting a part rather than *being* the character.

I looked over at the production assistant. Suddenly I noticed the huge greenish-blue eyes. The nose, small, but not Japanese anime small... still, it was tiny. Full lips, sensuous under a certain light, but here... he fit right in. Even his chin seemed to be receding as I watched.

Oh, fuck me gently with a chainsaw, I thought. I'd been had.

"You're one of them," I stated bluntly.

Indecision flickered across his features. I guess he'd been playing the worldly innocent for so long he couldn't quite decide if continuing the charade was the way to go.

"Not one of them," he finally said. "Not wholly. They called me 'half-breed...'"

"That's all you ever heard," I whispered.

"How I learned to hate the word," Micah supplied with a friendly smile. "Yeah, you got me, Lee."

"You drugged my coffee."

"Yup."

"You really a love child of a swampy Hatfield–McCoy feud or was that just a fun story to spin?"

"Little o' both," he admitted cheerfully. "But I told it to you backwards. Momma wandered a little too close to Castro land when she was still pretty much just a cub. Couple of the young Castro bucks, they thought it would be fun to take turns with her, then let her loose in the swamp again. Probably figured she'd die before she made it back home, considering what they all done to her." He shrugged. "But she didn't. Momma made it out of the bayou back to Marcadet land. Got magicked back to health... more or less. Her mind was never much good after that. But even though her momma tried to talk her into getting rid of her unborn baby, she wouldn't hear of it." Micah heaved a sigh. "And, well, here I am." He gave me a sideways glance. "You don't look particularly surprised."

"Oh, please," I retorted. "I've worked in Hollywood more than long enough to spot a half-assed plot twist a mile away."

"Yeah, well, it was more than a plot twist—" he put a sarcastic spin on those words "—to me. Angelique was the only one of her family to treat me right when I was young. Rest of 'em…" He spat on the ground, which sucked up the fluid as if it was thirsty. "I can't wait to see them torn apart, their outsides ripped off and their insides eaten, all while they're still alive. I wanna hear their screams."

"What is it about the name He Who Eats Worlds makes you think you're not gonna be on the menu?"

Micah shrugged again, wearing that grin I used to think was kind of charming, but now made me want to punch him in the mouth.

"We'll just have to see about that."

The low croak of voices took on new excitement. The water started to bubble and froth like the world's skankiest Jacuzzi with the jets on high.

"Ah," LeRoy said with a pleased smile. "And here is the Thaumaturge!"

What came bubbling out of the lagoon looked like it should have had a job guarding the Mines of Moria. It looked like a crocodile and a kraken got busy bumping uglies, possibly had a threesome with the Blob, and spawned a truly fucked-up offspring. Even with the bulk of its body in the water, its shape rose higher than the others, topped by a long crocodilian head bowed in reverence, hanging downward like a hood. The rest of its massive body descended into formless protoplasm, merging with the water. In the gelatinous mass around its middle, parts of former meals were still visible floating in the viscous jelly. I saw bits of snakes, frogs, and the jaws of an alligator that had to be at least four or five feet long before it had been bitten in half.

†

It had lain in a stupor after it ate its mate. Millennia together, feeding on the worlds in this dark dimension, then they ran out of food, and the honeymoon period was over. Since it had devoured its mate, no other food had come its way. Between them, they had long since eaten everything in this dimension. Truly, if it had not acted first, its mate would have fed upon it.

Their children had long ago been sacrificed on the altar of their parents' appetite.

After a while, there was nothing. No food. No light. No offspring. No mate. Just the endless ocean's sterile, stagnant depths. It became lonely. Hungry. It willed itself to shut down. To die before hunger and loneliness drove it mad. It fell into a torpor and slept, dreaming strange, dark dreams of gluttony interspersed with more disturbing visions of a different world. A different dimension. One where its appetites were small. Harmless.

Now it floated listlessly in the thick jellied waters of its home-turned-prison, letting its massive bulk drift wherever the currents took it.

Then something caught its attention. Something new. Something pricking at the edges of its consciousness. A light, perhaps, shining toxic rays through the endless blackness. A song, cut short, the ululating discordant wailing calling it into the first gateway. A scent, a stench of rot, of flesh falling from the bone.

Sweet perfume.

A thrumming rhythm, a steady blood-drenched pulse that called to it, leaving a trace of millions of heartbeats along the way.

It had felt similar calls before. Had started to follow them, but the signals had abruptly stopped, the gates had slammed shut and the way lost.

But now… the gates were opening again. And the beacons were strong and clear, guiding the way.

†

"O Adjurix," LeRoy intoned grandly, "thou glittering censer in the cold void! Let thy fragrant incense of the sacrifice go out into the black gulf of the heavens! Bring forth they that dwell in the darkness beyond all sight and thought…"

"*Rrrth-naa'bthnk, okhyoi oth-mhhg'-gthaa sll'-ha*," croaked the cultists in unison.

The foul reek of the Adjurix rose into the air.

†

Oh, the lovely smell of putrescence. Death and decay, an odor that stirred its appetite for the first time in many decades. It let itself follow the enticing aroma and its promise of a delectable feast, drifting up through the waters until it passed through the first Gate.

†

"O Haruspex," LeRoy said, "Diviner of the Flesh, Sanguinary Summoner! Decrypt the secret messages of the pulsating blood-tide! Read the hidden glyphs inscribed in the carnal codex and draw forth their wisdom…"

"*Har-ne'nhhhngr, ikhuyah g'r'l-uh yll'oktmyoi!*" The cultists raised their voices like a chorus of lunatic frogs.

The Haruspex pulsed, the sound like a heartbeat in a hollow drum.

†

The dimension beyond the first Gate was sterile, devoid of life and sustenance, but the smell had now combined with a throbbing pulse, something vaguely remembered as a heartbeat. A life force. Which meant food.

It went through the second Gate.

†

"Burn for us, O Lucifer, Beacon of Discord and Madness!" LeRoy cried. "Dance in the language of the cold starry host and show us the path!"

"*Thar-a-na-k nafln'ghft, g'nafln'ghft m'ai oktmyoi k'-yar-na-k!*"

The radioactive glow that emanated from the Lucifer lit up the entire clearing, its reflection turning LeRoy's face a ghastly green.

†

Light. An unholy, sickly glow that shone like a welcoming beacon, combining with the pulsing heartbeat and the sweet odor of death, pulling it onward through yet another Gate, closer and closer to a dimension rich with food and… and something else. Something remembered on the edges of its consciousness. Something from long ago.

†

"O Augury, Sign of That to Come, Portent and Foretoken of the Unfolding, Signal the Opening of the Way…"

"*Ka-dish-tugn-h'gua, gelac'voh'ma!*" came the answering chorus.

The Augury moved its wings in answer to LeRoy's invocation, creating subtle vibrations that nonetheless reached over time and space.

†

It felt something… ripples in a pond after a rock is cast into the water.

Subtle, but inescapable.

It went through the fourth Gate.

†

"Lift up thy voice, O Cantrix!" LeRoy practically sang the words. "Intone the jubilant song of pain throughout the gates between the worlds! Call forth that which waits upon our voice!"

"Ulnph-leg-eth, ftoku-gthaa gl'tkhabah'om vulgt-lagln!"

A weird burr sounded in the Cantrix's throat, building into an ear-splitting wail that pierced dimensions.

†

It had almost reached that point of frustration when something pierced through the veils of time and space, through the dimensional walls. A sound. A... singing, a voice raised in such pure agony that it pierced the very folds of time and space. Beautiful, it thought, and slowly drifted up as the sound pulled it up and through the fifth Gate.

It was almost home.

†

"By thy craft and might, O Thaumaturge!" LeRoy shrieked. "Shape the miracle! Work the passage and invoke the Final Gate and draw forth That Which Must Emerge"

"Wgah-'nthkhu, m'aig'thkhu ch'ng-luiu-gthaageb n'-thy-leii!
Wgah-'nthkhu, m'aig'thkhu ch'ng-luiu-gthaageb n'-thy-leii!"

The froggy chorus rose in volume, the last unintelligible words hitting my ears like bullets, while the Thaumaturge wavered octopus-like in the center of the circle, constantly stretching forth and retracting slug-like appendages in a hypnotic, swirling dance like a demonic carnival carousel. It responded to LeRoy's sorcerous commands, its movements somehow coordinating the ritual like an orchestra conductor.

That's when the shit really hit the fan.

CHAPTER TWENTY-SEVEN

It started as a speck hovering in the air above the crusty, scaled blob in the water, vibrating like a fly trapped in an invisible web. The vibrations increased, and the speck began expanding while at the same time going around and around in an ever-growing spiral, turning the air a dark and swirling cloud tinged with toxic greens and noxious grays. Wind whipped through the clearing, strong enough to catch and lift my braid. The end smacked Micah across the face with the thick ponytail holder. Despite everything, I smiled when he yelped in surprised pain.

The wind continued to rise, the sound blending with the Cantrix's song.

"Bring the woman here!"

Micah and one of the male cultists dragged me over to the platform where LeRoy stood, his voice rising above the unearthly wail coming from what used to be Tia and the answering shriek from the slowly expanding storm above the water. It looked as if a tornado had tipped over on its side, affording one a view of the inside as it spun. I half expected to see cows or the Wicked Witch of the West appear, but instead the thing just kept expanding, sucking the light out of the sky.

As it grew larger and the wind and the Cantrix shrieked ever louder, a truly foul smell emerged on the back of the warm, moist wind. Trash left out in the hot, humid sun. Rotting corpses, decayed flesh crawling with maggots. Mildew and mold. All these things and yet none of them—the putrid smell was not of this world. I would never complain about Langdon's breath again—if I lived to complain about anything.

The chanting increased in volume. The spiral deepened into a funnel, widening until it blocked out everything else. Suddenly the funnel ripped, and something began to emerge.

The Gate had opened.

The hands clutching my arms loosened as the cultist holding me went limp with terror. Guess seeing their precious Elder God wasn't all it was hyped up to be. He Who Eats Worlds wasn't pretty. Even the small glimpse we were getting as it worked its way through the Gate made that obvious.

It was the same noxious gray-and-green coloration as the plant life on this side of the Veil and the storm clouds, dripping with thick, gelatinous goo. Its skin had the texture of an adipocere corpse, as if it were rotting on the bone. Tentacles and random protrusions undulated in a jarring rhythm. Multiple eyes bulged on top of wriggling stalks above a wide chasm ringed with sharp, surprisingly small teeth that seemed to ripple inward in steady waves.

One Lovecraftian Elder God made to order.

"Oh, He Who Eats Worlds, whom I have summoned from across dimensions, through time and space, I offer you this woman as the first meal of many in your new home. Accept my humble offering and grant me a place at your side as you make this planet, this dimension, your kingdom."

Nothing about LeRoy's little welcoming speech was humble. He reeked of arrogance, his very tone and demeanor dripping with a sense of his own superiority. If I'd been He Who Eats Worlds, I'd have gobbled him up then and there.

Instead, the creature's eyestalks all turned, sending its multiple gaze in my direction. I gagged on the charnel-house stench that blasted out as the thing exhaled. Tentacles ribboned, unfurling like flags in a gale-force wind. Its mouth opened wide, impossibly so. Two of the tentacles undulated toward me. I was so screwed.

One tentacle slapped against the ground in front of me with a wet smack that shook the earth. The other waved and rippled like an enthusiastic pole dancer—

—and plucked the man on my right off his feet and into its mouth. I watched in horrified fascination as the teeth pierced the screaming man and then slowly, inexorably, fed him further down its gullet on the rippling escalator of the multiple rows of teeth. He vanished as his body hit the cutoff of the Gate. Thankfully, so did his screams.

Micah's slack fingers let go of my other arm completely as he took one stumbling step backward, and then another as the other tentacle lifted from the ground. I froze as it grazed one of my legs, the tip of the tentacle pausing and then almost caressing my calf. Then it coiled up like a fern before unfurling with blinding speed, wrapping itself around the production assistant's waist and pulling him off his feet. He screamed, his hands reaching out toward me as He Who Eats waved him in the air back and forth, as though it couldn't quite make up its mind what to do with him.

"Lee!" he wailed, all of his hate and hubris leached away by fear.

Acting on pure reflex, I reached for him, for the person I

thought he was before he betrayed me—and the rest of the planet. For the kid who'd uncomplainingly driven us back and forth, put up with all of our requests and demands—even some of Leandra's more unreasonable ones—on set. Micah, who I'd thought was my friend. I strained to reach him, my fingertips grazing his.

Then the tentacle retracted, carrying Micah straight into the mouth before I could do more than scream his name. I shuddered as he followed his Castro kinsman down the throat and into another dimension on the other side of the Gate.

There was no one holding me now, nothing to keep me where I was. And yet I didn't move, standing still as I stared up at He Who Eats Worlds, breathing through clenched teeth as the hell-stench wafted out of the Elder God's mouth.

I could have run, I suppose, but I don't know where I would have gone. The Veil was sealed, LeRoy had said so. Even though two of their own had just died horribly, the rest of the Castro clan showed no sign of running. If anything, the look of dumb worship on their slack-jawed faces had increased. No, they wouldn't let me get very far.

I stayed where I was and waited.

And then the back of my neck started itching as He Who Eats Worlds turned its full attention on me.

Mother…?

The thought penetrated my skull like a baseball bat hitting from the inside out, so loud I thought my ears would bleed. I cried out, put my hands over my ears and fell to my knees.

I could still hear LeRoy laugh.

Mother…

It was softer this time. As if the creature knew it had hurt me the first time.

Slowly, I took my hands away from my ears. Shut my eyes

so as to not see the hideous form in front of me, so I could see who *truly* spoke to me.

Tell me who you are, I silently beseeched it.

Mother, it said again, and then it showed me. A golden-sand beach. Water the color of lapis lazuli. Beautiful children playing under a golden sun, frolicking in the gentle waves. A little girl with long, dark curls reaching up to a woman who—

Who looked just like me.

This was not He Who Eats Worlds, an Elder God who had existed before my ancestress.

This hideous creature was one of Lilith's children.

Home now, it cooed, voice piercing my skull like iron spikes. I tried to ignore the mind-numbing pain and spoke to it again, silently.

You are home. What do you want?

Mother. Love. It gave a long quavering sigh. The smell was horrific.

Yes, I replied. *Love. What… What happened to He Who Eats Worlds?*

My mate? Nothing left to eat. He ate our children. I ate my mate.

Talk about a Dr. Seuss rhyme gone wrong. *Why did you answer the summons?*

I want Home. I want Mother. I want Love.

What else do you want?

Food. So hungry.

And there was the rub.

This monstrosity had been one of Lilith's original children by Ashmedai. Had been turned into this abomination by Yahweh's curse and had somehow ended up as an Elder God's live-in girlfriend in another dimension. Now all it wanted was home and its mother.

And to eat everything and everyone on the planet.

Well, hell.

You can't stay here. I didn't know if the sorrow I felt for the creature carried in my thoughts. I hoped so. I thought so, since its longing for its mother and home had pierced my heart.

Why? This is home. You are my mother.

I didn't argue the last. Trying to explain who I really was wouldn't help resolve this. *Because this world is not meant to be food for you.*

This is my home.

You've changed since you left, I said silently. *If you were to live here now, you would devour all life on this planet. I... I can't let you do that.*

But you are my mother. You feed me. You love me.

My heart cracked a little bit for this poor lost child. And my heart hardened even more against Yahweh, asshole god who'd condemn innocent children to such horrible fates simply because they were the offspring of someone who'd disobeyed him. What the hell, Yahweh?

I do love you. It wasn't exactly a lie, even if it wasn't the truth. *But I can't let you stay here.*

You would hurt me?

The betrayal in its voice hurt more than I would have thought possible.

You... You can go back to where you came from, I answered. *Live out your life there. I don't want to hurt you. But if you stay here, I won't have a choice.*

Mother. Its sorrow reverberated in my head.

"What are you waiting for? Devour her!"

LeRoy, still standing on his little platform above the harbingers, glared at me, face red with frustration. I imagined his expression was much like Yahweh's when Lilith had refused to go back to Adam.

The harbingers all stirred restlessly. Their part in the ritual was over and now they were probably hungry, just like the monster they'd helped summon. LeRoy ignored them. They'd done their job and now had no place in his attention.

What is this? Lilith's daughter asked.

This is the man who summoned you. He wants you to kill me.

All of its eyes swiveled toward LeRoy. He froze under the gaze of the creature he'd summoned, and then glared at me with centuries-long hatred.

"Kill her!" he screamed, spittle flying from his lips.

A tentacle lashed out. LeRoy threw himself to one side and it missed him by inches.

"You dare turn on me?" He got to his feet, brushing himself off as if his appearance mattered. "I summoned you. I created these harbingers to open the Gates that would allow you to come into this dimension. I did this. Me!" He pounded his chest for emphasis, like an angry gorilla. Behind him, the harbingers continued to stir uneasily.

The Cantrix—Tia—turned toward LeRoy, blind eyes somehow unerringly staring straight at him. That weird burr in her throat started again, the vibration building until another shriek burst from her throat. Not as ear-piercing or as ghastly as her last, but horrible and loud enough to make the other harbingers—even the Thaumaturge—turn in her direction… and then follow when she left her makeshift dais and started walking toward LeRoy, her steps horrible and lurching and deliberate.

At first LeRoy didn't move, his expression making it clear he couldn't believe his creations could mean him any harm. Guess the arrogant asshole was unfamiliar with Frankenstein and his monster. It was only when Tia reached him and reached *out* for him, the other five eagerly grasping for him as well, the Thaumaturge snaking its gelatinous tendrils out of the diseased soup of its home to brush the toes of LeRoy's polished shoes, that he realized he was in danger. That he'd lost his power over them.

And by then it was too late.

All six harbingers had their way with their creator. By the time the Thaumaturge dragged the now weakly screaming, dissolving man into its center mass, he'd experienced all the fear and pain he'd so willingly brought to their hosts. Even so, I don't think he truly believed his fate was sealed even as he disappeared, one grasping hand reaching toward the sky until it, too, vanished from sight as the Thaumaturge submerged under the thick, sickly gray-green liquid.

CHAPTER TWENTY-EIGHT

As their leader vanished under the water, the remaining Castro cult members stared in shock. This wasn't supposed to happen. It wasn't part of the script—if sicko doomsday cults even had scripts.

Before I could even think of what to do next, the creature squeezed yet further out of the Gate and began scooping up cultists and tossing them into its mouth like popcorn. The rest screamed, the sound a froggy chorus of the damned as they scattered, trying to run. They didn't get far, though, because LeRoy had closed the path into and out of the Veil. They scrabbled at seemingly thin air, trying to find an escape route. But they had nowhere to run.

Neither did I.

The creature finished snacking on cultists, withdrawing its tentacles in an almost dainty gesture as if it planned on wiping its mouth with a napkin. More of it had emerged from the Gate, long, undulating waves of gelatinous muscle interspersed with scales, crusted over with centuries of god knows what. If it got all the way out, would it be able to make its way through the Veil into the world beyond?

I couldn't take that chance.

What's your name? I asked, hoping to distract it.

It froze in the act of tossing yet another frog-faced cultist down into its mouth.

My name?

Yes. Do you remember your name?

There was an even longer pause. Then, *Ashurra. My name was… is Ashurra.*

Ashurra, you can't stay here. You can either go back where you came from, or… I'll have to kill you.

Kill?

I'm sorry. I don't want to do that. But you've been gone a long time and this is no longer the place you knew. And you're no longer the little girl you used to be. You don't belong here anymore.

Mother?

I shut my eyes, wondering where the hell the tears that sprung up had come from. I hated myself for lying, but I did it anyway. *Yes. I am your mother. But you can't stay here with me.*

It was silent. She… was silent. Ashurra. Once a little girl with ringlets of dark hair, huge dark eyes, the sweetest smile…

God, I hated this. I waited, giving her time to formulate whatever thoughts were in her head. Her slimy, tentacled head…

I know.

You know…?

Yes. I will stay here. I want to be with you.

I shut my eyes, heaving a sigh and opening them again. *Ashurra, you can't stay. I told you—*

I will eat you and then you will be with me always, like my mate and my children.

Oh, that was not good. The itching in my neck flared into a full-scale burn.

I leaped backward just as she lashed out with one of her tentacles. It smacked me across one hip, knocking me off balance. I fell on my ass, continuing the momentum and turning it into a backwards roll as yet another tentacle thwacked down where I'd just been.

I love you, she said.

Whomp. Another tentacle descended, missing me by inches this time as I rolled to the side.

Love. You.

Whomp.

I could not keep this up. She was only using one tentacle at a time and I was still running out of energy fast.

Ashurra, please, I pleaded, *you have to stop. You can't—*

Whomp. Even as I scrambled out of the way, I saw the harbingers turn—all of them except Tia—and start moving in my direction.

Oh hell, I was well and truly screwed.

Scrambling backwards on hands and feet, I turned and dove into the shed, kicking the door shut behind me. It stayed shut for all of a few seconds before something ripped it off its rusty hinges and tossed it aside.

An unearthly glow filled the doorway. I recognized the Lucifer. Close behind it came the Adjurix, the smell of sweet rot overwhelming in the enclosed walls of the shed. I'd no doubt that behind those two were the Haruspex and the Augury. I could hear the latter's wings beating and the pulse of the former's heart. I didn't hear the song of the Cantrix, but had no doubt it was out there too.

God, Tia…

I looked around the interior for something to fight with, any kind of weapon. Nothing but two cowering cultists, one male, one female, and a rusty shovel. Good enough.

I grabbed the shovel by its handle, lifted it up and jammed the blade of the shovel into the Lucifer's neck, swiveling it around and into one of the walls of the shed. Its eyes and roaring mouth blazed like angry white-hot suns. I used the momentum to drive the blade in even deeper, its metal edge glowing as it bit into the ripping skin, tearing a bright crack of white light until it suddenly burst completely into a blinding flash, bathing the entire interior of the wooden shed in a fiery white phosphorescent glare. I gave one last shove, separating the head from the Lucifer's body with a brilliant death-throe flash of lightning. The inner glow in its eyes and mouth died as the head hit the ground, the body crumpling next to it. The grass blackened and died beneath it.

The Adjurix shambled up towards me next, arms raised to attack, the stench of its perfume filling the shed and making me dizzy. I couldn't stand the thought of the rotting thing touching me, so I spun the shovel around and smacked the flat side against its head. The skull collapsed like a hollow chocolate Easter bunny, releasing even more rotting perfume into the air. The horrible decay-stench attacked my nose and mouth like a living thing, sickening fingers of corpse-rot inserting themselves into my nostrils and down my throat. I struggled for air. It was like trying to breathe through a mouthful of trash-water and vomit. Choking on the noxious fumes, my head reeling, I fought just to keep from bowling over and retching from the overpowering miasma. With a last desperate burst of strength, I pulled back the shovel and struck again blindly, driving the metal into its shoulder and impaling it against the wall where its fleshy human husk broke open like a smashed egg, its reeking insides oozing out in runnels of pus and watery blood.

I couldn't tell if they were easy to kill because I was just that awesome or if they were somehow drained of power from the summoning ritual. Either way, I was nearing exhaustion and had four more to kill, plus She Who Wants to Eat Me, and I didn't think I had that much energy or willpower left.

I had to try, though, because even if LeRoy hadn't opened the Veil before he died, I'd no doubt Ashurra would be able to find a way through and turn the planet into an all you can eat buffet, starting with New Orleans.

I'd barely taken a breath—a shallow one to avoid inhaling the toxic fumes emanating from the fallen Adjurix—when both the Haruspex and the Augury lurched through the open door, with the Cantrix staggering up behind them. The Augury's wings beat a steady rhythm in time to the Haruspex's pulsing heart, the latter reaching for me with sucker-encrusted fingers. The Augury's oversized mouth opened and closed, drool running out between the rings of teeth and pooling on the ground below. These things were just a never-ending source of gross bodily fluids.

I held out the shovel, keeping both harbingers at bay, protecting the two cultists cowering behind me. The last thing I expected was hands between my shoulder blades, shoving me forward into the harbingers as the ungrateful bastards ran out of the shed.

Well, hell.

The Augury crouched low and spread out its clawed wings, the talons stretched wide. Then its toothy gargoyle jaws yawned open impossibly wide with an ear-splitting screech of challenge, and it leaped to attack. But I was ready for it. As it launched forward I spun around, bringing the shovel edgewise with a terrific swing. Batter up. I clocked the creature perfectly in the head, the point of the shovel's blade sinking into its jawbone with a loud crunch, like a medieval executioner's axe. The avian monster shrieked with pain and crashed sidelong into the flimsy wooden wall, spilling a flurry of black feathers and a whip of spittle in the air. It flapped its wings erratically for a moment, then fell still and silent, its body hanging limply by its neck from the splintered hole in the wall.

The Augury wasn't the only one to scream at the impact—a jolt of pain raced through the nerves in my wrist and forearms. The impact had shattered both the Augury's skull and the haft of my shovel. The splintered wooden pole rebounded out of my grasp and clattered off the opposite wall.

Seizing its chance, the Haruspex hurled itself at me. The grotesque, lumbering body slammed into me, knocking me to the damp ground, crushing the air from my lungs. I hit the dirt floor hard without a chance to break my fall, struggling to draw breath again, nearly losing consciousness. With a gasp, I took in a mouthful of precious air, then barely had time to grab its big forearms by the wrists, using all my might to keep its relentless hands at bay. Every finger was a horrid little leech mouth, along with the bigger one on both palms, all squirming and sucking to get at my blood.

But worse than any of these was the giant maw where the neck had once been. Now it was humping up from the shoulders, a lipless ring of jagged needle teeth craning towards my face. I could see all the way down its wet, mottled, devouring gullet, quivering in anticipation. Using both hands I could keep the sucker-fingered hands off me—barely—but I had nothing left to defend myself from the horrible mouth, straining forward to engulf me.

It kept leaning in, using its engorged bulk against me, trying to press me down and feed. Its relentless, pounding full-body heartbeat reverberated through mine. I could only squirm and twist underneath it, struggling to push its thick fleshy mass off me. The thing's breath smelled like copper, clotted blood, and gastric juices—a sickening combination. I tried to pull my face away from the searching, groping mouth as its spiny corona of teeth scraped at my cheeks. I screamed as the needle-tips began to work their way in, penetrating the skin and muscles of my face.

A hideous ear-splitting screech, impossible for any human throat to make, shattered the air. The Haruspex stiffened suddenly, shuddered, and reared its headless torso back. No, it was being yanked back, by chitinous limbs covered in little spines. The Cantrix—Tia—was attacking it.

As her wings beat the air ferociously for lift, her insectile forelimbs seized hold of the Haruspex's clammy flesh, pulling the monster back—even as its half-human arms were mercilessly working and twisting the splintered shovel haft like a spear deep into the thing's veiny back. Crimson ichor spurted into the air. The pallid gray hide of its chest began to tent up—before the gory, jagged point of the haft came tearing out of it. The Haruspex's pulsating body spasmed, and then its thundering heartbeat seized up and stopped.

CHAPTER TWENTY-NINE

"Tia…"

Before I could say anything else, the Cantrix gave a wounded cry and vanished outside, around the shed. I followed her out in time to see Ashurra eat the two cultists who'd thrown me under the bus. I can't say I was sorry. My only regret was that she didn't take longer with her meal, because as soon as she'd finished, her attention—and her dozens of eyeballs—turned back to me.

An odd trick of the light caught my eye, somewhere high in the tree branches above the Thaumaturge—a glimpse of some kind of will-o'-the-wisp, a wavering little golf ball-sized greenish-gray spot of illumination that suddenly roared to life, becoming a shining circle of blue-white flame. Cayden was at the opening, gesturing, crackling blue electricity sparking from his hands like Dr. Strange, increasing the size of the circle until it was wide enough to let a linebacker through.

Instead, Mike'n'Ike crashed through onto the tree.

Holy shit, I thought. They'd found the rift the Thaumaturge had left in the Veil.

The twins gave a wild, hooting holler from up in the branches. Despite everything, I gave a startled laugh when

I realized both were stark naked. They stood proud as two Aussie Tarzans in the crown of the tree, challenging the monster below.

"Hey! Big Ugly! You think you're a croc, do you?" Ike called down.

"Not bloody likely, you fat lump, you!" Mike chimed in. "Great grotty blob of dog's breakfast!"

The Thaumaturge craned its head up at them, hissing and issuing a low, guttural growl from deep below its long crocodilian jaws. Pointing at it with outstretched fingers, the twins took up a singsong chant.

"What are you? What are you?

"Whatareyouwhatareyouwhatareyouwhatareyou?"

The creature seemed to realize their needling little mantra had power behind it. It began to snap its jaws at them and form thick, angry tentacles from its malleable flesh, thrashing in frustration.

The brothers stopped their chant, and leaned down to taunt the monster further.

"We are Illuka and Miro, descended from the line of Old Man Ginga himself," Ike called down. "Why, you're no crocodile at all, are you, Mr. Blob Lizard?"

"You are nothing but a mock croc," Mike pronounced with a shake of his head.

"No, that's not a croc," Ike said quietly. "This is a croc."

The twins' eyes suddenly gleamed in the dark, a glittering hue of flecked gold with inhuman slit pupils. Geometric lines of tiny dots and little triangles in bright white appeared, running up and down their chests and faces like tribal body paint. They both grinned and suddenly leaped from the branches, howling a challenge as they transformed in mid-air. Their muscular bodies and limbs grew even larger, becoming armored as their heads lengthened, and their spines sprouted raised double lines of horny upright scales all the way down to long new tails. Both kept their upright human stance, though now their feet and hands bore hefty claws.

And then the two werecrocs came down on their prey.

The Thaumaturge roared its defiance and whipped heavy tentacles at them, trying to envelop the brothers in gelatinous folds of thick rubbery flesh. I gasped as the Gingas were caught in the grip of the many powerful, constricting arms that quickly wrapped around them—but they were by no means down for the count. Both werecrocs fought back with crushing, saw-toothed jaws, biting down on what passed for the unholy creature's neck—the place where its scaled reptilian head emerged from the rest of the huge amorphous mass. Then they threw the weight of their reptilian bodies into a frenzied spin.

They had the Thaumaturge in an honest-to-god death roll.

Something wrapped around my waist and pulled me off my feet. Next thing I knew, I'd landed on what felt like a bed of nails as Ashurra's teeth began piercing my clothes and skin, pulling me further into her mouth toward the darkness that lay down that cavernous throat and beyond the Gate.

You feed me now, Mother, she crooned happily.

"Lee!"

I looked up in time to see Cayden leap from the other side of the Veil down onto the tree, knife in hand. In the time it took him to yell "Catch!" he sent the knife spinning in my direction, the hilt smacking into my outstretched palm. I shoved the blade into the roof of Ashurra's mouth, pulling it toward me as it carved through teeth and flesh as easily as if both were made of butter, and sending a shower of alien blood on top of me.

Ashurra screamed, the sound louder than the Cantrix's summoning wail and the winds beyond the Gate, punishing my eardrums, flaying my mind. I nearly dropped the knife to clap my hands over my ears, but I managed to keep hold of it, pulling it out to stab into the teeth below me, cutting them away to stop the mad conveyer belt before it pulled me to my death.

You hurt me! I hurt!

She spat me out, sending me sprawling on the gore-covered grass. The bulk of her rose up and more tentacles stretched toward me, their murderous intent clear. I slashed through them all, screaming along with her as I plunged the blade up to its hilt into Ashurra's body.

Her screaming stopped before mine did.

†

"Do you want to go back through the Gate? You can heal there."

But I will be alone again…

I sat on the ground next to the dying creature. Next to Ashurra, who once was as human as me.

No. If I stay here and die, I will be with you. I will…

The thought trailed off and Ashurra was silent. Her massive head drooped all the way to the bayou, sending foul-smelling water splashing up onto the shore, soaking me. I didn't care. I put one hand out, resting it on a space between eyestalks. The eyes were all dimming, their lights going out one by one until there was only one left. It stared at me. I felt peace coming from Ashurra as I sat with her. And I felt her life force leave her body once and for all. The light inside that last eye went out. When it did, the Gate vanished, and the wailing wind stopped. Just like that. No fuss, no fancy incantations, just… nothing.

I sat there, my hand still resting on the dead creature, for I don't know how long. Time had no meaning beyond the Veil. I was afraid that if I moved, feelings would break through my numbness. I didn't want to feel anything.

A hand rested lightly on my shoulder. "Lee?"

Cayden.

"We need to leave."

I looked up at him. "She wanted her mother," I said dully. "She wanted to be home. She used to be human."

"I know," he said.

"Well, I'm here to tell you, this really sucks."

With that, I burst into tears, the force of my sobs wrenching my insides. The hand on my shoulder shifted to my elbow, pulling me to my feet and then into warm, strong arms. He pressed my head against his chest, fingers caressing my scalp and hair. It felt good and it offered a comfort I desperately needed at that moment.

Then I took a step backward. Cayden's arms loosened, letting me go. I didn't look at him. I couldn't. Not yet. Instead I scooped up his knife from the ground, wiped the blade on one of the few non-goo or blood-spattered patches of grass, and handed it to him, hilt first. He sheathed it.

"Nice knife," I said.

Only then did I look at him. For once, the mocking grin was missing from his face and the manic gleam in his eyes was banked instead of blazing. In his expression I saw a comprehension of what I'd been through and how I felt that I never would have expected that from him.

"Come on," he said simply, and led the way to the tree leading out of this fucked-up clearing. A rope dangled down from the opening. I stopped.

"Where's Tia?"

Cayden nodded toward what was left of the shed.

"She's still alive then?"

"For now."

He followed me to the shed. A few wallboards still stood, the roof collapsed over them. I heard noises from underneath. Like muffled sobs filtered through a buzzing mask. Horrible sounds because I knew what—who—was making them.

"Tia?"

The noises stopped.

"Tia, please come out."

"Do you really think that's a good idea?"

"We can't leave her here." There was no room for argument in my tone.

"She's not fully human anymore," Cayden said with a lack of emotion I actually found comforting.

"But she's not one of them either," I shot back. "She stopped the Haruspex from killing me. She didn't transform all the way, something stopped it. Maybe… Maybe she can be brought back."

Cayden was silent, considering my words before finally saying. "We'll try."

Using one hand, he effortlessly flipped the piece of roof out of the way, revealing the Cantrix—Tia—cowering against what was left of the wall. I knelt by her side.

"Tia," I whispered. "We have to leave. You need to come with us. We can help you."

She shook her misshapen head.

"Yes," I insisted. "Please… let us try."

Slowly, painfully, Tia let me help her to her feet. Cayden called for Mike'n'Ike. Both were battle-scarred and bloody, but still moving. "She's injured. Can you help carry her out of here?" Cayden asked.

"I reckon we can," Ike answered. Mike nodded. The compassion I saw in their eyes earned them my loyalty for life.

I waited until the three men had lifted Tia through the opening in the Veil, using sheer strength and agility. Ike climbed out first, then hung down upside down so Cayden and Mike could hand Tia up to him. Mike scrambled up the rope to assist.

I was quiet as Cayden unlooped the rope and handed it to me. "Can you climb?"

"I'm a stuntwoman," I said.

With that, I gripped the thick rope in both hands, swung out over the soup that used to be the Thaumaturge, and pulled myself up, hand over hand, through the opening Cayden had made in the Veil, and onto the tree branch on the other side. I stayed there until Cayden climbed back through. We both sat on the branch for a few moments, covered with unspeakable muck and stinking of death.

I finally spoke. "How did you find me?"

"I went to your room to invite you to breakfast. Your friend showed me the note you'd left her."

"Eden?"

"Is that her name?" Cayden's tone was indifferent.

We fell silent again for a minute.

"You're a sorcerer, aren't you?" I said.

Cayden shrugged. "I have some skills."

I punched him on the arm, hard.

Cayden looked at me. "You, Lee Striga, are one of a kind."

I didn't argue with him.

CHAPTER THIRTY

We'd cleaned up at the location as best as we could, given that the only running water was cold, and then I'd hit the shower as soon as we'd gotten back to the hotel—those of us who'd been beyond the Veil still smelled kind of funky, and I pitied the poor tourists who'd had the misfortunate to ride up in the elevator with us. Cayden sent someone to retrieve my belongings out of Micah's Cadillac, which was predictably parked on the Castro's land. He told me Tia was safe for now, and he'd keep me in the loop with her progress. That was enough for the time being.

Now I sprawled on the couch in the production suite, listening to Devon, Cayden, and Jen run damage control on the shooting schedule.

"Basically," Devon said, "you're telling us that Angelique is out of play for three weeks, and Mike'n'Ike for what, a week?"

"That's what the doctor said," Cayden replied. "Could be less time for Angelique given her shifter metabolism and rate of healing, but we want to make sure her ankle is solid before putting any stress on it. She can still shoot, just no stunts. So we'll need to put off finishing the final battle until she's healed. As for Mike'n'Ike, you know how they are."

"They'll be back in play tomorrow then."

Grinning, Cayden nodded. "Yup."

"Excellent!" Devon said, rubbing his hands together. "What about Lee?"

"I'm good," I said, ignoring every ache and pain currently throbbing in most of my extremities. Nothing was broken, but I could use some painkillers and an hour or three in my room's tub. A few beers wouldn't go amiss either.

"That's my girl," Devon said happily.

Not your girl, I muttered silently. Devon's familiarity turned on and off as it suited his needs. He hadn't been there when the shit went down behind the Veil. True, Cayden had strongly discouraged Devon from joining him and the Ginga twins, wanting someone on the other side to keep watch in case things went bad and make sure the opening was closed. Fine, he hadn't been totally worthless. I just didn't have the same warm fuzzies for him that I did for my stunt team.

Jen, in the meantime, punched numbers into a calculator and scribbled notes rapid-fire, frowning all the while. "Do you think the Marcadets will give us a break on the price to extend the location rental?"

Cayden shrugged. "I'll see what I can do. There are plenty of scenes we can shoot in the meantime, and Lee can double some of Angelique's action scenes that don't involve Leandra too, if need be."

"Otherwise I'd be fighting myself," I commented helpfully from my prone position. "And I feel obligated to point out that Angelique won't be happy having someone else do any of her stunts." I liked Angelique. I didn't want to take work away from her or ruin our working relationship. Then again, maybe she'd be okay with it since she'd be dead if not for me.

"Nothing to be done about it," Devon replied. "I'm not

happy she's out of play, even temporarily, and neither is our budget."

"Damn straight," Jen muttered, once more attacking her calculator.

I gave them both the finger from the hidden safety of the couch back. Cayden saw it, however, and he grinned at me.

"Don't worry," Cayden said. "She'll be fine. And the more professionally that she deals with this, the more work she'll get in the long run."

Unless she kills a producer, I thought to myself. I yawned, a big jaw-cracking, hippo-rising-from-the-river-type yawn.

"Lee, there's no reason for you to be here unless you want to." I opened my eyes to see Cayden standing next to the couch.

"Did I fall asleep?" I asked. My eyes flickered to the wall clock—a good hour had passed. "Never mind."

I got slowly to my feet, feeling all the aches even more now that I was asking my body to move again.

"I'll walk you to your room," Cayden said. I was too tired to argue with him.

I waved at Devon and Jen, who were too engrossed in their work to notice.

Cayden was quiet as we walked to the elevator. Fine by me. I was too tired to talk anyway.

I shut my eyes and leaned against the back wall of the elevator, letting Cayden do the hard work of pressing the button. When the elevator stopped, I opened my eyes and followed him down the hall to my room.

"Is… Eden here?" I noticed the slight hesitation before he said her name.

"Nope. She's out playing tourist." I'd texted her to let her know I wouldn't be up to going out, that Tia had been found and that everything was okay. That last part was as close to a lie as I ever wanted to tell her, but I wasn't up to telling this story by text.

"Do you want company?" And there it was. Direct and to the point. I knew what he meant.

"I don't think that would be a good idea," I replied, equally blunt.

"Why not?"

I sighed. "We're working together. You're my boss. I sort of kind of am dating someone. You sort of kind of are dating… well, more someones than I am. Do you want me to go on?"

Leaning against the hallway wall next to the door to my room, he folded his arms and stared at me with those eyes, the banked flame of crazy flaring up a bit. His pose was relaxed, but I could sense the tension in his muscles. It made me nervous.

"Answer me this and I'll walk away. For now. But you have to be honest."

"Fine," I said, eager to end this and take my nap. "I promise to tell the truth, nothing but the truth, so help me Bourbon Barrel beer." He didn't say anything. "Seriously," I added. "I promise."

He straightened, all pretense of relaxation gone.

"Do you want me?" He didn't touch me, but the tension between our bodies practically crackled.

I gulped. I didn't expect anything that direct, and his proximity made it hard for me to think of a way to dance around the answer to his question. I didn't try.

"Yes." There it was. Honest and potentially dangerous. Oh, who was I kidding? There was nothing potential about this. Getting involved with this man was nothing but trouble.

"Then why are you running away from me?"

"I'm not," I replied shakily. "I'm just not running toward you."

"Why not?" He touched the side of my face, very softly with one of those oddly dexterous hands. Killer's hands, I thought again. The touch, almost feather-light, sent shivers down my spine. The good kind of shivers combined with a rising heat in my belly. If he could make me feel this much with one brief touch, what would it be like spending even an hour in bed with him?

"Please don't." The words felt forced even as I said them.

"Why not? Doesn't this feel right?" He brushed his thumb over my mouth. Again, the lightest of touches. I wanted to bite it, to suck on it. I wanted—

I wanted him.

"Yes," I said.

"Then let's do what feels right," he whispered, the pinpoint of flame in his eyes nearly hypnotizing me.

I shut my eyes. "I can't."

"Why not?" His breath was warm on my face, his lips brushing against mine.

"Because," I replied, stepping away from him even as my body screamed in protest, "it would be wrong. At least right now."

I swiped the room key. It blinked green and I pushed the door open. I stopped before going in, looked at Cayden and said, "I will never forget what you did for me. But if anything ever does happen between us, it's not going to be because you rescued me. And it's not going to be while we're working on a film together."

"What if I don't hire you again?"

I smiled. "That, my friend, will be your loss. But for now, what happened behind the Veil stays behind the Veil."

With that I shut the door, the sound of Cayden's laughter echoing in the hall as he walked away.

ACKNOWLEDGMENTS

This was a tough book to write. The reality of my mom's death hit hard, and debilitating pain in my hips and back took away going for long walks, my coping mechanism for stress of any kind. If I got a hundred words done in a writing session, it was a good day. Two hip replacement surgeries and subsequent recovery time later, enough of my writing mojo returned to finish *Blood Ink*.

So… to everyone who cheered me on through two surgeries and my transformation into a partially bionic woman, you are all the best. From cupcakes and cards to cat memes, to taking care of me when I could barely walk, to coming to my book events (special love to my stepmom, Gayle, for always showing up), to selling my books (Patrick N, looking at you), to hosting those book events (Mysterious Galaxy and Borderlands), you all played a huge part in raising my spirits. And special thanks to my "hip sister" Tori, for sharing your experiences and helping me manage my expectations!

Thank you, Steve Saffel, for giving me the gift of much-needed time, and for understanding that sometimes the creative gears grind to a halt when gummed up with grief and pain. You're awfully nice for a Dark Editorial Overlord.

Many thanks to the rest of the Titan gang, especially

Sam Matthews and Jill Sawyer, whose respective editing passes on *Blood Ink* helped make it a better, tighter read. As always, much appreciation for Katharine Carroll, Hannah Scudamore, Nick Landau and Vivian Cheung, Polly Grice, Gary Budden, Paul Gill, Laura Price, and anyone that I might have missed.

Oh, the performance anxiety of acknowledgments!

Hugs to Bill, my second dad and pal—our morning phone calls helped keep me going.

Much love to Jonathan and Sara Jo, who have brought so many wonderful things to my life, and who inspire me to keep reaching for the stars.

Thank you, Lisa, for being my beta reader and repeatedly telling me "you can do eeeeet!" I totally blame you for the craft beer. When I get through those hell dimensions I'm telling Mom on you!

And so much love for you, Dave, for learning to make coffee for me when I was healing and couldn't do it myself, and for pretty much being there for me 24/7 during the writing of this book. And for making coffee. Did I mention the coffee? No greater love hath a man who doth not like coffee than to learn to make it for his temporarily infirm wife. You da best, baby.

ABOUT THE AUTHOR

Dana Fredsti is an ex B-movie actress with a background in theatrical combat (a skill she utilized in *Army of Darkness* as a sword-fighting Deadite and fight captain). Through seven plus years of volunteering at EFBC/FCC, Dana's been kissed by tigers and had her thumb sucked by an ocelot with nursing issues. She's addicted to bad movies and any book or film, good or bad, which includes zombies. She's the author of *Spawn of Lilith*, the Ashley Parker series (touted as *Buffy* meets *The Walking Dead*), the zombie noir novella *A Man's Gotta Eat What a Man's Gotta Eat*, and the cozy noir mystery *Murder for Hire: The Peruvian Pigeon*. With David Fitzgerald she is the co-author of *Time Shards*, a trilogy of time-travel adventures, and she has stories in the *V-Wars: Shockwaves* and *Joe Ledger: Unstoppable* anthologies. She lives in San Francisco with husband (and co-author) David, their horde of felines, and their dog, Pogeen.